MW00480197

THE BLACK KNIGHT

Dean Crawford

Copyright © 2015 Fictum Ltd
All rights reserved.

ISBN:1519115415
ISBN-13:9781519115416

The right of Dean Crawford to be identified as author of this Work has
been asserted by him in accordance with sections 77 and 78 of the
Copyright, Designs and Patents Act 1988.
All rights reserved.

Also by Dean Crawford:

The Warner & Lopez Series
The Nemesis Origin
The Fusion Cage
The Identity Mine
The Black Knight

The Ethan Warner Series
Covenant
Immortal
Apocalypse
The Chimera Secret
The Eternity Project

Atlantia Series
Survivor
Retaliator
Aggressor
Endeavour
Defiance

Independent novels
Eden
Holo Sapiens
Soul Seekers
Stone Cold

Want to receive notification of new releases? Just sign up to Dean Crawford's newsletter via: www.deancrawfordbooks.com

Dean Crawford

I

Colorado Springs, USA

1899

'It is time.'

The silent blackness of the night sky twinkled with a thousand stars, like diamonds embedded in black velvet as Nikola stepped out into the fresh air and inhaled deeply. He closed his eyes, savored the sweet scent of it, so much clearer and cleaner than the chemically tainted smog of New York City. He had not slept for eighteen hours but his mind did not wander.

'Time to make history,' he said to the stars above.

He turned to where the windows of his laboratory glowed with electrical light: warmth from the darkness, power from the mysterious ether that surrounded mankind. The laboratory, situated just to the east of the city, was silent at this early hour, desks scattered with papers and wall cabinets filled with books on electrical engineering, physics, chemistry and other more arcane sciences. Inside one of the rooms stood a large spark-gap magnifying transmitter, an advanced version of the air-core Tesla Coil. The primary and secondary coils were wound around a fifty foot diameter frame. A third, eight foot diameter coil was placed within the other coils, magnifying the electrical effects via resonant rise and delivering an incredible eleven hundred amps and one million volts.

Nikola Tesla's friend and lawyer, Leonard E. Curtis, had offered to find land and provide power for his research from the El Paso Power Company of Colorado Springs. The next supporter to come forward was Colonel John Jacob Astor. With thirty thousand dollars of investment from Astor, Tesla had begun building the new experimental station near Pikes Peak. Joining Tesla were several assistants who were not fully informed of the inventor's plans, including his long-serving assistant George Scherff. Arriving at Colorado Springs in May 1899, Tesla had inspected the site some miles out in the prairie. He had told reporters that he intended to send a radio signal from Pikes Peak to Paris, but that had merely been the official story.

In the midst of Colorado's own incredible electrical displays, Tesla had sat and taken vast numbers of measurements. He had found the Earth to be literally alive with electrical vibrations and come to the conclusion that when lightning struck the ground it set up powerful waves that moved from one side of the planet to the other. If the Earth was indeed a great conductor, Tesla had hypothesized that he could transmit unlimited amounts of power to any place on the globe with virtually no loss. But to test this theory, he would have to become the first man in history to create electrical effects on the scale of lightning.

The laboratory that rose from the prairie floor was both wired and weird, a contraption with a roof that rolled back to prevent it from catching fire and a wooden tower that soared eighty feet into the air. Above it was a hundred forty two foot metal mast supporting a large copper sphere. Inside the wooden structure, technicians had begun to assemble an enormous Tesla coil specially designed to send powerful electrical impulses into the Earth.

On the evening of the experiment, each piece of equipment had been first carefully checked. Then Tesla had alerted his mechanic, Czito, to open the switch for only one second. The secondary coil had begun to sparkle and crack and an eerie blue corona had formed in the air around it. Huge arcs of blue electricity snaked up and down the center coil. Bolts of man-made lightning more than a hundred feet in length shot out from the mast atop the station. Thunder from the released energy was heard fifteen miles away in Cripple Creek. People walking along the street observed sparks jumping between their feet and the ground. Sparks sprang from water line taps when touched and light bulbs within a hundred feet of the lab glowed even when turned off. Tesla's experiment burned out the dynamo at the El Paso Electric Company and the entire city lost power. The power station manager had been livid and had insisted that Tesla pay for and repair the damage but Tesla was unrepentant, for he had the United States government on his side.

Several major corporations including the immensely powerful Marconi had shown interest in his work and now he was about to conduct the greatest experiment he had ever attempted.

'We are ready, Nikola.'

Tesla turned and saw George Scherff standing at the entrance to the laboratory, a slightly pensive expression on his features as he awaited the moment of ignition. The laboratory hummed with restrained energy as though alive. Tesla nodded once and raised his arms to the darkened skies above them as he cried out.

'Let there be light!'

George looked back into the laboratories, and with a curt nod relayed the command to Czito to open the switch. Tesla turned to watch and a moment later threw his hands up to shield his eyes as a tremendous blast seared the deserts as though the sky itself had burst into flame.

The tower lit up with a fearsome white light as bright as a thousand suns that blazed into the darkness and seared it away, the endless deserts illuminated in a stark halo, distant mountain ranges glowing blue. A thick, solid bolt of energy erupted from the laboratory and crackled in an instant up the tower before blasting into the night sky as a deafening crack of thunder shattered the silence of the night as though the heavens were splitting above his head.

Tesla felt himself laughing at the sheer spectacle of the writhing, snarling coil of energy blazing up toward space as he felt the thunder reverberate like war drums through his chest, felt the shockwave as the air itself burned around the lightning bolt and then hit him in the face and he staggered backwards a few paces, his hands clasped to his ears.

The fearsome, infernal bolt vanished and the desert plunged back into absolute blackness as the power was cut off, and Tesla realized that he was breathing fast as he lowered his hands from his ears and heard a rumble of thunder rolling away into the distant deserts. His ears rang and his eyes throbbed with pulses of light as he struggled to regain his night vision and swayed unsteadily on his feet.

A noise to his right attracted his attention and he saw horses from a nearby livery stable bolt from their stalls after receiving shocks through their metal shoes, orange sparks flying from their hooves as they galloped in panic across the plains. As the throbbing lights in his eyes faded Tesla saw what he thought were more flickering relics of that infernal blast in his eyes but then he realized that butterflies had been awoken, electrified, and were now swirling in circles around him in the darkness with blue halos of St. Elmo's fire around their wings.

Tesla staggered off balance again and felt pricks of static electricity spark from his shoes and vanish into the desert at his feet, his own hair tingling on his scalp as it was lifted by the energy still seeking to escape from his body. He was still trying to recover himself when the door to the laboratory opened with a bang and George Scherff dashed out.

'Nikola! You must come quickly! You have to see this!'

Tesla gathered himself and hurried inside, his thin six foot two frame stooping to pass through the doorway as he followed George into the laboratory. There, Czito was scrutinizing a read-out being produced by clattering ink-keys and graph pens nearby, some sort of return signal that he had not realized was being recorded.

'What is it?' he demanded.

Czito looked up at Tesla, his face as white as a sheet.

'The energy burst,' he gasped. 'We've had a reply.'

Teslav stared at Czito for a moment, his prodigious intellect struggling to digest what the mechanic was saying.

'What do you mean a *reply*?'

Tesla stared down at the data stream and then his mind went into overdrive.

There could be no mistake. Even though he knew that it was not possible he leaned forward and poured over the figures, his mind humming and his eyes itching with fatigue.

The signal was clear. He was already familiar with the bursts of energy produced by the sun, by the Aurora Borealis and the currents generated by the Earth itself, but this was none of those. Nikola looked up across the laboratory to the window, outside which soared the tower from which he had driven truly monstrous surges of energy into the atmosphere, and inside the laboratory he possessed instruments so sensitive that he could detect electromagnetic disturbances anywhere within a thousand miles of the laboratory. The entire experiment had been designed by Nikola with one true aim in mind: to make the first attempt at communicating with another civilization, to speak for the first time with beings inhabiting another world.

He had not expected to be the one doing the listening.

While in Colorado Springs he had been researching transmitters, receivers, additional smaller resonance transformers and tuned electrical circuits. He had become interested in the effects of the electrical waves that the Colorado Springs' lightning storms would create within the Earth itself and had discovered evidence of terrestrial stationary waves. In a moment of inspiration, he'd had the idea of sending these extremely low frequency waves into the Earth and as the waves bounced back, he would add a boost to create the resonance rise and charge the earth with electricity.

It had been then that he had detected the strange signals coming not from the Earth but from somewhere *beyond* it, from space itself. Nikola stared down at the data before him, at the rhythmic flow of signals far too orderly and consistent to be the result of anything in nature.

'What are you?' he whispered to himself.

'Nikola? Have you ever seen anything like this?'

Scherff was no expert like Nikola when it came to interpreting signals data, but he had learned enough in the years he had spent at Tesla's side to at least understand what he was looking at.

'Where is it coming from?' Czito asked.

Tesla's eyes shone as he worked with pencil and ruler, reflecting the flickering electrical lights in bright halos as he stood up and pointed to the ceiling.

'I have plotted an orbit of seventy nine degrees off the equator, an apogee of just over one thousand miles and a perigee of perhaps a hundred and fifty miles,' he said, and then his expression became somber. 'The object is orbiting our planet once every one hundred and four minutes.'

George Scherff slowly looked up from the data into Tesla's eyes.

'Orbit? You're telling me that this signal is coming from space?'

Tesla nodded. 'It's coming from space, George. It doesn't belong to us. It did not come from this planet.'

'Then what do we do about it?' Czito asked.

Tesla was about to reply when he heard galloping horses approaching the laboratory. For a moment he thought that perhaps the spooked horses that had bolted from the nearby stables had returned, but then he heard voices and the sounds of booted men dismounting. Before he could speak, the door to the laboratory burst open and armed soldiers flooded into the building.

Tesla knew that they could not have travelled from Colorado Springs so soon after the energy burst. They must have been waiting much closer by.

'Nikola Tesla?!' their officer demanded, his expression brooking no argument as he looked directly into Tesla's eyes, already knowing the answer.

'Yes?'

'You will come with us,' the officer ordered, his men arrayed behind him with their rifles held at port arms. 'All of this material is now confiscated.'

Tesla's eyes widened and he took a pace toward the officer.

'But we have just made an important discovery, one that could change the world and...'

A dozen rifles lifted to point at Tesla and stopped him in his tracks.

The officer moved to stand in front of the scientist, one hand resting on the butt of his holstered pistol.

'It's not a request, Mister Tesla.'

***

II

Cheyenne Mountain Complex, Colorado Springs

(Present Day)

'It's no big deal, okay?'

Sergeant Jenny Duvall twirled a pen in the fingers of one hand as she flashed a winning smile at Corporal Hank Fuller.

'I went last time,' Fuller complained.

Duvall, still smiling, shrugged. 'Fair's fair, okay? You snooze, you lose. I won three hands in a row so it's your turn.'

Fuller sighed and tossed a handful of cards down onto his work station, which like Duvall's was arrayed with four monitors, a keyboard and three phones. A desk between their stations served as a useful space for playing poker during the small hours when they were the only staff on duty.

'Coffee?' he asked as he got to his feet.

'What else?' Duvall grinned as she tossed her pen down onto her work station and crossed her booted feet at the ankle as she propped them up against the desk. Even wearing drab fatigues she looked good, her long brown hair in a pony-tail.

Fuller turned and walked out of the Watch Station, leaving Duvall to revel in the silence and reflect on the fact that she was seated in perhaps the safest place on Earth.

The Cheyenne Mountain Complex military installation and nuclear bunker was located in Cheyenne Mountain Air Force Station, which hosted the activities of several tenant units. The complex was built beneath two thousand feet of granite, its fifteen three-story buildings protected from earthquakes or explosions by a system of giant springs and flexible pipe connectors. The complex was the only high altitude Department of Defense facility certified to be able to sustain an electromagnetic pulse generated by a nuclear detonation. Protected by a twenty five ton blast door and designed to withstand a thirty megaton nuclear blast within two kilometers of the site, a network of blast valves with unique filters to capture airborne chemical, biological, radiological, and nuclear contaminants ensured that in the event of a thermonuclear war, nobody at Cheyenne Mountain would perish in the exchange and supplies of food, water and power would sustain the base for months and perhaps years in the wake of any such attack. Still, she none the less wondered why the hell the US government had chosen to build the facility way out in Colorado.

Duvall, an Air Force staff officer, was in charge of liaising with the nearby Peterson Air Force Base, where the North American Aerospace Defense Command (NORAD) and United States Northern Command (USNORTHCOM) headquarters were located. The center for the United States Space Command and NORAD monitored through a world-wide system the air space of Canada and the United States for unidentified missiles, satellites and foreign aircraft.

The military complex in which she sat, far below ground, included many units of NORAD; the U.S. Space Command, Aerospace Defense Command (ADCOM), Air Force Systems Command, Air Weather Service and Federal Emergency Management (FEMA) were all represented. Everything that orbited the earth, including deep space debris, was monitored by the country's Space Command Surveillance Center using Ground-based Electro-Optical Deep Space Surveillance (GEODSS) technology. Information gathered from around the world was processed by computers and displayed on maps of North America and the globe. National and military leaders were notified of missile attacks, whether incoming intercontinental ballistic missiles or short-range tactical missiles, into North American air space or in conflict areas, such as the countries involved in or impacted by the Gulf Wars. Defense Support Programs, early warning and satellite systems at NORAD and Space Command were operated via the communication links from Peterson Air Force Base that she monitored. The DSP satellites used infrared sensors to detect heat emitted from missiles and booster plumes, and were now fine-tuned to gather information about even short-range missiles. Information was then fed to world-wide operations centers and agencies.

At least that was the official line, but Duvall and other operators knew that far more went on behind the scenes at Cheyenne Mountain. With the decline of the Cold War and the reduced threat of a concerted nuclear exchange, Cheyenne Mountain's role had changed gradually to become dominated by both the monitoring of near-earth orbital debris and also of monitoring signals coming from the wider cosmos.

Although Duvall was not prone to conspiracy theories, she did know that from time to time suited men who wore no insignia moved through the base with complete authority. Inevitably nick-named the *Men in Black*, they showed up at unusual times and seemed to operate mostly from the Watch Station's Signals Intelligence Office, which had recently developed links to the Arecibo radio telescope in Puerto Rico. Whatever the hell they were looking at, they kept it well under wraps from junior officers like Duvall.

Despite the perceived glamor of the role and the exotic location, Cheyenne Mountain seemed to Duvall to be a base in decline. Its staff numbers had been slashed over the years to a fraction of their former number, the base seemingly a Cold War relic consigned to mundane debris observation and…

A small, insistent beeping noise broke Duvall from her reverie and she glanced at one of the signals screens before her. Arrayed across the walls of the Command Center, the screens showed a variety of images including maps of the Earth's surface reminiscent of those seen at Cape Canaveral, that depicted the orbital trajectories of whatever objects Duvall cared to select at her station.

However, she had not selected any objects and in an instant her eyes settled on a single transmission spike. It took her mind only a moment to assimilate three salient points of information from the track.

It did not belong to the United States as it bore no transponder code.

It did not belong to any other nation as it bore no identification code.

It was in space, as its velocity was being recorded as close to seventeen thousand miles per hour, placing it in low Earth orbit.

Duvall lowered her boots from the edge of her desk and leaned forward as she peered at the contact. It was tracking an unusual near-polar orbit, rather than the equatorial orbits favored by most satellites and space vehicles.

The sound of Fuller's voice broke through her thoughts. 'The machine's bust again, decaf only and…'

'We've got an infiltration signal.'

Fuller chuckled, more than used to the pranks played by bored operators on their colleagues. 'Yeah sure, maybe E.T's got some coffee we can borrow?'

Duvall did not reply to him as she scanned the data stream on her screen.

'Orbit is seventy nine degrees off the equator, apogee is one thousand seven hundred and twenty eight kilometres, perigee two hundred eighteen kilometres. Orbital period is one hundred and four minutes and thirty seconds.'

Fuller glanced at the main screen, saw the track, and dumped the coffee as he slammed down into his seat and slipped a pair of headphones over his ears.

'We've got a primary return,' he said as he saw the same track on his own screens. 'Records confirm it's not one of ours and it's not a catalogued piece of debris.'

'I've got data,' Duvall replied, 'object is approximately twenty four meters in length, approximately six metres in width. Data calculations estimate a mass of fifteen tons.'

Fuller glanced up at the screen. 'Damn that's big, real big.'

Duvall nodded as she held her own earphones to her head, squinting as she sought to determine what she was listening to.

'I've got audio,' she whispered, almost so quietly that Fuller didn't hear.

'You've got what?'

Duvall nodded to herself more confidently as she listened.

'I've got audio,' she repeated. 'I've got a signal. It's coming from the track.'

Fuller stared at her for a long moment and then looked up at the screens.

'What the hell is it?' he uttered.

Duvall reached out for her phone as she set her monitors to record every detail of the track. Without a transponder, identification and with signals being emitted or perhaps even received by the object, she wasn't about to put her career on the line by taking a chance that it was just an iron-rich meteorite captured by Earth's gravitational field that *just happened* to be deflecting satellite signals across the atmosphere.

She picked up the receiver and dialed a single number. The line connected immediately and she spoke clearly, trying to keep the nervous edge out of her voice.

'Primary Orbital Contact, signals confirmed, initiate Orion Shield. Repeat, initiate Orion Shield.'

Beside her, she heard Fuller curse beneath his breath.

Orion Sheild was the code name for the United States' missile defense system administered by the Missile Defense Agency. The major component was Ground-Based Midcourse Defense consisting of ground-based interceptor missiles and radar in the United States in Alaska, designed to intercept incoming warheads in space. Duvall knew that some GBI missiles were located at Vandenberg Air Force Base in California and could be supported by mid-course SM-3 interceptors fired from Navy ships, the Missile Defense Agency having some thirty operational GBIs. Those weapons would be augmented by the Aegis Ballistic Missile Defense Systems located on US Navy warships and designed to pick out incoming ballistic missiles in flight at high altitude, thus preserving the safety of the continental United States.

'Roger, *Orion Sheild initiated, stand by.*'

Duvall set the phone line to stand by as she heard boots running down the corridor leading to the Command Center and a low, mournful wailing siren as the entire base was alerted to the possibility that the United States was about to come under a nuclear attack.

Duvall prepared for the conversations that would follow: the Joint Chiefs of Staff on the line, conference calling as the President was awoken and informed of the crisis. She knew that they would be talking to her long before her boss was on site, and that as a communications specialist she was the most qualified person in the under-staffed base to conduct the assessment of the threat.

Then, just as she felt herself ready to conduct the assessment and as dozens of staff flooded into the Command Center, everything changed.

'It's not a missile,' Fuller said.

'How do you know?!' Duvall demanded, tension in her voice.

Fuller looked across at her. 'Because it just changed direction.'

Duvall looked up in shock at the main screen and saw the object's orbital track change by a few degrees.

'What the hell...?'

Fuller picked up his phone. 'We're not under attack,' he said to her, 'and I don't know what the hell that thing is.'

Duvall switched her headphones from internal to broadcast and then filtered the feed through to the Command Center's speakers. Above the rush of conversation a sudden sound of regularly paced beeps and growls echoed across the room and the conversation shuddered to a halt as every person in the building listened intently.

Duvall, along with everybody else in the Command Center, had been trained to recognize the countless signals emitted by both Earth-based installations and those from distant supernovae, neutron stars, black holes and quasars that blazed their high-energy emissions across billions of light years of intergalactic space.

What they were hearing now was none of those things.

The signal echoed around them like the chanting of monks drifting in haunting melody through the halls of some ancient abbey, both tuneful and yet without structure but for the rhythmic beacon accompanying it. Like a song from the depths of prehistory, something about it sounded familiar to Duvall, and she could see from the expressions of those around her that the rest of the team felt the same.

'It's like music,' Fuller finally managed to say, his jaw hanging open in shock.

Duvall recovered her senses and turned to the deck officer.

'Get a linguistics team down here as fast as you can, and open a channel to the Joint Chiefs of Staff. We may have initiated first contact!'

As the team scattered to perform their duties, Duvalls' own words echoed in her ears. *First contact*, the first verifiable signal from an alien species sent from an alien craft in orbit around the planet. She didn't have long to dwell on the gravity of the subject as Fuller spoke from beside her.

'Its orbital velocity is decaying,' he said, his features stricken and his skin pale as he stared at her. 'Whatever it is, it's coming down.'

***

III

Logan Circle,

Washington DC

The sound of incessant banging reverberated through the apartment and jerked Ethan Warner out of his slumber, dreams of helicopter blades and blazing guns vanishing as he opened his eyes and saw the feint light of pre-dawn glowing lethargically through the blinds of his bedroom window.

Ethan sat upright, unsure of whether he had actually heard something, and moments later he leaped out of his bed as he heard the front door of his apartment suddenly open despite the three sets of locks securing it in place. One hand reached for the Beretta M9 pistol he kept under his pillow and he whirled as two figures appeared to fill the bedroom doorway in the dull morning light.

'Ethan Warner? Defense Intelligence Agency.'

The brief, clipped tones imparted the information necessary for Ethan not to open fire on the armed intruders even as behind them another figure appeared in the doorway and hit the lights. Ethan squinted as he stood naked in front of the intruders, shielding his eyes with one hand as he stared at a tall woman with long auburn hair who smirked as she looked him up and down appraisingly.

'You didn't have to get your weapon out for me, Warner.'

Ethan turned away from former FBI Agent Hannah Ford and tossed his pistol onto the bed.

'False alarm,' he replied. 'I thought something exciting was about to happen. Don't you know how to knock?'

'We've been knocking for five minutes,' Ford replied as her two armed escorts moved to guard the apartment's door as Ethan dressed. 'You sleep soundly, which is something I wouldn't have expected.'

'I've learned not to give a damn any more,' Ethan retaliated. 'Where's the fire?'

Hannah leaned on the doorframe and watched as Ethan pulled on a pair of jeans.

'Doug Jarvis has called us in. I don't know why, but they're in one hell of a hurry so let's get moving.'

Ethan scowled as he glanced at a digital clock beside his bed. *5.26am.*

'Jesus, can't they have a crisis at a normal time for a change?'

Hannah didn't reply as Ethan padded into the bathroom and stood in front of a sink, yanking the faucet to let warm water fill it. A mirror reflected his wide jaw, gray eyes and scruffy light brown hair as he splashed the water across his face and tried to shake off the lethargy slowing his movements.

In recent years Ethan and his partner Nicola Lopez had been fortunate enough, or unfortunate enough depending on how he looked at it, to have been contracted by the Defense Intelligence Agency to investigate cases the rest of the intelligence community had rejected as unworkable. The connection to a high level agency like the DIA had come from a former colleague of Ethan's named Douglas Jarvis. The old man had once been captain of a United States Marines Rifle Platoon and Ethan's senior officer during his time with the Corps in Iraq and Afghanistan. Their friendship, cemented during Operation Iraqi Freedom and later, when Ethan had resigned his commission and been embedded with Jarvis's men as a journalist, had continued into their unusual and discreet accord with the DIA where Jarvis continued to serve his country.

Throughout this time he had performed his duties for the DIA alongside Nicola Lopez, as a part of their shared business *Lopez & Warner Inc.* The memory of Lopez slowed his movements further still and he stared in silence at his reflection in the mirror as he thought of her.

'How're you holding up?'

Hannah Ford's voice reached him from the distance. Ford had been an FBI Agent assigned to track both himself and Lopez in an attempt to arrest them for crimes they had not committed. It had taken a recent national incident for the FBI to realize the deception and cancel the operation, after which Hannah Ford had transferred to the DIA and joined the team. Her voice pulled him back into the present, and he sighed and dried his face.

'I'm fine.'

Nicola Lopez had been seriously wounded several months before during a gunfight with terrorists determined to assassinate either the President of the United States or the President of the People's Republic of China, during a major ceremony on the South Lawn of the White House. Both he and Lopez had been instrumental in preventing that tragedy, but success had come at a great price, with Lopez still on a life-support machine in a DC hospital. Ethan had moved from Chicago to be closer to both Lopez and the Defense Intelligence Agency.

'I checked in on her the other day,' Hannah said. 'She's still stable, still fighting.'

Ethan did not reply. It wasn't often that he had heard anybody refer to Lopez as stable – being a fighter ran strong in her Latino blood. They had shared several investigations for the DIA over the years, often facing death and coming out the other side by the skin of their teeth, each always covering the others' back. His world felt empty now without her constant bitching to color it.

Ethan pulled on his shirt, which helped to cover some of the scars his frame had garnered over the years, and then he pushed past Hannah and fitted his shoulder holster, slipping the Beretta into it before pulling on a leather jacket.

'Let's go see what the fuss is about,' he said, not wanting to discuss Lopez any further.

Outside the apartment two smart SUVs were pulled into the sidewalk, the sun rising in slivers of molten metal between gray clouds as Ethan climbed aboard one of the vehicles. Hannah Ford followed him and moments later the two SUVs were cruising south toward the Capitol, the driver eager to beat the early morning rush into the city center.

'Where's Vaughn?' Ethan asked.

Michael Vaughn was Hannah Ford's former partner at the Federal Bureau of Investigation, both of them having resigned their roles there to become agents within the Defense Intelligence Agency after the attempted attacks on the life of the President. A stocky, thick-necked and capable agent, Vaughn had followed Hannah willingly into the DIA.

'He's already at Bolling,' Hannah replied. 'Jarvis sent me to get you.'

'Why didn't he just use the damned phone?'

'Because you keep turning it off, Einstein,' Hannah pointed out. 'You haven't been on top form lately, Warner, so I guess he thinks you need me to pick you up and return you to your former joyful self.'

'He shouldn't have delegated that task.'

'I shouldn't have accepted it but I'm all heart, y'know?'

Ethan glanced out of the windows as he watched the city awakening around them, lights glowing in houses and twinkling across the Potomac. The SUV was closing in on Joint Bolling-Anacostia Airbase, located on the eastern shore of the river close to where it merged with the Georgetown Channel. The base was the location of the Defense Intelligence Agency's Headquarters and clad in secrecy.

'You got any idea at all what this is about?' Ethan asked, more to change the subject than anything else.

'Like I said, Jarvis didn't reveal much but I do know that this isn't just a DIA gig. Vaughn told me they've got a team of boffins from NASA assembling at the DIA Headquarters Building, and all of them are in a state of excitement about something.'

'Hellerman there?'

Hellerman was Jarvis's assistant, a scientist and verifiable genius who liaised with the agency on technical matters. A firm admirer of Lopez, he too had suffered since she had been shot months before.

The SUV pulled into the base, security checks delaying their passage as the vehicle and its occupants were thoroughly searched before they were allowed into the DIA's complex. The SUV pulled up close to the south entrance and allowed Ethan and Hannah to disembark. The dawn sky above was brightening quickly as two armed escorts approached them and hustled them inside.

The DIA's south wing entrance, in front of which was a fountain before broad lawns, made up only a tiny part of the agency's sprawling complex. Huge, silvery buildings with mirrored black windows contained some of the most sensitive intelligence gathering equipment in the world, including vast 24/7 *Watch Centers* manned by specialists monitoring events across the entire globe.

In all Ethan and Nicola had conducted eight investigations for the Defense Intelligence Agency since Ethan had been plucked from Cook County Jail by Jarvis and given a new life working for one of the most clandestine units ever created by the intelligence community.

Hannah took the lead as they moved through the intense security measures, including full-body X-Rays and pat down searches. They finally passed through the last of the checks in time for Jarvis to meet them in the main foyer of the building, the polished tile floor emblazoned with a large DIA emblem in the manner of all the senior intelligence agencies. For a change, Jarvis's characteristic easy smile and casual demeanor was absent, replaced by genuine concern and urgency.

'Ethan, how are you doing?'

Ethan shook the old man's hand. 'I'm fine. What's the story?'

'Come with me,' Jarvis replied. 'I'll show you.'

Ethan followed them, aware of the large number of civilian staff walking through the building. Uniquely to a highly secretive intelligence agency, two thirds of the DIA's seventeen thousand employees were civilian, which allowed selected freelance operatives like Warner and Lopez to act in concert with official employees like Jarvis. Represented in some one hundred forty countries and with its own Clandestine Service, to which Warner and Lopez were now attached, the agency's only weakness was a lack of influence in law enforcement, forcing them in past cases to work alongside, or against, local police and federal law agencies around the country.

Jarvis led them to an elevator shaft, which in turn carried them deep into the building's subterranean sections far from the prying eyes of even the most sophisticated surveillance cameras and electromagnetic scanners.

'A NASA Watch Station at Cheyenne Mountain, Colorado, detected an unknown signal this morning coming from Earth orbit,' Jarvis announced as they travelled down in the elevator. 'It's got the Joint Chiefs of Staff running about like headless chickens, and for now the President is out of the loop until we can provide a decent explanation for what the signal is and what it means.'

Hannah Ford frowned. 'What kind of signal?'

'You'll need to hear that to believe it,' Jarvis replied.

'I never like it when you say things like that,' Ethan said, recalling previous expeditions he and Lopez had conducted at the DIA's behest. 'It usually means something dangerous is gonna happen.'

The elevator doors opened and Jarvis led them out into a Watch Station used by the new department that Jarvis was heading up. Formerly employing only Ethan and Nicola Lopez, the events of recent investigations had brought the department to the attention of the current administration, with the result that staffing had increased. Ethan saw at least a dozen specialists working at computer stations before the large screens that dominated the walls, all showing news feeds from around the world.

'So what's so special about this signal?' Ethan asked.

Jarvis grinned conspiratorially as he led them to a briefing room, outside which awaited Mickey Vaughn. The former FBI Agent shook Ethan's hand and offered him a genuine smile.

'Good to see you back.'

Vaughn ushered them into the briefing room, where sat Lieutenant General J. F. Nellis, the Director of National Intelligence. Nellis was a former United States Air Force officer who had recently been appointed DNI by the current president. Jarvis had been selected by Nellis to run a small investigative unit designed to root out corruption within the intelligence community while remaining beyond the prying eyes of senior figures on Capitol Hill. Jarvis had been chosen due to his prior success in operating a similar unit within the DIA that had conducted five investigations into what were rather discreetly termed as "anomalous phenomena," which had attracted the attention of both the FBI and the CIA and eventually been shut down. Jarvis had spent some twenty years working for the DIA and been involved in some of the highest-level classified operations ever conducted by elements of the US Covert Operations Service. Most of them he would never be able to talk about with another human being, even those with whom he had served. Jarvis knew the rules and had obeyed them with patriotic fervour his entire career.

'Please,' Nellis gestured to seats around a long table with long, elegant hands. 'Take a seat.'

Ethan sat down among several scientists, all of whom were whispering excitedly among themselves as Vaughn shut the briefing room door and all eyes turned to Nellis. The tall general, gray haired and imbued with an air of great authority, spoke softly but clearly.

'My apologies for the speed with which you have been mobilized but there is little time and we need to act fast. At oh four hundred hours this morning, Eastern Seaboard Time, an anomalous signal was detected by NASA engineers at Cheyenne Mountain's Surveillance Base in Colorado Springs. This signal has now been confirmed by signals officers at Arecibo in Puerto Rico, and Signals Inteligence stations both at Joint Base Edwards and multiple listening posts across the globe. So far, we have been able to use our satellites to intercept these signals so that they cannot be detected by non-military or non-US assets on the ground.'

Ethan frowned.

'How did you manage that so fast?' he asked. 'Surely people could have detected the signals themselves? It will be all over the Internet by now.'

General Nellis smiled.

'That would be true had we not already known about the object making the transmissions. Fortunately, we have been aware of its presence for over a century.'

The scientists around Ethan gasped, their eyes wide as they stared at Nellis.

'A century?' Hannah Ford echoed. 'But we haven't had satellites in orbit for that long.'

'Indeed,' Nellis agreed. 'That's because the satellite does not belong to us, and we have been able to conceal its presence for decades because we already knew that it was there. The object was placed in orbit long before mankind first launched a satellite into space.'

Ethan's curiosity got the better of him. 'How long has it been there?'

General Nellis folded his hands before him.

'The object's rate of decay, when measured against its mass, provides scientists with the means to calculate how long the object has been in orbit around our planet by back-tracking its orbital path to the point where it was first captured by Earth's gravity.' Nellis breathed out softly as though unwilling to impart his next sentence. 'They have calculated that the object, now code-named Black Knight, has been in orbit around the Earth for approximately thirteen thousand years.'

***

IV

A silence descended in the briefing room that lasted for several long seconds, as every man and woman present considered just what that meant.

'Thirteen thousand years,' Hannah echoed. 'So it's not man-made?'

'Hardly,' Jarvis pointed out. 'Thirteen thousand years ago, mankind had just worked out how to throw spears a long way and make knives out of something other than chipped flint. There's no way Black Knight could have been produced by us.'

Mickey Vaughn, who had been leaning against a wall listening, spoke for the first time.

'What's it signalling, and to whom?'

'A good question,' Nellis answered as he picked up a remote from the table and pointed it at a television monitor mounted on the wall behind him. 'This is a recording of the signals detected from the object before it became silent again a half hour ago.'

Nellis touched a button and Ethan heard the strangest sound emerge from speakers mounted discreetly around the walls of the room. What sounded like a rush of distant ocean waves was followed by a harmony of whistling wind, then whoops and what sounded like trickling water. A series of long, low moaning sounds drifted in and out of range over the existing chorus, sombre and deep, followed by what might have been the sound of a crackling fire.

Ethan listened in fascination, actually closing his eyes as he heard the sounds and behind them all a digital warbling, a rippling cacophony that was clearly not natural.

Nellis switched the recording off as he set the remote down on the table. 'We have our finest cryptographers working on the signals at the moment,' he revealed to them. 'As yet we have absolutely no idea what the message means, but then again we always knew that any signal from an alien civilization might take a form that we could not comprehend, let alone translate.'

Hannah leaned back in her chair, one hand absent-mindedly twirling a strand of her long auburn hair.

'So it's alien and it's been up there for thousands of years, and NASA knew about it? How? Did one of the *Apollo* or *Space Shuttle* missions stumble across it?'

Nellis picked up the remote again and hit a button. On the screen behind him appeared the image of a young man, dark wavy hair and a thick moustache dominating a stern expression.

'Nikola Tesla,' one of the scientists gasped, a man with short white hair and rectangular spectacles that gave him the appearance of a physics professor. 'Damn me, I might have known!'

Nellis nodded.

'Indeed, Doctor Chandler. Nikola Tesla was an electrical and mechanical engineer and is widely regarded as one of the greatest geniuses ever to have lived. Born in Serbia, he moved to the United States and became a prolific inventor with some three hundred patents to his name. His research gave us alternating current, the Tesla Coil, induction motors and wireless communication. In short, he gave us much of our modern world.'

'And what does this guy have to do with Black Knight?' Vaughn asked.

'Tesla picked up the first verifiable repeating signal from Black Knight in 1899,' Nellis explained, 'while experimenting with electrical discharges into the Earth's atmosphere as a means of communicating wirelessly over long distances. His data showed that something else was present in the returning signals from Earth's orbit, and Nikola Tesla at the time made an announcement that he had detected the first signal from another civilization from outer space. It made quite a stir in the media of the time.'

Jarvis picked up the story from one corner of the room.

'In the 1920s, a small number of amateur HAM radio operators were occasionally able to receive the same signal. In 1928, scientists in Oslo, Norway experimenting with short wave transmissions into space began picking up what they called Long Delay Echoes, in which they received echoes several seconds after transmission. The phenomenon is still not well understood. Everything went silent again until 1954, when several newspapers including the *St. Louis Post Dispatch* and the *San Francisco Examiner* reported an announcement from the United States Air Force that two satellites were found to be orbiting the Earth at a time when no nation yet had an ability to launch such objects.'

General Nellis gestured to the image of Nikola Tesla.

'Tesla died in 1943, penniless. It turns out that after he first detected what we now call Black Knight, the government of the time took to employing him and ensured that none of the recordings he made of the signals reached public hands. Over the next few decades they made every effort to ensure that any tracking of Black Knight's signals were explained away as atmospheric phenomena.'

'By 1960 the United States and the Soviet Union both had hardware in orbit,' Jarvis went on. 'But in February 1960, newspapers everywhere reported that somebody else also had something in orbit. A radar system that had been designed by the US Navy to detect enemy spy satellites had picked something else up. It was described as a dark, tumbling object in a highly eccentric orbit that wasn't ours and didn't belong to the Soviets either.'

Nellis pressed a button on the remote and an image of something in orbit around the Earth appeared on the screen behind him.

'The Navy explained the detections away as the casing from an old *Discoverer* satellite launch, a half shell about eight yards long. Trouble was, the casing they used as an explanation was in a slightly different orbit to Black Knight's. Most people didn't notice that and the general public bought the story, which disappeared into obscurity once again until 1988.'

Jarvis moved closer to the screen as he spoke.

'When the Space Shuttle *Endeavor* made its first flight to the International Space Station during mission STS-88 in 1998, the astronauts aboard took photographs of a strange object which were widely available to the public on the NASA website for a brief time. This is what they saw.'

The image on the screen changed to a bizarrely shaped, black object that looked almost like a giant camera suspended in orbit above the curved surface of the Earth. Ethan leaned closer to the screen as the scientists around him gasped in amazement, peering at the object's unusual shape, almost like some kind of sculptured undersea creature.

'That's Black Knight?' Hannah asked. 'It looks a lot like space junk to me.'

'That's what NASA said it was later,' Nellis replied. 'Unfortunately, NASA took every single one of the images down beforehand. They reappeared later and it didn't take long for the conspiracy theorists to notice that the images had new URLs and had been digitally altered, along with new descriptions having been added explaining the images as space junk. A few of them asked NASA why astronauts would take some many photographs of a piece of junk that had supposedly already been identified, but NASA remained silent. That, of course, only fuelled the suspicion that the astronauts had photographed something real and mistakenly uploaded their images to the Internet.'

Ethan leaned back in his chair.

'How come this Black Knight's causing so much fuss now, if we've known about it for so long?'

'It's the signals,' Jarvis explained. 'All previous signals from Black Knight have been basic beeps and whistles. NASA has been trying to decipher them for decades with no success. But the new signals are completely different and are being emitted four times per orbit in all directions. The only reason they're not being detected by Russia or other global powers is because a prior space shuttle mission placed a small satellite alongside Black Knight designed to block most of those signals and direct them to only our own listening posts.'

Nellis sat back down at the table as he went on.

'Black Knight's orbit has begun to decay at a greater rate than we predicted, likely as a result of micro-meteorite impacts over thousands of years that have reduced its velocity. In short, it's coming down and soon. Our mission is to secure the object before anybody else can reach it, because while we can veil signals intelligence from Black Knight nobody is going to fail to see the re-entry burn when a fifteen ton alien satellite comes down through the atmosphere at hypersonic speed.'

'How come we haven't brought it down already, in the Space Shuttle?' Vaughn asked.

'Too big and too heavy,' Jarvis replied. 'Believe me, we would have had this thing down here long ago if it had been possible. There was apparently some talk in the 1990s of tethering it to the International Space Station for long-term study, but the *International* bit of that equation prevented us from doing so. Even today, nobody wants Russia or China getting their hands on whatever technology might be aboard that thing.'

'What's the plan then?' Ethan asked. 'Where is this thing going to come down and why are we here talking about it? Surely this is a military situation?'

General Nellis shifted uncomfortably in his seat and gestured for Jarvis to continue.

'Black Knight's signals are getting a reply,' Jarvis announced.

The scientists at the table almost erupted in shouts of delight and excitement, their faces beaming with astonishment.

'A *reply*?' one of them uttered, a young woman with brown hair in a neat bob whose name tag said her name was Amy. 'From *where*?'

Jarvis switched the image on the screen from one of the Black Knight to an orbital satellite image of a region of the globe that was instantly recognizable.

'The Antarctic,' he announced. 'The signals travelling up are much weaker than those coming down but there's no question about it: somebody up there is talking to Black Knight, and we have absolutely no idea who it might be.'

Ethan stared at the image of the return signal's source as Nellis spoke.

'Ethan, you have suitable experience in dealing with these kinds of phenomena, and with Nicola Lopez out of the picture for now I'd like you to take Hannah Ford down there with a research team and figure out what the hell's going on.'

Ethan glanced across at Hannah. 'I'm not sure that we can be of any help, and what about logistics?'

'We can't make a major assault force deployment to the Antarctic,' Nellis explained. 'The Russians and the Chinese would identify it in an instant and move assets of their own in order to figure out what we're doing. The best shot we have at this is deploying a small team to intercept and examine Black Knight and the source of the earth-bound signals, while we figure out a way of getting more support to you.'

'What about security, and firepower?' Hannah asked. 'It's not impossible that other people know about Black Knight no matter how well NASA thinks they've covered it up. The Soviets got into space before we did and may have some idea of what's up there.'

'We'll be dispatching you with a twelve man team from the US Navy SEALs,' Jarvis explained. 'They're trained for Arctic warfare and will be deployed to protect you all. You'll leave in an hour aboard an Air Force KC-135 bound for Port Stanley on the British Falkland Islands, and from there fly south to join the US Coastguard vessel *Polar Star* off McMurdo Sound, Antarctica. The SEAL support will likely involve whatever means we can produce of getting Black Knight out of the area and onto US soil.'

'If it survives,' Ethan said. 'There's no guarantee that it will endure the burn-up in descent.'

'We're acting on the presumption that it will,' Jarvis admitted. 'But once that thing hits the atmosphere it'll be leaving a trail of fire across the entire night sky. We might be able to announce it as a comet or meteor burning up in the atmosphere, but we can't forecast it or the Russians and others will of course search for it and the whole thing will be blown.'

Ethan nodded.

'Where is Black Knight predicted to impact?'

'That's the thing,' Nellis revealed. 'It's slowing down and appears to be preparing to touch down close to the source of the earth-bound signals.'

Ethan stared at the general.

'Slowing down?' he echoed. 'On purpose?'

'Yes,' Nellis replied. 'It recently changed direction. We think that it may be under intelligent control.'

***

Dean Crawford

V

Pierre Hotel, Manhattan,

New York City

Gordon LeMay stood in an apartment on the 39th floor of the Pierre Hotel and looked out over the expanses of the city's Upper East Side and Central Park. Despite being the Director of the Federal Bureau of Investigation and having the ear of the Joint Chiefs of Staff and the President himself, LeMay realized that he was intimidated by the sheer exuberance that he was witnessing.

The apartment contained five bedrooms, marble floors and walls, voice-controlled lights and facilities and a wall-mounted, concave screen seven feet across that probably cost more than LeMay earned in a year. But he was only in one apartment, of the many that were currently being rented. His employers, a cabal of men who were colloquially known as *Majestic Twelve*, had rented out the *entire* top floor of the hotel to ensure absolute secrecy. LeMay knew that the cost of doing so was in the order of half a million dollars per month, the rent coming with a butler service, twice-daily maid service and a chauffeur driven Jaguar.

LeMay had arrived via that Jaguar to a discreet entrance at the rear of the hotel to avoid being spotted or photographed by any journalists who might be lingering outside the hotel in the hopes of getting a shot of the latest movie star hogging the front pages of the news. LeMay's graying features and sagging jowls were well known to the media, frequent interviews and sessions in Congress or the Senate a feature of his role within the law enforcement and intelligence community. Likewise he knew that the existing members of Majestic Twelve would also arrive discreetly, even though their identities were unknown even to LeMay and that even were they to be photographed they would not be recognized by the ordinary man in the street. It was a curious irony when compared to the global media presence of Presidents and Prime Ministers that the people who held the greatest wealth and power in the world were virtually unknown and made great efforts to remain that way. Although they normally met only once annually under the cover of the Bilderberg Group meetings, today was an important day and LeMay had been summoned to New York to meet with them for the first time.

Few people knew of the existence, let alone the relevance, of the Bilderberg Group.

Members of the Bilderberg, together with their sister organizations - the Trilateral Commission and the Council on Foreign Relations, were charged with the post-war take-over of the democratic process. The measures implemented by this group provided general control of the world economy through indirect political means.

Bilderberg was originally conceived by Joseph H. Retinger and Prince Bernhard of the Netherlands. Prince Bernhard, at the time, was an important figure in the oil industry and held a major position in Royal Dutch Petroleum, otherwise known as Shell Oil.

In 1952 Retinger approached Bernhard with a proposal for a covert conference to involve NATO leaders in general discussion on international affairs. The meeting would allow each participant to speak his mind freely because no media representative would be permitted inside; nor would there be any news bulletin about the meeting or the topics discussed. If any leaks occurred, the journalists responsible would be "discouraged" from reporting it.

Prince Bernhard supported Retinger's proposal for an international meeting, and in 1952 Bernhard approached the Truman Administration and briefed them about the proposed conference. However it was not until the Eisenhower administration when the first American counterpart group was formed. From the outset the American group was influenced by the Rockefeller family, the owners of Standard Oil - competitors of Bernhard's Royal Dutch Petroleum. From then on, the Bilderberg business reflected the concerns of the oil industry in its meetings.

Bilderberg took its name from the Bilderberg Hotel in Oosterbeek, Holland, where the first meeting took place in May, 1954. The concept of Bilderberg was not new, although none attracted and provoked global myths in the way that Bilderberg did. Groups such as Bohemian Grove, established in 1872 by San Franciscans, played a significant role in shaping post-war politics in the US. The Ditchley Park Foundation was established in 1953 in Britain with a similar aim.

Around a hundred and fifteen participants attended the meeting, coming from government and politics, industry, finance, education and communications. Participants were invited to the Bilderberg meeting by the Chairman, following his consultations and recommendations by the Steering Committee membership. The individuals were chosen based on their knowledge, standing and experience - just like the members of Majestic Twelve.

LeMay heard voices approaching from outside the apartment and turned to face the door as it opened. A butler walked in, carefully holding the door open as a lone individual entered the apartment. LeMay remained silent and still as the door was closed by the butler and the new arrival looked him up and down appraisingly.

'Director LeMay, what a pleasure to finally meet you.'

'And you are?' LeMay asked.

The older man smiled. 'My name is Victor Wilms, and I represent Majestic Twelve.'

'I thought that they would be coming here in person,' LeMay said.

'They *are* here in person,' Wilms assured him, 'but new developments have resulted in them being delayed elsewhere in the city. Right now, I'm here to brief you on those new developments. If you will?'

Wilms gestured to one of the plush leather couches, and LeMay obediently sat down as Wilms perched on the arm of a couch opposite and continued on.

'The group have been concerned about the recent breaches of protocol at the FBI that you have endured, and of the increased risk of exposure.'

'I'm aware of that,' LeMay replied. 'The Defense Intelligence Agency has embarked upon a mission to bring me down and perhaps to expose the members of MJ-12. General Nellis is spearheading the initiative and they've proven most efficient at derailing our plans. I've recently lost two valuable agents to their cause and narrowly escaped a jail sentence myself.'

'Thanks to us,' Wilms reminded him. 'It was not a cheap venture to purchase the loyalty of a military court judge.'

'I'm aware of that also,' LeMay admitted. 'What can we do to put this all right?'

Wilms watched the director for a long moment as though assessing him. Apparently satisfied, he decided to continue.

'The Defense Intelligence Agency has begun an initiative to recover from orbit a relic of some kind that our members believe may hold the key to mankind's origins. As you know, we have in the past made it a mission to recover similar objects and artifacts, but this one has always been beyond our reach.'

'Do we know where it is?'

'Oh yes,' Wilms chuckled. 'It's some two hundred miles above our heads and it may soon be coming down to Earth. We would very much like to take possession of it.'

'It's in orbit?' LeMay uttered in amazement. 'Do you have a location for its landing area?'

'Somewhere in the Antarctic,' Wilms replied. 'It's only a matter of time before the CIA get word of the object, and when it re-enters Earth's atmosphere everybody is going to be scrambling to get to the landing zone.'

LeMay rubbed his temples. 'My biggest problem now is that with Aaron Mitchell out of the picture I don't have a trustworthy agent to undertake this mission.'

Wilms nodded as he glanced out of the apartment windows at the sprawling city.

'Mitchell began to question his place among the order of things, began to question Majestic Twelve's mission. He started to act as though his opinion mattered in the grand scheme, which it of course did not. A shame, but he will no longer be an issue for us.'

'Don't underestimate him,' LeMay warned.

'I trained him,' Wilms replied. 'He is incarcerated in the Florence ADX Maximum Security Facility. There is no danger of his escape and no reason to concern yourself. I have no doubt that within just a few weeks the isolation and his impotent rage will cause Mitchell to suffer a tragic demise of which the rest of the world will know nothing. It is all in hand.'

LeMay considered Wilms for a long moment.

'He'll be after my head should that tragic event not occur.'

'Your purpose is to ensure that Majestic Twelve's bidding is fulfilled by the Bureau of Investigation,' Wilms snapped.

'That's precisely what I do,' LeMay shot back, 'and it's precisely what Mitchell did for thirty or so years, and look where he is now! What guarantees do I have that should I be met with failure, I won't find myself incarcerated in a Black Prison somewhere?!'

Wilms' anger faded and the calm smile returned.

'Failure is not met with a price by Majestic Twelve,' he replied, 'only betrayal. Mitchell was in a position to complete his last mission and yet he deliberately failed to do so, for reasons that I myself cannot fathom. Combined with his age and apparent desire to subvert Majestic Twelve's mission, it was decided that he should be disposed of as quickly as possible, a mission made far easier by his arrest by agents of the Defense Intelligence Agency.'

Wilms gestured the city outside and the country beyond.

'You and I both know that this country is governed by its administration only to give the people the impression that they have some kind of control over their futures, some sort of influence on the politics of their day. It is an illusion that has served this country well, and many others, since the end of the Second World War. The people are not capable of self-governance and democracy is a poor means to effectively maintain peace and prosperity across the developed world. Far better to govern from behind the scenes, to allow business to dominate politics rather than the other way around – that's where Communism went wrong.'

LeMay winced.

'Nobody in this country's going to take a socialist hard-line, Victor, least of all me. This is all about survival and prosperity, right? You want me to recover this object of yours, then I'll need more resources than I've ever had before. It's a major operation.'

Wilms nodded in agreement.

'The funds will be at your disposal,' he promised, 'as will a reliable armed force of not less than one hundred men, with tactical support of whatever kind you and your connections are able to provide. Naturally, this must be done under the radar.'

LeMay was already thinking, names of people he knew popping into his head, former soldiers and specialists. Mercenaries.

'I can arrange the deployment of your force, and support should be possible via private mercenary units. I won't have the necessary power to enact a complete radio blackout of the region, however.'

'Leave that to us,' Wilms replied. 'We have enough influence to subvert even military monitoring of the local environment for a limited amount of time. The DIA is already in motion on this, so we must act fast. Forty eight hours, Gordon, to gather the forces required and deploy them to the Antarctic.'

LeMay felt a quiver of alarm at the limited time to perform such a gargantuan task, but knowing that money was no object would smooth the process and he was loathe to show any sign of weakness before Wilms at such a crucial moment.

'The force will be deployed on time,' he promised.

'Good,' Wilms said as he stood. 'You may use all of the facilities here at your disposal to arrange the deployment. All of the phones have been provided with suitable electronic shielding. Call me, when it is done.'

Wilms left the apartment without another word, leaving LeMay to ponder the magnitude of what he was being asked to do.

'Whatever the hell it is you're after, I hope it's worth it,' he uttered to himself as he picked up the phone and began to dial.

***

VI

Florence, Colorado,

Byron Thomas drove north along Highway 67 as the sun rose to the east across the barren deserts. The sky was a flawless light blue, and although the cool of the night still lingered he knew that within an hour or so the deserts would be once again scorched by the sun, the temperature forecast to be in the nineties.

He wore a prim tweed suit, a small bow tie against his tightly buttoned collar and square-rimmed glasses shielding his dark eyes, their arms resting alongside his gray temples. Although a physically imposing man, partly due to his African American heritage, Byron was an academic through and through, a student of both law and psychology and a career psychologist who had made his fortune rehabilitating some of the most violent criminals the world had ever known. But today, he was afraid.

Beside him on the passenger seat of his Prius lay a slim folder, within which were the medical history and doctor's assessment of a patient so dangerous that they had been incarcerated without charge in the most secure prison in all of the continental United States. The final words of the physician who had begun treatment on the patient some years before, written in bold letters across the bottom of his psyche report, sent a shiver down Byron's spine.

Aaron James Mitchell is without a doubt the most powerful and dangerous man I have ever attempted to treat.

ADX Florence, as it was known, was America's most secure Super-Max prison, designed to house the most feared inmates within the country's prison system. Sited on a thirty seven acre complex, the majority of the facility was above ground with a subterranean corridor linking the cellblocks to the lobby. Enshrouded both in secrecy and endless glittering razor wire fences, few journalists or outsiders were ever permitted entry. Its inmates were among the worst that humanity had to offer; mass murderers, terrorists and cult leaders with the blood of hundreds of people on their hands, Mafia dons and other hardened convicts so repulsively violent that it made Byron's stomach clench at the mere thought of being in the same building, let alone confronting them. And yet, today, confront them he must.

The low, white buildings and watch towers loomed before Byron on the side of the road, bathed in warm orange sunlight but still somehow clinical in their appearance, indicative of a place where memories and hopes went to die. Byron pulled slowly into the parking lot, stopped at the security gates and showed both his identification and his letter of admittance to the guards there before being waved through and parking in front of the southern block.

Byron killed the engine and took one last look at the file, even though he had read it a hundred times before. He knew that he was merely delaying the inevitable, but he could not help himself as he flicked through the pages.

An image of a dark skinned Afro-American, born August 12th, 1955 – *Aaron James Mitchell. Mother; Florence Mitchell, nee Spencer, an American by birth, Detroit. Father; Jackson. J. Mitchell, former soldier, service record; Pacific Theatre, Iwo Jima, decorated veteran. Devout Catholics, both now deceased. No other siblings. Aaron Mitchell, service with United States Marines, Vietnam, decorated twice, two tours of active duty, two further tours as instructor...*

Byron, as he suspected like many others, had initially felt a sense of relief upon first reading the file's opening pages. He'd believed that he was reading the operational file of an all American boy and veteran, a man whom he could harbor some hope of liberating from whatever madness had consumed him.

Wife; Mary Allen Mitchell. Daughter; Ellen Amy Mitchell, born 1972, Oakland, California...

Byron's relief had quickly turned to melancholy.

... died, 1978. Interred Oakland, California.

Aaron James Mitchell; Diagnosed with acute anxiety and depression, revised as Post Traumatic Stress Disorder. Original PTSD from combat service enflamed via suppressed grief after loss of family. Two years medical hospital, San Diego. Released 1981.

Mitchell's record vanished into vagrancy sometime after his release from hospital, as had sadly so many of America's Vietnam veterans, before being mysteriously picked up by the CIA and maintained under strictest security. Byron scrolled down rapidly toward the physician's report near the bottom of the file, written some years' previously.

Physically impressive. Doctor's note: Aaron J Mitchell is without a doubt the most powerful and dangerous man I have ever attempted to treat.

The rest of the medical report was heavily redacted, no doubt as a result of Mitchell's work within the military. Byron could only guess at the horrors faced by this patient in the steaming jungles of South East Asia, and then again perhaps in foreign countries undercover as an operative of some kind, perhaps a spy.

Byron took a deep breath as he looked up at the walls of the prison, unmarked, bleached it seemed, scoured of any trace of humanity and compassion. He only hoped that his mission here today would be worth it, worth more than the tremendous sum of money that had been deposited into separate bank accounts belonging to Byron over the last two months.

Byron stepped out of the air conditioned vehicle and into the hot sunshine, already flaring off the asphalt as the heat began to rise. He walked across to the block entrance, where the first of many security gates opened and then closed behind him as he walked through. Pinned between two steel gates, he was searched thoroughly by prison security teams. The guards checked his letter of admission in his pocket, his file and his pockets before waving him through to a reception area where he was required to leave his cell phone, wallet and other personal belongings.

An alarm sounded that made Byron flinch as the next set of steel gates rumbled open and he walked slowly forward, hating every footstep as he eased into the darkened maw of a sally port that led into the prison's interior.

'This way, Doctor Thomas.'

A sergeant, his khakis perfectly pressed, his hair immaculately combed, gestured for Byron to follow him as they walked through a cool corridor that descended beneath the block walls and led to more security gates. Each was governed by operators in remote stations and covered by security cameras – there were no keys, no means for a prisoner to escape even if they did somehow manage to get out of their cell.

They passed through the gates, and Byron saw an X-Ray machine sunk into a revetment in the wall that scanned him as they moved by. No alarm was emitted and Byron continued under the sergeant's guidance until they emerged into the cell block proper.

Unlike most prisons, Florence did not have any communal areas for prisoners to mingle, for they all spent their days on permanent lockdown. Byron had heard that even exercise time, a single hour per day, was strictly organized so that no prisoner ever crossed paths with another. Complete and utter solitude was the facility's answer to the incomparable brutality of its inmates - they could harm nobody if they never encountered a soul.

Byron was led through the pristine, silent block. Most normal prisons were never, ever silent, filled with complaining, cursing cons and stressed correctional officers, the stench of urine and faeces staining the air. But here it was almost peaceful, and Byron felt himself relax somewhat as he walked alongside the sergeant toward an austere interview room located on the south side of the block.

The sergeant held the door open for Byron and he walked in to see a small table, steel rings bolted into its surface and poured concrete pillars for seats on either side, more steel rings in the floor either side of the seats. The walls were likewise built from poured concrete, featureless and bare, the room utterly empty and even the table bolted into the floor.

'There are no cameras in here due to the need for absolute security,' the sergeant informed him. 'In the past, patients have been known to punch out the lenses and use the glass as a weapon. I'll have the patient brought through. He will be secured to the table by both wrist and ankle restraints and two guards will be right outside the door, which will be left partially open throughout the meeting. If you have any issues, or you fear in any way that the encounter is becoming dangerous or the patient agitated, you merely have to call the guard and they will intervene instantly. Do you have any questions?'

Byron smiled up at the guard and shook his head.

'No, thank you. Please do bring the patient through.'

The sergeant turned with military efficiency and marched off down the corridor.

Byron waited a moment and then he slipped from the corner of his mouth a slim, silvery object that he concealed in one hand. Then, he made sure that the envelope in his pocket was open and ready. Finally, he took a deep breath and waited.

For the first time in his life, Byron Thomas prepared to commit treason.

***

VII

The dawn light broke through the four inch vertical window slot, a brilliant halo of light against a perfect blue sky. The light washed across the face of Aaron James Mitchell as he lay on the concrete bed in his cell and thought of the world outside.

Aaron spent twenty three hours a day locked inside his cell and was escorted by a minimum of three officers for his seven hours' of private recreation per week. The cell had a desk, a stool and a bed, all of which were forged entirely from poured concrete, as well as a latrine that shut off if blocked. A shower ran on a timer to prevent flooding, as did a sink lacking a potentially dangerous faucet. A polished steel mirror was bolted to the wall, the cell illuminated with an electric light that could only be shut off remotely. In addition, the cell was soundproofed to prevent Aaron from communicating with other inmates via Morse code or by any other means.

It was going to be tough to escape from the facility, and something of a shame: he had enjoyed the peace, solitude and simplicity.

Aaron hauled himself off the narrow bed and padded to the window. Four feet tall and yet only four inches wide, the narrow window was designed to prevent inmates from knowing their specific location within the complex because they could see only the sky and roof through them, making it virtually impossible to plan an escape. Inmates exercised in a concrete pit resembling an empty swimming pool, also designed to prevent them from knowing their location within the facility. The pit was only large enough for a prisoner to walk ten steps in a straight line or thirty in a circle. Telecommunication with the outside world was forbidden. The prison contained a plethora of motion detectors and cameras and no less than fourteen hundred remote-controlled steel doors. Guards in the prison's control center monitored inmates twenty four hours a day and could press a "panic button" that instantly closed every door in the facility should an escape attempt be suspected. Pressure pads and twelve-foot-tall razor wire fences surrounded the perimeter, which was patrolled by heavily armed guards with silent attack dogs. In extreme cases of inmate misbehavior, the center of the prison housed an area known as "The Black Hole", which could hold some one hundred fifty prisoners in completely darkened and fully soundproofed cells.

Aaron looked out of the window at the thin patch of sky, his mind turning in the silence. The facility's location in Colorado gave Mitchell the ability to estimate where his cell was located within the complex due to the light from the rising sun to the east. The lighter edges of cumulus clouds drifting right to left across the blue told Mitchell that he was looking south, as the prevailing winds in the state were from the west. Moreover, ranges of hills to the east of the facility had a tendency to cause warm updrafts of air to disperse clouds during the late morning, further informing Aaron of his location. The final evidence however was a pair of red-tailed hawks he had observed flying back and forth across the sky above the prison. Carrying prey and twigs only one way and not the other, he knew that they were nesting somewhere nearby, and by good fortune he had been able to ascertain that their swooping climbs away toward the south east were aimed at the roof of one of the six watch towers surrounding the facility. A simple mental picture of the facility, combined with all of the evidence, yielded a cell on the southernmost tip of the prison.

Aaron straightened his posture, forced himself not to slouch in defeat as he washed in the tiny sink and relieved himself in the latrine before taking a shower. There was little rush as the strictly coordinated routine of normal prisons was not a feature in a maximum security unit – he would not normally be allowed out of his cell until after lunch, and then only for an hour of strictly supervised exercise. He wouldn't be making that appointment, as he would be long gone by then.

Mitchell had already memorized his location within the state of Colorado, and of the nearby towns he would be required to traverse in order to reach his desired refuge. From Florence he would travel to Penrose, and from there further north through Beaver Creek state park until he could reach the slopes of Cheyenne Mountain, just south of Colorado Springs. It was an irony not lost upon Mitchell that the main route through the state park was named the Vietnam Veteran's Memorial Highway.

Aaron dressed and waited patiently for the guards to hand-serve a breakfast of powdered eggs and sauce through a shutter on his cell's steel door. Then, Aaron sat cross-legged on his bed and waited in absolute silence as he calmed his mind and emptied his body of the silent rage that burned within. His time would come in just a few hours, when he was due to meet with his counsellor.

The silence of minutes turned to hours, Aaron motionless on the bed and in a deep state of meditation. His heartbeat slowed gradually until his mind went into a state of deep relaxation, all sense of time vanished as he explored the deepest neural tracts of his memory, relived moments from his past both distant and recent with complete lucidity. Some haunted him, his long dead parents talking to him it seemed from beyond the grave, but their presence also comforted him and immunized against the confines of the cell surrounding his physical body. Other memories stoked the flame of anger inside him, especially those of Victor Wilms and the voices of Majestic Twelve, they who had used him for thirty years and then abandoned him to die here alone and forgotten.

His rage seemed to ring like a claxon in his mind, and then he realized that the sound was that of his cell door opening. Aaron drifted from the comforting realm of his dreams back to full consciousness and slowly got to his feet. There were no words, only the opening of a small shutter in the steel door at waist height. Aaron walked across to the shutter, turned his back to it and placed his hands behind his back.

The gloved hands of a correctional officer closed a set of cuffs around his thick wrists, and then Aaron stepped forward as the steel door was unlocked and then opened before him to reveal two burly officers.

'Keep your back turned,' one of them snapped, as if Aaron needed telling, his back to the open door.

Aaron felt more restraints locked into place around his ankles, and then he was turned around by one of the guards.

'Time for your counsel meeting.'

Aaron allowed himself to be guided out of his cell and turned to walk down the featureless, silent corridors. The sound-proofing of the cells deadened all noise, unlike the rowdy halls of other prisons, and there was no stench of urine and sweat that stained penitentiaries across the United States. Aaron noted that every other cell in the block was sealed, and with no windows there was no way to tell who else was incarcerated within.

The two guards led him down toward the exercise area, but instead of continuing on they turned down a side corridor and led him toward an interview room located on the southern-most tip of the building. The door to the room was open, and as Aaron was led inside he came face to face with his counsellor.

Byron Thomas, a graduate of Harvard and regular visitor to Aaron since his incarceration, stood from his seat and waited as Aaron was sat in a steel chair bolted to the floor. His manacles were fastened to steel rings in the floor and on the table before the guards withdrew, pushing the door to the interview room close to the jam for privacy but never shutting it completely.

'Good to see you again, Aaron,' Byron said in a deep, melodious tone.

Aaron nodded in silence. Byron was, like Aaron, an African American with an impressive physique, six foot four and with broad shoulders. That one could be a former Special Forces soldier and Vietnam veteran, and the other the inhabitant of dusty libraries and law schools seemed impossible to

Aaron, but there it was. The academic and the killer, occupying the same room and yet worlds apart.

Precisely as planned.

'You have progressed well over the past few weeks, Aaron,' Byron said as he opened a file and then began to slip out of his jacket.

'It's peaceful here,' Aaron replied. 'I wonder why inmates fear it so much. The solitude is wonderful.'

'Most men are not you, Aaron,' Byron said as he began undoing his tie and pulled a slim, silver object from his pocket that he slid across the table to Aaron's fingers. 'People mostly do not naturally enjoy being alone.'

'Fools,' Aaron replied as he picked up the sliver of metal and turned it expertly in his hands, slipping it into the locking mechanism of the manacles at his wrists and deftly unlocking them. 'They leech upon the attention of others.'

'Leech,' Byron echoed. 'That's a strong word, Aaron. Do you really despise other human beings so much?'

'Give me a reason not to.'

Byron quietly slid out of his pants as opposite him Aaron silently unlocked his ankle restraints and stood, removing his gray prison slacks as he moved around the table. Byron walked around to the opposite side and sat down.

'Love, compassion, generosity,' he said.

'Hate, greed, apathy…,' Aaron replied, slightly adjusting his voice as he spoke and began putting on Byron's shirt, pants and jacket.

'… fear, shame, rage,' Byron continued smoothly as he slid into the prison slacks and began fitting the manacles about his ankles. 'I don't care anymore. None of it matters.'

'Everything matters,' Aaron said. 'You just have to begin to care about yourself enough to care about the world outside, the people in it.'

Byrson's voice darkened, more gravelly now.

'What the hell for? I'm inside for the rest of my life several times over. You think anybody out there cares a damn about me? You think I give a damn about them?'

'And yet you're progressing well inside this facility,' Aaron said as he reached into the pocket of Byron's jacket and removed a small envelope. Inside, beneath the letter it contained, was a fine dusting of gray powder. Aaron dipped his fingers into it and smoothed the powder across his temples, dusting his hair with the soft gray ash. 'Perhaps, with time, you will find yourself moved to less demanding surroundings.'

Byron licked his fingers and smoothed his own temples down, smearing away the powder in his own hair before he reached down and placed his hands inside the manacles on the table top. Aaron slipped the slim glasses on as he reached down and quietly clicked the manacles closed around Byron's wrists.

'Why the hell would I want to move?' Byron snarled. 'This place is perfect! I don't have to listen to idiots like you spouting your psycho-babble to anybody who'll listen! I don't have to watch war veterans spat on in the street!'

'The Vietnam War was a long time ago, Aaron,' Aaron soothed. 'The people revere and respect our servicemen now.'

Byron gestured to the cell around them with a hateful grin. 'Doesn't look much like that to me, does it?!'

'You're here due to the murder of several innocent civilians, Aaron,' Aaron said calmly. 'Surely you don't expect to walk the streets with…'

'I expect a goddamned trial!' Byron screamed as he shot up out of his seat and yanked wildly on the chains.

The door to the interview room burst open and the two guards rushed in as Byron thrashed and snarled, fighting uselessly against his captors as they wrestled him face down onto the desk.

'If I ever see you in here again, I'll kill you with my bare hands!' Byron screamed.

One of the guards looked up at Aaron as he struggled to keep Byron pinned down, fully occupied with the task.

'Get out of here!'

Aaron nodded, his eyes wobbling with fear as he hurried out of the interview room and turned down the corridor. Two more guards were rushing toward him and he pointed back toward the room.

'Hurry, they're struggling with him in there!'

The guards dashed past, night sticks in their hands as Aaron continued on. The desk sergeant at the first set of gates opened them immediately as a silent alarm, flashing red lights that would not agitate the other inmates, warned him of the unfolding drama back on the block.

'He gone crazy again?' the sergeant asked as Aaron walked through.

'Can't stand the solitude,' Aaron replied as he passed by. 'Blames everybody but himself.'

'Shouldn't murder people then, should he,' the sergeant replied as he filled out a form and passed it to Aaron. 'Sign here please, doctor.'

Aaron dutifully signed the form, having practiced the signature in his mind a thousand times. The sergeant compared it to another on file, and then opened the second security gate to allow Aaron to pass through.

'Have a good day, Doc'.'

'You too.'

Aaron passed through no less than twelve more gates, all manned by security staff who had seen Byron pass through a half hour before. Nobody challenged him, although he was subject to the same rigorous searches as Byron would have been on the way in. There was nothing to find, and ten minutes after donning the Doctor's clothes Aaron James Mitchell walked out of the prison's main entrance and into the parking lot.

The sun was up in the sky now, the fearsome orb flaring in the perfect blue sky. Mitchell inhaled deeply on the air, but forced himself to walk normally as he pulled the doctor's keys from his pocket and hit the central locking button. A silver Prius's tail lights flashed nearby and Aaron subtly altered course toward it, conscious of the watch towers arrayed around the prison and the armed guards likely watching him from within.

Moments later, Aaron drove out of Florence ADX and vanished toward the north.

**

VIII

McMurdo Sound, Antarctica

'Welcome to the bottom of the world.'

The voice sounded disembodied to Ethan's ears as he sat in an uncomfortable seat in the shuddering belly of a giant C-130 Hercules aircraft, the loadmaster speaking into a microphone that connected to the headphones Ethan wore to protect his ears from the tremendous roar of the engines.

Through a small window beside his shoulder Ethan peered out into the frigid atmosphere outside the aircraft. The wing stretched away above him, huge turboprop engines trailing turbulent vapor that glowed in the light of a sun blazing amid a stream of molten metal searing the distant horizon. Far below a featureless canvass of ice fields stretched away into infinity, cast into dark and frosty shadows.

'We'll make our final approach to McMurdo in the next few minutes,' the loadmaster said as he walked between them and tugged on their harnesses to check that they were secure.

Ethan saw his companions jab their thumbs in the air in unison. Hannah Ford, two scientists named Willem Chandler and Amy Reece and their two respective assistants, and twelve Navy SEALs occupied the interior of the aircraft along with their respective equipment, compact vehicles and weapons. The soldiers had been deployed from the Atlantic Undersea Test and Evaluation Center at Andros Island in the Bahamas, while the two scientists seemed to have been plucked from some mysterious back room at the DIA.

Chandler, he had learned, was employed by the DIA as what they called a *futurist* and was apparently an authority on conspiracy theories, while Amy Reece was an *exobiologist* and linguistics specialist who specialized in the search for life outside the Earth and the effects of extra-terrestrial environments on living organisms. Between them and their respective assistants, Ethan figured they represented the closest things to an expert opinion on Black Knight that the agency had been able to rustle up at short notice.

Ethan glanced outside as the Hercules dipped its wing and began a gentle turn. The beams of pale sunlight glowing through the windows into the aircraft's cavernous interior vanished as they were plunged into darkness. The engine roar subsided enough for Ethan to hear the flaps and undercarriage deploy to the sound of whining hydraulics, the huge aircraft dipping and bouncing in the wintry gales blustering across the vast ice plains. Ethan clenched his harness as a tight knot of anxiety in his guts threatened to eject his breakfast over his boots.

Through the open hatchway to the cockpit far to his left, Ethan spotted the green glow of cockpit instruments and a glimpse of twinkling runway lights stretching out into the dark void ahead. The Hercules bumped and gyrated as it descended, and then a thump reverberated through the fuselage as the aircraft touched down on the ice and the pilots deployed the spoilers and threw the huge engines into reverse. The aircraft thundered and vibrated as though it were coming apart at the seams, and then slowed as it turned off the runway and taxied toward a parking spot.

Ethan breathed a sigh of relief and closed his eyes. He heard the engines whine down as he watched the loadmaster get out of his seat and hit a large red button inside the fuselage. The rear of the Hercules yawned slowly open as a ramp dropped down onto the ice. Half a dozen soldiers, wrapped up in thick Artic camouflage and armed with rifles, strode up the ramp. The loadmaster pointed at Ethan's group and waved them over.

Ethan unstrapped himself from his seat and hefted a large holdall onto his back. He then pulled on thick gloves, tightened his thickly padded jacket and pulled the hood tight over his head as he looked about at their bleak surroundings.

The station owed its designation to nearby McMurdo Sound, which had been named after Lieutenant Archibald McMurdo of HMS *Terror*, which first charted the area in 1841 under the command of British explorer James Clark Ross. British explorer Robert Falcon Scott first established a base nearby in 1902 and built Discovery Hut, which still stood adjacent to the harbor at Hut Point. The volcanic rock of the site was the southernmost bare ground accessible by ship in the Antarctic, and the founders initially called the station *Naval Air Facility McMurdo* from its creation in 1956.

Ethan knew that McMurdo had become a center of scientific and logistical operations in the Antarctic. The Antarctic Treaty, signed by over forty-five governments, regulated intergovernmental relations with respect to Antarctica and governed the conduct of daily life at McMurdo for United States Antarctic Programs. The first scientific diving protocols were established before 1960 and the first diving operations were documented in 1961, with a hyperbaric chamber available for support of polar diving operations.

From his vantage point outside the Hercules aircraft as he trudged off the ramp, Ethan could see rugged hills and valleys through the dawn gloom, and a nearby slate and shale shore. The black water of the Ross Sea was encrusted with jagged chunks of ice and a large ship was anchored there, its deck lights blazing in the darkness.

'Polar Star,' Hannah said as she saw the ship, her breath forming dense clouds on the frigid air as she spoke. 'That's our ride, part of the US Coast Guard fleet.'

The Polar Star was a stocky, thick-hulled vessel, her paintwork red and white for high visibility against both the black water and brilliant ice floes. The ship's bridge was almost a perfect cube, spinning radar dishes perched atop its lofty heights and glowing interior lights hinting at blessing warmth within. Nearly four hundred feet long and with a maximum speed of eighteen knots, *Polar Star* could continuously break six feet of ice at three knots, and could break twenty one feet of ice if backing and ramming, so Ethan had heard.

'Let's get the hell aboard then,' Ethan said, glancing again at the bitter gloom surrounding them. 'The less time I spend out here, the better I'll feel.'

Ethan followed the SEALS and scientists as they trudged across the base, soldiers armed with rifles watching them and ensuring that they did not stray far from their assigned path toward the rugged, icy shoreline. Although McMurdo was as much a research station as a military outpost, the soldiers were under orders to shoot anybody who strayed too far. Bristling with sophisticated listening devices and other obscure military technology, McMurdo's military contingent was still shrouded in Cold War secrecy.

'There anybody else out here we need to worry about?' Ethan asked as they walked, weighed down by their heavy backpacks.

'The French have an outpost, Dumont d'Urville, about fifteen hundred nautical miles south of Tasmania, but they're a long way from us,' Hannah said. 'Our plan, according to Jarvis, is to use *Polar Star* to break a channel across McMurdo Sound and make it to Ross Island and the station there as part of a standard resupply and refuel operation conducted every year at this time. We'll deploy before *Polar Star* moves on.'

Ethan marched up a ramp resting on the ice that climbed up onto the ship's deck, the vessel entirely surrounded by the ice sheets but its crew apparently unconcerned. He could see her captain watching as the SEALS hauled their heavy weapons and wheeled several strange vehicles aboard the vessel, clearly unhappy with the volume of military hardware suddenly appearing on his vessel. A tall, broad shouldered man with the rugged features of the experienced seaman, he extended a gloved hand.

'Captain James Forrester,' he introduced himself as Ethan stepped aboard the ship.

'Ethan Warner. When will we get underway?'

'As soon as you're aboard,' Forrester assured him. 'We've established a link to your senior officer in Washington DC and your team will be briefed as soon as we're on our way.'

Ethan eyed the captain uncertainly.

'How many of the crew know why we're here?'

'None of them,' Forrester promised, 'and I've already signed a non-disclosure agreement. Our mission route is routine anyway, so it's not going to raise any eyebrows with Ivan or any other of the research stations out here.'

Ethan smiled inwardly. It had been a long time since he had heard the Russians described as *Ivan*, a Cold War moniker that Forrester had likely been raised using.

'I'll have the team assemble as soon as possible,' Ethan promised.

'Your quarters are ready,' Forrester said as he turned to oversee the rest of the crew. 'Ensign DuPont will show you the way.'

A young sailor beckoned for Ethan to follow him even as the *Polar Star's* crew hauled the boarding ramp up from the icy wasteland below the ship and he heard the sound of the vessel's powerful engines begin to reverberate through the hull. He followed the Ensign through a hatch beneath the bridge and felt a waft of blessed warm air envelop him as he and Hannah walked through the interior.

'Damn,' Hannah uttered behind him, 'I've just realized that I couldn't feel my face.'

'The temperature outside is seventeen degrees below zero,' Ensign DuPont explained as he strode through the ice breaker's myriad corridors. 'You kind of get used to it.'

'I'd rather not,' Hannah replied, and then looked at Ethan as she pulled the thickly lined hood of her jacket off. 'You got any idea what this briefing is about? I thought that Jarvis laid it all out back in DC?'

'No idea,' Ethan admitted, 'but it must be important to have it all set up, and the SEALS didn't look like they knew what it was about either.'

DuPont led them to their quarters, little more than a pair of bunks in a room barely larger than a broom cupboard.

'You won't be staying aboard for long,' the Ensign informed them, 'so this is really just a place to store your kit while we cross the sound. The briefing room is just a little further down the corridor, to the right.'

Ethan thanked the Ensign, dumped his kit and thick polar jacket on his bunk and then headed straight for the briefing room with Hannah close behind.

The briefing room was located a deck below the bridge and was dominated by a table covered with a sheet of Perspex, beneath which was a map of the southern hemisphere, the Antarctic at its center. Ethan figured that the captain and his officers used this room for detailed navigation and planning.

The SEALS were already in the room, leaning against the walls and trying to remain inconspicuous despite the air of restrained violence that often enshrouded Special Forces troops. Around the map table were Chandler and Amy, both of them wrapped in winter weather clothing and whispering excitedly as a wall-mounted monitor at the far end of the room glowed into life and Doug Jarvis appeared upon it.

'Ethan,' Jarvis said, 'I take it your team is in place?'

'The ship's already in motion and we should make Ross Island in a few hours,' Ethan confirmed.

'Good,' Jarvis replied, 'because we've uncovered more data regarding the Earth-based signals we detected answering those belonging to Black Knight.'

The SEAL team leader, Lieutenant Riggs, stepped forward. 'Can we expect any kind of resistance?'

Jarvis appeared non-committal.

'That's uncertain at this time, as we simply don't have enough data. What we do have is evidence that the signals are being emitted from a site that was originally occupied in 1946.'

Ethan stared at the monitor for a long beat before he could speak. 'Who the hell was up here in 1946?'

Jarvis appeared as stunned as the rest of the crew as he replied.

'According to what we've managed to uncover, the only country known to have established a base up here in Antarctica in the months following World War Two was Germany. Not only that, but we chased them up here in an attempt to destroy what they created.'

Hannah Ford spoke up. 'And what exactly did they create up here?'

'A subterranean base,' Jarvis replied, 'and we've been trying to locate it for seventy years.'

***

IX

'The Nazis had an Antarctic base?' Ethan asked.

The briefing room had fallen silent as the soldiers, scientists and *Polar Star's* Captain Forrester listened to Jarvis as he replied from the Defense Intelligence Agency in Washington DC.

'The Germans had been sending exploratory missions down to Antarctica since the early nineteenth century,' he said. 'The Antarctic Plateau was claimed for Norway by Roald Amundsen as the King Haakon VII Plateau when his expedition was the first to reach South Pole in 1911. The name Queen Maud Land was initially applied in January 1930 to the land between 37Â°E and 49Â°30'E discovered by Hjalmar Riiser-Larsen and Finn LÃ¼tzow-Holm during Lars Christensen's Norvegia expedition of 1929. Norway's claim was disputed by Germany, which in 1938 dispatched the German Antarctic Expedition, led by Alfred Ritscher, to fly over as much of it as possible. The ship *Schwabenland* reached the pack ice off Antarctica in January 1939. During the expedition, an area of about a hundred forty thousand square miles was photographed from the air by Ritscher, who dropped darts inscribed with swastikas every sixteen miles. Germany attempted to claim the territory surveyed by Ritscher under the name New Swabia, but lost any claim to the land following its defeat in the Second World War.'

Ethan frowned as Hannah replied.

'So if they were prevented from annexing the territory after their defeat then how could they have built any kind of operational base up here, much less kept it secret for seventy years? There are at least twelve research stations all across Queen Maud Land belonging to many different nations.'

'That's what's caused the confusion,' Doctor Chandler replied. 'The entire story of a German base being built in Antarctica at the end of the Second World War, which has been in circulation for decades, has always been rejected by historians based on the assumption that because the Germans spent so much time surveying Queen Maud Land, that's where the site of the base must be. These recent signals intelligence tells us that the assumption has been wrong.'

A digital image of Antarctica replaced Jarvis on the monitor as Chandler went on.

'The legend purports that the Nazi mission was supposed to establish a base on Antarctica in order to set up a staging post for further invasions of countries in the southern hemisphere prior to the invasion of Poland.

However, records show that the mission was merely an attempt to scout new territories into which the Nazi machine could spread as the war progressed. Historians have repeatedly pointed out that the supposed discovery by the Nazis of warm water and vegetation within Antarctica's wastes, which would have been used to sustain a population or a base of some kind, were false and that there were no such sources.' The image changed again to a portion of the continent's eastern shores, north west of the *Polar Star's* current location.

'That was until 2015,' Chandler said, 'when surveys conducted by scientific teams on the continent and orbiting satellites detected a series of subterranean pathways that were channeling warm water beneath the Totten Glacier, a seventy mile long and eighteen mile wide feature and the largest on the continent's east coast.'

Ethan watched as graphics taken from research published in the *Nature Geoscience* journal showed a trough some three miles wide that had formed a gateway deep underneath the glacier, along with another tunnel that could allow warmer sea water to penetrate the glacier base.

Captain Forrester nodded as he observed the graphics.

'It's is the most rapidly thinning glacier in East Antarctica,' he said. 'Our own surveys have shown that much, but we didn't know anything about a warm water channel beneath it.'

'During a voyage to the frozen region during the past southern hemisphere summer,' Jarvis replied via the screen, 'researchers found the waters around Totten Glacier were around a degree and a half Celsius warmer than other areas.'

'Doesn't sound like much,' Ethan pointed out. 'Would that have made much of a difference to the Nazis?'

'It could have,' Chandler said. 'The warm water channels to the eastern coast could have provided one of the most important access routes into the continent: subterranean sea channels, perfect for concealing the movement of German U-boats that could have been used to supply the base.'

'What does this have to do with Black Knight?' Hannah asked.

Jarvis reappeared on the screen as he spoke.

'As many people know, the Nazis and Hitler specifically were obsessed with the occult, the paranormal and pretty much anything other-worldly. The Nazi regime placed great stock in anything that supported their notion of an Aryan master race, from whom they were thus supposedly descended and destined to rule the world. You name it, they went after it: Atlantis, the Ark of the Covenant, the Holy Grail and many other artifacts both mythical and obscure. But one particular device caught the attention of investigators during the post-war period: something called *Die Glocke*, or The Bell.'

Jarvis spoke as the screen's image split into two and revealed an image of a large, metallic object shaped somewhat like an acorn. Ethan could see strange symbols written around the circumference of the object's base, almost like hieroglyphics.

'This object was reportedly part of the Nazi's most secretive research and development programs in progress toward the end of the war. The Germans were making truly tremendous strides in technology, pioneering jet engines, electromagnetism, superconductivity and other exotic discoveries that we're only really coming to terms with today. There were rumors among the allies that in the rush to conquer Germany and occupy Berlin in the final days of the conflict, the governments of America, the United Kingdom and Russia were also keen to confiscate German technology for themselves, acts which created some friction between them even as the last shots of the war were being fired.'

'You're saying that what might be up here is something that belonged to the Nazis?' Captain Forrester asked.

'Again, we can't be sure just what's up here,' Jarvis cautioned. 'The truth is that if the Nazis did have an Antarctic base then they may well have attempted to regroup there in the aftermath of the German defeat, and taken much of their technology with them. It's not often broadcast by NASA, but after the war the vast majority of former Nazi scientists were brought back to the United States. The men who had previously worked for the Nazis on rocket technology for their infamous V-Bombs ended up pioneering the race for the moon. Werner Von Braun, one of NASA's best known scientists during the space race and the creator of the Saturn V rockets, was a German scientist who worked for the Nazis.'

Ethan peered at the schematics of *Die Glocke*.

'That doesn't look like anything we ever sent to the moon, except maybe the lunar capsule.'

'*Die Glocke* was not a spacecraft,' Doctor Chandler replied, 'at least as far as we can make out. No evidence of it was ever recovered from Germany after the war, at least as far as official records reveal, and scientists like Von Braun never admitted any awareness of the project. However, there is a tantalizing trail of evidence supporting the notion that something was indeed created in Germany that matches *Die Glocke* in a number of ways. The Third Reich had an underground scientific laboratory in a facility known as *Der Riese*, or The Giant, near the Wenceslaus mine near the Czech border. Experiments conducted there refer to a device made out of a hard, heavy metal that was some twelve to fifteen feet high and nine feet wide, similar in shape to a large bell. The device contained two counter-rotating cylinders which were filled with a metallic substance somewhat like mercury but violet in color and code-named Xerum-525. Other *leichtmetall*, or light metals, like thorium and beryllium oxides are also referenced in the documents, as well as the extraordinary effects that the bell would create when activated. Supposedly, within a zone extended some two hundred meters out from the object crystals would form in animal tissue, blood would gel and separate and plants would decompose into a greasy substance. What sources we do have said that several scientists died while experimenting with the device, and that many feared even approaching it whether activated or not.'

As Jarvis spoke, the image of a concrete framework standing derelict in a thin forest appeared on the monitor, like a hollow Colosseum with arches intact.

'This object, The Henge, in the vicinity of the Wencelaus mine, is said to have served as a test-rig for the device, which remained tethered within while tests were being performed to determine its supposed anti-gravitational properties.'

Several of the SEALS tutted and shook their heads, Ethan catching their skeptical mutterings from where he stood.

'It's myths and fantasies,' Amy said, speaking for the first time. 'None of this supposed evidence has ever been substantiated in any way, all of it merely shared by conspiracy theorists on the Internet without any effort to check sources or interview witnesses.'

'It all sounds like conjecture to me,' Ethan said finally. 'And again, it doesn't reveal anything about the Black Knight.'

'Except that it does,' Chandler replied, ignoring Amy as she rolled her eyes. 'In 1936 an object is known to have plummeted out of the sky near Freiburg, in Germany's Black Forest, and was recovered by the Nazis there for study. Whatever the object was, its discovery coincided with the sudden rise in military might and technological prowess of the Third Reich. I had our data analysis team calculate the object's trajectory and then run it backwards to obtain orbital information, and its position would have coincided almost precisely with the current polar orbit of the Black Knight.'

Ethan's eyes narrowed as he tried to understand what he was hearing.

'So Black Knight deployed something? Or maybe there was more than one of them?'

'Perhaps,' Jarvis said. 'After all, according to orbital data it must have been up there for several thousand years and thus may have become unstable over time. If there was more than one, that's what the Germans may have ended up with'

'And this supposed German crash?' Hannah asked. 'Are you saying that what we're heading toward in Antarctica must be where the Nazis hid it?'

'All we can say for sure is that elements of the Third Reich fled to Antarctica via South America in the aftermath of their defeat, and that British and American forces attempted to pursue and destroy them in expeditions that ended not just after the war but some *decades* later.'

'Decades?' Hannah echoed. 'We were still chasing them so recently?'

'Many of the most wanted Nazis, those who served the SS and who ran the concentration camps, fled before the end of the war and many of them disappeared in South America,' Chandler pointed out. 'Israel especially spent many decades hunting down former war criminals and bringing them to trial.' He gestured to the map of the Antarctic on the screen beside him. 'The warm water channels into the Totten Glacier prove that no matter how outlandish it may seem, the Nazis could have travelled deep into the continent's interior and developed a staging post for their proposed domination of the world, perhaps using Antarctica for a surprise naval attack. The Nazis were extremely fond of their naval power, Germany itself being landlocked, and had very well developed expertise in building submarine pens in marine environments.'

Ethan looked at the map of Antarctica dominating the briefing room as Jarvis went on.

'I'll leave Captain Forrester to fill you in on what we think happened after the war, and I'll check back in again in twelve hours to find out what's happening. We need to get this situation under control by the time Black Knight re-enters our atmosphere, because the continent's going to get real busy once the Russians and who knows who else see the object come down and wander down there for a look around.'

'Roger that,' Ethan replied as the monitor went blank and he turned to Captain Forrester. 'So, what's your take on all of this?'

Forrester beckoned them to follow him from the briefing room.

'I'll show you.'

***

X

Telfs-Buchen,

Austria

The mountains of Innsbruck-Land soared above the quaint village nestled at their base, the dawn sunrise touching the sky with delicate shades that contrasted with the angular granite slopes of the Mieminger mountain chain.

Victor Wilms stood on the balcony of an exclusive hotel apartment, a cup of coffee in one hand as he shivered against the dawn chill and took in the extraordinary view. Despite the cold air he always performed this ritual with the sunrise, for it represented to him a brief glimpse into what the Earth looked and sounded like without the human stain upon its surface, without the noise and the conflict and the endless suffering of so many for the peace and prosperity of a small few.

The news had reached Victor at a most inopportune moment, on the very morning that he was due to first brief the members of Majestic Twelve on the momentous events about to occur on the opposite side of the planet in the frigid wastes of Antarctica. Despite his lofty position within the cabal, Victor had never before laid eyes upon the controlling members, had never before been accepted as one of their own despite half a lifetime of service. Now he was about to be accepted into the fold and yet once again had to be the bearer of bad news.

Aaron Mitchell had vanished. That it had occurred at all staggered Victor equally as much as it had put the fear of death into Gordon LeMay. Mitchell's escape from the most secure facility ever built in the history of the United States would have made front-page news were it not for the complete media ban placed on the event. Nobody would ever know that Mitchell had even been incarcerated there, much less that he had escaped and that his absconding had remained undetected for almost twelve hours. It had only been the keen senses of one of the security guards who had often been responsible for Mitchell's incarceration that had detected something odd about Mitchell after the visit from his psychologist – a change of gait, a slightly different inflection of voice, an unwillingness to come out of his cell for exercise.

Upon closer inspection it had been revealed that the psychologist had taken the place of the criminal in a deftly arranged deception that Victor knew Aaron Mitchell must have had in place for years, perhaps decades. That his former protege had possessed the forethought to somehow arrange the loyalty of a man who could not be much further removed from the former Special Forces soldier did not surprise Victor at all – Mitchell had been so successful in his role as Majestic Twelve's senior undercover operative directly *because* of his resourcefulness. What surprised Victor was that he had kept his doppleganger in play for so long, even now, in his advancing years. Victor had long ago thrown his hand in fully with Majestic Twelve, understanding that there was nothing else out there for him and no reason not to become devoted to the organisation for life.

A soft buzzing intruded on Victor's reverie and he turned with some reluctance from the stunning vista outside and closed the balcony doors behind him. He pulled the blinds closed to prevent any observation from other houses in the town, and then moved across to the door and opened it.

Outside stood a tall, gaunt looking man whom Victor recognized instantly although most people could have walked past him in the street and had no idea who they were looking at.

'Good morning Victor,' the man greeted him with a hand shake and a sombre voice. 'May we come in?'

'Of course,' Victor croaked as he backed away from the door and gestured for the men outside to enter.

One by one they walked into the room, each wearing a suit that would have cost Victor a month's salary, watches on their wrists worth more than some luxury cars and subtle colognes from brands too exclusive to even be available in malls.

For the most part Victor did not recognize the men as they filed into the room, accompanied by two younger men who were clearly armed escorts. The apartment door was closed behind them and they variously sat or stood as Victor turned to face them. Of those that he did recognize, he knew them to be reclusive billionaires who had forged their fortunes in the stock markets of the world, real estate, agriculture and military technology. Not one of the men was less than fifty years of age, and there were just eleven of them, not twelve. Their number had been reduced a few years previously when Dwight Opennheimer, a Texan oil billionaire, had met his maker deep in a cavern in New Mexico at the hands of Ethan Warner while searching for the elixir of life, now held safely in the hands of MJ-12.

'What news, Victor?' asked the tallest of them, colloquially known to Victor as Number One – the reference that had in the past allowed Victor to differentiate between one member of Majestic Twelve and another during audio conversations.

Victor started with the good news.

'Gordon LeMay has been successful in organizing and deploying a small, highly trained force of men to the Antarctic. They are operating under the pretence of a highly classified mission to liberate US possessions from enemy forces, who have seized those assets after a melting glacier exposed a secret US base.'

Victor detected an air of approval settle upon the men as they looked at him, their gazes seeming to appraise him. Victor had spent the better part of his life serving these men so they knew him well enough, and he recalled other voices long in the past that he no longer heard, founding members of the group who had long since passed away. Majestic Twelve was controlled by patriarchs, the most learned of their kind.

'Are those assets fully under LeMay's control?' asked another of the men. 'He has been somewhat unreliable of late and we all know about how the Defense Intelligence Agency has been attempting to expose us.'

'LeMay's tenure as Director of the FBI will likely end before the year is out, but at this time he remains a useful asset. We cannot predict who will be promoted to director upon his departure, but with the increase in surveillance of our interests we cannot guarantee that any future director will be allied to our cause.'

Majestic Twelve were more than aware of the efforts made by General Nellis, the Intelligence Director, in exposing them through the work of the Defense Intelligence Agency. Many of their most recent failures had been a direct result of the DIA's interference in their operations, and that led naturally on to the next question that Victor had been dreading.

'What of Aaron Mitchell?'

The tall, gaunt man's question was neither accusing nor casual. Victor knew that they would likely be aware of what had occurred, for MJ-12 seemed to have eyes everywhere. None the less, it was a failure on Victor's part – he should have ensured that Mitchell was killed when in custody.

'Mitchell escaped from Florence ADX Security Max facility yesterday morning. I have no information regarding his whereabouts. I take full responsibility for this failure. I should have had him neutralized when I had the chance.'

'And yet you did not,' the tall man said. 'Why?'

Victor took a breath before he replied.

'Mitchell has served us for almost thirty years,' he replied. 'In that time he has never failed us, but he is getting older and is not able to perform for us as well as he once did. He questioned our loyalty to him, believed that we might abandon him at any moment. I took that opportunity to attempt to assure him that our loyalty was as strong as his had been, by allowing him to live. That was a mistake and a loose end that may now prove difficult to tie up.'

The gaunt man nodded, caught a few glances from his companions before he replied.

'Loyalty, Victor, is a prized asset. Mitchell was worth giving the benefit of the doubt and his capture was regrettable. He did not kill the president at Travilah as he should have done, and thus now the only person who has failed us is Mitchell himself. We must move forward from this. How long before we have the artifact in our possession?'

Victor felt an overwhelming relief wash through him, a tension in his stomach unwinding as he sighed beneath his breath and spoke more easily.

'Our sources inform me that the object will impact East Antarctica within just the hour. Our teams will be in position ready to take possession of the artifact, although we have evidence that the DIA is also deploying a team via the McMurdo research station.'

The tall, gaunt leader of Majestic Twelve peered at Victor.

'Warner and Lopez?'

Victor nodded.

'Warner and Ford, as it is at the moment. Lopez was injured during their last mission and is recuperating in a hospital in Washington DC.'

'Then now is the time to strike,' the gaunt man said. 'Have somebody reliable finish Lopez off prior to our return to New York, while she cannot fight back. That will remove one thorn from our side for good while Warner is otherwise indisposed.'

Wilms nodded.

'I don't have many details but I think we can safely assume that given the sensitivity of the Antarctic mission the DIA will have deployed with armed escorts, likely Special Forces troops.'

The gaunt man frowned.

'We cannot afford to have a major engagement in Antarctica, such an event will not go unnoticed.'

'All media and military channels suggest that nobody outside of MJ-12 and select groups of NASA and DIA personnel are aware that the object is even in Earth orbit. For now, we have the advantage – I suggest that we use that and push forward in an attempt to beat the DIA team to the site. It has been many decades since Majestic Twelve assets have used the base.'

'The site was abandoned decades ago when scientific research teams began building their damned observation posts all across Antarctica,' the gaunt man lamented. 'We could not afford our operation being disturbed or located, and we did not predict that Black Knight would suddenly begin its descent into the atmosphere.'

Victor knew that MJ-12 had been formed in the aftermath of the Second World War after a series of extraordinary events involving unknown craft observed in flight around the globe. Although such unidentified flying objects had been observed throughout history, even back as far as ancient Egypt, it was only recently that any headway had been made in understanding what the craft actually were and the nature of their purpose. When one such craft had impacted the ground in New Mexico in 1947, close to a town called Roswell, and aviator Kenneth Arnold had observed what he termed "saucer like discs" flying at tremendous speed near Mount Rainier in that same year, the Eisenhower administration had formed Majestic Twelve to coordinate a covert study of the phenomenon. What the administration of the time had not fully appreciated was that the founders of Majestic Twelve were men who had been fully aware of the Nazi experiments with supposed extra-terrestrial technology in the years before and during the Second World War, and involved in spiriting that technology away from the United States Government after the fall of Berlin. Majestic Twelve was not just a cabal of industrialists intent on the control of governments – it was actively continuing the work of the Nazis.

'Do we have sufficient resources in place to recover the craft and secure it?' Victor asked.

The men of Majestic Twelve looked at each other for a moment before the gaunt man nodded.

'We do,' he replied. 'But it may prove difficult for the teams to gain access to the base.'

'How so?' Victor asked. 'Is the glacier damaging the facility?'

The gaunt man shook his head.

'The Nazis who built the base encountered something up there, which was why they never went as far as to occupy the location permanently.'

Victor felt a tingling on his arms as the hairs on the back of his neck rose up.

'Encountered something?'

Number One nodded, his pale eyes haunted.

'Our own people encountered the same thing years later, and we too abandoned the base and sealed it.'

Victor swallowed thickly. 'What's up there?'

The gaunt man shook his head.

'You don't want to know, but we can assume that neither our own or the DIA's team will make it out of there alive.'

***

XI

Wilkes Land,

Antarctica

Captain Forrester strode onto the bridge of the *Polar Star*, Ethan following as the captain barked an order to his crew.

'Give us the bridge.'

The crew immediately vacated the bridge as the captain moved to stand behind the wheel and gently placed his hands upon it. Ethan got the impression that Forrester would rather be guiding his ship by hand through the icy seas than letting computers and GPS satellites navigate their course. The captain made a few last checks of the computers, and then as the last SEAL onto the bridge closed the door behind him, Forrester spoke clearly enough for them all to hear.

'In 1947, as I'm sure you've all heard many times before, an unknown object crashed near Roswell in New Mexico. Captured by the United States Army Air Force, they announced proudly to the world that they had captured a flying saucer, that announcement appearing in several national newspapers. Within days the Air Force recanted that statement, claiming that what they'd found was a weather baloon.'

Ethan knew enough about the legend of what happened in Roswell to know that it was pretty hard to confuse the materials used to create weather balloons with those required to produce a flying metallic disc.

'What is rarely reported is that the alleged crash also conincided with Kenneth Arnold's sighting of similar objects near Mount Rainier in Washington State in the same year, both of these iconic events coinciding with a top secret United States Navy operation that was conducted in Antarctica in 1946 and 1947 as part of the Navy's Antarctic Developments Program. The project became better known in later years as Operation Highjump.'

'What was the operation for?' Hannah Ford asked.

Forrester accessed a screen on the bridge controls and relayed it to a monitor mounted high on the bridge so that everyone could see it.

'Operation Highjump was organized by Rear Admiral Richard E. Byrd Jr., USN. Its primary mission was to establish the Antarctic research base Little America IV. The objectives were ostensibly to prepare crews for fighting in frigid conditions and full-on Arctic warfare, as well as extending the sovereignty of the United States over as much of Antarctica as possible. The government of the time had already recognized the threat of a battle-hardened Soviet Union's ability to expand and consolidate its gains after the fall of Berlin.'

Ethan knew that after the cessation of hostilities and victory in Europe, the allies had begun to view the Soviet Union with great mistrust, a feeling shared by their erstwhile Communist allies. Facing each other over the smoldering rubble of Germany, the two massive armies had settled into an uneasy peace that would soon become the chill of the Cold War and the dawning of the thermonuclear age.

'Operation Highjump was to develop techniques for establishing, maintaining, and utilizing air bases on ice. The work would improve existing knowledge of electromagnetic, geological, geographic, hydrographic and meteorological propagation conditions on the continent.'

Hannah allowed a small smile to form on her lips.

'You don't sound like you think that was their main objective.'

Chandler and Amy had gathered on the bridge and were listening intently as Forrester went on.

'The initial expedition went as planned, reaching the arena in late 1946 and launching reconnaissance missions. It was about then that things started to go wrong. A PBM Mariner aircraft assigned to the recon' missions crashed with the loss of three crew members, along with the loss of another life on the Ross Ice Shelf in an accident. I suspect that you all are aware of the superstitious nature of seamen throughout the centuries, and already the station was gaining a reputation for ill luck, but by early 1947 the base Little America IV had a serviceable runway on the glaciers. At that point, according to the official reports the expedition was terminated due to the approach of winter.'

'But it wasn't?' Ethan guessed.

'The problem I and many others have with the official story is that the mission was considered a low-priority exploratory survey mission. Yet it was comprised of an aircraft carrier, twelve warships, a submarine, over twenty airplanes as well as a crew of four thousand men. Even Byrd himself suggested that the mission was high level and military in nature, despite the official announcements.'

Forrester gripped the *Polar Star's* wheel more tightly as he spoke.

'The region of the Antarctic to which we're heading has seen more vessels lost than the Bermuda Triangle,' he replied. 'The list of vessels and aircraft that have vanished or been destroyed is almost endless: the *San Telmo*, lost in the Drake Passage in 1819 with the loss of over six hundred men; the *Pisagua* in 1913, run aground and wrecked; an Air New Zealand flight in 1979 that collided with Mount Erebus with the loss of over two hundred fifty lives; *Explorer*, holed and sunk; *Insung 1*, sunk with twenty one lives lost; *Berserk*, lost without trace; *Jeong Woo 2*, lost without trace and a DHC-6 Twin Otter aircraft in 2013 that crashed into a mountain range with the loss of all lives on board. Those are just the cases I can remember off the top of my head but there are many, many others.'

Ethan frowned.

'So you think the American expedition pulled out for fear of their lives?'

'The leader of the expedition, Admiral Byrd, discussed the lessons learned from the expedition with International News Service aboard USS Mount Olympus, and warned of the danger of future wars resulting in foreign nations mounting aerial assaults via polar regions. Byrd said that the most important result of his observations and discoveries was the potential effect that they have in relation to the security of the United States. The fantastic speed with which the world was shrinking was one of the most important lessons learned.'

'Sounds reasonable enough,' Hannah pointed out.

'But then, having established that point, neither the Soviet Union or the United States ever established a permanent military presence in Antarctica,' Forrester went on. 'Not only that, but a single documented event in 1946 seemed to precede the following flying saucer events of 1947. The expedition had captured some seventy thousand photographs and had been scheduled for five months' duration, well through the Antarctic winter, but then it was abruptly and without public acknowledgement cancelled after just two months in what seemed to be a panic. No further announcements regarding the expedition were made by the Navy, and no further expeditions were conducted in the region.'

Ethan thought for a moment.

'They found something,' he said with clairvoyant certainty.

'They found what the Germans had done,' Forrester explained. 'In August 1945, a year and a half before Byrd's expedition, German U-boats U-530 and U-977 surrendered in the Argentinean harbor of *Mar del Plata*. The U-boats were from the so-called *Führer convoy*, an extremely secret formation whose exact mission remains unknown to this day. The crews of the submarines refused to talk, so we were able to learn very few details, although the captain of U-530 did supposedly speak of an operation by the name of *WalkÃ¼re 2*. In line with this operation, his ship set sail from Kiel in Northern Germany for Antarctica two weeks before the end of the war; thanks to the Walther snorkel, it only had to surface once during the entire voyage across the Atlantic.'

Forrester guided the *Polar Star* to the right of a gigantic chunk of polar ice trapped in the frigid waters.

'On board the U-Boats were passengers whose faces were allegedly masked, as well as important documents from the Third Reich. The captain of U-977, Heinz Schaeffer, confirmed to his captors that he sailed the same route with his boat shortly thereafter and in conducting their own research, we realized that numerous German U-boats travelled in the direction of Antarctica during the war and in its immediate aftermath.' Forrester looked at Ethan. 'Operation Highjump was a fully militarized operation to hunt down the last of the German Navy, believed to have been hiding beneath the Antarctic ice in a purpose-built base. So, one has to ask: what did Byrd's fleet encounter down there and why has nobody ever returned to the site?'

A silence pervaded the bridge for a long moment before Hannah shrugged off the chilly atmosphere the captain had created.

'Let's stick with what we *do* know for now,' she suggested. 'Do we have precise coordinates for this German base you're speaking of?'

'Not precise coordinates,' Forrester replied. 'The base is likely to have been designed to ride the glacier it's encased within otherwise it would have been torn apart by now. We've made a few calculations based on its likely position, seventy years after its construction. Your team will be deployed there from the shore as soon as we arrive.'

'Which will be when?' Ethan asked.

'Four hours,' the captain replied as he glanced up at a GPS display mounted to the ceiling of the bridge. 'We'll make the mouth of the glacier by dawn, at which point you'll be on your own.'

Ethan turned away from the bridge and looked at the commander of the SEAL team. Lieutenant Riggs was leaning against a bulwark and had watched the entire exchange in silence.

'We'd better get what rest we can,' he suggested. 'It's going to be a long day.'

***

XII

George Washington University Hospital,

Washington DC

The man stood across the street from the hospital and watched in silence as patients and loved ones filed in and out of the building. One of the busiest hospitals in the district, it would not be easy to get inside unobserved, find the target and eliminate them while leaving no trace. But he knew that the price paid for the taking of the life of Nicola Lopez would be well worth it, and that there would be nothing that she could do to prevent her murder.

He stepped off the sidewalk and strolled casually across the street, the bright winter sunshine enabling him to wear sunglasses which aided in shielding his identity from the myriad cameras dotted around the city's streets.

He kept his head down as he walked through the hospital's entrance and into the crowded lobby, the characteristic clinical scent of the wards filling the air as he weaved through the queues of visitors and patients and headed for the private wards.

At the first opportunity he made his way toward a public rest room and pushed through the doorway. The stalls inside were busy as he moved through and found an empty one, closed the door, and then slid out of his jacket and pants to reveal a doctor's uniform. From his pocket he slipped an identity badge and pinned it on his shirt lapel, and then a small pager to his belt as he rolled up his jacket, cap and pants and slid them behind the latrine cistern.

He walked out of the stall and turned for the exit, pushed through the doorway into the corridor and turned immediate right. A quick glance across the busy lobby revealed that nobody had noticed anything untoward, the staff far too busy to take any notice of another doctor hurrying to and fro.

He knew from his research that Nicola Lopez was no longer under armed guard in her room. The terrorists who had shot her had themselves been neutralized within a couple of hours of the incident, and the conspiracy that they had formed to murder senior politicians in the administration had failed. Thus, there was nobody any longer gunning for Lopez and no need for round the clock protection. Or so they thought.

He moved toward an elevator and then thought better of it, taking the stairs up to the third floor of the hospital where a series of private wards were located. Doctors and nurses milled this way and that as he walked toward a ward tucked away on the south west corner of the building.

His nearest escape route was the stairwell at the far end of the ward, with a secondary route to the elevator should he require it. He knew that he would only have a few moments to enter the room, complete his mission and escape without detection. He knew well the consequences of being identified– *Majestic Twelve* would spare no expense in removing him from the equation and preventing any connection between them and the murder of Nicola Lopez.

The corridor was deathly quiet as he moved through it and identified the room in which Nicola Lopez lay. Her name was emblazoned upon a chart resting in a plastic holder on the door, and he could see through a window into the room. Even the briefest of glances told him that she was alone, the nurses having already completed their rounds and moved on.

Comatose. That was the detail he had received from his discreet enquiries: that Nicola Lopez had been in an induced coma while her body recuperated, and was now on strong medications designed to maintain her in a sort of stasis, unconscious but not in a coma, to give her body the best possible chance of recovery from her ordeal. He had never before encountered Lopez in such a vulnerable state and now it would serve his purpose well.

He opened the door and walked in. The room was well ventilated, flowers arranged on a table near the bed where Lopez lay amid a tangle of intravenous lines. Her sheets were pure white, her long black hair neatly tied in a pony-tail and snaking like black oil beside her head. Her features were drawn, somewhat pale, her breathing soft and a gentle rhythmic beeping from the heart monitor informing him that she was still alive.

He pushed the door closed behind him and moved toward her bed, one hand slipping into the pocket of his pants to produce a slim syringe filled with a clear fluid. He reached up to the intravenous line plugged into Lopez's left arm, and carefully slipped the tip of the syringe into the line and squeezed.

In absolute silence the clear fluid emptied from the syringe and flowed into the line, and from there into Nicola Lopez's helpless body.

*

'I'm here to see Nicola Lopez,'

The woman leaned casually on the counter and smiled at the receptionist, a young African American nurse who began tapping on her keyboard as she scrutinized her files.

'Miss Lopez is on a private ward, level three. Do you have an appointment?'

'I do,' the woman said, flicking her long blonde hair out of her way as she reached into her handbag and produced a card and an appointment form. 'I'm Angela Raymond from Clearwater Insurance. We're acting for Miss Lopez's family in regard to the shooting that injured her. We'd like to visit her to assure ourselves of her condition so that we can make arrangements on behalf of her family.'

'And her family are where?' the nurse asked.

'Mexico,' Angela replied, 'Guanajuato, to be precise. They're hoping to travel here soon but we're working for them until they can reach the States and start proceedings. I'll only need a quick visit and a word with her physician to clarify her injuries.'

The nurse nodded and glanced at her screen.

'Level Three, Doctor Hazeem Reyen is the duty physician. He'll inform you of everything you need to know.'

Angela flashed the nurse a bright smile of gratitude and made her way to the elevators. Within moments she was travelling up to the third floor, the elevator humming as she held her card in one hand and waited patiently for the elevator to reach its destination.

The doors opened onto the third floor and Angela followed the signs to the private wards as she sought out some sign of Doctor Reyen. She spotted a Middle Eastern looking man near the reception desk and hurried over.

'Doctor Reyen?' she asked.

Hazeem Reyen turned to the attractive blonde in the smart suit and shook her hand, responding to Angela as men always did, surprised and delighted at her attention. Angela smiled back as the doctor introduced himself and she informed him of what she required.

'Of course,' Reyen replied, 'Miss Lopez is in room five. I'll show you there now.'

Doctor Reyen led the way to the ward and as he reached room five he glanced back at Angela.

'I didn't realize that there was any valid insurance claim for Miss Lopez's family? She survived the shooting and should make a full recovery, given time.'

'They're looking into legal action against the government,' Angela explained. 'Miss Lopez was unsupported when she tackled two terrorists in the Capitol, and they feel that her safety was neglected by the police.'

Doctor Reyen opened the door to room five and gestured for Angela to enter. She walked into the room and turned to look at Nicola Lopez, who was laying in silence before her, the heart monitor beeping softly.

'I'll just be a moment,' Angela said to the doctor.

Doctor Reyen smiled.

'That's fine, but I cannot leave you alone with the patient I'm afraid. I'll have to wait until you're done here before I can leave.'

Angela smiled gently. 'I understand. Could you close the door for me?'

Doctor Reyen turned and pushed the door closed.

The blade was slim and easy to conceal as Angela let it fall from the inside sleeve of her jacket and swung it overarm toward Doctor Nazeem's back, aiming for a spot directly between his shoulder blades where the spinal column travelled up toward the brain stem. The blade flickered in the light as it rushed down upon the doctor, but then something slammed into Angela's shoulder with tremendous force and hurled her aside.

Angela's head smacked into the unforgiving wall as the blade in her hand slashed down the back of the doctor's arm and he cried out in surprise and pain. Angela turned in the direction of the blow that had struck her and saw Lopez propped up on her elbows, her dark eyes flaring with rage and one leg outstretched where she had launched her attack.

Angela fought to get to her feet even as the door to the room was hurled open.

Doctor Reyen staggered backwards out of the way as a large man burst into the room, dark eyes glaring down at Angela.

*

Nicola Lopez hauled herself off the bed as she saw the blonde woman on the floor look up in terror as Aaron Mitchell's boot swung into her slim wrist with a hefty blow. The blade in her hand spun through the air as Lopez heard the brittle bones in the woman's arm snap like twigs.

The blonde woman screamed, the scream cut off abruptly as Mitchell's boot slammed down onto her face and silenced her with a brutality that sent a pulse of fear writhing through Lopez's guts.

Lopez slid off the bed in panic and almost fell as her legs betrayed her, weakened from lack of use. Mitchell loomed before her and she gathered her strength and swung her best effort at a punch to his jaw. Mitchell blocked the blow with ease and then caught her before she fell. Lopez sucked in air, her eyes aching and her limbs weak as she realized that the giant assassin held her life, quite literally, in his hands.

Mitchell turned and looked down at the injured doctor.

'Get your wound tended to and call the police,' he growled. 'Ensure that woman is restrained and detained before she regains consciousness! Believe me, she will kill anybody who tries to stop her!'

The doctor nodded frantically as he scrambled to his feet, one hand clamped around the bloody wound to his arm as he pushed through the door and out into the corridor outside, screaming for a security team.

Aaron Mitchell turned to look at Lopez, his dark eyes smoldering with restrained violence.

'Come with me if you want to live.'

***

XIII

'What the hell are you doing?' Lopez gasped, her voice a whisper, and despite the effort it required she still managed to add: 'Asshole?'

Aaron Mitchell did not reply as he carried Lopez out of the hospital and across the parking lot outside until he reached a non-descript sedan he had hired with cash he had withdrawn from a safety deposit box in Missouri. The journey from Colorado had been a long one, but he had long maintained a network of such caches in case of emergency. He opened the passenger door and lowered Lopez into the vehicle, strapped her in before he took his place behind the wheel and drove out of the lot.

Lopez was, by any standards, out of the game. She knew that Mitchell had slipped something into her saline drip to bring her back to consciousness, because she had seen him toss the empty syringe into a trash can on their way out of the building. Likewise, she also knew that the woman whose face Mitchell had brutally stomped had been there to kill her.

'I asked you a question,' she murmured as the car veered onto the beltway, headed south.

Mitchell grabbed a chilled bottle of water and handed it to her.

'Drink, as much as you can. We need to get you back up to strength.'

Lopez stared at the man who had opposed her and Ethan for so long, quite uncertain of what was going on. She took a small sip of the water from the bottle, and then immediately realized how parched she was and promptly guzzled the rest of the water down as Mitchell negotiated the traffic heading out of the district toward Maryland.

'Why did you get me out of the hospital?' she demanded, slightly more energetic now as the water hit her system.

Mitchell spoke in a serious tone that brooked no argument.

'How much do you remember?'

Lopez blinked, her mind reeling as she tried to recall her last moments of consciousness.

She had been near the White House, running down two terrorists hiding in a goods vehicle to the south west of the building. They had been using an advanced form of technology, one that she and Ethan had been searching for, that allowed the user to control the mind of an implanted human being. She struggled to recall the man's name: Hazeem? No, Abrahem – Abrahem Nassir.

'I was running toward a vehicle,' she said finally. 'Shots were fired at two cops coming from the opposite direction. They went down and the vehicle started its engine. I got to the rear of it, pulled on the door and it flew open, knocked me off balance. There were two guys inside and they got the drop on me.' Lopez hesitated as she realized that she had recalled the moment she had been shot. 'Two rounds to the chest,' she whispered.

Mitchell nodded, driving sedately amid the traffic in order to avoid standing out.

'That's the last thing you remember?'

'Before that woman in my room and you turning up,' she confirmed.

'Then you've got some catching up to do,' Mitchell replied. 'You were in an induced coma for four weeks, and unconscious for as long again. You were shot two months ago.'

Lopez stared into the distance for a moment and then yanked down the sun visor and looked into the small vanity mirror upon it. Her pallid skin, sunken eyes with dark rings and messy hair peered back at her.

'Jesus,' she gasped.

'You're alive,' Mitchell countered. 'You'll recover fast, provided the people who hired that assassin to take you down don't get to you first.'

'And who hired them?' Lopez demanded.

'Majestic Twelve,' Mitchell replied. 'They're moving to shut down any opposition they encounter, and both you and your friend Ethan Warner are at the top of their list.'

Lopez struggled to make sense of what Mitchell was saying.

'Then why haven't you put a bullet in my brain?'

Mitchell gripped the wheel tighter, as though it was a struggle to get his words out.

'There have been some developments of late,' he rumbled, 'that have caused me to question the role of Majestic Twelve.'

Lopez watched the big man for a long moment before a smile spread across her features.

'You turned coat on them?' she mocked. 'Wow, they must really have tugged your chain, Mitchell. Pension benefits from a criminal organization not what you were hoping for?'

Mitchell had in the past detected Lopez's sarcastic nature and was surprised to hear it return so soon, the fiery Latino swiftly reverting back to her natural self.

'Majestic Twelve has grown immensely in power over the past few decades,' he replied. 'Ventures that would have been unthinkable to them in the 60's are now commonplace, and it appears that they consider themselves the effective rulers of western civilization. MJ-12 considers the President of the United States to be merely a cypher, an official elected to appease the public, to make the population of our country believe that they actually have a say and influence on how the country is run. In truth the president has little real power and Majestic Twelve has enough of both the Senate and Congress in its pocket to ensure that any policy unpalatable to them is easily over-ruled.' Mitchell sighed. 'That's not what I signed up for.'

Lopez leaned toward him and jabbed a finger into his big, round shoulder.

'But you *did* sign up, didn't you?' she accused.

'I was deceived,' Mitchell growled back at her. 'We were signing up to serve our government. Most of us were Vietnam veterans, vagrants with nowhere to go and despised by our own people, the people we thought we had fought to protect from the advance of Communism. Instead, we were spat on and rejected.'

'Not our country's finest hour,' Lopez admitted as she leaned back in her seat.

'We were the perfect patsies, vulnerable to the promises of a cabal like Majestic Twelve, wealthy and powerful and able to indirectly control assets of the intelligence community. We were trained under the radar by former CIA operatives and deployed to serve the interests of big business instead of our country. Within weeks of accepting their offer I went from living in a cardboard box in Anacostia to earning five figures a year and having my own home again.'

Lopez shook her head.

'So it didn't ever cross your mind as odd that you never set foot in the CIA or FBI buildings?'

'Deniable assets,' Mitchell replied, 'paramilitary units attached to clandestine services. After Vietnam, they claimed that the government needed an arm of the military and intelligence community that could be used in complete secrecy without upsetting Congress, which was as keen as anybody to discredit both further overseas military action and appease the public mood. Majestic Twelve capitalized on that.'

Lopez watched the traffic passing them by as Mitchell drove, and realized that she needed to capitalize on this moment while she could.

'Tell me everything,' she said. 'Tell me what their end-game is, what they actually want.'

'Uncertain,' Mitchell said. 'Majestic Twelve was formed in 1947 as a result of the supposed crashed flying saucer incident in Roswell, New Mexico, but also in response to a series of events in the aftermath of the Second World War that occurred in Antarctica.'

'Antarctica?' Lopez echoed. 'What the hell happened up there?'

'It's a long story, which you'll hear about soon enough,' Mitchell promised. 'Point is, MJ-12 was an official and militarily supported group until somewhere in the 1970's, when it was shut down by the government of the time. That's why the trail of data that investigators follow always dries up and why MJ-12 is generally considered a myth – they officially were removed from all government documentation and all assets and references destroyed. The reason for the excise was that MJ-12 was considered surplus to requirements with the rise of the Black Budget and the expansion of highly secretive military facilities like *Area 51* at Groom Lake in Nevada, Edwards Air Force Base, Cheyenne Mountain and others. In essence, military contractors like Lockheed Martin and Boeing took over the development of highly classified projects and rendered MJ-12 obsolete.'

'So they re-formed outside of the government,' Lopez figured.

'Exactly,' Mitchell confirmed. 'The most powerful men among those ejected from the government's circle of trust continued the Majestic Twelve mandate but this time remained highly secretive in their own right. The idea was that employees of the group would serve, not actually knowing that they were serving Majestic Twelve. They recruited operatives, training staff and military hardware using contacts within the military-industrial complex, and needed their own paramilitary force to perform military actions when the United States government were unwilling to put troops on the ground in foreign countries, should the need be required to sustain profits in their business ventures outside of the US.'

Lopez leaned back in her seat as she digested what Mitchell had told her.

'They become ever more powerful, growing in influence and stature as they commit to profitable ventures around the globe, unhindered by the law, and eventually begin to rival the US government in power.'

Mitchell nodded as he eased off the freeway.

'Majestic Twelve now has the director of the Federal Bureau of Investigation in their pocket, the Speaker of the House, numerous other officials both here and overseas as well as at least four Presidents and Prime Ministers from around the world. They cannot directly influence the president as, remarkably, he managed to win the presidency without their financial backing. But they can and do guide US policy by pressuring Congress with political lobbying, financing the campaigns of politicians in return for policies favorable to their business ventures. When overseas they deploy their paramilitary forces to achieve by force what money cannot, which is why you're here.'

'Me?'

Mitchell nodded.

'I have been outcast by the group for failing to assassinate the President of the United States, or at least ensuring that he died at the hands of Abrahem Nassir.'

Lopez gasped and smiled again.

'I almost forgot – Ethan must have come through!'

'He did,' Mitchell acknowledged, 'as he annoyingly often does. But his success, and in part my failure, have forced MJ-12's hand and now they're on the warpath. The Defense Intelligence Agency's efforts to root them out have grown from a mild annoyance to a serious threat and they're acting upon that. I was incarcerated in Florence ADX without trial, and was forced to enact an emergency escape plan I've had in place for two decades. It was a one time thing, so I can't run it again. I've played my hand and by now MJ-12 will know it.'

Lopez blinked.

'You escaped from a security max prison?'

'Preparation is everything, Miss Lopez,' Mitchell replied. 'Now, Majestic Twelve has deployed a paramilitary force to Antarctica, hot on the heels of Ethan Warner and a smaller team sent by the Defense Intelligence Agency to the same location. We need to support them as soon as possible.'

'Ethan's in Antarctica?'

'Yes,' Mitchell confirmed, 'because whatever it is that MJ-12 wants is up there. I intend that they will not get hold of it.'

Lopez stared at him for a moment. 'What's my part in all of this?'

For the first time, Mitchell smiled.

'I'll need you with me to help prevent me from getting shot when I walk into the Defense Intelligence Agency.'

Lopez shook her head.

'I'll be damned,' she whispered, 'you're really switching sides?'

Mitchell looked at her, his dark eyes smoldering with restrained anger.

'Majestic Twelve lied to me when they recruited me and have betrayed me for a single decision of which they didn't approve,' he growled. 'That makes me very angry.'

Lopez's guts contracted slightly as she reflected on what a man like Aaron Mitchell might consider as being very angry. She said nothing more as Mitchell drove slowly toward the DIA Headquarters at Anacostia-Bolling.

***

XIV

Antarctica

General Andrei Veer stood in the cavernous rear of a C-130 Hercules transport aircraft and surveyed the men seated before him. There were one hundred of them in total, each crammed onto the narrow seats lining the fuselage of the gigantic aircraft, and between them were rows of tightly packed ATVs – All Terrain Vehicles, each with four am-tracks and rear-mounted machine guns, and each capable of transporting two armed men across the ice at high speed.

Veer was a giant of a man and stood with his arms folded across a barrel chest, his face half concealed by a thick, dark beard. Cold gray eyes that seemed a reflection of the bitter Antarctic continent far below them scanned the faces of his men and saw neither hubris nor doubt in their gazes.

'We deploy in ten minutes!' he boomed, his thick Slavic accent loud enough to be heard above the roar of the Hercules' four massive turboprop engines. 'Our target is in the north of Queen Maud's Land and the Totten Glacier, and we know that an armed force of unknown origin has been deployed to prevent the United States of America from achieving its objectives. It's our job to ensure that they do not succeed!'

A roar of *Hoo-Rar* filled the interior of the aircraft as the soldiers, a mixture of former Marines, Army Rangers and other highly skilled units clenched their fists as one and punched the air. Dressed in white Arctic camouflage and with M-16 rifles clutched to their chests, they were heavily armed and well suited to the task at hand.

'Our primary mission is to recover a highly classified military satellite that is descending out of orbit prematurely toward the glacier,' Veer shouted above the roar of the engines. 'The enemy is made up of scientists and soldiers of unknown allegiance but we should not underestimate them: they will be well armed, highly paid and highly motivated, just like all of us. The difference is that the satellite belongs to our country, and we will get it back from them!'

'*Hoo-Rar!*'

Veer pointed to the ATVs and the aircraft around them.

'Expect hostile action! Deploy with full and lethal force! If there are no survivors from the enemy team, then our President will not have to explain to the world what happened up here and the security of our country will remain inviolate!'

'Hoo-Rar!'

Veer reached for a face mask that lay on the rear of an ATV beside him. He prepared to don the mask and then shouted:

'Thirty seconds, open the doors!'

The C-130's loadmaster punched a series of large buttons attached the fuselage wall, and instantly a huge ramp at the rear of the aircraft began to slowly lower and provide a vertiginous view of the world below. The sky above was a deep indigo blue flecked with stars, and behind the aircraft's massive turboprop engines swirling vapor trails glowed gold in the sunrise as they billowed into the distance in the aircraft's wake.

The air was cold enough to take Veer's breath away, ice clinging to his eyebrows and beard until he donned the mask. Oxygen flowed from the mask, allowing him to breath in the bitter cold and the high altitude, low pressure air as he strode to the ATVs. His men lined up on either side of the aircraft's fuselage, where two hatches were manned by the loadmasters.

A red light high on the fuselage wall suddenly turned green, and the loadmasters opened the hatches to allow a freezing gale to flow through the aircraft as Veer roared into his microphone.

'Go, now, now, now!'

The troopers deployed one after the other, hurling themselves out of the open hatches either side of the aircraft into the frigid air thirty thousand feet above Antarctica. Veer turned and watched as the loadmasters, all of them protected by masks and Arctic survival clothing, began pushing the ATV's out of the Hercules.

The vehicles fell away behind the craft one by one, large parachutes deploying behind them and billowing out to slow the vehicles' descent toward the ice far below. Veer watched for a moment longer as his men poured from the Hercules into the void, and then he sprinted down the fuselage, running faster than the ATVs rolling off the back of the aircraft as he reached the point of no return and hurled himself off the back ramp of the Hercules into the abyss.

Antarctica was sprawled below him, a vast continent of ice bathed in an orange glow from the rising sun behind Veer as he plummeted away from the Hercules. The roar of the aircraft's engines faded swiftly into memory as he reached terminal velocity, following the black specks of his men as they rocketed in freefall down toward the barren, frigid wastes far below.

The Antarctic coastline demarked clearly the mouth of the Totten Glacier to their south, the glacier tiger-striped with long dark shadows from ridge lines and ranges of hills spreading for miles across the empty, desolate continent.

The roar of the Hercules' engines was replaced by the scream of wind rocketing past Veer as he plummeted ever downward. He checked his altitude and then squinted down at the icy wastes far below, seeking any sign of their quarry. Within a few moments he spotted a series of glowing streaks, perhaps twelve trails or plumes churned up by vehicles travelling far below them on the surface. On his visor, a small blinking red light marked the location where the signals his employers had detected from what they called *Black Knight* had been.

Veer spoke into his microphone, loudly enough to be heard over the roar of the wind buffeting past him.

'Enemy seen, deploy between them and the target. Repeat, cut them off!'

Veer tucked his arms and legs in and tilted his body down, accelerating as he sought to catch his men up and be the first to touch down on the Antarctic wastes. His massive body raced downward and he plummeted past some of his men, who quickly accelerated along with him as they plunged through thin veils of cirrus cloud, the surface of Antarctica increasing in detail below them. Veer could see the vehicles' plumes more clearly now, the machines heading north toward the same spot marked on his visor with the red icon.

A last glance south revealed the presence of a fairly large ship many miles away, anchored near the coast. Veer grinned inside his mask, knowing that the team on the ice would believe themselves the only people even aware that Black Knight even existed.

They won't know what's hit them.

***

XV

Totten Glacier, Wilkes Land,

Antarctica

'All call signs report in!'

Ethan gripped hold of the ice glider's handles as he glanced back over his shoulder. The *Polar Star* was anchored in the frigid black water of the glacier's mouth, surrounded by immense chunks of flat, floating ice that had calved off the enormous glacier into the Antarctic Ocean.

The low morning sun flared across the horizon behind the ship, the ocean sparkling like burnished copper beneath its glare as the SEAL team deployed their equipment and maneuvered their vehicles into position at the head of the convoy.

The ice gliders they were using were extraordinary tandem twin-seat vehicles, set on three skis in a tricycle configuration, with the two independently suspended outboard skis located at the end of curved arms in the manner of a seaplane's wings and floats. Behind Ethan, who sat in the rear cockpit of one such craft, was a bio-fuel powered Rotax 914 aircraft engine attached to a three-bladed pusher-propeller with variable pitch. The four-cylinder turbocharged engine pushed out a hundred horsepower and was capable of driving the glider at an incredible eighty miles per hour across the ice.

In the enclosed cockpit, a GPS-enhanced radar system designed to detect voids in the ice and report coordinates to the rest of the team was allied to a computer-controlled aiming system for the two machine guns embedded in the glider's nose. Ethan checked his harnesses and reveled in the warmth billowing into the cockpit from the engine as the driver, Lieutenant Riggs, looked over his shoulder.

'All set?'

Ethan offered the soldier a thumbs-up and then Riggs opened the throttle and as one the twelve ice gliders soared away from the coast, following a path alongside the glacier as they headed in-land toward the source of the signals detected by NASA and the Defense Intelligence Agency.

'The location of the signals is just over a hundred miles in from the coast,' Riggs reported. 'We'll be there in a couple of hours, so just hang on and enjoy the ride.'

Ethan gripped hold of the sides of his seat as the glider accelerated across the ice, which was sparkling white in the low sun and striped with deep blue shadows stretching away from them, cast by low hills and jagged, angular outcrops of solid ice shaped by the winds that frequently scoured the barren snow fields.

On a monitor in front of him Ethan could see the GPS display mapping the frigid Antarctic wastes, and on it a small red spot that blinked on and off, demarking their destination deep in the ice fields. Ethan knew that each ice glider carried a small amount of personal baggage along with the SEAL's weapons and equipment. Weighed down by the excess gear the vehicles were limited to around sixty miles per hour across the ice, much of which was maintained by their momentum once moving. The engine behind him roared, his ears protected by a headset that allowed him to communicate both with the driver and the other members of the team.

Ethan looked out of the long, tear-drop shaped canopy and saw other ice gliders blazing across the ice nearby, their propellers whipping up spiralling vortexes of snow behind them that glowed and sparkled in the sunlight. He turned back to the view forward and almost immediately he spotted something on the display before them.

Another, small and intermittent contact flickered in and out of view as the glider bounced and careered across the ice.

'There's a new contact on the monitor,' he reported to the driver.

The SEAL looked at his display and frowned.

'Could be an artifact of some kind, a reflection,' he replied. 'The data is coming in via a downlink to a military satellite and we often get anomalous reflections appearing and then disappearing. It's not a perfect system, especially down here with all the cold weather and ice. Don't worry, the nearest people are hundreds of miles of us!'

Ethan frowned.

'There are people on the glacier?'

'There's a Russian research station at Lake Vostok, a subterranean lake more than two miles beneath the ice. The Ruskies drill bore holes down there, looking for life forms different to those we're familiar with. The station is manned year-round, but we're not going to be going anywhere near them.'

Ethan held on grimly as the ice glider seemed to almost fly across the sheer white surface of Antarctica, occasionally hitting rises in the terrain that felt as though they were in a vehicle that had hit a pot hole in the road.

Ethan's arms began to go numb from the vibrations as he held on and hoped that the constant juddering wouldn't give him the mother of all headaches by the time they reached their destination.

On the GPS display appeared a second warning screen and this time Ethan spotted a countdown timer appear, showing just two hours and seven minutes.

'That's the object', Riggs identified the new display. 'We're getting live tracking information from NASA. It's coming down, whatever the hell it is.'

'We need to get established and ready to pick this thing up,' Ethan replied.

The ski gliders thundered across the icy wastes for another bone-jarring two hours, Ethan peering at the empty wilderness around them, bathed in the orange glow of the low sun and slashed with giant crevasses that plunged into chilly blue depths, forcing them to find alternative routes.

Ethan's bones and joints were aching by the time the SEAL lieutenant began to slow, and Ethan looked up to the GPS monitor and saw that the flashing icon denoting the position of the signal was almost now in the center of the screen and that they were within five nautical miles of its position. The ski glider's motion across the ice smoothed as Riggs began bothering to pick less rough routes across the surface of the ice, and Ethan peered up into the blue sky above that was laced with high cirrus clouds glowing like angel's wings in the permanent sunrise.

'Four miles now,' the driver said. 'Firing team, weapons hot, stay sharp.'

As they travelled, Ethan saw Riggs slide an M-16 rifle out of its slot inside the canopy rail of the glider and allow it to rest across his thighs as with the other hand he flipped up a protective cover over the arming switch of the two cannons built into the glider's nose. Ethan heard a humming sound begin to emanate from where he guessed a belt-fed drum contained the guns' ammunition, the drum spinning up ready to fire.

It was then that he looked up into the sky above and shouted a warning.

'Incoming!'

Riggs looked up and his voice echoed over the communications channel. 'Holy crap!'

Across the vivid, deep blue vault of the heavens a fearsomely bright flare of light rocketed through the atmosphere. A trail of glowing debris followed it as it plunged across the sky, leaving a billowing cloud of smoke behind it that glowed in the low sunlight as it streaked overhead. Ethan saw a faint concave shockwave of vapor ahead of the object enveloped by the bright halo, and a moment later above the sound of the ski glider's engine he heard a terrific crash as the sonic boom hit the air around them.

'Black Knight is down!' Riggs yelled.

Ethan saw the bright object plummet toward the Antarctic and then a brilliant flare of light burst like a second sunrise ahead of them as it hit the ground at tremendous speed. A broad cloud of debris churned up from the impact burst into the air a few miles ahead of them as the object ploughed into the deep ice.

Ethan looked up at the roiling cloud of debris left behind by Black Knight's terminal descent, and then saw an aircraft flying high over the Antarctic, the vapor trails from its four engines glowing like golden needles across the chill blue heavens.

'There's an aircraft up there,' Ethan said.

Riggs looked up at the aircraft.

'The only thing that's going to be allowed to over fly this area is a military aircraft, and we haven't been informed of any support for this mission yet.'

Moments later, through the billowing debris cloud emerged the shapes of parachutes with vehicles descending slowly toward the ice fields before them, and other fast moving specks plummeting toward the surface.

Riggs keyed his microphone and called out to the entire formation.

'We've got company!'

***

XVI

'They're coming down ahead of us!'

Ethan saw the specks plummeting toward the ground before them, and then suddenly black parachutes billowed into life as the freefalling soldiers pulled their 'chutes and slowed dramatically.

Ethan recognized the tell-tail method of a HALO jump – High Altitude, Low Opening, the preferred insertion method of Special Forces soldiers into enemy territory, usually at night under the cover of darkness. Too small to be detected by radar, and dressed all in black, the soldiers would normally be invisible to their enemy as they descended.

'That looks like half an army,' Riggs uttered in dismay from the front of the cockpit. 'I count at least a hundred.'

Ethan nodded, scanning the beautiful skies now marred with dozens of billowing parachutes.

'They're trying to cut us off short of the target and get there first,' he replied.

They saw a few of the parachutes plummet to the ground in flames, and Riggs' features twisted into a grim smile.

'Looks like a few of them got torched by Black Knight on the way down, but they still have almost seven times the number of men we can field,' Riggs pointed out. 'We're going to have to get creative here.'

'I've got vehicles deploying!'

The call came in over the radio from one of the other SEALS, and Ethan craned his head up higher into the sky to see the larger, black objects still descending through the dawn sky, each suspended from three large parachutes.

'Damn,' Riggs cursed. 'Who the hell are these people? How did they even know we were here?'

Ethan did not have the time to give Riggs an extensive debrief of the history of Majestic Twelve, and he was pretty sure that revealing the Director of the FBI to be one of their number and the likely reason for the enemy force's well equipped arrival would be a step too far in exposing state secrets.

'They're part of something known as Majestic Twelve,' he replied. 'They have a lot of money and a lot of connections. We've been working with the DIA to dismantle their organization for some time.'

'Not with much luck by the looks of it,' Riggs uttered in reply, and then keyed his microphone to speak to the rest of the team. *We need to get past them before their vehicles land and they can direct heavy fire! Push through at maximum speed!*

Ethan gripped the canopy rails of the glider and hoped that Riggs and his men could get them through in one piece.

*

General Veer hauled down on his guidelines as the icy terrain of the glacier loomed before him, glowing orange in the low sunlight as he swept in like a dark bird of prey and lifted his boots. Veer hit the ice running and swiftly slid to a halt and hauled his parachute in as his men thumped to the ground all around him.

'Attack positions!' he bellowed as he pulled his M-16 rifle from over his shoulder and dashed toward a low ridge of ice.

The gliders were still almost a mile away, spiraling vortexes of ice crystals billowing out from behind their propellers like jet exhausts as they raced toward Veer's men. The soldiers were still thumping down onto the ice sheets and hauling in their parachutes, deploying in large numbers and spreading out as Veer glanced over his shoulder.

The C-130 Hercules transport had deployed them a few miles to the south of the signal's source, giving them the chance to cut the DIA team off before they could reach it. He looked up and saw their ATV vehicles floating down on larger parachutes, drifting with the light winds toward the north.

'Get to the vehicles!' Veer roared, pointing at a small group of his men deploying toward the onrushing gliders. 'Get them here and those big guns deployed!'

The group of a dozen or so men shifted course and began running to intercept the vehicles as they descended, and Veer sprinted to a low ridge line with his men and threw himself down into a prone position as he flicked the safety catch of the rifle off and took aim down the rifle's sights.

The ski gliders rocketing toward them immediately began splitting up, aiming for opposite ends of General Veer's line of men. Veer smiled grimly as he called out new orders.

'Switch to fragmentation grenades! Hit the ice in front of them!'

His men responded instantly, switching their rifles to the underslung 203 grenade launchers beneath the rifle barrels and taking aim. General Veer heard a series of soft thumps as one by one grenades arced out across the ice, invisible to the onrushing gliders.

*

Ethan gripped the canopy rail as he saw the line of MJ-12 soldiers spread out across the ice.

'They're spreading too wide!' Ethan snapped at Riggs. 'Open fire on them!'

Riggs's reply came back from the front cockpit, angry and intense.

'Stand by!'

Ethan watched as the formation of ski gliders split up, Hannah's glider rocketing away to the east with four more, others splitting to the west as they broke up and attempted to pass by the troops amassing before them.

Ethan was about to say something when he spotted a tiny black speck appear on the ice sheet to their left.

'Grenade, ten o'clock!'

Riggs responded instantly, jerking the controls to the right. The glider snapped right as Ethan flinched his head away from the sudden explosion of ice and metal fragments as the grenade detonated some twenty feet away on the ice.

The glider shuddered as the icy debris clattered against its hull and canopy, tilting over with the shockwave as the blast hit it. Ethan's head slammed left and right as the vehicle skittered out of control across the ice at sixty miles per hour and Riggs almost lost control. The SEAL struggled with the glider for a moment and then its skis dug into the ice once more as they continued east.

Ethan saw another blast send a fountain of ice up into the air, the grenade narrowly missing a glider as it frantically fought for control. A third blast slammed into the ice sheet to their left and Ethan heard a cry of panic as the nearest glider was showered with debris and its engine billowed a cloud of oily black smoke.

The ski glider careered to its right and slammed into another, both vehicles spinning into the air and crashing down onto the glacier in a cloud of ice and smashed metal as they tumbled to a halt in flames.

'Return fire wherever you can!' Riggs ordered his team.

Ethan heard the ski glider's guns clatter as Riggs opened up on the soldiers on the low ridge ahead, the ice no defense against the glider's cannons. Ethan almost cheered in delight as he saw the bullets rip into the ridge and the soldiers there hurl themselves away from the gunfire that smashed across the icy terrain.

Ethan looked to his right and saw the gliders sweeping far away, their positions betrayed by the plumes of ice crystals glowing in their wake. Two more grenades thumped down alongside the glider and exploded as Riggs desperately turned away from them.

The blasts hammered the glider's hull as a hail of automatic fire swept the ice sheet around them. Ethan hurled himself down into the cockpit as bullets screamed by, two of them punching holes in the glider's carbon fibre hull.

'They're going to annihilate us!' Hannah shouted from her cockpit, her glider some two hundred yards away from Ethan's.

'Stand by!' Riggs yelled again. 'Do not deploy until the last moment!'

'Deploy what?!' Ethan asked.

Riggs did not reply as they rocketed toward the MJ-12 soldiers, Riggs firing controlled bursts as he kicked the glider's rudder left and right, sweeping the ridge line with gunfire. Tiny black figures jumped clear and Ethan felt sure that he saw several of them cut down as other gliders opened fire alongside Riggs's machine.

Fresh grenade blasts ripped through the formation and Ethan saw another glider hit directly, the enemy's aim getting better as the gliders closed in. The grenade detonated just ahead of the glider in a blossoming ball of flame, and the shockwave from the blast lifted the glider's nose too high. The vehicle shot into the air as it turned over and slammed back down onto the ice, the cockpit crushed as the engine burst into flame, a sparkling trail of ice crystals behind it stained with black smoke and flames.

'Whatever you've got planned, I'd do it now!' Ethan snapped.

Ethan cursed as more bullets flew by past the glider's canopy and then he heard Riggs' cry over the intercom.

'Deploy, now!'

Ethan saw Riggs pull hard on a lever in the cockpit, and suddenly his heart leaped into his throat and his stomach plunged inside him as he heard an explosive detonation from somewhere directly over his head.

The glider's engine wailed and the vehicle's nose soared into the air as Ethan held on grimly, convinced that they had taken a direct hit under the nose. The ski glider rocketed up from the ice sheet into the frigid air and Riggs turned violently to the right as Ethan braced himself for the crash.

To his amazement the ski glider remained airborne as a shadow passed over the cockpit, and Ethan looked up to see a parachute billowing above them, attached to the glider with high-tensile cables.

'Damn it Riggs,' Ethan snapped, 'you could have said something!?'

'Where's the fun in that?' Riggs asked grimly as the glider climbed away.

The gunshots faded as Ethan looked around and saw eight of the ski gliders now airborne with them, the remaining four reduced to smoldering black specks on the ice sheet below that trailed long pillars of smoke away to the south.

'We're four down with eight left,' Ethan reported. 'And they've got a hundred men behind them.'

Riggs turned the glider through the air as he lowered the nose.

'Time to even the odds,' he growled back.

***

XVII

'They're airborne!'

General Veer heard the cry go up as he sheltered behind an icy outcrop from the ice glider's gunfire blasting the ridge line. He peered around the edge of the outcrop as the gunfire ceased and saw the gliders soaring into the air on explosively deployed chutes, turning the gliders into armed paragliders.

'Get to the vehicles!' he yelled. 'Don't let them get ahead of us! Shoot them down!'

The soldiers broke away from the ridge as the paragliders climbed out of rifle range, the sunlight glowing through their gracefully arced parachutes as they eclipsed the sun, their shadows racing over Veer's position. He looked out to the south and saw four smoking piles of wreckage burning on the ice fields.

'Ten men to the south!' he roared. 'Get out there on the ice and take any prisoners you can find alive!'

Veer whirled as several of his men split away and began sprinting toward the debris field, their rifles held before them. He ran across the ice, his boots gripping the surface easily as the metal studs dug in and looked up to see the paragliders passing overhead, their engines humming distantly as they continued to climb. The leading machine suddenly tilted its nose down and Veer bellowed a warning.

'Incoming!'

The glider's nose lit up as two small-calibre machine guns blasted the ice sheet, the bullets pursuing Veer's men as they sprinted for their own vehicles. Veer ducked down and threw himself toward the glider, making it harder for the pilot to nose down and track him at such low altitude, and the bullet streams passed by him as he hit the unforgiving ice.

Veer turned and saw several of his men hit by the hail of gunfire that hammered into them from above with dull thumps, their bodies tumbling awkwardly down as the glider ceased fire and raced by overhead. Four more followed it, their bullets slicing into Veer's troops before they pulled up again into a zoom climb away from the ridge.

Veer took aim with his rifle and fired half a dozen shots at the receding gliders, but saw no impacts as he scrambled to his feet.

Veer cursed as he ran, saw ahead his men hurrying to where the All Terrain Vehicles they had brought with them had landed. They were hauling off the parachutes that were draped across the vehicles, all ten of which were specially adapted for cold weather environments: fitted with enclosed cockpits and armed with an M2HB fifty calibre machine gun, they were slower than the ski gliders but infinitely more durable.

'Get those guns into play, now!' Veer shrieked as he reached the vehicles, the soldiers scrambling to start their engines.

He looked up and saw the gliders sailing high overhead, each travelling at perhaps forty knots. Veer jumped onto the back of the nearest ATV and grabbed at the machine gun, pulling the locking pins out as he turned the weapon and aimed it up into the frigid blue sky at the nearest of the gliders and squeezed the trigger.

The deafening clatter of the machine gun split the air as it began spitting used shell casings out onto the pristine ice.

*

'Jesus!'

Ethan heard Riggs shout in alarm as beside them a stream of gunfire ripped through the formation. Ethan looked left as a sharp crack caught his attention and one of the glider's engines spilled a plume of black smoke and began to descend rapidly toward the ice below.

'*We're hit!*' Hannah shouted over the radio.

Ethan felt his guts convulse as he watched the glider go down.

'We need to go after them!' he shouted.

Riggs' reply was without compromise.

'Our objective is the site of the crash. We go forward.'

'And just how do we get back if there's nobody left to carry the damned artefact out of there?!' Ethan shouted. 'At this rate, you'll be the only man left!'

Ethan heard Riggs curse as he called out a fresh command.

'All call signs, hit them while they're in their vehicles! Cover the damaged glider!'

Ethan grabbed the manoeuvring handle to steady himself in his seat as the glider wheeled about in mid-air, Riggs turning steeply as he swung around and began lining up for a fresh pass at the troops streaming toward the recently landed ATVs.

Ethan could see a large calibre machine gun firing up at the gliders passing overhead, and then his vision jarred as Riggs opened fire once more and sent bullets spraying into the packed soldiers as they tried to get their vehicles into motion.

Riggs pulled up and away from the target and Ethan heard a *whump-whump* sound of impacts as the ATV's large calibre machine gun pumped rounds into the air. The glider shuddered and the canopy shattered as a bullet shot up through the floor of the cockpit and smashed its way out through the Perspex canopy.

Riggs swore as he saw the canopy above them tear open, a ragged gap appearing in the center as he pulled through a hard turn to escape the onslaught.

'That's going to cost us!' he shouted back at Ethan.

Ethan looked over his shoulder as they continued around the turn and saw several of the gliders make daring passes over the ATVs far below, gunfire raking their enemy. He could see bodies lying on the snow, gunfire billowing up toward them as the soldiers abandoned their attempts to board the vehicles and opened fire with their rifles.

Ethan looked to his left and saw the smoke trail of the damaged glider fleeing to the north, almost down on the ice now as its pilot attempted to land.

'There!' Ethan said. 'They're down!'

Riggs looked left and saw the glider thump down onto the ice a half mile away.

'All gliders pull out and turn north!'

The gliders pulled up from the ATVs and turned away, several of them with ripped parachute canopies and trailing feint lines of grey smoke from minor damage to their engines. Ethan watched as he saw the MJ-12 soldiers again board their vehicles and start the engines to pursue the gliders, then turned and looked ahead as he saw Hannah's glider bumping along the ice far below.

'There won't be enough time to get them back in the air,' Riggs insisted, 'and we don't have enough seats to get them into the other gliders. There's nothing we can do.'

Ethan's mind raced as he sought some way of preventing Hannah and her pilot from being captured or killed by Majestic Twelve's mercenaries. He watched as Hannah's glider slid to a halt and its parachute billowed uselessly in the Antarctic winds, tucked in close to the glider where the pilot had drawn it in to prevent the winds from hauling the glider backwards and out of control across the ice.

'I've got an idea,' he replied. 'Land us to the north of them, as close as you can get.'

He could almost feel the scowl developing on Riggs's face as they began to descend toward the crippled glider.

'I have a bad feeling about this.'

*

'Get out, now!'

Hannah Ford punched the buckles of her harness and scrambled from the warmth of the glider's cockpit and out into the frigid cold, her legs slightly numb after the continuous vibrations inside the craft as her Navy SEAL pilot jumped out and cocked his rifle. Going by the name of Del Toro, the chunky Latino soldier had already revealed himself to be something of an emotionless automaton driven only by the need for the mission to succeed.

Hannah looked up and saw a handful of smoky clouds on the horizon as the vehicles she had seen on the ground began making their way toward the crippled glider. High above, she saw their colleagues sail overhead and continue on toward the north.

'This is only going to go one way,' Del Toro snapped at her, 'and it doesn't involve us escaping. But we can take down as many of them as possible before they over run us.'

Hannah blinked. 'It's your positivity that I admire.'

'The engine's shot and we're outnumbered,' the soldier growled. 'Our team won't come for us, it's not part of our mission. Do you want to be captured, tortured, raped and murdered, or would you rather shoot a few of these assholes before they get to us?'

Hannah scowled and pulled out her 9mm pistol.

'I thought you Special Forces guys could out-fight entire armies, conquer countries and stuff?'

Del Toro smiled grimly.

'Don't believe everything you see on television. Special Forces teams are trained to go in quietly, create havoc and leave without ever being seen. We're not typically well equipped for open battle against numerically superior forces.'

Hannah was about to reply when a sudden clatter of gunfire erupted from the south and bullets hammered the ice around her. She turned and hurled herself into the meagre cover provided by the crippled glider as the bullets smashed into the hull, Del Toro throwing himself down alongside her and aiming his rifle and the onrushing enemy.

'This is where the fun begins,' he said with a tight smile as he took aim.

The large calibre weapon firing at them had a much greater range than the soldier's M-16 rifle, and Del Toro did not fire for what felt like an age as Hannah kept her head down and listened to the sound of bullets peppering the glider's hull and impacting the thick ice below it.

'We're going to get pulverized here!' she shouted above the gunfire, now able to hear the sound of the vehicle's engines boring down upon them.

The SEAL did not reply, aiming carefully. He had propped the M-16 onto its tripod, the barrel arced high up into the sky as he switched to the underslung 203 grenade launcher and held his breath for a brief moment before firing.

The grenade popped out with a thump and rocketed out across the ice plains. Hannah watched it until it was too small to see, and then she saw it thump down in front of the onrushing ATVs.

The grenade detonated, a distant blast of shrapnel and flame that burst directly in front of the ATV. The vehicle shuddered and swerved and she could see that its windscreen had been shattered, but it kept coming.

'The grenade didn't kill them,' she said.

'It wasn't supposed to,' the SEAL replied quietly from over his rifle's sights. 'I wanted that glass out of the way.'

A moment later he fired two shots in rapid succession and Hannah saw the ATV swerve again, the tiny distant form of the driver slumped over his controls as the vehicle slowed to a halt on the ice.

'Good shot,' she murmured.

'It's only delaying the inevitable,' he snapped back. 'You wanna start shooting that thing or are you gonna use it as a peace offering?'

Hannah scowled and fired off a couple of shots at the stricken ATV as its passenger tried to remove his dead driver from his seat and take the controls. The shots forced the passenger to shield behind the vehicle, taking him out of the race.

The SEAL fired again, a grenade slamming into a second ATV and this time he got lucky, the blast tearing apart the vehicle's tracks and sending it spiralling out of control to the right.

'Two down,' the SEAL said grimly, 'ten to go.'

Hannah looked up and saw the gliders sailing overhead, ignoring their plight as they continued on toward the north.

'See?' Del Toro chortled almost gleefully. 'They're not coming down here for us.'

One of the glider's engines in the sky above suddenly changed note, and she looked up to see it descend from the formation as it passed overhead, changing direction and aiming for them. She could not prevent the smile that curled from the corner of her lips as she realized without a doubt that Warner was on board.

'You're forgetting,' she said, 'that not everybody up there is a Navy SEAL.'

Del Toro did not reply, firing again and sending grenades arcing across the ice to explode close to the ATVs closing in on them. Hannah heard the roar of the glider's engine as it soared down over the ice and then its skis rasped as it touched down, slowing dramatically as the power was reduced. She fired two shots and looked over her shoulder to see the craft turn on the ice and hurry toward them.

'See?' she said. 'They've come for us.'

'It won't do any damned good!' Del Toro shot back. 'There's four of us and only two seats!'

***

XVIII

Hannah fired her pistol at the onrushing ATVs as a shower of gunfire raked the ice before them. Warner's pilot skilfully guided their own glider into the cover of the damaged machine, and the canopy opened as Ethan Warner jumped out and sprinted across to them.

'Get back inside your glider!' he yelled.

Hannah did not hesitate to obey, running for the cockpit as Del Toro looked at Ethan in amazement.

'It's useless!' he shouted. 'The engine's shot!'

Ethan clipped a pair of rappel lines to the glider's frame. 'The parachute still works and the wind's with us. Get inside and loosen the 'chute now!'

'One glider won't have the power to pull us!' Del Toro protested. 'The enemy will capture four people instead of two!'

Ethan secured two more lines and then without another word he dashed past the SEAL and leaped into the glider in front of Hannah.

'Fine, you run, I'll stay with Ford!' Ethan shot back.

'Get the hell out of here!' Hannah screamed at Del Toro.

The SEAL cursed and fired several more shots at the onrushing ATVs as they loomed closer, Hannah able to see the gunners manning the machine guns mounted on the rear of each vehicle, trying to aim as the ATVs bounced and skittered on the uneven ice.

The SEAL jumped into the cockpit of Riggs' functioning glider and slammed the canopy down as Hannah heard the glider behind them roar as it accelerated away. Almost immediately the rappel lines were pulled taut as Ethan reached down and pulled a lever to release the parachute.

Hannah strained to look over her shoulder and saw the parachute billow outward once again as it filled with the frigid Antarctic wind. The combined force of the wind and the glider's engine hauled their stricken vehicle into motion.

'Damn,' Hannah smiled, 'not bad for a humble Marine, eh?'

Ethan grinned at her as he saw the parachute bloom against the sky behind them.

'Now we've just got to hope that Riggs doesn't cut us loose if we don't move fast enough.'

'We're moving a damned sight quicker than we were before!' Hannah pointed out, and then recalled Del Toro's words. 'How about you start shooting, or are you going to use those cannons as a peace offering?!'

'Yes ma'am,' Ethan saluted brusquely as he yanked the safety catch of the glider's cannons off and opened fire on the ATVs, showering them with bullets that forced the formation to split up in chaos to avoid the incoming fire as the glider was hauled backwards across the ice.

Hannah looked over her shoulder to see Rigg's glider accelerating, sliding this way and that as their momentum gradually began to build.

'We need to slow them down,' Ethan snapped as he fired another burst at their pursuers. 'They'll keep gaining on us otherwise!'

Hannah shook her head as she reached for the canopy lever.

'No, we need to lighten the load a little!' she replied as she forced the canopy open and unbuckled herself, holding on to the safety rails as she turned in her seat and reached for the baggage straps securing their weapons and equipment behind them.

'You jettison that lot and we'll be down on ammunition and supplies!' Ethan shouted above the wind and engine noise howling around them.

'If we get captured it'll belong to the enemy anyway!' Hannah shouted back. 'You got any idea of a way of detonating this little lot?!'

Ethan fired another clattering burst of gunfire at the nearest ATV and then shouted back to her above the noise of the wind.

'They might have remote detonators for C4 charges if we're lucky! The charges are lit by electrical current, so if the SEAL team set the batteries into the charges then we can blow the crap out of the ATVs!'

'And if they didn't put the batteries into the charges?!'

'Then we might as well hurl snowballs at them!' Ethan replied. 'Either way, it's better than doing nothing!'

Hannah scrambled in her seat and opened the top of one of the SEAL's ammunition baggage, rummaging inside until she pulled something out that looked like a long, metal stick.

'What's this?!'

'It's a thermite grenade!' Ethan shouted as he glanced over his shoulder at Hannah. 'Lodge it in there and the whole lot will burn. Only thing that won't is the C4 charges!'

Hannah turned and jammed the thermite grenade down into the baggage, then hunted around among the medical supplies, ammunition and explosives until she found a detonator pack. She pulled it out and then re-sealed the baggage before turning and handing the detonator to Ethan as she slid back into her seat and pulled the canopy back down.

'Is that it?' she asked, her face numb from the cold.

A grim smile spread on Ethan's face.

'Oh yeah,' he replied, 'that's it. Did you see any C4 charges? They're about the size of house bricks, wrapped in...'

'I know what they look like,' Hannah replied, 'and there are ten of them.'

*

'Full power!'

General Veer's voice boomed like a cannon across the ice, overpowering even the engines of the ATVs as they thundered across the rugged terrain in pursuit of the gliders.

The ATV on which he stood bounced and jerked this way and that, but Veer stood on long, strong legs that soaked up the bumps as he aimed the machine gun and opened fire on the stricken glider even as it was being towed away from them.

The gun rattled and shook as spent cartridges sprayed into the back of the ATV and across his boots. He could see his rounds churning the snow and ice around the glider but the shaking of the ATV was too intense to draw an accurate bead on them.

'Encircle them before they get away!'

The ATVs at the outside of the formation began to accelerate, pushing ahead and trying to outpace the two gliders. Veer looked up into the sky ahead and cursed as he saw the remaining gliders pushing on toward their destination. He had hoped that they would turn about and defend their fallen comrades, but then he should have known better: the Navy SEALs would prioritize the success of their mission above all other considerations, even their own brethren. Veer would have done the same in their situation, but the presence of non-military personnel had swayed one of them to turn about and attempt a rescue. Veer knew that the key to success was to play the bleeding heart civilians against their military escort, and he already felt sure that he already had prisoners to play with.

'They're not moving fast enough!' Veer's driver yelled above the wind and the noise. 'We're gaining on them!'

'Keep pushing!' Veer roared in reply as he released the machine gun, knowing now that the enemy could not escape. 'They can't get away.'

He stepped aside from the machine gun and was about to prepare for close quarter combat with whoever was inside the gliders when he spotted a small, angular imperfection on the ice sheet before them. Nature did not create objects that were angular, and indeed rarely produced any kind of dimensional symmetry, a handy way of detecting man-made structures in the wilderness. He squinted at the tiny speck left in the wake of the fleeing gliders and almost immediately recognized it for what it was.

'Break left!'

The ATV swerved hard left across the ice, but the other vehicles in the formation did not respond as quickly. Veer dropped down into a crouch and covered his head as he saw the tiny speck suddenly flare brilliantly as the square of C4 detonated directly in the path of two of his ATVs.

The blast ripped beneath one of the ATVs and hurled it into the air, smashed tracks and shattered glass blossoming out within the fireball as the vehicle was torn apart by the ferocious blast and hurled in different directions amid a roiling cloud of flame and black smoke.

Veer huddled against the wall of the ATV in which he crouched as metallic debris showered the vehicle. He squinted as he saw a second vehicle engulfed in flames career across the ice and slam into the wreckage of the first as it plunged back down onto the glacier, billowing clouds of smoke and flame blazing inside it as the driver and gunner burned alive.

A second detonation followed as another C4 charge exploded and shattered the chassis of another ATV, flame and smoke snapping from the vehicle as it rocketed along the glacier and crashed through an icy outcrop, the vehicle tumbling in a ball of flame as its burning occupants were hurled out onto the ice.

'Fall back!' Veer yelled.

The ATVs slowed dramatically and turned away from the chase as Veer stood up once more and roared in fury, one thick fist slamming down onto the roof of his ATV as he watched the gliders pull away and escape to the north.

*

Ethan pulled the canopy shut and huddled inside his Arctic jacket as he watched the ATVs fall away from them, the sunlit horizon smudged now with drifting clouds of black smoke from the burning wreckage of three ATVs.

'That'll learn them,' Hannah said triumphantly.

Ethan shook his head.

'They won't stop there,' he assured her. 'Majestic Twelve will have paid them handsomely to finish their mission. They'll regroup and continue to pick us off one by one until they get what they want.'

He keyed the microphone.

'Lieutenant Riggs, our tail is clear for the time being. How much farther?'

'*We're within a couple of miles,*' Riggs replied. '*Combat spread, go!*'

The ice gliders flying ahead and above them descended gently toward the ice sheet and landed, their parachutes billowing behind them for a moment until their pilots spilled the wind from them and drew them in.

The gliders began to spread out on the ice, just like an infantry unit would when approaching an enemy position to prevent that enemy from taking out entire platoons using mortar fire or grenades. Ethan looked across to his right and saw an identical glider, its driver focusing intently ahead as they gradually closed in on what looked like a low ridge of hills protruding from the endless ice sheets. It took almost fifteen minutes to reach the edge of the hills.

'No visual,' Riggs reported as he surveyed the ridgeline. 'We'll have to go in on foot – those slopes are too rough for the gliders and we don't know what's on the other side.'

Ethan peered out to his left and right. 'No way we can send a couple out to the sides, see around the edges first?'

Riggs's reply was adamant.

'This feature extends for miles, and with MJ-12 right behind us we don't have enough time for an extensive recon' of the area. We go in here and now.'

Ethan said nothing more as the glider coasted to within a hundred yards of the low hills, and from his vantage point he could now see that the hills were in fact a ridge of loose boulders of snow and ice, as though a gigantic hoe had torn through the surface of the ice sheet and churned it over.

Riggs guided the ski glider alongside the rough edge of the mound and then allowed it to slide to a halt as he shut down the engine, Ethan and Hannah's glider likewise sliding to a halt. Ethan pulled the headset from his ears, grateful to get it off his head as he saw the remaining ski gliders pull in at various spots down the length of the ridge, canopies opening and billowing clouds of warm vapor puffing from their interiors onto the frozen air in the golden sunlight.

Ethan unlocked the canopy and pushed it open, felt the fierce bite of the cold against his skin as he stood up in his seat and climbed out. Hannah jumped out onto on the ice with him and stretched her legs as the SEALs jogged to the edge of the ridge, their weapons at port arms as they began scaling the unstable slopes.

Doctor Chandler emerged from his glider, and Ethan looked about in alarm. 'Where's Amy?'

Riggs shook his head. 'Porter's glider went down with Amy,' he informed Ethan. 'We lost a few good people already and we haven't even found Black Knight yet.'

Ethan found himself mourning the spirited young scientist's loss, but he knew that they had no time to grieve. Majestic Twelve would catch up with them again soon enough.

'Is that the impact crater?' Hannah asked as she looked at the ridge.

'I guess so,' Ethan replied, 'Black Knight is about the only thing that's crashed down here.'

It was the voice of a scientist behind them who corrected Ethan.

'It's not something that's come down,' he replied, 'it's something that's come *up*.'

Ethan peered curiously at Doctor Chandler as together they began clambering up the slopes of the ridge until they reached the top, broken chunks of glacial ice embedded in mounds of loose snow.

Ethan moved alongside two of the SEALS, who were lying prone on the ridge top with their weapons held before them as they looked at something. He heard their voices just before he reached them.

'We've got a problem.'

Ethan rested alongside them and looked down and his heart leaped into his mouth.

Opposite the ridge was another similar ridge, and below them plunged a deep chasm of glowing blue ice, a canyon ripped into the glacier as though a giant's sword had plunged down from the heavens and sliced into the continent for miles.

Hannah looked at the wrecked gliders, the vast freezing wilderness and the plunging chasm, and then at Ethan. 'I bet you ten bucks we don't make it out here here alive.'

***

XIX

Defense Intelligence Agency,

Anacostia-Bolling,

Washington DC

Nicola Lopez held out her identity card to the security guards manning the entrance to the huge base, one of them scrutinizing it for a long moment. The soldier looked at the image of Lopez on the ID card, arrogant and full of vigor, and then at the weary looking woman sitting in the sedan in front of him.

'You got an appointment here, ma'am?' he asked.

Lopez managed a smile despite her uncertainty over just how the DIA was going to react to her sudden arrival with one of their most wanted fugitives sitting alongside her in the vehicle.

'Contact Doug Jarvis,' she said simply. 'Tell him that Nicola Lopez is here with Aaron James Mitchell. He'll understand.'

The soldier nodded and moved off to the command post as Mitchell glowered across at her.

'You just sold me out?'

'You think they're going to just let us walk in there?' Lopez challenged. 'I'm supposed to be in a coma and you're a wanted man. Better to let them understand that we're here together, by choice, than let them think you're trying to infiltrate one of the most secretive locations in the entire continental United States, no?'

Mitchell shrugged and returned to silence as Lopez waited and wondered what kind of greeting they would get once word reached Jarvis of their arrival. She got her answer a minute or so later when the security guards burst from the command post, fanning out and bellowing at the top of their lungs.

'Show us your hands! Out of the vehicle and get down on the ground, *now!*'

Mitchel looked at her, and now it was Lopez's turn to shrug.

'It's not so bad – they didn't just open fire on us.'

Lopez carefully climbed out of the vehicle and put her hands on her head. Mitchell mirrored her actions nearby as the soldiers advanced, glaring at them down the barrels of their rifles as from the buildings beyond the checkpoint dozens of DIA agents sprinted with weapons drawn toward them.

Lopez placed her hands behind her back and crossed her legs at the ankle as the soldiers moved in. She winced as one of them thumped a knee into her back to pin her down as he cuffed her, several more soldiers piling in on top of Mitchell and cuffing him before they were both hauled to their feet, Lopez's hair in disarray as two dozen DIA agents surrounded them, weapons drawn, stern faces glaring at Mitchell.

'Hold your fire,' Lopez said, hoping that enough of them knew who she was and would listen to her. 'He's on our side.'

None of the agents replied or even looked at her. She was wondering whether anybody at the damned agency even knew what she had been through in the name of national security when she saw a familiar figure striding toward her across the lawns.

Doug Jarvis, for once, was not sauntering along with his hands in his pockets but was hurrying at a spritely pace for his age, his gray hair whipping around in the breeze as he reached the command post and the ring of armed guards parted for him.

'Hold your fire,' he said.

To Lopez's chagrin the armed agents immediately obeyed and lowered their weapons, still watching Mitchell. To her absolute amazement, Jarvis seemed to barely even notice the big man as he hurried up to her and threw his arms around her.

'Nicola, I thought we'd lost you!'

Lopez blinked, unable to return the embrace with her hands manacled behind her back. Jarvis held her for a moment longer and then stepped back, one hand holding each of her shoulders as he looked her up and down with a broad smile on his face.

'You look like shit,' he pointed out.

Lopez struggled to conceal the smirk that ached across her face.

'And you still can't hold a candle to me,' she replied.

'What happened? When did you wake up, and what's this asshole doing here?'

Jarvis tipped his head in Mitchell's direction and Lopez sighed.

'It's a long story, but if Mitchell here hadn't turned up at the hospital I'd be dead. Mitchell wants to come over to us, Doug. Looks like MJ-12 have decided he's past his sell by date.'

Jarvis released her shoulders and turned to confront the huge operative, who merely regarded him in stony silence with eyes as dark as night.

'Give me one good reason not to have you dragged into those bushes over there and ventilated with bullet art?'

Mitchell's reply was as sombre as it was unintimidated.

'Because you need me,' he said. 'Majestic Twelve have taken their gloves off and they're coming for all of you, for all of us.'

Jarvis sneered at the big man. 'So you finally get out of your depth and then you come running here?'

Mitchell smiled without warmth.

'You put me in the highest security facility available in the entire country, and as soon as I was ready I escaped without problem. If I was your enemy I would have continued running, but it was MJ-12 who were prepared to let me rot in there. I knew that by doing so they had changed their plans, and by leaving me where I was they were clearing up loose ends. That meant that they would pursue all of you, and remove the itch in their side. I decided to scupper that plan and come here to show you that my work for them is done.'

Jarvis peered at Mitchell for a long moment and then at Lopez.

'You believe any of this?' he asked her.

Lopez shrugged.

'Got no reason not to,' she replied. 'MJ-12 sent a female assassin to take me down, that's all I know right now. But given everything that's happened over the last few months it sounds plausible that MJ-12 is looking to remove us from play.'

Jarvis made his decision.

'Put him in custody,' he ordered his agents. 'Nicola, come with me. There's a great deal you need to catch up on.'

*

'Hey, brainbox!'

Lopez saw Hellermen before he saw her, the scientist completely consumed by some kind of marching robotic device at his work station inside one of the DIA's secretive Watch Centers. Hellerman whirled, his jaw dropping as he heard her voice.

'Lopez!?'

Hellerman's robot marched off his desk and clattered onto the floor as the scientist launched himself at her. Lopez hugged Hellerman tightly, always amused to see the younger man's unveiled affection for her. When he drew back, she was surprised to see tears welling in his eyes and many of the other employees sat behind their work stations watching discreetly, the ranks of television monitors arrayed across the walls of the Watch Center glowing with news feeds from around the world.

'When did you wake up?' he asked, his voice constricted.

'I got woken up,' she said. 'Looks like I'll pull through.'

Hellerman nodded, took off his spectacles to clean them and then blew his nose as he recovered his senses and the smile appeared once more.

'It's good to have you back. For a while there I...' He stuttered slightly and shook his head. 'Can we get married now?'

Lopez placed a hand gently on his cheek, his tin beard rasping against the skin of her palm as she smiled back at him. 'One thing at a time, Romeo. Where's Ethan?'

'Oh, *him*,' Hellerman replied. 'The competition. He's in Antarctica.'

'Where abouts in Antarctica?'

Jarvis walked into Hellerman's office, his hands once again in his pockets as he spoke.

'Ethan was dispatched on a new mission for us while you were still napping at the hospital,' he said, all pretence of affection already vanished. 'A lot's changed while you've been gone.'

'I'll say,' Lopez shot back. 'I hope he's not out there on his own. Have you got somebody covering his back?'

'Ethan's been partnered with Hannah Ford, formerly of the FBI.'

'*Her?*' Lopez uttered in horror. 'What's she doing working with Ethan?'

'Like I said,' Jarvis repeated, 'a lot's changed. After you went and got yourself shot up in DC, both Hannah Ford and Michael Vaughn resigned their positions at the FBI and joined us here at the DIA. Essentially, they both now knew what Director LeMay had been up to and wanted to join the fight against Majestic Twelve. I signed them up to this department with the blessing of General Nellis, knowing that they would have considerable personal motivation for vengeance against both LeMay and MJ-12 as a whole.'

Right on cue Lopez turned as Michael Vaughn, a stocky, dark skinned man and former partner of Hannah Ford walked into the office with his hands in his pockets and a welcoming smile on his face. Lopez was struck by how his casual manner seemed a mirror to that of Doug Jarvis.

'Good to see you back on your feet, Nicola,' he greeted her with a warm handshake.

'Just about staying upright,' she replied with a grin, and then turned to Jarvis. 'So if this is the new team, then what's the plan? If Ethan's in Antarctica then I need to get the hell out there to support him.'

'Not enough time,' Jarvis countered. 'The mission will be complete long before you could reach the site. I have a different task for you, if you're up to it?'

Lopez straightened slightly and lifted her chin. 'All I need is a shower and a shot of coffee and I'll be ready for anything.'

Jarvis raised an eyebrow and glanced at Vaughn, who smiled.

'Just like Hannah.'

'Something I should know about here?' Lopez demanded.

'Your target is FBI Director Gordon LeMay,' Jarvis said. 'We know that Majestic Twelve will want to speak to him now that Black Knight has descended and Aaron Mitchell has escaped from custody. Mitchell is dangerous to them should he genuinely have decided to switch sides, and Black Knight represents a coup for them that they cannot afford to ignore. They'll go full throttle to acquire it and that may be what we need to identify them should they meet LeMay in person.'

Lopez frowned. 'Surveillance? I'm out of the game for a couple of months and now you want me to sit in a car watching LeMay?'

'If you'd been here when the Black Knight case first emerged believe me, you'd have been deployed with Ethan, but it's too late for that and besides, no matter how invincible you may think you are you're not yet in shape enough to start charging around shooting the bad guys. Michael here is itching to get into the field and you clearly are too, so this is the perfect first case for you two to work together. Find LeMay, follow him. By definition he can't meet members of Majestic Twelve inside the FBI building, so it'll have to be somewhere far from prying eyes – that's when they'll expose themselves and I want the both of you there to see and record it.'

Lopez looked at Vaughn, who shrugged.

'I'm not Ethan Warner ma'am, but I'll do my humble best.'

Lopez sighed, not willing to brush Vaughn off without first giving him the chance to prove himself. She reached for her cell phone and began composing a text message.

'Fine, let's do it,' she said as she tapped. 'What about Mitchell?'

'I've got my own plan for him,' Jarvis assured her.

***

XX

Antarctica

'How the hell are we going to get down there?!'

Hannah Ford's voice echoed down into the plunging chasm before them as Ethan surveyed its depths.

The pristine blue ice of the first couple of dozen feet changed slowly to a deep, darkening blue that finally vanished into blackness far below. Ethan judged the limit of his vision as probably no more than fifty to sixty feet – beyond that was the impenetrable darkness that had likely not witnessed light for millions of years.

'It's a subterranean warm water vent,' said Chandler. 'We've seen these active on Jupiter's moon, Europa.'

'You mean it's not from Black Knight's descent?' Hannah asked.

'The initial chasm is, yes,' Chandler went on, 'but this is too uniform to have been carved so recently. The object must have broken through the ice here and crashed down into an existing cavity.'

'I don't care what it is,' the SEAL commander said, 'Black Knight went down into it and we're going down there too. Break out the climbing gear and let's get on with it.'

With practiced military efficiency the SEAL team unpacked climbing ropes and tackle from their ski gliders and began securing rappel lines to large boulders of ice and hammering metal stays into the rock-solid glacier.

Ethan strapped into a climbing rig, fastening his harnesses into place as he looked across at Chandler.

'We're not on Europa,' he said. 'What caused this cavity, if not the satellite?'

'It's the result of warm water rising and weakening the surface of the glacier, which eventually breaks free and rolls back either side of the warm water, leaving these ridges either side of the breach. Somewhere down in this chasm there must be a warm water channel just like the satellite surveys suggested, and at some point it must have reached the surface of the glacier.'

Hannah Ford frowned in disbelief.

'The ice here is supposed to be kilometers thick, right? How could warm water have made it up this far?'

'Because the continent below the ice is solid land, just like the rest of the world. It has contours, mountain ranges, ancient forests and other debris now crushed beneath the ice that could direct a flow of water close enough to the surface to breach it.'

'Forests?' one of the SEALs, a man named Saunders, asked. 'What forests?'

'Not now,' the Lieutenant Riggs snapped. 'Warner, you're a former soldier, right?'

'Fourth Marines,' Ethan confirmed.

'Good, you're with Saunders. Down you go.'

Ethan masked his own dislike of heights by turning away from the team as he clambered with Saunders to the edge of the chasm and looked down. The gloomy depths of the glacier served to conceal the true height of the fall. Ethan turned in unison with Saunders, and with a nod to each other Ethan crouched at the knees slightly and then walked backwards over the edge of the ridge, his hands controlling his descent on the rappel lines.

The vertiginous canyon opened up beneath him and Ethan felt its icy breath gust by as he gently descended with small jumps, letting out no more than two feet of cable at any one time. Beside him, watching closely, Saunders descended alongside him as above the SEAL team began preparing the scientists for their own descent while two more soldiers appeared over the edge and followed Ethan down.

To Ethan's surprise the air grew a little warmer as they descended, the endless winds at the surface falling silent. He realized that the noise of the journey out in the ski gliders and then the endless buffeting winds had been assaulting his ears for almost three hours. Now, the silence seemed deafening.

The ice before him was perfectly blue, light from above illuminating its depths as though he were looking into a cliff forged from some exotic jewel. Light sparkled within, but below him jagged outcrops of ice as hard as granite threatened to slice his lines in two.

'Stay sharp,' Saunders said with a gruff voice that echoed alarmingly inside the crevasse. 'Watch your route down.'

Ethan obeyed as they descended further, and now the light began to fade as they rappelled down. Ethan reached up and carefully activated a small light attached to his jacket at the same time as Saunders, the brilliant LED glow causing the glacier walls to sparkle as though the ice were encrusted with a thousand diamond chips.

Ethan looked up, saw more of the soldiers and scientists following them down from the bright sliver of sky above, and then the ragged outcrops of ice blocked his view and he followed Saunders down deeper into the glacier's depths.

They were more than eighty feet down when Ethan heard a soft hissing sound coming from far below, sounding closer than it was due to the confines of the crevasse.

'Running water,' Saunders figured as they descended. 'Maybe the scientist was right.'

Ethan peered down between his boots but saw nothing but inky blackness, the air frigid with cold.

'Warm water my ass,' he said finally. 'There's nothing warm down here.'

They descended for another minute, two feet at a time, easing their way around dangerous chunks of ice until Ethan realized that the air had become saturated around them with a thin mist.

'That's steam,' Saunders uttered in amazement.

Ethan shook his head, unwilling to believe it, but then the lights from their jackets caught on something far below and he looked down to see the lights reflecting off of a rapidly shimmering surface.

'Water,' Saunders cautioned. 'Slow your advance and we'll try to find a place to set down. If you get caught up in that flow, you're as good as dead.'

Ethan nodded as below them the water channel slowly emerged from the absolute darkness. He realized quickly that the scientist had only meant that the water that had created the chasm was warmer than the ice itself, the water flowing through the channel likely sub-zero, remaining a fluid only because of the pressure of the glacier above preventing it from freezing.

Saunders took the lead, guiding Ethan down, and then a moment later their boots thumped down onto a ledge some five feet above the water flowing by in a channel roughly ten feet wide. Ethan unclipped his harness from the rappel line and stepped clear with Saunders to provide space for the others coming down above them.

'Wow,' Ethan murmured as he looked around them, and his exclamation echoed into the distance in both directions.

The water had carved a tunnel complex beneath the glacier that was probably twenty feet in width and height, with perfectly smooth walls of glistening ice as clear as glass. Ethan's light shone onto the ice above his head and was both reflected by it and also penetrated at the same time, the beam a fuzzy ray piercing the ancient glacier.

Below them, but above the flowing water, were a series of perfectly formed steps carved into the ice that led down to the water's edge.

'You're kidding me?' Saunders uttered.

Ethan looked to his left and right, saw the steps follow the contours of the tunnel far into the darkness, and saw identical steps on the far side of the water.

'You think that somebody hacked these steps out for access?' he asked.

'Don't be ridiculous!'

Doctor Chandler gestured to the glacier walls around them, his voice echoing through the tunnels as he landed on the icy path beside them.

'The water's risen and fallen back in discrete stages recently,' he observed, 'and created these ledges one at a time as it eroded the walls of the cave. I suspect that this channel was the result of warm water finding a way towards the Antarctic Ocean via gravity, just as all rivers do, which means it likely follows the path of some ancient river that once flowed before the continent froze.'

Ethan peered into the water's depths.

'But how would Black Knight have known to come down here? How could a signal have guided it? Antarctica has been covered by ice for millions of years.'

Chandler smiled as though pitying Ethan's naivety.

'Humans have only existed for a few million years,' he replied, 'but throughout that history we have recorded technologies witnessed by people that exceed anything we have today. If Black Knight is thirteen thousand years old, it may be a more recent example of extra-terrestrial involvement in our evolution.'

Ethan glanced at Saunders, who shrugged. Lieutenant Riggs landed on the ice with more scientists, soldiers and Hannah Ford alongside him, and unclipped himself from his harness. He immediately checked his radio, and Ethan saw him wince.

'Not a chance,' he said finally. 'We're out of radio contact while we're down here.'

'Then let's move fast,' Saunders suggested. 'Sooner we're done, the sooner we can get the hell out of here.'

Saunders took the lead as he began following the cave upstream, still heading toward the signal's source. Ethan turned to follow him with Hannah at his side as they walked carefully alongside the rushing water, their lights patches of illumination in an otherwise deeply black universe that picked out the glowing ice around them and gave the impression that the entire cave system was constantly moving, the ice bending and warping the lights as they walked.

'How far did we descend?' Hannah asked as they walked.

'A hundred feet at least, maybe one fifty,' Ethan replied. 'I don't want to think about how much ice there is above us right now.'

'A lot,' Chandler replied unhelpfully from behind them. 'Millions of tons in fact, and glaciers are always moving so it's generally unstable ice too.'

'Thanks Doc,' Hannah shot back, and then was cut off as she saw something poking out of the ice ahead. 'What the hell is that?!'

Ethan spotted a thick cylinder of some kind jutting out over the path ahead and saw Saunders slow as he illuminated it.

'It's a tree,' Saunders said in disbelief.

The group slowed as they looked at the thick tree trunk poking out of the ice before them, its surface black as night.

'It's a *petrified* tree,' Chandler corrected them in delight as he edged forward and examined the surface of the object. 'A fossil probably several million years old.'

'What the hell is it doing down here?' Ethan asked.

Chandler looked over his shoulder at Ethan with a knowing smile.

'One hundred million years ago, the Earth was in the grip of an extreme Greenhouse Effect. The polar ice caps had all but melted; in the south, rainforests inhabited by dinosaurs existed in their place. These Antarctic ecosystems were adapted to the long months of winter darkness that occur at the poles and were truly bizarre. Robert Falcon Scott, an Antarctic explorer, first discovered fossil plants on the Beardmore Glacier at eighty two degrees south, in 1912. Take a look up there, at that dark line up in the ice.'

Ethan peered up into the glacier's depths and saw a thin line running through the ice parallel to the horizon.

'That's a sedimentary layer,' Chandler explained. 'If we went up there and excavated it we'd find soil, twigs and leaves embedded within it, all of them three to five millions of years old. The ice here is a relatively recent geological event – prior to this, Antarctica was a tropical rainforest.'

'You're telling me that Antarctica was like Brazil?' Hannah uttered in amazement.

'Scientists routinely excavate petrified logs from the depths of glaciers just like this one that must have come from extremely large trees. We're even able to slice into the fossil trees and count the rings demarking their growth. The most amazing thing about that is the requirement for many of those species to have coped with the Antarctic winter, during which it's dark for six months of the year.'

'Trees grow through photosynthesis don't they?' Ethan said. 'Wouldn't they die?'

'Experiments at the University of Sheffield in the United Kingdom showed that planets like the Ginkgo, an ancient species considered a "living fossil" by science, could survive in simulated Antarctic conditions quite well. Although they used up food stores in the winter, they more than made up for this by their ability to photosynthesise twenty four hours a day in the summer.'

Saunders ducked under the tree and moved on, Ethan following as Hannah spoke to Chandler behind him.

'So if Antarctica was a normal land mass before the ice, then wouldn't it have had animals living on it?'

'Many,' Chandler confirmed, 'and as we're talking about a period from one hundred million years ago, then there would have been dinosaurs roaming this continent just like any other.'

'Dinosaurs?' Hannah echoed. 'Seriously?'

'Absolutely,' Chandler said. 'Researchers at the Victoria Museum in Australia have found many dinosaur fossils in southern Australia at a location that was once positioned just off the east coast of Antarctica. Their work has shown that not only did dinosaurs live on Antarctica, but that they did so year-round. Specimens of the species *Leaellynasaura* showed adaptions of the skull which indicate that the animal had enlarged optic lobes, designed to offer acute night vision well suited to the prolonged winter darkness.'

Hannah smiled nervously.

'Let's hope that none of them are left wandering about down here then, shall we?'

Saunders chuckled.

'The species died out tens of millions of years ago, and was a plant eater no bigger than a kangaroo,' he said. 'You'd have had nothing to fear from it.'

Ahead of them, Lieutenant Riggs slowed as he looked down at a scanner he held in his hand.

'Well, something's ahead of us,' he said. 'I'm getting a much stronger signal now. We're close.'

***

XXI

The ice channel's water glistened in the glare from the team's mounted flashlights as Ethan followed Saunders over a series of rugged, icy boulders blocking their path, likely deposited by the fast moving waters that had forged the tunnel.

Ethan could see that the water itself was still icy cold, possessed of a faint blue hue that betrayed its frigid depths as not much above freezing.

'This water,' he said, glancing back at Saunders, 'how come it's warmer than the rest? Something must be heating it?'

Ethan found it tough to believe that rainforests haunted by small dinosaurs once flourished where the thick ice sheets now existed, but he knew that the evidence of science never lied.

'The geological record provides irrefutable evidence of dramatic climate fluctuations that have occurred throughout our planet's history,' Chandler replied, scrambling over a rocky boulder. 'In the past fifty years the Antarctic Peninsula has warmed by nearly three degrees Centigrade, faster than any other part of the world. These ice channels may now be common beneath the ice sheets but normally we just can't see them, and so we can't tell if they're flowing in from the oceans around Antarctica somehow, or are coming from within it and spilling into the oceans around the continent instead.'

Ethan surveyed the depths of the tunnel ahead thoughtfully.

'Water doesn't typically flow into continents from outside, it falls as rain or snow.'

'Correct,' Chandler replied, 'and that leaves only one possible cause of the warming we're seeing here: volcanism.'

'There are volcanoes here too?' Hannah uttered. 'You're really selling the place.'

'Mount Erebus is currently the most active volcano in Antarctica and is the current eruptive zone of the Erebus hotspot. The summit contains a persistent convecting phonolitic lava lake, one of only five long-lasting lava lakes on the planet. Scientific study of the volcano is also facilitated by its proximity to McMurdo Station. Mount Erebus is classified as a polygenetic stratovolcano – that is that the bottom half of the volcano is a shield and the top half is a stratocone like most volcanoes. The whole system has been active for some time.'

Ethan tried not to consider what that meant for the expedition, currently some two hundred feet beneath the ice of an unstable glacier being weakened by volcanically warmed water rushing by just feet from where they walked. He was about to change the subject when Saunders called out.

'Hey, you guys see that?'

Ethan looked up ahead, and in the gloom he saw something shimmering against the ice. The team stopped and stared ahead in silence at the glistening light, as though a star had fallen through the ice and was sparkling where it had become trapped. Ethan squinted, tried not to look directly at the glow but to one side of it where his eyes could detect it more easily.

'Is it a reflection of some kind, from our lights?' Hannah asked.

Lieutenant Riggs called out. 'Everybody shut off your lights.'

Ethan obeyed instantly, turning his LED light off as did everybody else in the team. The tunnel was plunged into an absolute darkness so deep that Ethan was forced to put a gloved hand onto the ice wall alongside him to keep his balance. He peered into the distance as his eyes adjusted to the darkness, and saw the soft blue glow spread across the tunnel far ahead of them.

'What's causing that?'

Hannah's voice sounded disembodied in the blackness, echoing back and forth within the confines of the chamber as Ethan noticed the glow getting brighter, his eyes adjusting quickly to the gloom.

Then Saunders' voice echoed from somewhere ahead.

'It's getting brighter, and it's coming closer.'

Ethan's eyes widened as he realized that the light was closing in on them, illuminating the tunnel around it in a blue halo of light. Lieutenant Riggs reacted instantly.

'Everybody down, stand by!'

Ethan crouched down, one gloved hand resting on the 9mm pistol holstered on his belt as he watched the light growing in intensity before them. Like the hazy halo of a blue sunrise it reflected off the ice of the tunnel and seemed to sparkle as though alive, shimmering through the glassy ice. Ethan's first fear that it was some kind of man-made light attached to a craft on the water began to dissolve as he realized that the light had no natural proximal source.

'I can't see a target on the water,' Saunders whispered harshly, sighting the glow down the barrel of his M-16 rifle's telescopic sight.

It was Lieutenant Riggs who replied.

'It's not on the water,' he said. 'It *is* the water.'

Ethan stared in amazement as from the darkness the water flowing through the tunnel suddenly began to glow a bright blue, illuminating the ice cave around the team with enough light for Ethan to make out the way far ahead.

'What the hell is going on?' Hannah asked, her voice hushed as they watched the bizarrely glowing water swirl past them in flickering eddies of light.

Doctor Chandler stepped forward and crouched at the edge of the flow as he peered down into the water.

'It's mareel,' he said as he identified the source of the glow. 'The water's filled with bioluminescent bacteria and dinoflagellates called *Noctiluca scintillans,* or perhaps a similar species called *Vibrio harveyi.* I've heard of Navy pilots coming in to land on aircraft carriers at night being helped by this glow of the water in the wake of the ship, the glowing wake guiding them in the absence of any other light source. It's caused by a disturbance in the water and is often seen by mariners out in the oceans at night.'

Ethan stared down at the glowing water, which was now illuminating the team's faces in a neon blue light as though they were all staring at computer monitors. The ice cave around them was bathed in the blue glow, the ice sparkling vibrantly above their heads.

'What's causing the disturbance?' he asked.

Chandler shook his head.

'I've heard of the discharge of pollutants into water being capable of generating algae blooms that then glow as a result of the chemicals on which they feed,' he said thoughtfully as he looked up river toward the glowing depths of the cave. 'But the ice below this glacier should be pristine unless the volcano itself is discharging chemicals into the water.'

Lieutenant Riggs peered into the distant tunnels.

'You think that it's likely to erupt soon?'

Chandler shook his head.

'Mount Erebus is notable for what are called ice fumeroles, ice towers that form around gases that escape from vents in the surface of the volcano. The ice caves associated with the fumaroles, like the one we're standing in, are usually dark because polar alpine environments are starved in organics. The life is sparse, mainly bacteria and fungi which is of special interest for studying *oligotrophs* - organisms that can survive on minimal amounts of resources.'

'That's not what I asked,' Riggs snapped.

Chandler glared at the soldier, apparently unintimidated.

'I hadn't finished. The caves on Erebus are of especial interest for astrobiology as most surface caves are influenced by human activities, or by organics from the surface brought in by animals or ground water. The caves at Erebus are high altitude, yet accessible for study. There is no chance of photosynthetic based organics or of animals in a food chain based on photosynthetic life, and no overlying soil to wash down into them. Organics can only come from the atmosphere, or from ice algae that grow on the surface in summer, which may eventually find their way into caves like this one through burial and melting. As a result most micro-organisms here are chemolithoautotrophic - microbes like *Chloroflexi* and *Acidobacteria* that get all of their energy from chemical reactions with the rocks and don't depend on any other lifeforms to survive.' Chandler shook his head. 'But they would not be present in such numbers and concentrations through natural sources as we're seeing here. Something must have happened upstream to cause this.'

Lieutenant Riggs pushed his point.

'Something man-made, like a chemical leak?'

Chandler stood up and nodded.

'Something exactly like that,' he agreed. 'This cave could become highly poisonous at any time, and we know that it has broken close to the surface above us in recent months, perhaps recent weeks. If it floods again…'

'We get the picture,' Riggs cut in. 'Keep moving.'

Ethan followed Saunders as they picked their way forward through the tunnel, the glowing waters now illuminating their path as they advanced ever deeper into the glacier. Ethan knew that the water had to be flowing downhill to reach the ocean somewhere on the Antarctic coast, so technically they were going uphill. Thus, the immense mass of ice above them would likely be getting thicker with every step that they took. He had read somewhere that at its thickest the Antarctic ice sheet was three miles deep, all of it snow compacted until it became as hard as granite. The thought of the warm water weakening that immense mass of ice and bringing it down on the team, either crushing them instantly to death or trapping them to freeze for all eternity was too terrible to contemplate, so he put his head down and pushed on, Hannah just behind him.

They walked for several more minutes until Saunders' harsh voice snapped just loudly enough to be heard over the rushing water.

'Enemy!'

***

XXII

Ethan's response was almost as swift as that of the SEALS. In an instant he dropped into a crouch, his pistol appearing in his hand as he drew it and aimed alongside Saunders, who had dropped into a similar crouch and was holding his rifle tight into his shoulder and aiming down the tunnels. To Ethan's surprise and delight he saw Hannah's pistol just to the right of his head, the former FBI agent covering him and aiming in the same direction.

The rest of the SEAL team had mirrored their actions, all eight of their rifles aiming over or around their civilian charges as they sought the enemy that Saunders had seen.

Ethan peered into the shimmering blue depths ahead of them and saw a figure standing on the ledge, the clear shape of a rifle in his grasp. Ethan aimed at the figure as he heard Saunders challenge the man.

'On your knees, put your weapon down *now*!'

Ethan watched the figure, waiting for him to capitulate as he identified the soldiers massed before him, but the man was either suicidal or fearless for he did not move.

'Last chance!' Saunders snapped. 'Down on the ground!'

The command echoed above the freezing water rushing by them, rolling into the empty darkness, and was answered with silence. Ethan peered at the shadowy figure for a few moments longer and then Saunders fired a single shot.

The crack of the rifle was ear shatteringly loud in the tunnel's confines, and even in the faint bioluminescence of the blue water he saw the shot impact the man in the center of his chest with a sharp secondary crack and a brief flash of light.

To his amazement, the figure did not move and Saunders lowered his rifle and looked over his shoulder, somewhat confused.

'Sorry, trick of the light I guess.'

Ethan frowned. 'Had me fooled too.'

It was Hannah who spoke up in the SEAL's defense.

'That's no trick of the light, stay sharp.'

The SEALS did not respond except to keep their weapons trained on the shadowy figure and begin advancing as one, edging their away around the scientists crouched on the path and moving toward the figure.

Ethan moved into position behind them with Hannah alongside him as they crept forward and began to emerge onto a slender ledge that jutted out on a curve in the tunnel, where the water had once washed around a smooth bend and scoured from the ice a wider platform. Ethan lowered his pistol as he saw the SEALs relax, and then his jaw dropped as he realized what Saunders had seen.

The light from the water was piercing the ice walls of the tunnel, creating an illusion of open air instead of the solid ice that confronted them. There, trapped within that ice was the shape of a man, a rifle held in his long dead hands. Ethan heard Hannah gasp as she noted the uniform the man was wearing.

'That's a German soldier!'

Her exclamation echoed down the tunnel and within moments the scientists were hurrying to join them and staring at the frozen corpse. Ethan had recognized the distinctive shape of the German *Wehrmacht* helmet just a moment before Hannah, and then the gray uniform replete with collar insignia, the winged Swastika and belt kit the soldier had worn when he had died. Near his grasp was a pristine Sturmgewehr 44 rifle, suspended in the ice a few inches beyond his hands, which were outstretched as though trying to shield himself from something rushing toward him.

Ethan could not help himself as he marveled at the perfect preservation of the body. The soldier's face was contorted in pain and fear, his mouth wide open and his eyes squeezed shut, his head turned away from whatever had been threatening him. His skin had turned leathery and black, probably as the result of the freezing that had damaged his soft tissue at the cellular level but otherwise preserving his body as though he had died the previous day.

'Remarkable,' Chandler uttered as he managed to get a good look at the grisly frozen corpse. 'Perfectly preserved, he must have been frozen shortly after death.'

Lieutenant Riggs looked at the ice surrounding the body.

'Looks like he was drowned and the water froze rapidly with him trapped inside it,' he suggested.

'Almost certainly correct,' Chandler agreed, 'as was my conjecture that this cave is susceptible to regular floods, the water freezing as soon as it stops flowing.' The doctor looked at the curve in the tunnel and nodded to himself. 'He drowns, is caught in this corner of the tunnel by a vortex of spinning water curling around on itself on the outside of the turn, and then when the tunnel is full of water it freezes, enveloping him forever.'

Ethan looked at the water flowing past them and still glowing with its unnerving blue light.

'Now the warm water has eroded some of the ice away and exposed him again,' he said. 'All the more reason to push on and at least this solves one mystery: there definitely were German soldiers up here during or after the Second World War.'

'We must be close,' Lieutenant Riggs agreed. 'Del Toro, Sully, up front with Saunders, the rest of you back at the vanguard.'

The SEALS deployed rapidly as Lieutenant Riggs positioned himself ahead of the scientists but just behind Ethan and Hannah as they advanced deeper into the tunnel. The glow from the water was beginning to fade now as the bioluminescent bacteria in the frigid water passed by. Ethan switched on his light once more and glanced over his shoulder to see the other-worldly glow fade away behind them, as though the headlight of some ghostly blue train were steaming away into the darkness.

The depths of the tunnel ahead were plunged once more into absolute darkness, the harsh white beams of the flashlights cutting this way and that and passing through the clear ice close to the tunnel walls in shimmering shafts of dispersed light.

Ethan trudged along behind the SEALs at the head of the team, and was lost in his thoughts of Lopez for what felt like several minutes. It was tough for him to be on deployment knowing that his partner of so many years remained in a hospital ward back in DC, as though somehow he were betraying her. He was so consumed by his thoughts of her that he barely heard the command echo down from the darkness ahead.

'Stay alert.'

Ethan looked up and saw ahead the three flashlights of the leading SEALs reflecting off something ahead of them that was not ice. He could hear the rush of the water still but now above it there was another sound, more violent, as though water were spilling from a great height and crashing down upon something and the sound of the impact dispersed across a great area.

The noise of the water grew louder and he saw the flow of the subterranean river becoming more turbulent and disturbed, the black water roiling and swirling as it plunged into the tunnel. Ahead, the beams of the SEAL's flashlights suddenly stopped breaking up in the tunnel ice and he realized that they were walking out into a more open area, the sound of their footfalls changing despite the deep blackness.

Ethan saw the tunnel open out into a vast cavern, the beam from his light vanishing into the gloom around them. To his right he could hear water thundering down and crashing into the floor of the cavern before flowing away down toward the tunnel itself, and suddenly he realized that he was walking not on ice but on a solid, uniform surface. He looked down as he heard the spikes on his boots crunch into crumbling asphalt.

The SEALs slowed as Lieutenant Riggs pulled two flares from his belt kit and without hesitation pulled their caps and tossed them ahead of the team. The two flares arced through the air and burst into life with brilliant, fierce orange glows that illuminated the vast cavern in a flickering sunset hue.

Ethan almost toppled sideways as he saw the huge cavern glowing in the light from the flares, the ceiling sloping down toward an immense fissure in the walls to his right where water crashed out from somewhere else in the glacier and flowed away toward the tunnel entrance across a vast asphalt dock.

The ceiling looked as though it had partially collapsed, making the entire cavern appear lop-sided and putting Ethan and the team off balance until the second flare illuminated two long, low docks extending away from them, each filled with icy black water that shimmered like oil in the light from the flares. The two docks ran parallel to each other and ahead was an immense fortified building encased within the ice, walls of stone and steel sheened with frost that glistened in the light from the flares.

'This is it,' Chandler said in awe. 'We found it.'

Lieutenant Riggs looked at his scanner.

'The signal is coming from inside, from beyond the dock,' he said. 'They must have had some kind of power source in there to maintain it for so long. This base must have been here for at least seventy years.'

Ethan looked at the docks.

'Submarine pens,' he identified them. 'This is how they must have built the base. That tunnel was here for decades, perhaps centuries, carved out by the warm water channel. The Nazis used it for access to the interior of the ice sheet and then built the base right under the ice where it would never be found.'

Doctor Chandler nodded in agreement.

'The volcanism of Mount Erebus has been ongoing for centuries, millennia perhaps. This chamber may have been a natural consequence of warm water passing through the glacier and excavating this cavern. The Germans could have monopolized on that and built this facility within the existing cavity.'

Lieutenant Riggs surveyed the entrance to the base, massive steel doors left wide open, the interior as black as deep space and every bit as cold.

'Let's get going,' he ordered. 'We only have a few hours left.'

A voice prevented any of them from moving as Trooper Del Toro crouched down by something on the asphalt nearby.

'You might want to hang tight a moment,' he said as he looked over his shoulder at them. 'I don't think we're alone down here.'

'What do you mean?' Chandler asked. 'Nothing significant could survive in this cavern, there simply aren't sufficient resources.'

'Then how do you explain this?' Del Toro asked, and gestured to something lying on the asphalt at his feet.

Chandler and the rest of the team edged their way closer, and Ethan realized what he was looking at. On the asphalt and contrasting starkly with the ice and water was a large mound of animal scat. Ethan stared at it for a moment before speaking.

'There's something alive down here.'

Del Toro nodded

'And it was here recently,' he said, 'because this scat hasn't frozen yet. My guess is that whatever it is heard us coming long before we got here, especially after Saunders fired that shot.' He looked into the blackened depths of the Nazi base. 'It knows we're here.'

**

XXIII

DIA Holding Cell

Washington DC

Doug Jarvis walked down the corridor of the holding cells with no less than eight armed men escorting him, all of them professional soldiers and DIA agents. Ahead, three security gates stood between them and the cells, of which there were just ten.

The security guards accessed the gates one by one, always sealing the last behind them before entering the next, until Jarvis was admitted to the cells. Only one was occupied, a red light active above the cell door. He waited as the guards approached the door and shouted their commands.

'Mitchell, step up to the door, hands behind your back!'

Jarvis heard the shuffling of chains as Mitchell obeyed the commands, and through a hatch in the six-inch thick steel the guards manacled his wrists together before daring to open the cell door.

Jarvis watched as they stood back and beckoned Mitchell out, the towering man shuffling into the corridor. Even in prison fatigues Mitchell still cut an impressive figure for his age, standing a head above the guards who were not themselves small men. Jarvis wondered how such a physically imposing individual could have remained hidden, allegedly dead, for so many decades.

Mitchell turned to Jarvis, locking eyes with him as he stood in silence in the corridor and waited. Jarvis chose his words with care, uncertain of the assassin's motives.

'You turned yourself in,' he said simply, 'not what I would have expected from a lifelong servant of Majestic Twelve.'

'Like I said,' Mitchell rumbled in response, 'things have changed.'

'Haven't they just,' Jarvis said as he sauntered across to a heavily-barred window and perched on the ledge. 'You've put me in an interesting position, Aaron. On the one hand I now have a captive who could tell me a great deal about Majestic Twelve, and on the other I have to ask myself what you have to gain by being here?'

'Majestic Twelve sold me out,' he replied. 'They were willing to let me rot, and I wasn't willing to trust that they would extricate me from the security max facility in which the FBI deposited me.'

'And on whose orders do you believe you were incarcerated?'

Mitchell's sombre features cracked into a smile. 'You know that's not how this game works, Mister Jarvis.'

'You're well informed,' Jarvis replied, 'there aren't many people outside of the DIA who know my name, which merely tells me that you know a great deal more besides and that you're not in any position to negotiate terms of any kind.'

'I didn't come here to negotiate.'

'Just as well,' Jarvis said, 'as we know damned well who put you in the security max, just as we know of the connection of various senior level FBI operatives to Majestic Twelve. Your employers' little scheme is beginning to unwind, Mitchell, and your arrest and incarceration is just the beginning.'

'The Antarctic is where it will end,' Mitchell said, 'and you don't have long to put a stop to it.'

Jarvis managed not to let his expression slip as he kept his gaze on Mitchell.

'The Antarctic,' he echoed, 'and what would that have to do with Majestic Twelve?'

'Like I said,' Mitchell repeated, 'that's not how we play this game.'

Jarvis looked at his shoes for a moment in thought before he replied.

'You know, of course, that handing you over to the Feds would be a wonderful way of placing an operative inside the enemy on the pretence of defection?'

Mitchell nodded.

'Which was why I ensured that Lopez was not harmed,' Mitchell replied. 'I knew that as soon as I escaped from custody MJ-12 would initiate a clean-up mission to prevent me from gaining leverage to seek refuge with their enemies. That's why they attacked Lopez when they did, and it was only good fortune that I got to her in time or I would not be standing here.'

'Where would you be then?'

'Forgotten,' Mitchell replied. 'Even today, it's possible to disappear completely if you really want to.'

'Majestic Twelve would find you eventually,' Jarvis countered.

'Perhaps, but then that's why I'm here. I didn't want to spend the rest of my life looking over my shoulder. You help me to retire in peace and I'll help you dismantle Majestic Twelve one piece at a time.'

Jarvis weighed up the pros and cons of Mitchell's likelihood of deception. This was a man who had once crushed another beneath a twenty ton shipping container in Dubai. He had killed, repeatedly, murdering Stanley Meyer and many others during the long course of the Defense Intelligence Agency's mission to expose and destroy MJ-12, and now he was standing before Jarvis and offering his assistance.

'You're going to have to give me something to work with that I can verify and fast,' Jarvis demanded. 'I'm not about to open our doors to a paid killer on empty promises.'

Mitchell nodded.

'I wouldn't expect you to, and besides, I have a personal reason to expose as many of MJ-12's assets to you as possible at an early stage. I know that one of them personally was responsible for my incarceration in Colorado.'

'Whom?'

Mitchell took a breath.

'Gordon LeMay,' he replied finally, 'Director of the Federal Bureau of Investigation. He is the primary senior officer within the intelligence community currently in MJ-12's pocket and responsible for...'

'Tell us something we don't know,' Jarvis cut him off wearily. 'We've known about LeMay for months. Tell me something new and interesting or I'll have you sent for a swim wearing concrete slippers.'

Mitchell's expression darkened.

'Then perhaps you should look into a man who goes by the name of Victor Wilms,' Mitchell said.

'Who is Wilms?'

'He's a former Green Beret, served in the earliest days of the Vietnam War before transferring to MJ-12, or perhaps what he thought was a government branch at the time. He was responsible for recruiting me in DC forty years ago, and still holds a position of great trust within MJ-12.'

Jarvis eyed Mitchell suspiciously for a moment.

'To what degree would this handler of yours be useful to us?'

'I believe that he knows personally the founders and leaders of Majestic Twelve.'

Jarvis raised an eyebrow as though the revelation was no big deal to him, but his mind was already turning rapidly. With LeMay their single lead in hoping to identify the leaders of MJ-12, and with the embattled director likely now as much of a liability as an asset to the cabal, there was no guarantee that he would be meeting senior figures within MJ-12 any time soon. Dispatching Lopez and Vaughn to watch the director was costly in terms of time and manpower, and a long shot when there was no immediate likelihood of him meeting Majestic Twelve's shadowy leadership.

But if Mitchell could identify and lead them to Wilms, a man with a far more likely chance of encountering the heads of MJ-12, then the DIA would have achieved a considerable intelligence coup against one of the most nefarious criminal organizations that had ever existed.

Jarvis offered Mitchell a wry smile.

'And I take it that in order to expose this Wilms, if that's his real name, you would have to be released to make contact?'

Mitchell nodded.

'Yes,' he replied. 'Wilms and I are not on the best of terms, but as I'm on the loose he may fear for his life as a result. The same will be true of LeMay – both have betrayed me, and Wilms has already voiced a fear of retribution on my part. If I attempt to meet with him on his own terms, to give him the confidence that I don't intend to ice him, then you'll be able to identify and tail him.'

Jarvis frowned. 'You think that MJ-12 will respond to that?'

'They will not want to lose Wilms as an asset, and if Wilms can be convinced that I'm no longer a threat then they may be more comfortable meeting him,' Mitchell replied. 'All that's required is that MJ-12 believe that I have acted alone and that I am not in your custody. Your agents will be able to follow me and track me as much as they wish, I'm not running anywhere.'

'You've displayed a remarkable knack for evading arrest,' Jarvis said. 'My superiors are not going to want you walking the streets at all, monitored or not.'

'I can't bring you Wilms while I'm shackled in a cell,' Mitchell pointed out. 'The longer I'm here the more chance there will be of MJ-12 learning of my location and realizing that I'm now working for the DIA, or worse closing ranks and making themselves even harder to locate.'

Jarvis bit his lip, unsure of whether Mitchell's plan would be enough to convince Nellis to cut Mitchell loose.

'They'll need more,' Jarvis said. 'How much do you know about Antarctica?'

Mitchell tilted his head as he replied.

'Not as much as I'd like right now,' he admitted, 'but the plan to recover Black Knight has been years in the making. I take it that you have personnel involved in an attempt to recover the device as we speak?'

'We have a team in the region,' was all that Jarvis was willing to share.

'Then they will be going toe to toe with a man named General Andrei Veer,' Mitchell said. 'He's an American of Lithuanian descent and former Army Ranger recruit who was thrown out of his training cadre shortly before graduation for striking a senior officer. He's built himself a nice little career heading mercenary units in countries like Bosnia, Syria, Afghanistan and others. Wilms uses him for paramilitary ventures that need to be kept under the radar, operations funded by Majestic Twelve.'

'How do you know this?' Jarvis enquired.

'Because I hired him,' Mitchell replied. 'Veer is a blunt instrument, the difference between a lock-pick and a grenade. He's not stupid however, and he has the ability to raise hundreds of men to his banner if the price is right, mostly disaffected soldiers who were thrown out of their own regiments for various crimes. He always picks from elite units: airborne, rangers, Special Forces even if he can recruit them, and they rely on superior numbers and firepower to achieve their objectives. How many people do you have on the ground in Antarctica?'

Jarvis smiled tightly.

'We deployed an advance force of twelve Navy SEALs, supporting a small team of scientists.'

Mitchell stared at Jarvis as though he was insane.

'You sent twelve men on one of the most important recovery missions in human history?'

'We needed to be discreet.'

'They'll need a damned miracle,' Mitchell shot back. 'Where's Ethan Warner?'

'Embedded with the SEALs,' Jarvis replied, 'along with Hannah Ford.'

Mitchell nodded and held up his wrists.

'Wilms is the man holding the sword of Damocles over the Antarctic,' Mitchell explained. 'If things go wrong for them down there, he'll destroy the entire site and everything in it.'

'How?' Jarvis demanded.

'Like I said, that's not how we play this game,' Mitchell said as he held up his manacled wrists. 'If you want me to get Wilms we're going to have to move fast because if I can't get him to help you identify MJ-12, your boy Warner and his team are as good as dead.'

***

Dean Crawford

XXIV

Antarctica

The SEALS gathered at the entrance to the subterranean base as Ethan peered into the inky blackness of the interior, the steel blast doors hanging open where they had been presumably left more than seventy years before.

'What the hell could be living down here?' Hannah asked the soldiers urgently.

The pile of scat on the dock was large enough to belong to something of significant size, but there were no visible prints or any other traces of a large animal that Ethan could see as he surveyed the area.

'There's nothing down here,' Riggs insisted. 'We've got more important things to worry about.'

Ethan turned and looked at the lieutenant. 'Such as?'

'Time,' Riggs replied. 'It's only going to be a matter of time before those soldiers find their way in here after us, and when that happens we don't have anywhere left to run.'

The SEALs acknowledged this with a grim silence and a brief exchange of understanding glances that Ethan deciphered as a tacit agreement that the mission would be completed regardless of casualties or the danger of the entire team not making it out of Antarctica alive.

Lieutenant Riggs cocked his rifle and turned toward the entrance to the base.

'On me,' he ordered. 'Del Toro and Saunders, rear guard.'

Two of the SEALS repositioned to the rear of the team as Riggs set off into the base and was consumed by the darkness. Ethan followed with Hannah alongside him, her voice carrying in the bitter cold.

'I don't like this one damned bit,' she uttered. 'This wasn't what I signed up for when I agreed to work for Jarvis.'

Ethan smiled grimly as they entered a cold corridor, dripping water echoing in a symphony around them and the floor of the tunnel slick with frigid water and a thin crust of ice. Above their heads, icicles as hard and sharp as swords forested the interior.

'Get used to it,' he said, 'working for this department of the DIA means being ready for just about anything.'

'Is this the kind of thing you and Lopez used to do?'

Ethan fought off a pall of sadness as he was again reminded of his partner lying unconscious in hospital.

'Every time we deployed for the DIA we got shot at, abducted, attacked, pursued or otherwise harassed by people who would rather we were dead. It's not your average nine to five job.'

'You're not kidding,' Hannah sighed, 'my first deployment and I'm freezing to death a hundred fifty feet beneath the ass of the world. It's not the march of hope and glory I had in mind.'

Ethan said nothing more as they followed Lieutenant Riggs and the SEALs through the darkened corridor, which ended at an open blast door. The door was more like a hatch, hanging on thick steel hinges and glistening with crystals of frost that sparkled in the flashlight beams.

The corridor beyond was walled with metal panels, a thin film of ice encrusting the floor as the soldiers peered inside.

'This looks like the spot where the docks end and the base starts,' Riggs said. 'We'll keep heading inward toward the signal until we find it.'

The corridor was featureless as they walked through it, several of the metal panels having fallen aside to reveal interior walls built from concrete that had in places cracked with the bitter cold and the expansion of frozen water trapped within them. Chunks of ceiling masonry littered their path as they eased their way inside, and Ethan watched closely as Riggs and another soldier led the way down the corridor to a junction, this one marked with German writing stencilled onto the wall opposite.

KOMMANDOZENTRALE

'Command center,' Hannah interpreted the sign.

'Not just a pretty face then?' Ethan smiled as he glanced at her.

He could not tell if Hannah was appalled or embarrassed by his comment as she averted her eyes and pushed on in pursuit of Riggs. They turned right and followed the corridor to a stairwell that led up toward another hatch, this one sealed shut.

Lieutenant Riggs reached it and examined the locks.

'Steel bolts, turned in from the other side,' he reported as Ethan joined him.

'Can we cut through them?' Ethan asked.

'Yeah, we've got a torch but it'll take time we don't have,' Riggs replied. 'We'll use the thermite.'

Ethan knew well the power of thermite, a pyrotechnic composition of metal oxide and a metal powder fuel, usually aluminum. Ignited by heat, the thermite underwent an exothermic oxidation process that produced an extreme burst of heat inside a very small radius, as useful for welding as it was for melting and breaching metal structures.

Ethan eased back out of the way as the SEAL team's explosives expert, Sully, hurried forward, examined the door for a few moments and then attached three slim thermite cylinders to the reverse side of the locking mechanism that was concealed from them on the far side of the door. He wedged the cylinders into place, Ethan guessing that the door was locked shut with three sliding bolts sunk into receptacles in the walls.

'Fall back,' Riggs ordered.

The team descended the stairs as the explosives expert finished his work and hurried back down the corridor. He swiftly activated a battery-operated detonator in his webbing, and then flipped a switch.

Ethan saw a bright light flare at the top of the stairwell as the battery-powered igniter inside the first thermite cylinder activated, followed by the second two in fearsomely bright bursts of light and heat. A hissing sound echoed down the corridor and Ethan saw a swirl of blue smoke that was followed by an acrid smell, the taint of burning metal filling the air.

The light faded out and Lieutenant Riggs ascended the stairwell once again. Ethan followed and saw three patches of glowing red metal shimmering in the darkness as he watched Riggs grab the door's handle and heave back on it.

The heavy door rattled against its locks and then suddenly it swung open as two SEALs aimed their rifles into the darkened interior. Their flash lights illuminated a command center as they rushed in, their weapons sweeping the darkness efficiently.

'Clear!'

At the harsh whisper Ethan and Hannah advanced with their weapons drawn and entered the command centre.

The center looked something akin to the bridge of a ship, with a central console running the length of the room and overlooking windows that gazed out over the submarine pens and the cavern itself. Ethan could see that the window glass was thickly frosted over, one or two of the panes smashed out to reveal the panorama beyond.

At the back of the command centre was a large map, and this was the sight that really attracted his attention.

'That's Antarctica,' he said with some surprise, 'but not with the ice on it?'

Doctor Chandler removed his glasses and peered up in amazement at the large map dominating the wall.

'Good Lord,' he uttered, enthralled. 'That's the Piri Reis map.'

'The what?' Riggs asked.

Chandler gestured to the map as the rest of the scientists and soldiers entered the command center.

'It was found in 1929 by a group of historians,' he said, 'drawn on a piece of gazelle skin. It was a genuine document drawn in 1513 by an admiral of the Turkish fleet by the name of Piri Reis, who said that he'd compiled the map from older maps in the Imperial Library of Constantinople that dated back to the fourth century BC and even earlier.'

Hannah frowned at the map.

'But that map shows mountain ranges, forests, lakes and stuff. How could he have known that was there if Antarctica was covered in a couple miles of ice?'

'That's the great mystery,' Chandler said. 'How could a fourth century map contain data that we have only recently discovered using orbital satellites and advanced technology? The latest possible date that the region of the Antarctic Piri Reis recorded was ice free was around four thousand BCE.'

'What's BCE?' Ethan asked.

'The modern form of historical dating, standing for Before Current Era,' Chandler replied. 'Historians, like scientists, have long since accepted that biblical history did not record real history, so they replaced BC with BCE, and AD, or *Anno Domini* – the Year of Our Lord, with Current Era, or CE.'

'So this map was historically recent, recording ancient data,' Hannah said.

' It's well known that the first civilizations, according to traditional history, developed in the fertile crescent of the Middle East around the year three thousand BCE,' Chandler confirmed, 'and was followed within a millennium by the Indus Valley. Accordingly, none of the known civilizations of the time could have surveyed an ice free Antarctic.'

Ethan looked up at the map with interest.

'The Nazis were obsessed with the occult, the paranormal and such like. Maybe they got on board with this and figured that Piri Reis knew something worth pursuing?'

'The Nazis chose this area of the Antarctic for their expeditions because of this map?' Hannah asked. 'Would they really have gone so far based on something scribbled on a piece of gazelle skin?'

'They did far more bizarre things than that,' Doctor Chandler pointed out. 'But right now, all that interests me is that they had this map here and they constructed an enormous subterranean base at great expense and considerable difficulty. They wouldn't have gone to these lengths without a damned good reason.'

Lieutenant Riggs stood in the centre of the room and frowned as he looked at the display he held in his hands.

'This says the signal should be coming from this room,' he said. 'We're right on top of it.' Ethan glanced up at the ceiling of the command centre and saw a panel embedded in it.

'Maybe it's some kind of mast,' he said. 'It might protrude up through the ice to emit a clear signal from the surface.'

Lieutenant Riggs was about to reply when from somewhere in the depths of the base a deep, reverberating moan shuddered through the facility. Ethan felt his guts contract involuntarily, saw anxious glances exchanged between the scientists as the bizarre roar soared through the abandoned tunnels and corridors and echoed away through the subterranean cavern outside to vanish into the glacier's icy depths.

A long, deep silence followed the unearthly noise as Doctor Chandler removed his spectacles.

'I fear that Saunders was right,' he announced. 'We may not be alone in this facility.'

Lieutenant Riggs shot the scientist a concerned look.

'Well thanks Doc, I'm glad you're here to tell us these things.' The lieutenant turned to his men. 'Cover all points, permanent rotating watch fore and aft. I get the feeling that something's going to come looking for us.'

'What about Black Knight?' Ethan said. 'We still have to recover it.'

'One thing at a time,' Riggs insisted. 'If we don't figure out a way to get that thing and ourselves out of here and past those soldiers, recovering Black Knight won't do us much good because we'll be dead.'

***

XXV

Manhattan Island,

New York City

Nicola Lopez sat in a Lincoln pool car and watched across East 94th Street, where a mid-range hotel was situated on the borough's Upper East Side, just south of Harlem and where the exclusivity of Manhattan began to deteriorate.

'Good choice,' Vaughn suggested, 'anonymous.'

Lopez nodded as she watched the hotel. 'Doesn't mean I like it. We've spent years trying to put Mitchell behind bars and now he's wandering the streets of NYC without a care in the goddamned world.'

'LeMay is in the city and Mitchell flew directly here,' Vaughn pointed out. 'Can't be a coincidence, right? Jarvis knows what he's doing.'

'Doesn't he just.'

Lopez had never really trusted Doug Jarvis. She liked the man himself well enough, although she never passed up the opportunity to give him a hard time, but she knew that his loyalty to his country surpassed all other considerations. Jarvis had repeatedly taken huge risks with the lives of the people under his command in order to achieve the objectives set him by the government and the DIA, and in that Lopez had often wondered just how much Jarvis differed from the immensely powerful and ruthless men they were trying to bring to justice. There was a fine line between honor and criminality, and Jarvis had spent much of his DIA career skirting the line far more closely that she would have...

'Visual,' Vaughn said. 'He's here.'

Lopez was mildly surprised to see Mitchell walking down the street on the far side, his hands in his pockets and a sepulchral air surrounding him. Other pedestrians gave him a wide berth as though he were carrying concealed weapons, somehow subconsciously aware of the barely contained violence within.

'This is a bad idea,' she insisted as she watched him stride into the hotel. 'First chance he gets, he'll bolt.'

'He could already have done that,' Vaughn reminded her, 'the moment he escaped from the facility in Colorado.'

Lopez continued to watch the hotel as she replied.

'That doesn't mean he hasn't got a plan. What I want to know is what the hell he's got in mind.'

*

Aaron Mitchell walked into the hotel and bypassed the reception desk, heading instead for the stairwell. The elevators were closer but Mitchell never allowed himself to be completely cornered: elevators had cameras, advance warning for anyone with the wherewithal to monitor the feeds and prepare for his arrival.

He climbed the stairs two at a time and faster than was necessary, deliberately pushing himself physically. It was a hard habit to break, to continually test himself in even the smallest things. He felt once again a pinch of mild pain from his ribs where, a year ago, Ethan Warner had fractured them during a bitter fight in Nevada. Healing was slower now, pain from injuries plagued him for longer, and he knew that his time as an effective field agent was finally coming to an end. He could not afford for this to go wrong.

He left the stairwell on the fourth floor and turned right onto a corridor. Plush red carpets and soft lighting, pictures on the walls. Rooms were numbered in brass, and as he reached room number *37* he knocked without hesitation.

There was a moment's pause and then he saw the light from the peephole blocked as somebody approached from within. The door opened and a young guy of about thirty with lank brown hair peered out at Mitchell.

'Can I help you?'

'Yes,' Mitchell replied, and slammed his body weight into the door.

The younger man was thrown back in surprise and Mitchell all at once surveyed the room in a single glance as he strode in. Double bed, a young girl asleep on it, wine bottles and beer cans strewn about the room, expensive suits tossed across the backs of chairs and the stale smell of cigarette smoke. Probably an after-office party, or an affair, or just some guy got lucky at a bar downtown.

The guy's protest and angry expression was silenced as Mitchell's left fist flicked out and struck the man on his temple. The impact snapped the man's head back long enough for Mitchell's right fist to roundhouse against his jaw with a loud crack. The man's eyes rolled up in his socket as he slammed down onto the bed and fell silent.

The girl awoke and sat up in bed for a brief moment, just long enough for Mitchell to loom over her and wrap one hand over her mouth as the other arm wrapped around her neck and squeezed, pinching off the flow of blood to her brain. The girl fought for only a few moments before she slumped unconscious in his arms, her low blood pressure from being so recently asleep hastening her collapse.

Mitchell released her and spent a moment or two securing the pair, binding them to the bed before borrowing their room key. He ensured that all of the room's windows were sealed before he turned and exited the room. Moments later, he stopped in front of room *43* and knocked.

The door opened promptly and two armed men with close-cropped buzz cuts and plain gray suits confronted him.

'Are you alone?' the first asked.

'I am.'

'Are you armed?'

'I am not.'

One of the men kept a pistol aimed at Mitchell as the other patted him down and waved a wand designed to detect listening devices across his body. Satisfied, they allowed Mitchell into the room and closed the door behind him. Mitchell walked into the room and saw Victor Wilms standing beside the window, looking out over the Manhattan skyline to the south. Wilms turned and gave Mitchell an appraising look.

'Well, Aaron, I'll admit that I'm both relieved that you called this meeting and equally surprised. There was some concern that you would start a war against us.'

'I still might.'

'Oh come now, you know how foolish that would be,' Wilms said. 'You could not hope to succeed. The government has been trying to eradicate Majestic Twelve for decades and has failed. What could you possibly hope to gain?'

Mitchell did not entertain the conversation.

'You have two choices,' he said, his voice deep and his expression cold and uncaring.

Wilms' casual demeanor vanished and his jaw stiffened. 'And what would they be?'

'You surrender to the American government and reveal the names of every member of Majestic Twelve, along with everything that they've done, in return for immunity from prosecution on your part.'

Wilms blurted out a laugh.

'Then you're asking me to commit suicide, Aaron, for such an act would never go unpunished. Even if the cabal were down to its last dime they would ensure they exacted a due and dispassionate revenge, as you have experienced yourself.'

'Allowing the attempted murder of a former president was a strategic mistake by the cabal,' Mitchell replied. 'They have become too confident of their power, too arrogant. It only takes one whistleblower to bring their whole operation down.'

'The FBI tried that route,' Wilms pointed out, 'and it came up empty.'

Mitchell knew that the FBI had investigated documents purporting to elaborate on some elements of Majestic Twelve back in 2002, but that the investigation had concluded that the cabal was the imaginary creation of conspiracy theorists and fringe lunatics.

'You will become the next whistleblower,' Mitchell repeated.

'What's my other choice?' Wilms asked, mildly amused as he glanced at the two agents flanking Mitchell, both with pistols drawn and aimed at him.

'You die here and now,' Mitchell replied. 'A tragic fall from that window behind you, just like Stanley Meyer.'

Meyer had been an inventor who had created a remarkable device known as a fusion cage which would have rendered fossil fuels irrelevant overnight, a drain on Majestic Twelve's resources that they could not allow to reach the public and an act of homicide that Mitchell had bitterly regretted ever since.

'You're outnumbered,' Wilms snarled as hatred twisted his features. 'I have ten more men outside waiting for you. If anything happens to me in here, you'll be nothing but a piece of damp bullet art the moment you walk into the street.'

Mitchell did not move, his senses focused on the two men just behind him. He could hear their breathing, could smell their cologne, could sense their presence. Wilms took a pace closer to Mitchell and reached for a pistol beneath his own expensive suit.

'You're nothing, Aaron,' he growled, 'no matter how important you think that you may be. You're a spent force, too old to be of use any more in the field. The only person who will die here today is you.'

Mitchell nodded. 'So be it.'

The two guards had made a mistake that so many made, supposed experts in close protection who used their weapons and physical prowess to intimidate instead of common sense and good training to control a situation. Their mistake was in keeping their weapons with range of Mitchell's long arms and vice like grip, even though they were behind his shoulders and technically out of sight.

Mitchell whirled right as he dropped down into a crouch, his hands landing on the pistol barrel of the guard behind his right shoulder and twisting the weapon onto its side as he pulled it down. Mitchell twisted and grabbed the guard around the neck, putting his body between himself and the other two men in the room to foil their aim. The other guard tried to counter the movement and aiming for Mitchell's head, moving to his left as Mitchell's prisoner struggled.

Mitchell's hand was still wrapped around the guard's pistol as he slipped his finger over the guard's trigger finger and pulled hard. The trigger closed and the gun fired as Wilms drew his pistol and rushed in.

The shot hit the second guard in the chest and he staggered to one side as Mitchell flicked his right boot out and it impacted Wilms in the stomach with enough force to fold the old man up, his pistol still in his hand. Wilms' breath rushed from his lungs in a wheezing gale as he collapsed to his knees.

The fallen bodyguard tried to aim again, the 9mm in round in his chest not enough to stop him dead. Mitchell hurled the man in his grip toward his comrade and the bullets slammed into his body with a double thump that Mitchell felt in his own chest through the bullet-proof vest he wore as he threw the gunman to topple onto his companion. The guard's weight slammed down to pin his companion on the floor and block his aim, his gun arm pinned pointing away from Mitchell.

Mitchell stepped forward and slammed his boot down on the guard's face, a dull crunch echoing through the room as his skull was fractured. The other guard stared lifelessly into eternity as blood poured from his chest in copious floods across the carpet, one of the bullets having evidently pierced his heart.

Mitchell turned to see Wilms valiantly try to lift his pistol. He took a single pace and grabbed the weapon, wrenched it from Wilms' grip and then stepped back. The whole event had taken seconds, but now both guards were neutralized and Mitchell held the only available weapon. He held one finger to his lips as he looked at Wilms and then beckoned him to follow, knowing for certain that the room would have been bugged and that support for Wilms would be here within moments.

Wilms, his guts convulsing, staggered to his feet as Mitchell pulled him along and out of the room. He closed the door to the room and dragged along Wilms behind him to room *37* and shoved him inside. The two young occupants were conscious now, their eyes wide with fear and their mouths silenced by gags as Mitchell stormed back in with Wilms and quietly closed and locked the door behind them.

'You'll never get away with this, Mitchell,' Wilms spat above his pain.

Mitchell slid the pistol into the waistband of his pants and grabbed a plastic biro pen from a shelf as he strode toward Wilms. One thick hand grabbed Wilms' collar as the other drove the pen into his body.

Mitchell knew all about pressure points, used to create excruciating pain with minimal effort. He clamped one giant hand over Wilms' face and drove the tip of the pen up under the old man's ribs. Wilms' face tightened and his eyes flew wide as he screamed in agony, the pen grinding against his innards without breaking the skin.

'You'll do what I say,' Mitchell growled as he lifted Wilms off his feet and across to the window.

Outside the room, Mitchell heard the thunder of boots running down the corridor as MJ-12 bodyguards rushed to the room where the gunshots had been heard. Somewhere in the distance across the city, Mitchell could already hear wailing sirens closing in on the Upper East Side.

'I can find you, anywhere,' Mitchell went on, twisting the pen this way and that. 'I can hunt you down and kill you at leisure, so don't you ever tell me what to do again. Those days are over. You will gather Majestic Twelve here in the city with LeMay among them. He will be the patsy, the reason that MJ-12 is exposed to surveillance, not you. Do this and you will be immune to prosecution. Fail, and I will find you.'

Mitchell slammed Wilms' head against the wall with enough force to knock him unconscious. Carefully, he laid the old man on the ground and then opened the window. Outside, the sirens were growing louder and he knew that the MJ-12 bodyguards would not linger and await the arrival of law enforcement that had most likely been called by the panicked owners of the hotel upon hearing gunshots upstairs. Mitchell pulled his cell phone from his pocket and took a single picture of Wilms lying on the floor at his feet.

Moments later, he heard the bodyguards leaving, hurrying down the corridor outside again to avoid being caught on the scene. As he had figured, they also used the stairwell. Mitchell glared at the two captives, both of them stricken with terror as he approached them and opened the man's wallet, which had been left on the bedside table. He slid a credit card into the wallet and closed it again.

'You're in no danger and if you do as I say you'll never see either of us again,' he assured them both. 'This man is an enemy of the state and highly dangerous. If he wakes up and is able to identify you, he will have you killed. On that card is an account containing fifty thousand dollars. It's yours, if you check out of this hotel this very minute and say nothing to anybody about what's happened.' Mitchell leaned close to them as he loosened their bonds, his dark eyes burrowing into theirs as he drew the pistol from his waistband. 'But if you fail to comply with my demands, guess who'll you'll be seeing again?'

The guy, faced with a dilemma, forced a look of heroic and reluctant defiance onto his face. The girl simply stared at the gun for a moment and then at the wallet, already spending the money inside it. Mitchell let them think about the gun for a moment longer, and then he stood up and moved to the open window. Room 37 faced to the north east, as opposed to the entrance to the hotel on the south west side. Mitchell climbed out of the window and hurried down the fire escape and onto an alley between the hotel and a small shopping mall.

Moments later, he vanished into the crowds heading north.

*

A swarm of police hazard lights flashed in the street as Lopez stood alongside the pool car with Vaughn and watched as two bodies were carried from the hotel in body bags.

'We can't walk in there with all of the police around,' Lopez said into her cell phone as they watched from afar. 'It looks like Mitchell met with this Wilms and then must have got bounced by MJ-12 agents or something. Both the agents are dead, Mitchell's missing and they're releasing the hotel's residents one by one.'

Doug Jarvis's reply came back over the line.

'Police radio reports are suggesting an argument gone wrong between two men,,' he said. *'Nobody's mentioned anybody else in conjunction with the attacks matching Mitchell's description.'*

'He's gone,' Lopez snarled as she clenched her fist in exasperation. 'He must have fled before the uniforms arrived and somehow Wilms must also be gone, if he was here at all.'

She was about to curse again when her cell beeped and she looked at the screen. An image had appeared, that of an old man lying on a carpet, perhaps dead, perhaps unconscious. The message had been sent from Mitchell's cell phone, the one handed to him by the DIA for tracking purposes. Beneath it was a message from Mitchell.

STAY ON HIM. I WILL BE CLOSE BY

'Wait one,' she said to Jarvis as she accessed the picture and showed it to Vaughn.

'Who is he? Wilms?'

Lopez looked at the picture for a moment longer and then up at the hotel. Moments later she saw a smartly dressed man walk out of the foyer, his face identical to that of the image on her cell phone. She watched as the old man strode along the sidewalk toward a smart SUV parked on the opposite side of the street. He crossed toward it and a door opened to let him in.

'Doug,' she said into her cell, 'I think we've got an eye on Wilms. He must have enough connections to get him out of trouble like this, the police are letting him go.'

'*Stay on him, don't let him out of your sight.*'

'What about Mitchell?' Vaughn snapped. 'He's nowhere to be seen.'

'*Leave him,*' Jarvis replied. '*Wilms is the priority!*'

'Mitchell's the key to everything! This could be a deception!' Lopez shot back as she turned for their car.

'*Wilms can lead us to Majestic Twelve,*' Jarvis insisted. '*If he does, Mitchell will no longer have any leverage over us! Get on Wilms and keep him in sight! I'll have his identity checked out.*'

Lopez cursed, and jumped into the car as Vaughn pulled out and followed the SUV at a discreet distance toward midtown.

***

XXVI

Antarctica

General Veer held onto the railings in the rear of the ATV as it slowed at the head of a convoy of eight vehicles, those that had survived the tactical descent onto the ice fields and the gunfight with the Navy SEAL team.

Before them was a long, low ridge that rose up off the glacier, churned ice and chunks of snow littering its banks. Veer could see as he jumped down off the ATV that the disturbance was recent and that the ski gliders had stopped nearby, their tracks in the snow clearly visible.

The other ATVs switched off their engines and his men dismounted, already down from their original hundred to about eighty five. Three had still been alive after the SEALs had dumped the C4 charges out on the ice fields, badly injured and in need of urgent medical attention. General Veer had ensured that they received the best possible care during a time of such urgency by personally executing them where they lay. Now his men stood and watched him in silence as he clambered up the ridge line and peered down into the shadowy blue depths of the chasm below him.

Rappel pins were still lodged in the rock hard ice, the lines descending down into the fissure and vanishing into the blackness far below. Several of Veer's officers joined him on the edge of the ridge and peered down inside it.

'No other way out,' one of them observed. 'They've taken a hell of a risk leaving us such a clear trail.'

Veer looked up across the plains.

'They managed to conceal their vehicles though,' he observed. 'Send a few men out to find them. They won't have gone around an obstacle this large, they wouldn't have had enough time, so they must be under cover somewhere to the east of here.'

An officer immediately hurried down the ridge again and began giving orders as Veer crouched down on one knee and ran his gloved hand down his thick beard as another officer, a former Green Beret, spoke up.

'Whatever the hell they're looking for, it's important enough for them to virtually guarantee their deaths here. They're barely bothering to disguise what they're up to.'

General Veer nodded thoughtfully. He had been contacted forty eight hours before by a man named Victor Wilms. Well connected and supremely wealthy, or at least his benefactors were, Wilms had made Veer an offer he simply could not refuse: raise a team of one hundred men, get them to Antarctica and recover an American satellite from rogue forces attempting to sabotage United States interests in the region. The price? Ten million dollars now to raise the group, a further ten million after successful completion of the mission. No taxes, no fuss and no questions asked.

It had taken all of Veer's mental strength to demand fifteen million dollars or there would be no deal. He had got it without question and immediately wished he'd asked for twenty. Even at that early stage, he had wondered whether the mysterious object he was being asked to recover would not be worth more to him than the payment from Wilms.

'They must have further support,' Veer decided as he looked along the length of the ridge, which extended into the distance toward the south east. 'The SEALs must be an advanced force, with maybe a Naval vessel or two on its way to back them up. We need to move fast or we'll get boxed in and it'll be us who are outnumbered.'

Veer stood and strode back down the ridge.

'Bring me the prisoners!' he boomed.

His officers hurried to the back of one of the ATV's , in which lay huddled two hostages pulled from the wreckage of several ski gliders damaged in battle, both of them injured and bound hand and foot. The soldiers hauled them up onto their feet and dragged them out onto the ice.

General Veer could see at once that neither of the captives was a military soldier, which pleased him greatly. SEALs were notoriously tough and trained to be able to withstand interrogation techniques of all kinds, whereas the scientists that had evidently travelled with them were civilians, the weak link in the chain.

The man was middle-aged and virtually bald, the other a young girl with bobbed brown hair who stood shivering on the ice. Veer had ordered their Arctic jackets removed to expose them to the bitter chill, which according to the read-out on his digital watch was a fresh minus twelve in the wind. He moved to stand before them.

'I'll make this simple,' he said. 'If you don't tell me what I need to know, I will kill you both. It's quite likely that your remains will still be here in a thousand years' time, because I won't shoot you – I'll have you buried to your necks in the ice.'

Veer let that fact sink into their minds, let them dwell on how long they would spend being cold before hypothermia would finally lead to death. In truth it probably would not be long but Veer liked toying with the idea of prolonged agony.

'Your names,' he demanded.

'Harrison,' said the man.

'Amy,' the woman replied, her voice barely audible above the bitter winds.

'Tell me why you are here with those soldiers.'

The balding man looked up at Veer with pleading eyes, his words stumbling from his blue lips as he tried to speak.

'Please.., I have two children…, don't leave us out here.'

Veer gestured to his officers. 'Bury him over there.'

The balding man's eyes flew wide and he screamed as he was dragged away across the glacier by several soldiers, all of them chuckling grimly at his protests. Veer looked at the young girl.

'Last chance,' he said, 'to save yourself and your friend over there.'

'It's called Black Knight,' the scientist gabbled, struggling to get her words out fast enough amid the freezing cold and the desperate cries of her colleague from nearby. 'It's a satellite that came down.'

Veer took a pace closer to her. 'Now tell me something I don't know.'

'It's not ours,' she mumbled. 'It's not Russian, or anybody's. It wasn't built by humans.'

General Veer stared at the girl for a long moment and then looked at his officers. 'That explains the rush to get down here.'

'It's been in orbit for thousands of years,' the scientist went on, 'and now it's come down and we're trying to retrieve it for the government.'

'Whose government?' Veer demanded.

She frowned. 'Our government, the United States. We're employed by the Defense Intelligence Agency.'

The general peered at the girl before him for a moment, and then he realized that she was telling the truth. If the Navy team was indeed working for the US Government, then that meant that Wilms had been…

Veer turned away from the scientist and walked out across the ice to where the other scientist was being forced to dig his own ice grave on the glacier, weeping and shivering as the soldiers around him waited impatiently. Veer strode up to the scientist and grabbed him by the throat, lifting him up onto his toes as he growled into his face.

'Who are you working for?' he demanded.

The scientist croaked his response, his eyes bulging. 'Defense Intelligence Agency.'

Veer released his grip and the man collapsed to his knees on the ice as the general considered what he had been told. Wilms was a liar and had just spent ten million bucks on an armed force to recover his mysterious alien box of tricks for him under the pretence of Veer working for the government. The fact that FBI Director Gordon LeMay was in on the deal had convinced Veer of Wilms's credentials, but now…

Veer looked at the ridge line. He had a choice: he had already pocketed four million of the ten million dollars he had been paid by Wilms, the cash squirrelled away in some off shore accounts for when he got back. He could have hired another twenty men with the cash, but he hadn't reckoned on coming up against Navy SEALs so he'd figured *what the hell*. Wilms had promised him another ten million on completion, but Veer now wondered just how likely that payment would be. If Wilms was not working with the FBI, then who the hell was he working for and what were the chances of them honoring payment? If the scientists were right, and Veer had no reason to think otherwise seeing as their lives were in his hands, then such a device, an alien satellite, would be worth a hundred times what he was being paid.

Veer looked down at the scientist sobbing on his knees and was overcome with a sense of regret and compassion. He couldn't let the father of two freeze in the ice alone out here.

Veer stepped back, drew his pistol and aimed it at the scientist's head. Before the man could respond and beg for his life Veer fired. A spray of crimson blood splattered the ice behind the kneeling man and he toppled onto the glacier, his eyes staring lifelessly at the blue sky above as Veer holstered his pistol and strode back toward the remaining scientist.

The girl collapsed in horror to her knees and promptly vomited onto the ice as Veer strode across to her.

'He refused to help me,' Veer growled. 'For your sake, I suggest you decide otherwise. Can this Black Knight satellite be transported?'

The scientist's head bobbed frantically up and down as she nodded, her face twisted with fear and disgust.

'It's solid and it survived aeons in deep space, it can be moved.'

Veer nodded and turned to his men. 'Get her a coat and hot coffee. I want her on her feet and moving with us within twenty minutes!'

The troops hurried to carry out their orders as Veer turned to his officers.

'I want ten men up here to guard the entrance to the chasm,' he snapped. 'If they try to come out before us then blow them all to hell. The rest of us will go down there and retrieve the object with maximum force, no considerations, understood?'

The officers nodded.

'Get to it then!' Veer boomed.

The soldiers dashed to prepare for their mission as Veer turned and surveyed the wilderness around them. At best, he reckoned he had twenty four hours before the might of the United States Navy descended on the area. At worst he would walk away from the mission with four million bucks tucked away, but if he could recover this *Black Knight* and get it out of the continent he would make a hundred times that, or even more.

All he had to do was ensure that Navy didn't take it from him.

***

XXVII

Ethan stood at the control panel of the old submarine pens and looked down through the shattered windows at the dock below. The SEALs had placed a handful of glow sticks around the docks to illuminate the vast chamber with an eerie orange glow that reflected off the icy walls of the cavern and contrasted with the strange blue glow of algae plumes that periodically drifted through beneath the water. It sometimes seemed as though the entire chamber was alive, shimmering with mysterious glowing beings rippling down the walls toward the exit tunnel ahead.

'I can't believe the Nazis built something like this out here,' Doctor Chandler said as he examined the control bunker. 'The sheer effort required to build a base of this size is almost unthinkable.'

Chandler leaned forward and peered out of the windows, his breath condensing on the freezing air as he spoke.

'Where did the Black Knight go? It's a sizeable object according to NASA's sensory data, and even if it shed its protective shell after re-entry and halved in size it should still be easy to locate, so why can't the soldiers find it?'

Ethan shrugged, uncertain of what they were dealing with and equally unsure of what it might be capable of. Ethan had a passing interest in *Unidentified Flying Objects*, which was a category that Black Knight surely belonged to. He had watched many television documentaries on them, had seen video clips shot by nervous civilians depicting strange glowing objects traversing the skies, most of which could be explained away quite easily. Yet there were others that defied all rational explanation; encounters that left witnesses with severe burns and radiation sickness; observations supported by radar records and multiple witness testimony that correlated with the reports of experienced pilots both military and civilian, and first-hand accounts by those who had worked within the military and had testified on oath that they had been involved in cover-ups of UFO sightings around the world.

'This bell that we were told about,' Ethan asked Chandler. 'Why do they seem so sure that it has something to do with Black Knight? Surely the Nazi connection isn't enough on its own to suggest we know that shape and size of the object we're looking for?'

Chandler gestured to the tunnel through which they had travelled to reach the submarine pens.

'That tunnel was about the right size for an object matching Die Glocke's size to have travelled through it, perhaps even created it,' he pointed out.

'Yeah, but we found a Nazi in the ice that had been there for decades,' Ethan pointed out, 'so the tunnel itself is also old, right?'

Chandler removed his spectacles and attempted to clean their foggy lenses as he spoke.

'Die Glocke was never identified as having been in the German's possession, although many references to it were found in the secret bases at which they were purportedly testing the device. However, we also know that in the wake of the Second World War our government spirited away countless Nazi machines upon which they had been working. Many of their finest minds came too such as Werner Von Braun, the inventor of the dreaded V2 rocket bombs, without whom we would have possibly lost the space race. Von Braun was the chief designer of the immense Saturn V launchers that took our astronauts to the moon.'

Ethan leaned on the control panel and folded his arms.

'So you think that the bell was taken out of Germany by our own people and…, what, worked on?'

Chandler shrugged. 'I wish I knew, but I don't. The only thing that I know for certain is that within two years of the end of World War Two the modern UFO phenomenon grew rapidly. From Kenneth Arnold's iconic sighting in 1947 to the alleged Roswell incident and others, flying saucers became more commonplace in human history after the end of the war. I don't consider that to be a coincidence.'

'I don't consider it to be evidence,' Hannah pointed out as she entered the control room.

Chandler smiled. 'Good, that's the right way to think: extraordinary claims require extraordinary evidence, as the late, great Carl Sagan famously said. It's why religions don't stand up to scrutiny, for instance. But Die Glocke does have further evidence to support its existence, and the fact that it may now belong to our own government. It was known as the Kecksburg Incident.'

'What happened?' Ethan asked.

'The Kecksburg UFO incident occurred in December 1965 in Kecksburg, Pennsylvania,' Chandler explained. 'A brilliant fireball was seen by thousands of people in several states and across Ontario in Canada, much like the one we witnessed as we travelled here. It passed over Detroit, Michigan and reportedly deposited hot metal debris over Ohio, starting grass fires in the process and caused sonic booms in the Pittsburgh area. It's fair to say that something real happened that night.'

'Sounds like a meteor or comet or something,' Hannah said.

'That's what the Air Force thought,' Chandler agreed. 'It was assumed and reported by the press to be a meteor after the authorities discounted other explanations such as a plane crash, failed missile test or satellite debris. The problem was that eye witnesses in the town of Kecksburg, roughly thirty miles south east of Pittsburgh, reported that something crashed into the woods near the town. Several people reported seeing an object go down, feeling the impact as an earth tremor and seeing smoke in the vicinity. They alerted the authorities, thinking that an aircraft had crashed, and the fire department was scrambled to the area. What they found in the woods has since gone down in legend as one of the best documented UFO encounters in history.'

Chandler replaced his glasses.

'The volunteer fire department guys reported finding an object in the shape of an acorn about as large as a Volkswagen Beetle, a description that closely matches that of *Die Glocke*. Writing resembling Egyptian hieroglyphics was also said to be present around the circumference of the base of the object. Before they could spend much time examining it they reported an intense build-up of military personnel and then the United States Army ordered all civilians out of the area, secured the object and removed it on a flatbed truck. They later claimed that they searched the entire area and found nothing.'

Hannah shrugged.

'Could have been a downed satellite,' she suggested. 'They come down from time to time, right?'

'Yes they do,' Chandler admitted, 'and they're very delicate objects that would burn to a cinder long before they reached the ground. The object the firefighters reported was solid and intact and shaped nothing like a satellite. The Greensburg *Tribune-Review* later reported the object sighting and the Army's sealing off of the area, including interviews with military personnel who said that their superiors were interested in examining the object. However, a later report in the same paper said that nothing was found, suddenly following the Army's official line of explanation which was that the fireball was caused by a meteor which exploded in mid-air before reaching the ground, the sonic boom causing the ground tremor that witnesses reported. When pressed, the reporter involved revealed that he had been pressured by government agents to alter his original report to match that of the Army.'

'So you're saying it was a cover-up?' Ethan said.

'NASA went back on its original explanation in 2005 and said that the object was in fact the remains of a Russian satellite. This was immediately rejected by a former NASA scientist who revealed that the orbital mechanics of the satellite in question revealed that it could not possibly have been responsible for the event. Furthermore, when pressed with a law suit and a court order to reveal the files surrounding the incident, NASA stalled for three years before revealing that the files had been *lost*, if you can believe that.'

Ethan looked out of the windows again.

'So if you think that the Kecksburg incident object was Die Glocke, then what could we be looking at here? A similar device?'

'It's only a hunch,' Chandler replied, 'but I don't think that the Germans built Die Glocke. I think that they captured it after the UFO crash in Germany in 1936 and began trying to reverse engineer the device. It would explain some of the incredible advances they made in short time spans during their war effort, and the advanced research they were doing in the later stages of the conflict. Some of the scientific advances made by the Germans during the Second World War are only really being understood today. If they had been successful in developing some of the technology they were working on and had weaponized it, they could have completely changed the outcome of the entire conflict, perhaps even defeated the United States of America.'

Ethan knew that the Germans had developed the V2 missile, which they used to attack Britain from afar. Another couple of years of development could have seen longer range missiles used to strike the United States, certainly Russia and likely even the Far East with impunity.

Ethan's mental image of Nazi missiles arcing across the Atlantic toward America drifted across his field of vision, following the lines of light raining down the walls, and suddenly he took a breath as he realized what he was seeing.

'Damn, it went beneath the water,' he gasped.

'What?' Hannah asked as she looked at him.

Ethan did not reply as he dashed from the control room and hurried down the stairwell outside, heading for the docks. He almost slipped twice on patches of black ice in the poorly illuminated corridors as he hurried outside, Lieutenant Riggs and two of the SEALs looking up at him as he dashed past.

'Where's the fire?' Riggs asked, standing up.

Ethan reached the edge of the nearest submarine pen, and then he reached down onto the dock and pulled free a chunk of ice. He turned and lowered the ice into the water and watched as the rest of the team joined him on the dock.

Ethan stared down at the chunk of ice in the water before him, and as he watched so it began drifting down toward the tunnel entrance. Hannah watched it go with him, and understood immediately.

'The warm water channel isn't in the fissure in the wall,' she said. 'It's passing beneath the pens.'

Ethan nodded, watching as the chunk of ice slowly began to melt before his eyes as it travelled south down the dock.

'If Black Knight came through here, it went below the base. It's somewhere down there,' he said as he pointed toward the frigid black water.

Lieutenant Riggs cursed as he peered down into the dock.

'How the hell are we going to get it out?'

Ethan was about to answer when another of Riggs' men called out in a harsh whisper.

'Enemy!'

Ethan whirled to where he could see Del Toro and Saunders near the tunnel entrance, their weapons pointed down into the impenetrable darkness.

There, just visible to the naked eye, Ethan could see the flickering of distant lights as the MJ-12 soldiers advanced toward them.

'We're running out of time,' he said to Riggs.

Another voice called out to Riggs from up on the command center.

'Lieutenant? You'd better take a look at this!'

**

Dean Crawford

XXVIII

Ethan hurried up the stairwell in pursuit of Riggs as they rushed toward the command center. Riggs had placed two fresh SEALs near the tunnel entrance to relieve Saunders and Del Toro, ready to ambush the MJ-12 troops once they arrived, and now they dashed into the command center to see Sully beckoning them to follow.

'This way.'

Ethan followed the two soldiers down a narrow flight of steps that headed away from the main docks, descending down until they reached a steel door that had been burned open by the SEALs, the harsh odor of burning metal hanging in the air.

Sully led them out onto a smaller, secondary dock, and this time the dock was not empty.

Ethan slowed as he stared at the submersible moored alongside the dock, a metallic device that reminded him of a U-Boat except that it was only around twelve meters long, its black hull and red stencil markings looking cruel and dangerous in the minimal illumination offered by their flashlights.

'I'll be damned,' Riggs said, 'it's a *Seehund*.'

'A what?' Ethan asked.

'It's a German midget submarine,' Riggs replied, 'two man crew, two torpedoes. They were deployed toward the end of the war and sank a fair few vessels before Germany surrendered at the end of the conflict. They were also known as Type Twenty Seven U-Boats, and were based on a British design used in an attempt to sink the German battleship *Tirpitz*.'

Ethan looked at the submarine, which had almost certainly been abandoned in the dock since the end of the war.

'Is it serviceable?' Ethan asked.

Riggs looked the submarine over. 'It's floating, but I don't know whether she'll hold water once submerged.'

Ethan saw that the submarine had a clear dome atop her bridge, allowing for visual inspection of her surroundings, and that her torpedo shoots were empty.

'It's too small to have come all the way down here from the North Atlantic,' Ethan guessed. 'That means it must have been brought here for a reason.'

'The warm water channel,' Riggs picked up on Ethan's train of thought. 'They built this base and planned to investigate the channel, and this submarine would be the only vessel that was small enough to do the job.'

'And that's not all,' Sully added. 'Take a look at this.'

Sully led them back inside the base to a hatch that Ethan had not taken much notice of when they had walked in. Inside the door entrance was a large box-like structure suspended in mid-air within an underground chamber.

'It's an anechoic chamber,' Sully explained, 'although what the hell they'd have built one of these down here for I have no idea.'

An anechoic chamber was a form of room that was isolated from exterior sound or electromagnetic radiation sources, preventing the reflection of wave phenomena. The chamber was supported slightly above the floor using tensile springs and surrounded on all sides by sound-proofing layers of anechoic tiles, a concrete shield and a full six inches of near vacuum-pressure air.

Ethan stepped inside and looked around. 'It's quite small, no more than ten men.'

His voice sounded dead, monotone, its vocal resonance lost within the room as though Ethan were listening to it underwater. He stepped out and walked with Riggs and Sully back to the *Seehund* in the rear dock.

Ethan peered into the black water and then looked at Riggs.

'If we want to recover Black Knight, we're going to have to go down there. Do you think that this sub' could bring it back?'

Riggs was about to reply when Hannah burst into the dock.

'They're travelling up the tunnel toward us!' she said urgently. 'We need everybody in the pens, now!'

Ethan ran with Riggs and Sully as they sprinted up the stairwell back toward the command post. Riggs posted the team's sniper, Saunders, in the command center, looking down on the submarine pen entrance as he and Ethan hurried down onto the docks and across to where the ice cavern's mouth extended into the blackness of the tunnel carving its way south through the deep glacier.

Ethan let his eyes adjust to the gloom for a moment, and gradually he began to detect the distant flashes of light that drifted like ghosts through the pristine ice.

'They're still some way off,' Doctor Chandler reported as he observed the slowly shifting lights. 'The ice down here is so clear that some of the glow from their flashlights is making it this far. Incredible.'

Riggs did not share the scientist's enthusiasm for the lights as he crouched down and surveyed the walls of the tunnel.

'Best thing we can do is bring the tunnel down on them,' he said finally. 'Set charges around the walls, work in darkness so they don't detect either our flashlights or our night vision goggles.'

Hannah frowned. 'They can see the light from night vision goggles?' she asked.

'The goggles fire a laser beam to illuminate the darkness and capture reflected light artifacts to build a picture for the wearer,' Riggs explained. 'If somebody else happens to be wearing one, they can also see the laser beam although it's invisible to the naked eye.'

Sully, Del Toro and Riggs began unpacking explosive charges from their kit as Ethan eyed the tunnel.

'If you blow this tunnel we lose our only way out of here,' he pointed out. 'Not to mention the fact that you might bring the rest of the cavern down with it.'

Riggs unpacked one of the C4 charges and lodged it into the ice near the tunnel entrance as he replied.

'We're not isolated,' he said. 'The Navy knows we're here and will send support. One way or the other, all we have to do is survive long enough to be located.'

Ethan shot the tunnel another glance. 'I'd rather they found us and rescued us rather than found us and dug our frozen corpses out of the ice.'

'You all knew the risks,' Riggs snapped back as he worked.

'Reassuring,' Hannah said as she peered into the gloom at the oncoming soldiers. 'They'll be here within the hour. It didn't take us much longer than that to reach the base and they're not encumbered with scientists.'

As if on cue, one of the scientists burst from the base and hurried across the slippery ice to Doctor Chandler's side.

'You've got to see this!' he insisted in a harsh whisper, conscious of the way sound might travel down the tunnel and alert their pursuers.

'See what?' Chandler asked.

'The algae plumes,' the scientist replied. 'We've analyzed them and it's like nothing we've ever seen before. There's new life down here.'

Chandler turned slowly to look at his colleague. 'New life?'

'New life,' the scientist confirmed. 'Completely new. We could have used Amy Reece here.'

Chandler stared at the younger man for a long moment and then turned to Lieutenant Riggs.

'Lieutenant, you cannot blow the tunnel in now. There are new forms of life present in this cave system that demand greater study and...'

'The tunnel's going,' Riggs snapped, cutting the old man off. 'You won't be able to study anything if you're dead. Your call.'

Chandler did not budge as he replied.

'You don't understand, Lieutenant. New life means that this glacier is a perfect preserve for...'

'For anything that dies inside it,' Riggs shot back. 'You're not here to study, doctor, only to advise us in any way possible on how to recover Black Knight. That's all.'

'But that's what I'm saying!' Chandler implored. 'You cannot seal that tunnel because by doing so you risk trapping us inside a cavern that floods not occasionally but on a *regular* basis.'

Ethan looked back at the base and suddenly he realized why the interior of the construction was filled with heavy blast doors.

'It's a submarine in itself,' he said. 'That's why there are pressure doors all through it.'

'Precisely!' Chandler said. 'There is a fresh water channel running through the glacier from somewhere to the north and it routinely floods this cavern system. That's why we found the Nazi soldier pinned in the ice – he was one of the ones who probably didn't make it back to the base during a lockdown.'

Riggs looked at his fellow SEALs for a moment before he replied.

'And how often does this chamber flood, do you think?'

Chandler gestured with an oddly casual jab of his thumb to one side, at the pristine walls of the chamber.

'Look at that ice,' he said. 'It's mirror smooth due to the passage of warmer water polishing its surface on a regular basis. You remember those steps inside the tunnel, the ones that looked hand carved that were created by gradually receding flood water? They were each two or three inches deep – water receding gradually. But the walls were also mirror polished. It's my guess that this cavern floods perhaps every few days and then the water recedes over a few days, leaving the steps in the ice. There cannot be much warning of a deluge as otherwise no soldier would have been so slow as to be drowned down that tunnel.'

Ethan began looking around them at the cavern system and at the water gushing from the ragged fissure in the east wall of the cavern.

'The Nazis must have placed a warning system of some kind into the tunnels, or perhaps out here, something to give their soldiers at least a chance of making it inside the base.'

Lieutenant Riggs was about to reply when from the deep black water they heard a thunderous moan shudder through the cavern. Ethan felt the hairs on the back of his neck rise up as he turned instinctively toward the hellish groan, as though the entire base was shifting position and wrending the very metal from which it was built.

Lieutenant Riggs stood up alongside him as Ethan's eye caught on the black water of the docks before them.

'Look at that,' Hannah said as she pointed at the water.

To Ethan's amazement he saw the water shivering in miraculously symmetrical waves, rippling as though sound were travelling through it, and he realized that it actually was.

'The water is cavitating,' Chandler gasped as he observed the phenomenon, raising his voice to be heard above the reverberating moan. 'Something is emitting enough power to cause all that water to shiver in response.'

The sound slowly died away, fading into the darkness as the rippling water settled down once more.

'I don't want to meet what caused that,' Hannah said as she backed away from the water's edge a few paces.

Doctor Chandler walked in the opposite direction. 'I most certainly do,' he replied. 'Do you have any idea how much energy was required to achieve that? Any biological form capable of such an emission must be gigantic, far larger than a Blue Whale.'

Lieutenant Riggs turned back to his explosive charges as though nothing had happened but Ethan could sense him thinking fast as he worked.

'We'll rig the charges anyway, but we'll hold off for as long as we can before detonating them. Only if the MJ-12 team breach the entrance do we blow them, understood?'

The SEALs all acknowledged the order as Doctor Chandler turned to his colleague, his features taut with excitement.

'You said that you found new life down here?'

'Yes,' the scientist replied, momentarily distracted by the unearthly moan they had heard coming from beneath the water, his eyes still fixed warily upon the dock. 'It does not share a genetic code with any known life form in our database.'

That caused even the SEALs to stop working and glance across at Chandler.

'No known genetic match?' Chandler echoed.

'That's right,' the scientist replied. 'It's a form of life that might not have originated on this planet. It's exo-biology, an alien life form.'

***

XXIX

Ethan and Hannah followed Doctor Chandler into the command center and through to a large back room that had once probably been used as a planning or operations center, the room dominated by a large table where Chandler's scientists had prepared a simple laboratory in the glow of luminous light sticks.

'How much work have you completed?' Chandler asked.

'We have performed nucleic acid sequencing and have deduced the metabolic pathways of the bacteria represented in the flowing water we sampled and, by extension, in the chambers that may lay beyond further inside the glacier,' the younger man replied. 'We have already found over a hundred unique gene sequences, ninety per cent or so from bacteria with the rest from Eukarya. Taxonomic classifications are underway for most of the sequences.'

'And how would you classify what you have found so far?' Chandler asked urgently.

'The taxa are similar to organisms previously described from lakes, brackish water, marine environments, soil, glaciers, ice, lake sediments, deep-sea sediments, deep-sea thermal vents, animals and plants. There are multiple sequences both aerobic and anaerobic, psychrophilic, thermophilic, halophilic, alkaliphilic, acidophilic and desiccation-resistant. Autotrophic and heterotrophic organisms are present, including some multicellular eukaryotes.'

Both Ethan and Hannah stared bug-eyed at the scientists.

'So, *in English*, what does that all mean?' Ethan asked.

Doctor Chandler stared into space for a moment and then he walked past them without another word and back into the command center. Ethan exchanged a glance with Hannah and then followed Chandler into the center to see him staring at the Piri Reis map on the wall there.

'Let me guess,' Ethan quipped, 'you don't have a clue and you're just covering up.'

If Chandler heard Ethan, he didn't respond to it directly.

'I think I know where the water's coming from,' he said finally.

Ethan felt a pulse of excitement. 'Good. If we can shut it off we'll prevent the chamber from flooding, right?'

A ghost of a smile flickered across Chandler's features. 'You won't be shutting this flow off, my boy,' he replied.

'You wanna start telling us what's going on?' Hannah demanded. 'Y'know, lives on the line and all that?'

Chandler roused himself from his reverie and gestured to the map.

'This map, as you know, may or may not show Antarctica ice-free. However, we know that the continent was indeed ice free in the distant past and that it was filled with all manner of life including dinosaurs.'

'I got today's history lecture,' Hannah confirmed. 'Cut to the chase.'

'Then Antarctica drifted south as a result of natural plate tectonics and became shrouded with ice that is now several miles thick,' he went on. 'That means, logically, that biologically preserved material and perhaps species were trapped within and beneath that ice in completely unique environments.'

Ethan glanced at the map on the wall and began to understand where the scientist was going with this.

'You think that something else has evolved under the ice?' he suggested.

'Not *something*,' Chandler corrected, 'but an entirely different and isolated ecosystem, a *Lost World* of sorts. Antarctica has been frozen beneath an ice sheet for at least fifteen million years, more than enough time for new and novel species to have adapted through natural selection to the conditions encountered beneath the ice.'

Ethan frowned.

'But how could anything get out if it's trapped beneath miles of ice?'

Chandler reached up to the map and pointed to a small oval that looked like a lake, drawn on the surface of what was presumed to be Antarctica.

'Lake Vostok,' he said finally. 'It's a submarine lake, trapped beneath the glaciers of Antarctica for fifteen or more million years. Its water is said to be utterly pristine, totally sealed off from the rest of the world for eons. If biological remains of species made it into the lake before the ice sealed it in, there could be anything lurking down there.'

'Anything?' Hannah echoed.

Chandler's assistant spoke up.

'Most of the larger forms of life that existed in prehistoric times did so because the atmosphere of the time was markedly different from today's and contained a far greater proportion of oxygen, allowing the existence of very large species like dinosaurs and insects with wingspans larger than today's birds of prey.'

Ethan smiled as he saw Hannah shiver.

'I've seen artwork of dragonflies as big as eagles,' he said, enjoying Hannah's discomfort, 'and millipedes as big as anacondas.'

'That's right,' Chandler went on, 'species grew on an immense scale back then, but the changes in atmosphere of today mean that they would be unable to survive for long as they would suffer the same kind of problems as humans at very high altitudes. They simply would not be able to breathe properly and would be rendered comatose and die very quickly. It's one of the reasons why, despite all you read in the news, dinosaurs such as *Tyrannosaurus Rex* could not be brought back to life even if the genetic sequence of such a species were fully decoded. They would die long before they reached their adult size.'

Hannah seemed relieved as she looked again at the Piri Reis map.

'So what do you think is in that lake and what does it have to do with this base?'

'If the Nazis thought that this area was holding something unique, such as new and novel forms of life, then it may have been an extra reason for them to explore the region, given their fascination with anything unusual that could be weaponized.'

'But if these species are genetically so different from anything on Earth then how could they manipulate them with technology from the Second World War?'

Chandler's eyes danced with excitement, glittering in the dim light as he spoke.

'In the Pacific Ocean west of the southern tip of South America, the United States Navy laid an array of hydrophones to monitor the passing of Soviet submarines during the Cold War. The network was called SOSUS, an acronym for Sound Surveillance System. The phones lie deep below the ocean surface in what's known as the deep sound channel, where temperature and pressure allow sound waves to keep travelling and not become scattered. In 1997 the sensors detected a sound that freaked out everybody who ever heard it. The varying frequency of the call bore the hallmark of a marine animal and was confirmed as a biological species by marine biologists who examined the recording. The call rose rapidly in frequency over a period of one minute and was of sufficient amplitude to be detected on multiple sensors.'

Hannah raised a cautious eyebrow. 'So?'

'The sensors were more than five thousand kilometres apart,' Chandler revealed. 'The frequency of the sound means that the living creature that made the call would possess a mass five times greater than that of the Blue Whale.'

A silence filled the room as they digested the implications of what Chandler was saying.

'A noise a bit like what we've been hearing in this chamber?'

Chandler nodded. 'Enough to cause cavitation in the water itself,' he replied. 'The land mass of Antarctica may not be able to support large species any longer, but there is nothing to prevent them surviving at sea.'

'It's not the only time it's happened,' the assistant confirmed. 'The US National Oceanic and Atmospheric Administration have even given names to the disturbing sounds they've detected, calling them things like Train, Whistle, Upsweep and Slow Down. Upsweep turned out to be an undersea volcano. But the 1997 sound was confirmed as biological, and they named it *The Bloop*. Likewise, Slow Down was recorded in the same area as the Bloop, lasted for seven minutes and was powerful enough to be detected on sensors two thousand kilometres apart.'

'Every other possible cause of the noises has been eliminated,' Chandler continued. 'Ice floes calving in Antarctica, submarine earthquakes, volcanoes and man-made events. Whatever made those noises is alive and five times larger than a Blue Whale and it's living in the deep ocean right now.'

The scientist stared up at the ancient Piri Reis map as he spoke.

'Sailors from around the world have reported tales of huge monsters of the deep for thousands of years. For the most part it was always dismissed as the effects of re-telling and alcohol, but those same sailors would also speak of rogue waves a hundred feet high that would rear up and swallow vessels whole. Science dismissed those tales too until an orbiting satellite detected rogue waves all across the world's oceans and large vessels started filming their encounters with them.'

Ethan, mesmerised by the tales, looked at Chandler.

'So you're saying that the *Kraken* might actually exist?'

'No,' Chandler smiled. 'We're saying that sailor's tales of a gigantic sea creature able to take down large vessels were born of encounters with something very real. Dead giant squid have been washed ashore that were sixty feet long, but there is no theoretical limit to the maximum size for a cephalopod, and great white sharks over twenty feet in length have been filmed off South Africa – that's the same size as the supposedly impossibly large predator featured in the movie *Jaws*.'

'And that's not all,' his assistant said. 'Scientists created the first synthetic life form, a micro-organism with a different genetic code to all other forms of life on Earth back in 2014.

The semi-synthetic microbe, a genetically modified E. coli bacterium, was endowed with an extra artificial piece of DNA with an expanded genetic alphabet – instead of the usual four "letters" of the alphabet its DNA molecule had six, a pair of extra base pairs, denoted by X and Y, which pair up together like the other base pairs and are fully integrated into the rest of the DNA's genetic code. This shows that other solutions to storing information are possible and, of course, takes us closer to an expanded-DNA biology that will have many exciting applications, from new medicines to new kinds of nanotechnology.'

Ethan reeled with the volume of information, but he could understand the basic gist of what the two scientists were trying to say.

'So life can exist in forms that don't or haven't yet occurred naturally on Earth, and Lake Vostok might contain forms of life that we haven't seen before,' he said. 'That still doesn't connect them to this base, right?'

'Wrong,' Chandler said. 'Lake Vostok is a hundred and sixty miles long, thirty miles wide and at its widest point and covers nearly five thousand square miles. At fifteen hundred feet deep and with such a volume of water, it could contain life forms of considerable size. It's an oligotrophic extreme environment, one that is supersaturated with nitrogen and oxygen to a degree fifty times higher than those typically found in ordinary freshwater lakes on Earth's surface. The lake is under complete darkness, so there is speculation that any organisms inhabiting the lake could have evolved in a manner unique to this environment. If there exists a subglacial channel that maintains a permanent flow to the open ocean…'

Ethan got it immediately.

'Then species could move in and out of the lake, perhaps move across large regions of Antarctica, and would have a native environment with enough oxygen to allow supr-sized growth.'

Chandler nodded.

'In 2005 an island was found in the central part of the lake, and over the past few decades some hundred forty lakes have been identified beneath the ice sheet. It is suspected that these Antarctic subglacial lakes may be connected by a network of subglacial rivers. Centre for Polar Observation & Modelling glaciologists have proposed that many of the subglacial lakes of Antarctica are at least temporarily interconnected, and because of varying water pressure in individual lakes, large subsurface rivers may suddenly form and then force large amounts of water through the solid ice.' Chandler gestured to the cavern outside. 'That would explain the flooding regularly occurring here in the past.'

He walked to the map and pointed to some of the rivers marked upon it.

'Research by scientists from the Lamont–Doherty Earth Observatory of Columbia University suggest that the water of the lake is continually freezing and being carried away by the motion of the Antarctic ice sheet while being replaced by water melting from other parts of the ice sheet under high pressure conditions. They estimated that the water in the lake is replaced every thirteen thousand years.'

Hannah looked at Ethan. 'Isn't that the same amount of time that Black Knight was estimated to have been in Earth orbit?'

'Exactly the same amount of time,' Ethan replied, thinking fast. 'Doctor Chandler, what's the chances that whatever Black Knight is, it was placed in orbit at the same time as something descended onto the ice sheet in Antarctica thirteen thousand years ago?'

Chandler stared briefly up at the ceiling as he considered this.

'It could simply be a coincidence? Why should a correlation be found when there is no causation known?'

'Because we're assuming that Black Knight is some kind of alien craft and that it was piloted here by something. But what if that's not the case?'

'What do you mean?'

Ethan thought back to Iraq and Afghanistan, to the unmanned aerial vehicles that had soared through the skies and targeted the Taliban and *Al-Qaeda* from high above, and the satellites and GPS stations that had made the weapons of the United States' forces so accurate during the conflict.

'What if it's not a manned craft at all, but a drone, something looking for life and sending the signals back to wherever it came from?'

Chandler stared at Ethan in amazement.

'That's how Nikola Tesla found it,' he said. 'He didn't detect its signals - it detected *him*!'

'And began signalling, when it realized that mankind was becoming technologically advanced,' Ethan added. 'Maybe we're looking at more than just a crashed alien craft here. It might be possible that it's a communication device to whatever species created it.'

***

XXX

Manhattan

'This isn't going to work.'

Michael Vaughn drove the pool car through the densely packed streets north of the Upper East Side and Central Park. The Pierre Hotel was just visible through the trees as Lopez peered at it and replied.

'It's going to work better than sitting around waiting for these people to just show themselves to us. Majestic Twelve aren't going to file out of the front entrance waving at the crowds, y'know, and this is where Wilms went after we lost Mitchell. He hasn't come out since.'

'I didn't suggest that they would,' Vaughn countered. 'Just that their surveillance would have ensured that every single point of access and egress would be covered in an area like this. We won't be able to get anywhere near enough to them to record any visual or audio.'

Lopez smiled to herself. 'You leave that to me.'

Vaughn shook his head as he drove. 'It's really just like having Hannah sitting here.'

'Hannah Ford is a pale imitation, literally,' Lopez replied without interest as she surveyed the street ahead. 'Accept no substitutes.'

Vaughn turned south on 5th Avenue, the trees of Central Park on one side and pale sunlight flickering through the leaves as Lopez searched for a suitable spot. She knew that they could not risk driving directly past the front of the hotel – MJ-12 would not have neglected to post guards who would most likely be on the lookout for her after the failed assassination attempt. That left Michael Vaughn, who would be able to monitor the location while Lopez got to work.

'There,' Lopez said as she saw one of the city's distinctive yellow cabs pull away from the sidewalk.

Vaughn pulled into the gap left by the cab as Lopez opened her door and got out before climbing back into the rear of the vehicle. Vaughn killed the engine and watched her in the rear view mirror as she grabbed a large ruck-sack and opened it.

'You really think that thing will get us a good enough look at MJ-12 to break the cabal open?'

169

Lopez unpacked a glossy black device, eighteen inches square with a horizontal four inch blade on each corner set into the frame. Along with it she produced a control unit, similar to those used by the operators of remote-controlled aircraft.

'Hellerman is a genius,' she replied as she set the drone down beside her on the seat and opened the battery compartment. 'He's bred real bees that he hooks up to electrodes and flies around, controlling their brains. Modifying one of these things is child's play to him.'

'Why not just send one of his bees in instead?' Vaughn asked.

'Too small,' Lopez explained as she installed the batteries and then began checking the cameras attached to the underside of the drone. 'They can't record footage easily, so we needed something big enough to carry a high-resolution camera and a solid state drive to record the data. Hellerman figures it'll fly with the camera working for about thirty minutes on these high-density batteries before we'll need to land it.'

Vaughn looked down the street at the edifice of the distant hotel.

'If they spot it they'll shoot it down,' he pointed out. 'If they get hold of it the whole thing's a bust.'

'Full of optimism, aren't you?' Lopez murmured from the back seat as she worked. 'The drone's fitted with a data relay device which will send everything it records back here to my laptop computer, which you'll be monitoring. Once we have a good shot of the group, we're out of here.'

Vaughn said nothing more as Lopez finished setting up the drone and the computer and then looked at a cell phone attached to the dash of the vehicle. Upon the screen was a small red dot moving through Manhattan and closing in on the Pierre Hotel. Doug Jarvis had deployed a small team of DIA operatives to track Gordon LeMay as he went about his business outside of the FBI, and that business had led them to Manhattan. Whatever the Director of the FBI was up to, he'd decided to fly to New York City and that had coincided closely with Mitchell's encounter with Wilms, before the enigmatic agent had vanished into thin air.

'Almost there,' Vaughn said as he scanned the screen. 'You ready?'

Lopez leaned across the back seat and opened the driver's side rear window, the sound of the bustling traffic and a gust of cool air flooding the car as she flipped a switch on the drone and activated her control unit.

The drone's ducted-fan engines spun up with an electric whine and the drone lifted up off the seat alongside Lopez as she deftly hovered the craft in the rear of the vehicle and guided it toward the open window.

'Stand by,' Vaughn said as he glanced in his rear view mirror. A flow of vehicles, cabs and goods trucks eased past their car, and then a gap appeared in the traffic. 'Go!'

Lopez pushed the control column forward and the drone hummed out of the window and over the street outside. Lopez immediately increased the power and the drone ascended rapidly out of sight into the bright sky above as she switched her attention from the drone to another laptop propped against the rear passenger door opposite her.

Through a camera attached to the bottom of the drone she could see the busy street below the drone as it climbed ever higher into the sky. The densely packed buildings to its right contrasted sharply with the angular expanses of greenery to its left as Central Park came into view. She smiled mischievously as she saw their own vehicle tucked in against the sidewalk.

'This is cool,' she whispered as she flew the drone.

'Stay focused,' Vaughn replied as he watched the traffic flow. 'LeMay's coming past us right now.'

Lopez forced herself to focus on the screen and not look outside as she hovered the drone three hundred feet above Manhattan.

'Passing us…,' Vaughn said, '…now.'

'Got him.'

Lopez saw the silver Mercedes in the drone's sights as it passed by, heard the whisper quiet engine and the hum of its tires on the asphalt as it passed them on its way to the Pierre Hotel.

'You think that you can pick him up once he goes inside?' Vaughn asked. 'We won't be able to see him inside the hotel, and the DIA only bugged his vehicle not his clothes.'

Lopez nodded, replying as she kept her gaze fixed to the screen.

'He's meeting Majestic Twelve. I figure nothing else will do for them but the Penthouse Suite.'

*

Gordon LeMay checked his tie one last time as he walked through the foyer of the Pierre Hotel and into an elevator, the bell hop pressing the button for the top floor without the need to be asked. The hotel had been informed of LeMay's arrival by the driver and the door staff, and everything prepared for his smooth passage through the hotel.

The elevator hummed quickly up to the top floor and opened onto a thickly carpeted corridor. The bell hop did not follow LeMay out, under strict orders along with all of the other staff to remain clear of the top floor. The elevator door closed behind LeMay and he turned toward the only open door before him at the far end of the corridor.

Somehow, he knew that there would be no turning back after this. Once he had been fully welcomed into the fold of Majestic Twelve there could be no leaving, no changing his mind, which was damned well fine with him. He was done with the stress of the intelligence community and more concerned with ensuring his own survival of any Congressional investigation into his conduct as Director of the FBI than anything else. Membership of Majestic Twelve would ensure that such irritations would be swept away and his future secured.

LeMay walked through the open door and saw a figure close it behind him. Victor Wilms was standing with his hand on the door handle, sealing LeMay into the elaborate room, which was occupied by eleven men that at a glance he knew represented Majestic Twelve.

'Gentlemen,' he greeted them.

'What news from Antarctica?' asked the tall, gaunt leader of the group.

No greetings. No ceremony. Down to business it was then, LeMay realized, but as a man who often gave the President his daily intelligence briefing he was used to being prepared.

'The team have accessed the tunnel system beneath the ice and have reached the base concealed within,' he reported. 'Communications are patchy at best, but I have it on good authority that the DIA team dispatched before us is now pinned inside with no means of escape. There have been casualties, but there will be no evidence of our presence at the site.'

Another of the men peered at LeMay.

'The DIA reached the artifact before your men?'

'Yes,' LeMay replied, 'an unfortunate eventuality but not one that could be avoided. They are, as you are no doubt aware, supported by US Navy SEALs and well equipped. But their success in reaching the base first means nothing if they cannot escape.'

The gaunt man shook his head.

'Support will reach them soon, likely a nuclear submarine or perhaps even a major fleet,' he cautioned. 'It is imperative that this is brought to a close before such reinforcements can arrive in the area.'

'It will be,' LeMay assured them. 'My people are under strict instructions to either escape the area with Black Knight in their possession, or if that proves impossible to destroy all trace of the site and the DIA team. We either get what we want, or nobody does.'

The leader of the group nodded and then stood. Despite his obvious advancing years he projected an aura of menace and competence that unnerved LeMay as he glared down at him.

'Your work has impressed us,' he said, 'and your commitment to our cause has not gone unnoticed despite the danger to your own career. You are certain, Gordon, that you have not been tracked to this location?'

LeMay realized that he had not until now been called by his given name, that the act of doing so was likely a major concession in the silent war of wills between them.

'Nobody knows that I am here with you,' LeMay assured him. 'I am visiting family in the city.'

'Good,' the tall man said, 'then it is time for you to come out of the cold. We know that your position as Director of the Federal Bureau of Investigation is coming to an end as a result of the work you have done for us. We will ensure that your exit will be without any political or criminal *discomfort*.'

LeMay beamed. 'That would be much appreciated.'

'Furthermore,' the gaunt man went on, 'we should like to hold a small ceremony, a tradition if you will, that has been a part of our history and will formally welcome you among our number. You, my friend, will become Number Four.'

LeMay's eyebrow raised in surprise. 'I am to replace a member?'

The gaunt man, evidently Number One, chuckled although LeMay could detect no true humor.

'We have a great deal of power,' he replied as the rest of the members got to their feet, 'but we do not yet have control over our longevity. I am not the first leader of this cabal and I shall not be the last. The previous Number Four was a man named Dwight Oppenheimer, who ironically was involved in searching for the elixir, the fountain of youth, several years ago in New Mexico. He died at the hands of a man whom I believe you to be familiar, one Ethan Warner?'

LeMay's expression darkened. 'I know of him.'

'Then your first mission, once our Antarctic business is complete, will be to eradicate Warner and his partner, Lopez. You will be a part of our future, Gordon, and we shall celebrate that formally tomorrow. But for now, congratulations.'

Number One extended a thin, wiry hand laced with purple veins that Gordon LeMay shook vigorously as the other men in the room clapped politely and Victor Wilms handed LeMay a champagne flute.

***

XXXI

'Keep it steady.'

'I'm trying!'

Lopez worked the control unit furiously as she guided the drone alongside the rear of the Pierre Hotel. The calm air at ground level near Central Park had been replaced by the faster free winds three hundred feet above the city that buffeted the drone as Lopez sent it whizzing across the rooftops toward the top of the hotel.

The dizzying height and the drone's instability in the wind began to take its toll on Lopez's ability to control the device, and she realized quickly that such unsteady footage was not going to be sufficient to identify the members of Majestic Twelve. Jarvis, and indeed the President, would need clear images of the group combined with the audio obtained from LeMay's implant in order to ensure that any convictions stuck.

'I'm going to have to switch on the auto-stability that Hellerman included in the package,' she said as she struggled to control the drone.

'Won't that use up more power?' Vaughn asked.

'Yeah, but at this rate we'll get nothing, it's too damned windy.'

Lopez's thumb moved briefly off the control column and flipped a switch on the top of the controller. Almost immediately the drone levelled off and began returning a crystal clear image of the city.

'Damn, Hellerman,' she smiled as she worked the controls and brought the drone back onto course toward the hotel's penthouse suite.

The top floor of the hotel, so she recalled had once been up for sale for around a hundred million dollars, a sum so vast she wondered why anybody would bother paying so much money for something so comparatively small. She knew that the suite held three bedrooms, two bathrooms, an expansive lounge and terraces that overlooked Central Park in its entirety, but she knew that any folk with funds like that could buy a five bedroom mansion outside the city and be blissfully happy in retirement for the rest of her life for a tenth of that sum.

'How the other half live, eh?' Vaughn said, clearly thinking the same thing as her.

'I wouldn't want to be any one of them,' Lopez replied. 'So much money that you no longer have any sense of its value.'

Vaughn raised an eyebrow. 'I'd give it my best shot.'

The drone was now behind the penthouse suite, where two terraces looked out to the west over the cityscape. Lopez guided the drone closer to the terraces.

'Take it easy,' Vaughn cautioned, 'we don't want them to see it.'

'I'm on zoom,' she replied calmly as she flew the drone around the south side of the suite, seeking the lounge windows. 'I doubt they'll ever know the drone was there.'

The drone drifted around to the east side, moving back over 5th Avenue and Central Park as Lopez fought to get a good line of sight into the building. The large windows reflected the bright morning sky, the sun behind the drone and the reflected light obscuring the interior of the suite.

Lopez's heart skipped a beat as she saw movement among the light playing on the windows, the reflections of clouds translucent enough to see suited men standing inside the building.

'Here we go,' she said as she guided the drone in closer.

The interior of the suite was colored in shades of magnolia, the dark suits of the circle of men within contrasting sharply with their surroundings. Lopez peered at the gathering and thought she saw a single gray suit among the black.

'Almost there,' she whispered.

The drone hovered, descending slightly, and as Lopez got her first glimpse at the men's faces so the sun broke through the clouds and a brightly reflected flare of sunlight ripped across her field of vision.

'Damn!'

Lopez guided the drone to the right, hoping to change the angle of view of the drone and lose the reflected sunlight. The drone flew sideways and she glanced at the power bar to see that it was already two thirds depleted.

'Less than ten minutes,' Vaughn warned her. 'Get the footage, Nicola.'

'Stand by,' Lopez replied in a whisper that she barely heard herself, manipulating the controls carefully.

The brilliantly flaring reflection of the sunlight faded out as the drone maneuvered to one side, and then the image cleared and Lopez gasped. She saw Gordon LeMay standing in the center of a group of men, all of them clapping and smiling as one of them handed LeMay a flute of champagne.

'I've got you now, asshole,' she chortled in delight as she watched LeMay sip from the flute as he shook the hand of a tall, sepulchral looking man dressed all in black.

'We're getting half of them,' Vaughn said from the front as he watched the display and the faces of the men upon the screen. 'Damn, we've got Majestic Twelve on film.'

*

Gordon LeMay sipped the champagne in the flute and acknowledged the smiles of greeting on the faces of the men with whom he was sharing the most expensive apartment in the western world. Truth be told he was completely amazed that he had been allowed to even enter the same room as these men, all of them worth billions, perhaps trillions of dollars each, all of them wielding more power than Presidents and Prime Ministers the world over, all of them part of a shadowy network of businessmen shaping world events to suit their own needs. Perhaps that was how they had become so wealthy and so powerful, by joining the cabal, and suddenly he found himself thinking that he too might become as wealthy and as powerful as the men around him.

'So, how does it feel to finally be here?' Wilms asked LeMay as he approached him.

'It feels good,' he replied, 'I'm relieved to be here, for sure, I don't mind saying.'

LeMay took another sip from his champagne and glanced out of the window across the stunning vista of Central Park and the city, and almost immediately his eye caught upon the black speck on the immaculately polished glass windows, sharply contrasted against the vibrant New York morning sky.

LeMay had spent the last thirty years working for the FBI and knew just about every surveillance trick in the book. To believe for even an instant that any agency would have been foolish enough to place a bug on the outside of the window itself seemed so outlandish that he could not even begin to entertain…

LeMay saw the speck move across the sky and then come to an abrupt halt, and in a moment of clarity he realized that he was not seeing a tiny object at the distance of the window but a larger one outside the building. He turned to Wilms, his eyes wide as he opened his mouth to speak, but no sound came forth.

LeMay tried again, but his voice was a mere croak that whistled from somewhere deep inside his throat. He felt his legs start to lose rigidity beneath him, swayed as Wilms snatched the champagne flute from his grasp as two more men moved in behind LeMay.

LeMay toppled sideways, unable to control himself as he was caught before he hit the thickly carpeted floor of the apartment. The two men lay him down on his back, and LeMay stared helplessly up at them as the members of Majestic Twelve moved into a circle around him and stared down with a strange, detached interest.

For a brief moment LeMay wondered, hoped, that this was all some bizarre ritual, a part of his acceptance into Majestic Twelve, but somehow he knew that it was no such thing.

Number One looked down pityingly at LeMay as he spoke.

'Dear Gordon, such a shame to have been deceived in such a way, but I'm afraid that deception is what we're all about. Surely you must have known that a man with such shamefully limited financial means could never expect to become a member of our cabal?'

LeMay tried to answer, his mouth gaping open and closed.

'He looks like a beached fish,' Number Three said as though examining an injured insect. 'For God's sake, put him out of his misery.'

'Not yet,' Number One replied, 'we can't allow the Defense Intelligence Agency the luxury of recovering his body with that implant in place, can we? Better that we remove it soon and ensure that they don't learn anything of our identities.'

LeMay felt tears flood his eyes as he tried to understand what they were referring to. He tried again to speak but nothing came out, his body completely paralyzed and his heartbeat feeling slow in his chest.

'Pancuronium bromide,' Victor Wilms explained, staring down at LeMay. 'It's used with general anesthesia in surgery for muscle relaxation. Side-effects include moderately raised heart rate, excessive salivation, apnea and respiratory depression, rashes, flushing, and sweating. Did you know that in Belgium and the Netherlands, pancuronium is recommended in the protocol for euthanasia? After administering sodium thiopental to induce coma, pancuronium is delivered in order to stop breathing.'

LeMay knew that he would die if he did not do something to prove his worth to the group, and he looked at Wilms and swivelled his eyes back to the suite's main windows. Wilms frowned for a moment as LeMay repeated the motion, and then he turned his head and stood up and he noticed the speck hovering outside the suite.

Wilms's composed expression collapsed into panic.

'We're being watched!'

The twelve members of Majestic Twelve whirled to look out of the window, and in an instant they all saw the drone staring back at them. For a moment it hovered there right before them and then it suddenly descended and shot out of sight toward the north.

'Get the security team out there!' Wilms shouted. 'And get LeMay out of the building, now!'

**

XXXII

'They're onto us!'

Vaughn started the car's engine as Lopez fought to bring the drone down to street level as fast as she could as the car jolted to the right, Vaughn cutting up a small goods vehicle as he struck out into the flow.

Lopez had seen everything: the faces of the men in the room, LeMay among them, who had collapsed in their midst. The expression of one of the men, Wilms, as he pointed directly at the drone before Lopez had cut the throttle and let the device plummet out of sight.

She turned the drone in mid-flight and swung it around to point the cameras at the elaborate entrance to the hotel, where she instantly saw a dozen men burst out onto the sidewalk of 5th Avenue, all of them looking up into the sky above Central Park. Dark suits, designer sunglasses and likely concealed weapons beneath their jackets.

'Multiple agents,' she reported as Vaughn drove down the avenue toward the intersection close to the hotel. She saw one of the agents point up at the drone and then the men sprinted across the street. 'They're onto the drone.'

Vaughn nodded as he saw the agents cross the street a hundred yards in front of them, heard a salvo of horns honking them as they dodged the traffic and vaulted over the wall into the park. 'How much battery do you have left?'

'Less than ten per cent,' she replied. 'We need a way to get that drone back into the car.'

Vaughn offered her a tight grin in the rear view mirror. 'Nice to hear you've planned ahead. Is the downlink working?'

Lopez blinked as she looked at the screen. 'Yeah but it's slow, I need another couple of minutes.'

Vaughn drove past the hotel, the lightly tinted windows of their vehicle effectively concealing them from observation as Vaughn turned right onto the Plaza and then followed East Drive, the trees surrounding them concealing the vast city that enveloped the park.

'You got a bead on the agents?' Vaughn asked.

Lopez turned the drone and looked down to see the four agents sprinting through the forest, following trails between the trees as they pursued the tiny drone.

'They're not going to make it,' she said. 'Head to the far side and we'll pick up the drone and get the hell out of here.'

Vaugh nodded as he accelerated toward the center of the park, where Terrace Drive would pick up 5th Avenue again and let them head north out of Manhattan. Lopez descended the drone, skimming the treetops as she flew it toward the park exit. Vaughn was almost there when she spotted the two glossy black SUVs pull into the park and block the entrance as armed agents got out and began waving vehicles down and peering inside.

'Damn, that was fast' she uttered. 'They've got support and they're checking vehicles, stay off Terrace.'

Vaughn did not reply, simply slowing down and easing the vehicle past Terrace and further into the park.

'How the hell did they figure this out so quickly?' he asked. 'We could have been anywhere in the city.'

'Majestic Twelve,' Lopez murmured. 'They've likely got tech just as advanced as some of our own. Maybe they scanned for the drone's controller signal and picked it up coming from out of the park.'

'We need to get out of here,' Vaughn snapped. 'If they identify us in this vehicle we're done.'

Lopez focused on the drone as she sought a way out of the park.

'They're following the drone right now, not us,' she insisted. 'I can give them the run around while you drive out of here.'

'If you get too far out of range with a low battery we could lose the drone,' Vaughn warned her. 'If we lost that downlink and the drone gets picked up...'

'It won't,' Lopez insisted. 'I've got an idea. Drop me off.'

'They'll see you.'

'Just do it.'

'The drone is the priority,' Vaughn insisted. 'We can't lose you or it!'

'Then pull over now!' Lopez shouted. 'Get the car out of the park on Terrace and I'll meet you on Central Park West!'

Vaughn yanked the car into the sidewalk and braked as Lopez got out and slammed her door behind her and dashed across the street into the trees. She heard Vaughn pull away as she ducked into some bushes and hurriedly unfolded her laptop to see the view from the drone as it flew overhead.

To her surprise she could hear its engines buzzing somewhere above her, and gently she began turning the drone to the north, continuing on over the park toward the Reservoir. She ducked down as she heard running feet pounding the path nearby, and peered through the trees to see four agents run past her, one of them speaking into a microphone as he stared up at the speck in the sky.

'Run *Forrest*,' Lopez smiled to herself as she watched them sprint desperately after the little drone.

She toyed with the idea of turning the drone in a big circle to tire the agents out further, but quickly scratched that from her list as she realized that it would give the game away and force the agents to search for controller's signal instead. The battery was low, five per cent now and falling fast and the downlink had not yet completed.

'Come on, damn it!' she whispered, urging the downlink to hurry.

Moments later, a warning signal appeared on the screen.

DOWNLINK FAILED – SIGNAL LOST

Lopez hissed an expletive as she slammed her fist into the soft earth beside her, and then she saw through the drone's lens Vaughn's vehicle stop at the exit of Terrace Drive, four agents surrounding the vehicle.

*

Vaughn dropped the window of the car as two armed agents with stern expressions peered down at him.

'Is this your vehicle, sir?'

'Yes it is,' Vaughn replied, affecting the air of a New York businessman on his way to work. 'Is there a problem?'

One of the agents walked to the rear doors of the car and opened one of them, leaning inside.

'No problem sir,' came the reply, 'we're looking for somebody.'

Vaughn knew damned well that law enforcement officers could not simply open the doors of a citizen's vehicle and search inside without a warrant, but he also knew that revealing too much knowledge of the law might arouse suspicions as to his identity.

The agent behind him rummaged around and lifted out a charger attached to a series of wires.

'What's this?' he demanded, looking at Vaughn.

'It's my laptop's battery charger,' Vaughn replied. 'Why?'

The agent peered at the device as though uncertain. If he looked in the trunk, Vaughn knew that he would find the rest of the drone's paraphernalia and then he'd be done. The agent climbed out of the vehicle and pointed at Vaughn.

'Pop the trunk, sir.'

Vaughn frowned, cursing mentally. 'Don't you need a warrant for that?'

'We don't need warrants to arrest you and impound the vehicle,' the other agent assured him as he produced a US Marshall's badge. 'Pop the trunk.'

Vaughn glanced at the badge, which appeared genuine enough although he knew that the men confronting him were most likely not US Marshalls. Vaughn glanced past the men at the sidewalk and saw two police officers strolling their beat on the sidewalk. It was illegal in the state of New York to fly drones, for obvious reasons, but facing down that charge with the DIA behind him was far preferable to being apprehended by the MJ-12 agents starting to surround the car.

'Hey!' he shouted. 'Officer!' The two cops looked in Vaughn's direction as he called to them. 'These guys are impersonating Marshalls!'

The effect was startling. The agents scowled and immediately dispersed toward their vehicles as the police officers changed their route and began marching quickly toward the entrance to Terrace Drive.

Vaughn put the car into reverse and pulled gently away as the officers attempted to intercept the SUVs, both of which were pulling out of the park and onto 5th Avenue. Vaughn saw the officers speaking into their radios as he turned away and drove north. He drove for thirty seconds before he then pulled the car into the sidewalk, killed the engine and jumped out. He locked the vehicle and then abandoned it, knowing that to use it further would be suicide as it would be tracked by MJ-12. He crossed the park toward the west and hoped against hope that Lopez had gotten the downlink sorted before escaping the park.

He walked as casually as he could, fighting the urge to sprint for the west side of the park among the joggers and dog walkers as he sought the nearest exit. He was headed for the denser trees of the Ramble, which would take him to the footbridge over the lake and onto West Drive and West 77th, perfect for losing himself on Central Park West and finding Lopez.

He crossed the footbridge and turned onto West Drive, then stopped as he saw two agents making their way toward him. Both reached for their weapons in an instant, aiming at him. Vaughn looked over his shoulder at the footbridge and the lake, but one of the agents shook his head.

'You won't make it,' he snapped. 'Hands on your head!'

Vaughn complied, glancing up and down the road but seeing no pedestrians, no police officers or any other source of assistance that he could use to scare off the agents. One of them maintained their aim at him as the other hurried forward and produced a pair of handcuffs.

'Where's the drone?' he demanded as he fastened one cuff around Vaughn's right wrist.

Vaughn's arm was yanked down off the top of his head and pinned against the small of his back.

'What drone?'

A grim chuckle and the agent behind him reached up for the other wrist. Vaughn dropped his head forward and then snapped it back, the back of his skull smacking into the agent's nose with a dull crack that echoed among the silent trees. Vaughn spun around, swinging his free left arm around to grab the agent and pull him against his chest as a human shield, the other cuffed wrist slammed up into the man's throat and pitching him backwards and off his feet as Vaughn reached beneath his jacket and drew the man's pistol from its holster and jammed it against his jaw. The entire move took no more than two seconds, far too fast for the other gunman to pick his target without fear of hitting his comrade.

'Walk,' Vaughn snapped at the gunman, 'or I'll sink him in the lake.'

The gunman shrugged.

'Sink him then but you'll go down with him. There's no escape pal, the rest of our team will be here soon.'

Vaugh betrayed no emotion as he cursed silently and sought an escape route.

'You're done,' the gunman insisted. 'Drop the weapon or I'll shoot you straight through him.'

Vaughn knew that he had no option but to kill both men and hope that he didn't take a bullet in the process. Lopez and the drone were the priority and he knew that he could not afford for them to fail in escaping MJ-12's agents.

A sudden whining noise roared in from nowhere and Vaughn saw something streak across the sky above them in a blur of motion. The other gunman threw his hands up in front of his face as the drone rocketed down and smashed into his head at full speed. Vaughn turned the agent in his grasp and rammed one knee into his thigh, crippling the man's leg with a single blow. The agent crumpled onto the path as Vaughn drove his boot down onto the man's face, incapacitating him and then he dashed forward.

The gunman hit by the drone tumbled onto the pathway, his face bleeding profusely as he tried to aim his gun at Vaughn. Vaughn swung his boot and it impacted the gunman's wrist with a loud crack like a snapping twig as the delicate bones shattered under the blow.

The gunman's pistol flew from his grasp as he cried out in pain. Vaughn jumped over him and dashed to the drone, which had smashed into the pathway and was now scattered into dozens of pieces all along the bank.

Vaughn saw the drone's camera drive and grabbed it, ripped it from the drone's frame as he turned and sprinted down West Drive toward Central Park West. He tossed the guard's gun into the bushes as he hurried out onto the main street and saw Lopez on the sidewalk opposite, beckoning him to follow.

Vaughn dodged the traffic as he jaywalked across to her.

'We lost the drone!' he snapped. 'You're lucky I got the drive.'

'You're welcome,' Lopez replied without concern as she turned and walked swiftly away down West 77th Street. 'And you lost the damned car.'

'The agency will sort that out,' Vaughn said. 'Did the download complete?'

Lopez smiled as they walked and hailed a cab.

'Oh ye of little faith,' she murmured as the cab pulled in alongside them. 'You think I'd trash the drone without first pulling the data from it?'

Under her jacket Lopez held her laptop.

'You downloaded it directly?' Vaughn asked in surprise. 'What about the agents on foot who were chasing it?'

'I led them into the trees and then turned around,' she said. 'Only took a moment to land the drone, plug it into the USB port and download everything directly, then send it back up again. They never knew a thing.' She looked at the cab beside them. 'Ladies first, right?'

Vaughn stared at her for a moment and then shook his head with a smile as he opened the cab door. They hadn't even got inside when Lopez's cell rang. She recognized the voice instantly.

'Wilms is on the move.'

'Where to?'

'Lexington. He's left the hotel via a back door and is on foot, moving quickly. If you hurry, you can intercept him.'

'What's your play in all of this, Mitchell?'

'Just get there, I'll take care of the rest. I know which vehicle he arrived in. Have LeMay's original driver meet us there.'

'And do what?' Lopez asked as the cab pulled away and Vaughn, able to hear the conversation, directed the driver to head for Lexington.

'It's all in hand,' Mitchell replied. *'Trust me, once I'm done with him, there won't be a thing he won't tell us. But if he escapes the city, we'll never see him again.'*

***

XXXIII

Antarctica

Hannah stared at Ethan in amazement.

'You're kidding, right?' she uttered. 'You're trying to tell me you think that Black Knight is some kind of UFO and that its owners might be listening in, that they picked up Nikola Tesla's signals and started transmitting?'

Ethan gestured to the Piri Reis map.

'*Somebody* had to tell those cartographers that there was a continent beneath Antarctica, because they sure as hell couldn't have known about it. Quite apart from that, we know that most UFO sightings occur not over the land but over and beneath the ocean.'

Again, Hannah appeared stunned.

'And we "know" this *how?*'

Ethan leaned against the control panel and folded his arms against the cold penetrating his Arctic jacket.

'Let's just say that Lopez and I spent a fair amount of time chasing around the globe in pursuit of artifacts for the Defense Intelligence Agency that support the existence of alien life in our universe. In the course of that work we've found that most craft described as UFO's originate from maritime environments – they come out of the sea, or in some cases, the ice.'

Doctor Chandler agreed.

'Sightings of UFO's coming in and out of the water are not new. Christopher Columbus recorded such a sighting in October, 1492. Crew members of the *Santa Maria* and *Pinta* sighted a strange light over the ocean shortly before the landing on Guanahani. The light was reported in Columbus' journal, Ferdinand Columbus' *Vita del Ammiraglio*, the proceedings of the Pleitos Colombinos and some other sources. Columbus described the light as a small wax candle that rose and lifted up, which to a few seemed to be an indication of land. He received a royal reward for the sighting. His son Ferdinand also characterized it as a candle that went up and down, and Columbus wrote that *"there exists the possibility of never leaving this legendary sea. My compass acts strangely. This sea seems to have the ability to draw things in from all over the Atlantic like a catch-basin.'*

'In June 1945,' Chandler's assistant went on, 'the Malta Times reported on a sighting by the brigantine *Victoria* nine hundred miles east of Adalia, where her crew saw three luminous bodies emerge from the sea into the air. They were visible for ten minutes a half mile from the ship. There were other witnesses who saw this same UFO phenomena from Adalia, Syria and Malta. The luminous bodies each displayed an apparent diameter larger than the size of the full moon.'

'March 22nd, 1870,' Chandler said, 'in the equatorial waters of the Atlantic Ocean, the sailors of the English corvette *Lady of the Lake* saw a lenticular cloud with a long tail advancing against the wind. This form was visible for an hour, wrote Captain F.W. Banner in the ship's log. The drawing by Banner in his log looked extraordinarily like a flying saucer.

Commander Graham Bethune, U.S. Navy, was flying his military plane from Iceland to Newfoundland on February 10, 1951 when he saw a UFO coming out of the water. He was about 300 miles from his destination when he and his crew saw a glow on the water like approaching a city at night. As they approached this glow it turned to a monstrous circle of white lights on the water. Then they saw a yellow halo, much smaller than whatever it was launched from, about fifteen miles from them. As the UFO approached the plane and flew alongside it, he could see what he described as a domed craft which emitted a coronal discharge.'

'But even that was nothing compared to three different occasions lasting a total of forty six days when an unidentified submarine was hunted by some fourteen Argentine warships, including an aircraft carrier, and thirty Navy planes,' the assistant said. 'The submarine, though audible and occasionally visible to the naked eye, could not be triangulated by sonar, sonar buoys, hydrophones or radar. Despite intense bombing and depth-charging by the most up-to-date US explosives, torpedoes and naval gunfire, it proved impossible to damage or sink the submarines, and the hunt was abandoned on each occasion without success. Captain Ray M Pitts, the leader of the U.S. Navy anti-submarine warfare team involved in the third hunt, confirmed afterwards that it had definitely been some kind of submarine, but he was prevented from saying more by the Navy.'

Doctor Chandler scanned the map as he spoke.

'The Shag Harbour UFO incident was the reported impact of an unknown large object into waters near Shag Harbour, a fishing village in the Canadian province of Nova Scotia on October 4, 1967. The reports were investigated by the Royal Canadian Mounted Police and Canadian Coast Guard, the Royal Canadian Navy and Royal Canadian Air Force as well as agencies of the Government of Canada and the U.S. Condon Committee.

The Canadian government declared that no known aircraft was involved and the source of the impact remains unknown to this day.'

'They made an official admission?' Hannah asked.

'That's right,' the assistant confirmed, 'although today they say that all documentation regarding the incident was *lost* – no surprises there, and it's remarkable how governments keep losing such valuable and explosive documents don't you think? What we do know was that the craft was about sixty feet long and was hovering while flashing orange lights, then it tilted to about a forty five degree angle and entered the water. The Royal Canadian Mounted Police were notified about the incident. A yellow light was reported in the water moving about and leaving a trail of yellow foam. The Canadian Coast Guard was dispatched but by the time they arrived along with other vessels at the point of entry the yellow foam was all that remained.'

Chandler nodded thoughtfully.

'At least eleven people saw the low-flying lit object head down towards the harbor. Multiple witnesses reported hearing a whistling sound like a bomb, then a whoosh and finally a loud bang. Some reported a flash of light as the object entered the water. Thinking that an airliner or smaller aircraft had crashed into the Sound next to Shag Harbour, some witnesses reported the event to the local Royal Canadian Mounted Police detachment. The unknown flying object was never officially identified and was therefore referred to as an unidentified flying object in Canadian government documents, the ones that can no longer be found. A Canadian Naval recovery effort immediately followed during which divers allegedly encountered not one but two objects, which later moved off.'

Ethan glanced at the Piri Ries map.

'But if Black Knight arrived here thirteen thousand years ago then there can't be any life forms aboard, right? They'd have long since died out.'

Chandler nodded.

'I would imagine not,' he replied. 'But if they were an aquatic species, and found refuge beneath the ice...'

Hannah shook her head.

'I'm not buying that. Thirteen thousand years? If they'd survived they would have bred, and surely if they were capable of such technologies as Black Knight they would have found their way off the planet in spacecraft or something?'

'I don't know,' Chandler admitted with a wry smile, 'but I do know that it's not just a human experience for things to go plain wrong.'

Even as he said it, a low, ominous moan shuddered through the complex once again. Ethan felt the deck beneath his feet vibrate with the force of it, saw the glow sticks around them bounce and dance about, sending their glow shimmering across the ice covered walls.

'Damn it, what the hell is that?' Hannah gasped.

Ethan's eyes caught on a large schematics diagram on the wall next to the one that bore the Piri Reis map, the light from the glow sticks briefly illuminating it. He glimpsed the shape of the base itself, and then extending out to the north a series of conduits or tunnels, some kind of cave system perhaps.

The hellish moan subsided once more and Ethan hurried across to the image, grabbed a glow stick on his way and held it up to the schematic. He wiped the ice from its surface, the schematic itself sealed inside a plastic sheath, and shone the light directly on it.

The base was depicted as a small, angular construction in the center of the image, with the tunnel they had used to access it departing to the right of the map. To the north, Ethan could see a complex series of tunnels, many of them winding tightly beneath the glacier and extending many miles into the glacier. He could tell just by looking at them that they were not man-made, their structure devoid of the sharp angles and precisely uniform corners that was the hallmark of humanity.

'What is it?' Hannah asked as she joined him.

Ethan continued to shine the light up at the image, and finally he began to understand what he was looking at. Markers on the map depicted bore holes drilled down into the ice that appeared to intercept many of the tunnels leading south toward the base, and small images superimposed on the tunnels portrayed blocky devices and tubes, strange objects that had been inserted into the tunnels by the Nazis decades before.

Ethan looked at the tunnels, the inserts and the cables running from them to the base and he finally realized what he was looking at.

'Power,' he said finally, 'hydroelectric power. The Germans were generating electricity from the water flowing beneath the glacier.'

Doctor Chandler looked at the map.

'You're right,' he said. 'They must have run the base using the generators as back up for the hydroelectric power produced by this system of channels and ducts.'

Ethan traced some of the lines up and down the map.

'If we could reactivate this system we could re-seal the base and prevent Veer and his men from getting inside.'

Hannah shook her head.

'This glacier is moving,' she pointed out. 'Those tunnels and power cables are most likely nothing more than debris now.'

'It wouldn't take them all to seal the base,' Ethan suggested, 'just enough of them to mean that Riggs and his men only had to cover the entrance through the windows of the control center. From that elevated position, they would be unassailable even to a numerically superior force.'

Chandler appeared concerned.

'We'll be burying ourselves beneath the ice with no means of escape,' he said. 'They'll blast the entrance and leave us here.'

'No,' Ethan replied. 'They're here for Black Knight, just like we are. They won't want to leave without it, so blowing the entrance is the last thing they'll want to do.'

'And what are we going to do about Black Knight?' Hannah asked. 'Case you hadn't noticed it's why we're down here too and we have no way of getting close to it.'

Ethan grinned and turned away from the schematic. 'I've had an idea.'

'I don't like it when that happens.'

***

XXXIV

'Fall back to the base!'

Lieutenant Riggs's harsh whisper echoed across the submarine pens as the SEALs began withdrawing back from the tunnel entrance. Ethan could see the flashlights from the advancing MJ-12 soldiers clearly now as he emerged from the base, shimmering beams drifting like ghosts through the crystalline ice surrounding the mouth of the tunnel.

Lieutenant Riggs retreated toward them.

'I've got an idea about that *Seehund*,' Ethan said.

'It'll have to wait,' Riggs snapped back.

'We may have a way to seal the base and prevent Veer's men from overrunning our position.'

'Can it be implemented now?' Riggs demanded.

'No, it'll take time,' Hannah replied.

'Then it'll have to wait, because they're here. Get into cover and shoot at anything that isn't us!'

Hannah followed Ethan at a run as they made their way back to the walls of the base, the SEAL's forming a protective semi-circle around them as they crept back inside. Lieutenant Riggs and his men settled into their defensive positions, their rifle sights trained on the tunnel mouth as they prepared to open fire. Ethan hugged the frame of the base's main entrance and held his pistol in both hands, Hannah alongside him and mirroring his actions as they took aim and waited for the MJ-12 troops to emerge from the blackened maw of the tunnel.

The flickering lights shifted this way and that, warped by the bending of the light by the ancient ice as they advanced, and as Ethan squinted he thought he could see the shadowy forms of men advancing toward them through the gloom. His finger slid into place behind the trigger as he stilled his mind and focused.

'Here we go,' Hannah whispered, her voice taut.

Ethan watched the lights flickering around the tunnel mouth, and then suddenly they vanished as one as though somebody had pinched out a candle flame and plunged the tunnel into darkness. Ethan let his eyes begin to adjust to the gloom in time to see something clatter down onto the docks before them.

'Flash bang!'

Ethan squinted his eyes shut and saw a bright, red flare beyond his eyelids and heard two deafening cracks that echoed around the cavern and a hissing sound in their wake as from the tunnel mouth erupted a blaze of gunfire.

Ethan opened his eyes as rounds peppered the walls of the base nearby and clipped chunks of ice off the docks before them with a deafening clatter. Near the tunnel mouth, clouds of smoke billowed from the two grenades to create a smoke screen that shielded the tunnel mouth from view as the MJ-12 troops poured into the cavern.

'Open fire!' Riggs yelled, although his men required little prompting.

The SEAL's opened up with their M-16s on the tunnel mouth, bullets cascading through the smoke to smash into any human being trying to access the cavern. Ethan fired controlled shots into the darkness, the mouth of the cavern now completely obscured by the smoke grenades and returned fire ripping back toward them. Bullets zinged off metal railings a few yards from where Ethan stood in the bunker doorway, Hannah flinching as she fired in return as bullets hammered the bunker walls inches from her head.

'Tactical retreat!' Riggs shouted.

The front-most four of the SEALs pulled back in a low run as they were covered by the comrades, then dropped into prone positions a few yards behind their firing line as Riggs and his men jumped up and ran back further toward the base. Ethan fired between the running soldiers as they retreated while maintaining a constant rate of fire against the enemy.

The roar of gunfire echoed back and forth across the cavern in a deafening cacophony as Ethan and Hannah held their position and covered the SEALs' retreat.

Riggs switched to his grenade launcher and fired off two of the weapons, both aimed either side of the tunnel to avoid bringing it down and cutting off their own escape route. Ethan knew that the MJ-12 soldiers would be fanning out either side of the tunnel to avoid the withering fire from the SEALs, and the smoke screen they had created concealed the incoming weapons just as effectively as it veiled them from the SEALs' fire.

Two blasts thundered through the smoke and reverberated around the cavern as the grenades detonated, and Ethan heard above the gunfire the wretched screams of injured men cut down by the blasts.

'Inside!' Riggs yelled. 'Before they return the favor!'

The SEALs broke ranks and filtered into the bunker past Ethan as he fired a few more shots and then turned and dashed into cover. Hannah followed him as Riggs fired a couple more shots into the smoke and then backed into the base.

The SEALs heaved the blast door closed, slamming it shut and then driving crowbars they had found through the locking wheel and the braces to hold it shut.

'Good enough for now,' Riggs said, Ethan hearing him despite the infernal ringing in his ears. The MJ-12 troops were still shooting outside, the SEALs listening intently.

'Poor command structure,' Saunders said. 'They don't even know we've ceased fire.'

'Those grenades took out a few of them,' Del Toro agreed. 'They should have stayed well back in the tunnel and used grenade launchers to flush us back into the base.'

'They might fear bringing the tunnel down on themselves,' Ethan pointed out. 'A frontal assault is the only real choice they had.'

Moments later, the sound of gunfire ceased.

'Let's go,' Riggs said.

Ethan ran up the stairwell with the soldiers and they dispersed at once through the control center, other members of the team already in place with their weapons aimed out of the broken windows and down toward the docks below.

Ethan found himself a corner beside a shattered window and peered out across the dock. He could still see the smoke drifting across the black water below and figures huddled around the mouth of the tunnel as well as several bodies lying on the icy dock nearby.

Through the darkness, a keening cry of agony wailed like some hellish bird of prey seeking a way out of the cavern. Ethan squinted and saw one of the bodies move, hands cradling the stump of a leg severed at the knee, a man's face grotesquely twisted in pain as he clutched at his wound.

'That'll slow them down,' Riggs said. 'Nothing like an injured team member to test the morale of your team.'

As Ethan watched, the injured soldier began dragging himself inch by painful inch back toward the tunnel mouth. He left a trail of dark fluid behind him, his blood loss horrendous as he tried to reach the safety of the tunnel.

He was halfway there when a tall figure emerged from the gloom and a single gunshot ripped across the cavern. The injured soldier shuddered and fell abruptly still. Ethan stared in silence as the shadowy figure retreated back into the tunnel and a deep voice boomed across the cavern.

'The game's up! There's no escape and we outnumber you ten to one. Surrender your positions, come out with your hands up and we'll let you leave in peace.'

Ethan could see Riggs shake his head slightly before he called back.

'The only people leaving here will be you and your men. The cavern is rigged to blow – either clear out or we'll take the whole damned place down with us!'

A thunderous laugh echoed across the cavern before the man replied.

'You won't,' he uttered in a dismissive tone as though scolding a wayward child, 'because you can't leave here without Black Knight and you won't kill your own people, either those in that base with you or the ones we have captive right here in the tunnel with us.'

Ethan's eyes widened momentarily as he heard a scuffle taking place inside the tunnel, and then the man's voice returned.

'So, just how many limbs will I have to pull of this young lady before each and every one of you surrenders?'

Ethan felt a premonition of doom sweep over him as through the last of the smoke spitting from the grenades on the docks he saw the big man holding a diminutive figure with one hand clamped around their arm. Even across the distance, he could hear her protests and recognized her voice.

'They've got Amy,' Hannah uttered.

The shadowy man pressed what Ethan guessed must be a pistol against Amy's head, and he heard her small but defiant voice echo across the chamber.

'Don't come out, ignore him!'

A sharp crack and a muffled sob answered her cry and she collapsed to her knees beside the big man, who called out again to the SEAL team.

'Sixty seconds boys, or she's gonna lose all that fight along with an arm!'

Ethan looked across at Riggs and Del Toro. 'Can you get him with the sniper rifle?'

'Wouldn't matter if I could,' Del Toro replied, 'another'll just take his place and we're back to square one.'

'We don't negotiate,' Riggs added firmly. 'We don't have time for this.'

'They've got Amy!' Hannah repeated.

'You all knew the risks,' Riggs snapped at her. 'I don't like it, but our mission is to recover Black Knight and get the hell out of here and that's what we're going to do.'

'The mission is compromised,' Ethan said as he stood and got in Riggs's way. 'That means a change of plan.'

'That's not your call to make,' Riggs shot back as he jabbed a thick finger into Ethan's chest. 'You're a passenger here Warner, and you answer to me. Mission priority is not Amy, it's Black Knight, and even if every other member of the team were captured in the next ten minutes it would remain my priority. We're going to activate that submarine, collect the artefact and leave one way or the other.'

'I know,' Ethan said, 'which is why you've got Hannah and me here. We can deal with the other side of things.'

'What *other* side of things?'

Ethan turned to Hannah. 'Let's go out there and see what they have to say for themselves.'

'Are you kidding?' Hannah asked in amazement. 'That guy just shot one of his own! We walk out there we're as good as dead!'

Ethan turned to Sully, the SEAL team's explosives expert. 'The C4 charges in that tunnel, are they rigged to detonate in series or individually?'

'Both,' Sully replied. 'It depends on what buttons I fancy pressing.'

'Good,' Ethan said, 'if I get down on my knees with my hands on my head, blow one of them.'

Sully shrugged but agreed nonetheless. Riggs looked at Warner.

'You'll get yourself killed,' he insisted.

'You just worry about that submarine,' Ethan replied. 'Get it working and get the job done, I'll try to buy you some time and maybe get Amy back too.'

'You tryin' to be a hero, Warner?'

Ethan shook his head.

'No, I want to get Amy to safety and I want to get a better look at our enemy out there. The more we know about them, the more chance we've got of evening the odds and maybe getting out of here alive.'

He turned to Del Toro. 'Cover us?'

'You got it.'

Ethan looked at Riggs. 'Call back, say you're coming down. He won't know the difference between your shouting and my talking when I get down there. Might convince them the team leader's in front of them.'

Riggs smiled in bemusement, somewhat intrigued by Ethan's sly thinking as he called down out of the shattered windows.

'Stand by, I'm comin' down!'

Riggs pulled back from the windows and waited expectantly.

'Let's go,' Ethan said as he holstered his pistol and led Hannah out of the control center.

***

XXXV

Larchmont,

New York

Paralysis. Gordon LeMay could not move an inch from where he lay on the back seat of a luxurious SUV driving north out of the city. He got the occasional glimpse through dry eyes of a road sign outside the tinted windows as it passed by, the asphalt humming beneath the wheels outside.

His heart beat felt slow, a dull nausea infecting his guts due to low blood pressure even though he was lying on his back. The motion of the vehicle on the road exacerbated that nausea, which in turn was infected with a fear that he was facing the last moments of his life.

Majestic Twelve had betrayed him, of that much he was sure, but he could not for the life of him fathom *why*. He had not failed them – had they suspected that he was behind the drone that he had seen filming them? He recalled lying on the thickly carpeted floor of the apartment as the members of MJ-12 looked down at him over their champagne flutes and laughed. Thus, LeMay's drugging had been premeditated, his betrayal born of some other failure that he could not possibly conceive of.

LeMay was overcome with a regret that threatened to swamp him and squeeze the life from his body long before MJ-12 managed to finish him off. He thought of his wife and their kids, three teenagers just about to venture out into the world, and his grief overwhelmed him as tears trickled down his cheeks. He had struck a deal with the devil – not the fanciful, mythical devil of biblical tales but the true evil among humanity, that of men with no cares but their own wealth and power.

He had been tracked, they had said, somehow, and LeMay could only guess at how the DIA might have managed to follow him so accurately. Wilms had seemed as surprised and shocked as LeMay and the others at the sight of the drone however, and yet that suggested they could not possibly have known in advance of its presence.

The vehicle turned off the road and into the drive of a large country mansion. LeMay knew that they were probably in Larchmont, an exclusive area just a few clicks out of Manhattan and near the Connecticut border. The car slowed and then waited before easing forward into a large garage,

LeMay glimpsing an electric door opening above them as they moved inside.

The engine was shut off and the doors of the vehicle opened. LeMay was dragged out by strong hands, his body pliant and loose, heavy and sagging. Unable to do anything except watch through eyes that would not close, and hope that his body retained enough physical control to keep breathing, LeMay was carried through the interior of a house that contained no furniture. He figured in a moment of abstract reverie that the property was one of countless hundreds owned by the cabal as safe houses and places where they could do their work without interference from the outside world.

LeMay was heaved by four men into a large room on the ground floor, and he heard the sound of their boots suddenly grinding on plastic as he was hefted up onto a table and swiftly bound to it using lengths of tough para cord. LeMay struggled to speak, to beg for his life, but all that his throat emitted was a series of odd growls, drool spilling from his lips as he wept openly and silently.

The four men completed their work and moved off in silence, leaving LeMay alone on the bench for a few seconds until he heard the approach of two more men. He looked down past his own chest to where he saw Victor Wilms and another man whom he did not recognize, who was wearing a surgeon's smock, a cloth mask over his mouth and nose.

LeMay's stomach turned inside him and he let out another strangled cry of panic as Wilms stood watching him, a faint smile on his face as though he were regarding a scolded child.

'You failed us Gordon, on so many levels,' Wilms intoned without passion. 'Did you really think that we would let somebody like you, somebody with absolutely no financial power, no real influence, no real use in the world into a cabal like Majestic Twelve?'

LeMay struggled to answer but Wilms winced as he looked down at LeMay.

'My God, you really are a pitiful, disgusting little creature Gordon. Let's get this over with and leave this sorry episode behind us, shall we?'

LeMay saw Wilms stand back as the surgeon moved forward, and LeMay saw that in his hand was a shiny, long chrome device like a narrow pair of forceps that glinted in the harsh light from the ceiling. LeMay's breathing accelerated and he struggled to move, but his body barely shifted an inch as the surgeon reached out with one gloved hand and pinned LeMay's head firmly in place.

LeMay let out a last desperate, pinched scream of desperation as the surgeon pressed the tip of the forceps alongside the septum inside his nose and then the man grimaced as with a hefty shove he rammed the device up into LeMay's nostril with a crunching sound. White pain seared Lemay's skull and he heard his own agonized scream soar despite the drugs coursing through his veins as the forceps crunched up through cartilage and plunged deep into the frontal lobes of his brain.

*

'There, through there!'

Lopez yanked the wheel of their vehicle as Vaughn pointed down a broad street lined with Colonial style mansions sheltering behind ranks of towering aspen. Behind Lopez a stream of police pursuit vehicles thundered, their lights flashing like a galaxy of bursting red and blue stars as they swerved into line behind her.

'It's got to be one of these,' Vaughn said as he surveyed the lines of houses.

Lopez keyed her microphone as she drove.

'Search the databases for any unoccupied premises in the area,' she ordered. 'If he's been taken out here it'll be some kind of safe house.'

Lopez slowed, peering up the long drives and across spacious lawns at the various properties in the upscale neighborhood. As she did so she spotted a house that had no blinds in the windows, trash cans that looked immaculately clean and no sign of decoration or adornment that was the hallmark of an American home.

'That one,' she snapped as she accelerated toward it. 'We'll try there.'

'It could be a rental, somebody travelling abroad,' Vaughn pointed out.

'Then we'll find nothing. Either way, we're taking a look.'

Lopez drove straight up onto the drive and leaped out of the vehicle as Vaughn joined her, his weapon drawn as behind them the six pursuit cars slid into the sidewalk and armed officers leaped out in support.

Lopez, her pistol held double-handed before her and her gaze fixed on the windows of the house, hurried up the lawn and peered inside the large bay window on the front of the house. Even in the gloom of the interior she could see what she was looking for within an instant.

'He's here!' she bellowed. 'Drop the door!'

A police sergeant called back to her. 'We're waiting for the warrant ma'am, it should be here in just a few…'

Lopez dashed to the front door and aimed at the lock, then fired twice, the two bullets smashing into the door handle and shattering it in a spray of wood and metal. The gunshots were shockingly loud in the otherwise quiet, leafy street as she then stepped back and hurled herself shoulder-first into the door.

The door splintered on her first charge, and then she hit it again and it swung open as she lunged inside and aimed into the house.

'Police, get on the ground!'

No sound but for the hollow tone of her voice in the empty property greeted her, and she dashed forward with Vaughn close behind as she hurried toward the front room where she had seen the table and the plastic on the floor and the blood.

Lopez hurried into the room and dashed to Gordon LeMay's side. To her horror, his face had been reduced to a bloated, bruised mess of blood and bone that had spilled in thick loops onto the plastic at her feet and across LeMay's chest.

'Call an ambulance!' she yelled at Vaughn as he reached for his cell phone, police officers rushing through the house with weapons drawn.

Lopez saw that LeMay's eyes were drifting open, bloodshot and greasy with sweat and tears that streamed even now down the sides of his face. She stared down at him, his nasal bridge split in two and blood spilling in thick floods from the cavity torn through his skull between his eyes.

'Who did this to you?' she asked. 'MJ-12?'

LeMay's jaw worked but no sound came out but a ragged, tortured whisper that Lopez had to leanb close to hear.

'Wilms… Victor Wilms…. Kill.'

Lopez looked down into LeMay's eyes. 'Wilms?'

Although it probably caused him great pain to do so, LeMay nodded once as he gasped again.

'Wilms, K-I-L, satellite.'

Lopez reached out to stem the flow of blood from LeMay's face, but as she looked into his eyes once more she realized that the light of life was already fading from them. She saw his chest sink as the last breath left his body and heard the death rattle in his throat as he died.

She turned to Vaughn and shook her head. 'He's gone.'

Vaughn turned to the police officers behind him.

'I want every home in the street canvassed. They all have security systems and it's likely they'll have surveillance cameras. Confiscate the footage and then get onto the traffic cameras too. I want to know who did this!'

The police turned and dashed away as Vaughn turned back to Lopez. 'Did you get anything out of him?'

'Wilms was here,' she said, 'and he said something about a satellite, called K-I-L, that belongs to Wilms.'

'I'll get Jarvis onto it,' Vaughn said as he hurried away.

Lopez looked down one last time at LeMay's body, and then with one hand she closed his eyes for the last time. Even as she did so, her cell rang in her pocket. She answered, and heard Mitchell's voice on the line.

'Wilms is heading back toward Manhattan.'

***

XXXVI

Antarctica

Ethan reached the main blast door of the base with Hannah alongside him and Del Toro behind them both, and together they slid the braces out from behind the door and opened it a crack. Ethan saw the docks extending away from them, the tunnel in the distance dimly illuminated by the fading light of the glow sticks scattered across the dock, and could just make out the shadowy forms of men hiding in the darkness within.

'This is pretty much suicide,' Del Toro whispered. 'They're gonna shoot you down rather than let you go.'

Ethan pushed ahead through the open door.

'I'm hoping that their curiosity will get the better of them,' he replied.

Hannah followed him reluctantly out onto the dock as Del Toro slammed the blast door shut behind them. Ethan noted that he heard only one brace being slid back into place on the far side of the door, Del Toro likely standing by in case they had to run to get back inside.

'What the hell are you going to say to them?' Hannah asked in an urgent whisper. 'Pretty please can we have our friend back?'

'I hadn't got that far in my thinking yet,' Ethan said as he walked at a steady pace, hoping to veil any sign of nerves as they closed in on the tunnel entrance.

'Reassuring as always.'

Ethan kept walking until he reached a spot perhaps twenty yards from the tunnel mouth, where he came to a stop and waited patiently. A few moments later the deep voice boomed out across the cavern.

'Ethan Warner, I figured you'd show up sooner or later.'

Ethan did not betray any surprise that this man knew his name. Given their repeated encounters with agents of Majestic Twelve, it in fact only confirmed that they were indeed facing MJ-12's mercenaries and not the military of some other country hell bent on beating America to the Black Knight.

'Like a bad penny,' Ethan replied, peering into the darkness but unable to see much. 'You know that you're being paid to walk to your deaths up here, right? You know who your employers are, don't you?'

'Need to know basis,' came the reply, 'and we're being paid well enough to have no problem in icing you and your team. Our government knows that we're here.'

Ethan smiled.

'That's strange, because it's our government that sent our team here too, so how come you're firing on fellow Americans?'

'Our mission is our priority! Surrender your positions and you'll be allowed to leave peacefully!'

Ethan glanced at the corpse of the MJ-12 soldier lying nearby, a ragged bullet wound in his skull bleeding black blood onto the icy dock.

'Like your comrade here?' Ethan asked. 'Nice of you to put him out of his misery.'

'He was no longer an asset,' boomed the reply.

Ethan grinned, keen to sow dissent among this man's followers.

'Neither is our friend Amy,' he replied, 'but we're standing here hoping to get her back, not putting a bullet in her head for being an *inconvenience.*'

'My men are behind me,' came the reply, 'and they're not going to walk away from me, so you can quit the divide and conquer routine.'

'You're no military commander,' Ethan said, 'you're a fake who hides behind his men, a coward.'

Ethan heard a rustle of movement and from the shadows loomed a huge man with a thick, black beard that was laced with ice. He peered at Ethan from the mouth of the tunnel, radiating hatred from his every pore.

'It's been a long time since anybody dared call me that.'

'So it's happened before then,' Ethan replied. 'Got us a pattern developing there, don't we?'

The figure took a pace closer and Ethan spotted a glint of light coming from a pistol the big man held in his hands.

'Surrender your positions or die,' he rumbled.

'Sorry, no can do,' Ethan chortled in response, covering his fear of death with a bizarre carefree attitude that surprised even himself considering the dire circumstances. 'Amy won't make a damn of difference because our priorities match yours. Give her up and maybe we can work together on this little problem of ours.'

The big man's eyes widened for a moment and then he chuckled, shook his head.

'Here's what I intend to do with them if you don't surrender your positions.'

The big man whistled briefly, and two of his soldiers marched out with a thin, pale man clutched between them. The victim was half naked, shivering with cold, his skin an unhealthy shade of blue. Before Ethan could even speak, the two soldiers suddenly rushed forward and hurled the hostage into the freezing water of the dock.

Ethan instinctively moved to help as Amy cried out in horror, but he knew that to enter the water was suicide. The thin man cried out in agony as he surfaced and gasped for air, his lungs and limbs paralyzed with the cold and unable to swim to safety.

'Get him out of there!' Amy screamed at the man holding her.

'Surrender your positions!' he boomed back at Ethan.

Ethan was about to cry out to the SEALs to surrender, to save the poor man's life as he thrashed weakly in the water, when suddenly the black water surged and something enormous loomed beneath the thin man. Ethan's heart skipped a beat as the scientist suddenly screamed in fresh pain and was yanked under the surface.

The entire chamber fell abruptly silent as the water lapped near the edge of the dock. Ethan stared at the surface of the water as Hannah's voice broke the silence.

'What the hell was *that*?'

Ethan could not break his gaze from the dock as something rose up and broke the surface. He heard Amy gasp in horror and recoil away as a severed leg, its skin a pale blue, emerged to float upon the icy water amid a cloud of scarlet blood.

The big man holding Amy twisted her to face the black water.

'So, shall I send her for a swim?'

Ethan heard from behind the big man a ripple of agreement, saw a series of tiny red points of light bloom into life on his chest and Hannah alongside him as infrared sights lined up on his body.

'No escape,' the big man rumbled as he raised his pistol to point at Ethan, 'and now I have three captives instead of two. Get down on the ground, lay flat. You move, I'll blow your goddamned heads off!'

Ethan slowly began to raise his hands above his head, Hannah beside him doing the same as he prepared to get down on his knees.

'They'll blow the tunnel,' Hannah whispered beneath her breath.

'You grab Amy,' Ethan whispered back, 'just get her back to the base.'

Ethan got onto his knees, Hannah alongside him, and was about to lay flat when the cavern suddenly shuddered and a soaring moan erupted from the walls as the black water of the docks once again rippled in perfectly symmetrical eddies.

The moan soared louder and Ethan felt it once again reverberate through his chest as he almost toppled sideways, the vibrations shuddering through the dock beneath him as before him he saw the big man sway to one side.

'Now,' he whispered to himself, hoping against hope that Sully would time his detonation well.

Ethan squeezed his eyes shut and ducked his head as he moved his hands from his head to cover his ears, and a moment later a blinding flash seared his vision as behind the big man a blast thundered through the tunnel as the C4 charges were detonated.

Ethan scrambled to his feet with his eyes still shut and his hands over his ears in time to feel the shockwave from the blast hammer into him. He drove into it, opened his eyes and reached for his pistol as he saw the big man hit the dock face down before him and Amy spin away to one side and tumble to her knees on the icy dock.

Ethan lunged for her, reached out with one hand and grabbed her wrist as he yanked her to her feet and almost threw her at Hannah, who staggered upright and reached out for Amy's hand.

Ethan ducked as a withering hail of fire erupted from the SEALs inside the base and plunged over his head into the mouth of the tunnel. A cacophony of screams and shouts of alarm roared from the tunnel as injured men regained consciousness enough to start screaming and others shouted commands and tried to get further back into the tunnel and out of sight.

Ethan saw Hannah and Amy running for the base as he turned and saw the big man dash out of sight into the blackness of the tunnel, firing blindly behind him as he went. Ethan whirled and sprinted down the dock, the whole cavern shaking as though it were about to tumble down around him, and he realized that the detonation of the C4 charge may have been the trigger necessary to finally bury them beneath billions of tons of ice.

The base door opened before him and he saw Hannah and Amy plunge through the opening as Del Toro appeared and aimed his rifle at Ethan. Ethan flinched as shots whizzed past, aimed not at him but at the tunnel behind to cover his escape, and moments later he plunged into the base as Del Toro retreated inside and slammed the door shut.

The rumbling and trembling began to subside as Ethan paused to catch his breath at the base of the stairwell.

'You're too lucky, Warner,' Del Toro observed as he checked the magazine of his rifle. 'Those quakes are getting more frequent.'

'Yeah,' Ethan gasped in reply, certain that without the unexpected tremor he and Hannah would have likely been hit.

Amy leaped across to Ethan and flung her arms about his neck. He could see that she was injured, blood trickling from her ears where the shockwave from the blast had hit her hard, but otherwise she appeared okay as he returned the embrace and then looked down at her.

'His name's Veer,' she said. 'Andrei Veer, and they'll follow him wherever he goes. They don't care about who lives and who dies, they're being paid too much money. They executed one of my assistants right outside on the ice.'

Ethan nodded.

'Mercenaries don't care much for the lives of others,' he replied, 'these guys are in this for the money and Majestic Twelve sure has plenty of that.'

'It's only a matter of time before they launch an assault against the base and overrun us,' Hannah pointed out, 'especially now they're under threat of being blasted into pieces inside that tunnel.'

Del Toro nodded and was about to speak when Doctor Chandler hurried down to meet them.

'You need to see this, right now,' he said.

The team followed the Doctor, who hurried up the stairwell and into the control center where Riggs and the rest of the team were keeping watch on the docks. Ethan helped Amy into a chair as he looked up expectantly at Riggs.

'How's the sub?' he asked.

'It'll hold water and the batteries are on charge,' Riggs replied, 'which is why you need to hear this.'

Riggs looked at Chandler, who gestured to the map of the base pinned to the far wall that Ethan had found.

'I've had a chance to study this schematic,' Chandler said, 'and I'm afraid that it does not bode well for us.'

'We kinda figured we were up the creek without a paddle already, genius,' Hannah uttered in reply. 'Get to the point.'

Ethan suppressed a smile. It was almost like having Lopez alongside him.

'The chamber was indeed supplied with energy by a series of turbines, which had been inserted into deep water channels upstream from the main base where we now stand,' Chandler explained. 'The glacier's weight, along with the force of water reaching us from Lake Vostok and other subterranean bodies of water, mean that the flow is under extremely high pressure. This was an advantage for the Nazis, who were able to harness that pressure to ensure a good flow of electrical energy to this facility. However, decades of being abandoned have weakened the structures they put in place to protect the turbines and now they're all on the verge of failure.'

'Which means what?' Ethan asked.

'The turbines are mostly locked in position at this time as a result of rust and seizures,' Chandler explained, 'which means that instead of turning with the flow of water and generating power they're effectively acting like dams, holding the flow back. Because the water is no longer flowing it loses what little heat it has and freezes, blocking the channels. The cavitation in the water of the docks and the low frequency emissions we're hearing are not the sounds of some gigantic beast as we first feared, but of the entire base coming under increasing pressure from the build-up of high pressure water behind the blockages.'

'I think I know where this is going,' Ethan murmured as he looked at the map.

'It's why the entire cavern system periodically floods,' Chandler explained. 'The turbines fail and are crushed beneath the pressure, and the water flows past once more and rushes into the cavern and docks, flooding it until the pressure equalizes once more and the excess flow drains away out of the tunnel we used to enter the base.'

Hannah leaned against a wall.

'How long?' she asked. 'Before it happens again?'

Chandler's features had paled slightly.

'It could happen next week or in the next two minutes, but it's imminent.'

'Any other ways out?' Ethan asked Riggs, already knowing the answer.

'Nope,' Riggs replied, 'and that submarine only has two seats. Truth time, people – we're not getting out of this base alive.'

***

XXXVII

'This is *not* a good idea.'

Hannah Ford stood on the dock beside the *Seehund* midget submarine as Lieutenant Riggs and his SEALs hurriedly prepared her for diving. The U-Boat was an ugly black vessel emblazoned with the red stencil numbering of the Nazi fleet, the *Kriegsmarine*.

'If this is your plan,' Riggs added as he worked, 'then your plan sucks.'

Ethan shared their concerns but he knew that there was no option but to use the tiny submarine to get below the surface and recover Black Knight. What he could not be sure of was what they were going to encounter beneath the waves. Not only would they have to contend with the frigid Antarctic waters, the danger of glacial collapses, the limited energy supply of the submarine and its antiquated controls, but they would also have to be ready to encounter something that was not of this world.

'We'll just go down, grab it, and bring it back to the surface,' Ethan assured her.

'Sounds easy if you say it quickly enough,' Hannah mumbled in reply.

Lieutenant Riggs jumped down from the sub's hull and looked her over one last time.

'She's good to go. The hull is secure, no leaks that I can find, so she's in good shape considering how long she's been here and you're lucky – most *Seehunds* didn't have ballast tanks but this one has been modified to carry them. My men are trained for this sort of thing and should be the ones going down there, and your experience is only barely enough to control the *Seehund*. Are you sure you want to go through with this?'

Ethan shook his head.

'Hell no, I want to be at home with a beer watching the damned game but we're here so we might as well get on with it. You're going to need all the firepower you can get up there on the docks, so it makes sense to send somebody else. Get the hell out of here and get on with it.'

Riggs nodded and looked across at Doctor Chandler, who was standing nearby with his hands shoved in the pockets of his Arctic coat, his head almost completely concealed beneath his hood.

'Are you all hooked up and ready to go?' Riggs asked him.

Ethan had arranged for the doctor to provide a digital communications link to the dock, so that if they encountered anything that they could not overcome they could fall back on the scientist's knowledge to help them through.

'The data link is in place, and communications should be possible to some extent through the water,' Chandler confirmed. 'However, there is a common phenomenon in deep water known as thermal layering, whereby denser cold water can move below warmer water and create a barrier to communications. Given what we know about the flow from Lake Vostok beneath the glacier, you may find that at times we cannot communicate.'

'Perfect,' Hannah replied. 'Anything else we might need to know about?'

Riggs gestured to the torpedo clamps on the submarine's hull, and at the bow section.

'The clamps are definitely strong enough to lift whatever's down there, given what we know about its size and mass, but when you resurface you'll have to come up real careful or you'll smash the artifact against the dock wall. Do that and you might compromise the hull, which will likely sink you.'

'Smashing,' Hannah uttered.

'There's a watertight section of the bow that used to contain a depth charge device that might help you to hook onto whatever's down there, but you'll probably have to improvise once you get a look at this thing.'

Ethan was about to grab Hannah's arm and guide her as gently as possible aboard the submarine before she finally lost her nerve when Amy appeared at the dock hatch and hurried down toward them.

'Wait for me!' She hurried across and pointed at the submarine. 'You need me on this one.'

Ethan shook his head. 'This is too dangerous.'

Amy shot Ethan an accusing glare. 'Yeah, right, and being in an unstable Second World War secret Nazi base beneath a moving glacier while under attack from gunmen is the safe option, right?'

'This submarine might not make it back to the surface and we don't know what we'll find down there,' Ethan replied. 'It's not your risk to take.'

'It's every bit my risk to take,' Amy insisted. 'You can't take Doctor Chandler, you don't have any experience in sub-aquatic Arctic environments and Hannah is clearly scared out of her wits!'

'Hey!' Hannah protested. 'I'm just a little concerned about being dunked in a rusting tin can under ten billion tons of ice is all. Cut me a break!'

'I'm not concerned,' Amy insisted to Ethan. 'This is *my* specialty - it's why I'm here. You need me down there and they need Hannah up here. She can shoot, I can't. It makes sense and you damned well know it.'

Ethan bit his lip and glanced at Riggs, who shrugged.

'Don't argue with a woman,' was all that he could say.

'Damn it,' Ethan uttered as he released Hannah's arm. 'Okay, you're up.'

Amy's face beamed with delight as she clambered gamely up the submarine's hull, a chunky digital camera dangling on a strap about her neck as she called back to Chandler.

'Use the sonar buoy to increase the communications signal beneath the ice! It might help to burn through any thermal layers we encounter.'

Chandler's features lit up and he called back. 'Good idea!'

Hannah looked at Ethan. 'Looks like you're in good hands.'

Ethan smiled with a confidence he did not feel. 'Cover our asses,' he replied. 'I don't want to come back with Black Knight and have to hand it over to Veer and his men.'

'Over my dead body, literally,' Hannah assured him. 'Be careful.'

'You too.'

Amy's voice called to him from the submarine's entrance hatch, where she had attached a small digital video camera attached by a lead to a laptop computer that was tucked under her arm.

'Are you getting on board or what?!'

Ethan took a deep breath and then clambered up the hull of the U-Boat and climbed carefully into the narrow confines of the tower. He reached over and took one last look at the dock before he pulled the clear dome hatch over his head and closed it, sealing it shut.

The interior of the submarine was cramped and dark, Amy moving into the engineer's position at the front while Ethan took the commander's position right behind her. His seat was provided with a periscope and a view through the clear acrylic dome for navigational purposes which could survive depths of almost a hundred and fifty feet, and he familiarized himself with his surroundings as he prepared to dive the vessel. The batteries were in the keel of the pressure hull, while a twenty two horsepower diesel engine was fitted for surface use, which Riggs had figured would give a maximum speed of around five knots. Below the surface, a twenty five horsepower electric motor provided a submerged maximum speed of seven knots.

Ethan reached out and activated the batteries by flipping a series of switches. The German inscriptions didn't help matters, but Riggs had been familiar enough with such submarines to be able to give Ethan a guide as to which switch did what.

The *Seehund* hummed into life as the batteries fed power to the electric motor, and a few small indicator lights lit up green as pressure gauges whipped into life and various other meters began indicating oxygen reserves and other essential information.

'Time to go,' Ethan said. 'Ready?'

'Ready,' Amy confirmed, giving him a gloved thumbs-up over her shoulder, her face buried in the laptop as she scrutinized the visuals from the underwater camera she had attached in front of the dome.

Ethan closed his eyes for a brief moment and hoped that this time he had not taken a step too far. He truly wished that Lopez were with him, or that Hannah had prevailed and not given up her seat to Amy.

Then, he pulled a lever. The ballast tanks issued forth a rush of compressed air that bubbled upon the water's surface as it was allowed to bleed from vents along the hull, and with alarming speed the *Seehund* sank beneath the waves.

Ethan looked up and caught a last glimpse of the dock, Riggs and Hannah watching them vanish beneath the water, and then they shimmered into a rippling image of light and darkness as bubbles streamed past the acrylic dome and darkness consumed the submarine.

Ethan reached out and, cautious of draining the submarine's batteries too quickly, illuminated only a single navigation lamp. A beam of harsh white light scythed into the blackness and flared off the walls of a vertical shaft hacked into the glacier itself.

'It's man-made,' Amy marveled. 'The Nazis cut down into the ice and made this dock.'

'Delighted for them,' Ethan murmured in reply as he concentrated on controlling the submarine and preventing either the bow or stern from bumping into the walls of the shaft.

He glanced periodically at the pressure gauges, which told him both the pressure and the temperature outside the hull. The acrylic dome could only take so much pressure, and with the water being compressed in places beneath the ice he knew that one false move could breach the dome. Their lives would be measured in seconds if such a catastrophic breach were to occur.

The lights continued to reflect off the walls of the shaft, and then suddenly the light that was illuminating Ethan's acrylic sphere weakened as the submarine descended out of the shaft and into complete darkness, the light beam spreading out and vanishing into the black water.

'Sub-glacial chamber,' Amy reported. 'This is the water that provides the entrance to the main base's submarine pens. It must flow on beneath the entire facility and exit into the Antarctic Ocean further down the glacier'

Ethan nodded, looking over his shoulder into the darkness to the south east, or so his magnetic compass told him. 'That's how the Nazi U-Boats would have got in and out, if the channel is still navigable.'

'We won't have time to check that out,' Amy advised him. 'The signal is coming from dead ahead, about two hundred yards.'

Ethan closed the bleed valves, the stream of bubbles from the vents clearing and the vibrations through the hull ceasing as the pressure equalized and the submarine hung in the blackness. For a few moments the silence was eerie and Ethan realized that he could just as easily have been in deep space as beneath the Antarctic ice sheet.

'What are you waiting for, a red carpet?' Amy snapped. 'Let's go.'

Ethan gently engaged the electric motor and the hum from the stern became a vibration as the screws began to turn and the submarine eased forward through the freezing blackness toward the distant signal blinking on Amy's laptop computer.

Ethan found himself glancing over the pressure gauges every few seconds, obsessed with the clinging fear that the dome would fail and freezing water would rush in under immense pressure, killing them both instantly. Although his common sense told him that it would all be over long before he could even begin to comprehend what was happening, somehow the knowledge that he would never be found, that they would both be frozen solid for millennia beneath the glacier seemed a fate too horrible to bear.

Ethan leaned forward and peered over Amy's shoulder to look at her laptop's screen and take his mind off his morbid thoughts, the blue glow from it illuminating the cold and dark interior of the submarine with an unearthly glow.

'A hundred fifty yards,' she said without looking over her shoulder, her breath condensing in clouds on the cold air. 'Keep it steady.'

Ethan nodded, saw the blue glow growing brighter from the screen, and then he realized that the laptop was not responsible for the shimmering blue white glow. Ethan jerked back upright, his head bathed in a glorious halo of light as the blackness around him was banished by a mass of pulsing blue creatures flooding through the icy depths.

***

XXXVIII

Manhattan

Nicola Lopez sat in a pool car on the corner of Lexington and 75th and waited patiently for her mark to arrive. The windows of the sedan were lightly tinted, sufficiently so that she knew she could not easily be observed or identified by passers-by on the street. Beside her sat Vaughn, likewise watching a single vehicle parked along the sidewalk further down the street.

The take down would have to be swift and slick to avoid detection, but Lopez already knew exactly how she would do it. Most agents would have attempted a risky grab and run from an apartment, an elevator or some other concealed location where there would be no witnesses to the hit. Lopez knew better. The more normal something looked, the less likely it was to attract attention.

What she didn't like was the fact that Mitchell had arranged the take down and was calling the shots. She didn't trust Mitchell as far as she could throw him, and she would rather he was locked up in…

'I've got him.'

Vaughn was looking across the street at a man walking in a long, dark coat buttoned up against the brisk winds buffeting the sidewalk. Lopez spotted him immediately and checked his appearance against a screenshot from her drone's camera.

'That's him,' she confirmed, 'that's Wilms.'

'He's going to run,' Vaughn observed with interest. 'But he's not in much of a hurry.'

'Trust me,' Lopez said as she reached for her door handle, 'when people have this much power they become convinced that they're above the law, above everybody else. This guy's got the bug all right, what I don't know is whether we can trust Mitchell with what he's got in mind.'

'We've got no choice now,' Vaughn said. 'Grab him while you can.'

Lopez stepped out of the car and pulled a baseball cap down low over her eyes, her black hair tied in a pony-tail behind her head, her leather jacket zipped up with the collar popped as she thrust her hands into her pockets and strode toward Wilms. She aimed to his right, not wanting to alert him to her presence too early, and saw him heading for a glossy black limousine parked near the hotel from which he had emerged.

'Now, Michael,' she whispered into her microphone.

She crossed the street, dodging the traffic as she hopped up onto the sidewalk a few paces behind Wilms. The Majestic Twelve agent reached his vehicle and reached out for the rear door handle.

'Victor!'

Lopez's delighted cry made several heads turn, including Wilms'. The old man stared directly at her from less than two yards away, and to her genuine delight Lopez saw a brief tremor of panic flicker behind his eyes. The momentary lapse revealed a powerful man who was weak within, cosseted and protected from the vengeance of those he controlled and victimized.

The panic dissolved as Wilms straightened from the door, Lopez knowing that he could not get into the vehicle faster than Lopez could tackle him.

'Nicola,' Wilms replied with a smile devoid of warmth. 'Good to see you up and about.'

Lopez closed to within a couple of feet of Wilms, her hands still in her pockets as she fought the urge to swing a right hook across this asshole's jaw.

'No thanks to you,' she hissed back. 'How much did the assassin cost you, Victor?'

'Me? Nothing,' he replied. 'Don't worry yourself, Nicola. You're not worth an expensive hit, and before you even think about it we can't be recorded. There are enough digital distortion devices in this vehicle to prevent any external monitoring.'

Lopez wasn't interested in Wilms' ride.

'We got you,' she said simply. 'Got Majestic Twelve on film, right here in the city and in the company of none other than Gordon LeMay, Director of the FBI. That'll look good on the evening news, don't you think? Federal boss cavorting with billionaires in Manhattan Penthouse suite, being drugged by them and abducted.'

Wilms did not shift an inch.

'You have footage of a man in the company of friends, Nicola, nothing more.'

'Then where is he?'

'Somewhere safe,' Wilms replied, 'a private hospital. Not one of the grubby halls that you and your kind fester in, believe me.'

'My kind?'

'The unwashed masses,' Wilms sneered.

'We're coming for you,' Lopez said. 'One at a time, we're going to bring every last one of you down to *our* level and see how long you last, starting with you.'

'Is that so?' Wilms taunted as he looked about them. 'And how are you going to do that, Nicola? You have no power of arrest over me, and even if you did I would be out within hours. I have friends so powerful the President of this country would piss his pants if they so much as looked at him.'

'And where are they, right now?' Lopez asked casually as she too looked about the street.

'Go ahead,' Wilms challenged her as he thrust his wrists in her direction and scowled. 'Arrest me and see how long it is before I'm out and your life as you know it is over. I can have your face all over the media within hours, arrested for crimes you haven't even heard of. You'll spend the rest of your life rotting in some forgotten cell and nobody will give a damn about you.'

Lopez smiled but said nothing as she turned and walked away, Wilms shouting behind her.

'You're nothing, Lopez! You're not even history because you're not important enough!'

*

Wilms climbed into his vehicle and slammed the door shut, enveloped in a cloud of anger as he snapped at the driver.

'JFK, right now! My jet is waiting.'

The driver slipped the vehicle into drive and pulled out into the flow of traffic as they headed north out of Manhattan. It was only moments before Wilms noted that they were headed in the wrong direction.

There was no need to scold the driver, no sense in arguing about which direction they were taking, for Wilms knew that he would not be taken to JFK in this car. He did not know how it had been done, but he did know that this vehicle could not be the one in which he had arrived at the hotel.

Wilms dove for the door handle but it was already locked. He reached for his pistol, concealed as it always was beneath his coat, but it was already too late for that as he saw the driver point a pistol over his shoulder at Wilms.

'Don't be a fool,' the driver snapped. 'Sit still.'

The driver pulled into the sidewalk again and the door opposite Wilms opened. A large form climbed into the vehicle and slammed the door shut,

219

and Wilms' guts contracted involuntarily as he looked into the eyes of Aaron Mitchell.

'I did what you said,' Wilms uttered in feeble defiance. 'I gave you MJ-12!'

Mitchell reached out with one giant hand and retrieved the pistol from Wilms' hand, then passed it to the driver who stashed the weapons before he drove back into the flow of traffic and headed north.

'You're making a mistake,' Wilms uttered to Mitchell, masking the dread in his belly with a thin veil of defiance. 'I'll be free within hours.'

Aaron Mitchell sat with his hands folded in his lap as he considered his reply for what felt to Wilms to be hours. When he spoke, his voice was quiet and yet seemed as threatening as ever.

'No, you will not,' he rumbled. 'You will tell me where Gordon LeMay has been taken.'

Wilms scowled.

'You think that I know that? You think that even if I did I'd tell you? This is a game far too big for you to handle, Aaron. You're a spent force, too weak to be of any value. MJ-12 will find you no matter what you do to me, and when they do they will crush you without mercy.'

Aaron smiled and looked across at Wilms.

'So much for the idea of an MJ-12 *family*,' he replied.

'You walked away from us.'

'You betrayed me,' Aaron countered as his voice dropped to a growl. 'And now you'll pay the price.'

Wilms scoffed and sat back in his seat.

'Thumb screws and electricity?' he snapped. 'None of it will do you any good Aaron, I don't know where LeMay is and I don't give a damn. The fat ass had it coming and if I'd had my way we'd have liquidized him years ago.'

Aaron inclined his head.

'I don't doubt it, Victor,' he said. 'Of course, you do understand that this vehicle is not being driven by your normal driver and that all of the distortion devices have been deactivated, so in fact every word you've been saying to me and to Nicola Lopez has been recorded.'

Wilms' features paled, outrage quivering like sheet lightning behind his eyes.

'It doesn't matter!' he spat back. 'You can't touch me!'

'No, we can't,' Aaron replied. 'But we can touch Timothy Morris.'

Wilms stared blankly at Aaron. 'Who? What the hell are you talking about?'

The vehicle was leaving the city, and with a sudden jolt of fear he spotted the signs heading out of the Upper East Side that the driver was following.

'What are you doing?!' he demanded.

Aaron smiled, his eyes as cold and black as oil as he leaned closer to Wilms and replied.

'You're coming back down to Earth with a thump,' he growled, 'and you're going to spend the rest of your life where you should have been all along. With the scum of the Earth.'

Wilms looked at the signs passing them by, his blood running cold in his veins.

RIKER'S ISLAND

'Timothy Morris,' Aaron said, 'sixty two years old, a convicted pedophile and murderer. You were arrested in the company of two pre-adolescent girls trafficked from Lithuania, both of whom were strapped to your bed in your apartment, the victims of repeated rapes. Your fourth arrest across several states, which means that you're going down for life without parole, although it'll take at least a year for your trial to be heard.'

Wilms' stared in horror at Mitchell.

'That's insane! MJ-12 will not tolerate such a..,'

'They'll drop you just as they dropped me,' Aaron growled back, 'because like you said to Lopez, you're not important enough. Besides, they won't even know where you are. As we speak your vehicle is being driven to JFK and your jet will depart on time. You just won't be on it, Victor. The jet will experience a fatal *accident* half way through its flight and you will be recorded by the Air Accident and Investigation Board as having died in the crash, the pilots exonerated of any responsibility for your demise.'

Wilms realized that Aaron had executed the perfect abduction and concocted a suitable fate for him, one where nobody would be searching for him and nobody would listen to his cause or his pleas that he had been set up.

Located on an island in the East River between Queens and the Bronx, Riker's Island was a city of jails, with a population of fourteen thousand inmates, all awaiting trial. As a new arrival, Wilms would be housed in the New Admissions Cells where he would be kept in a sort of quarantine until the results of tests for tuberculosis and other diseases came back from dedicated labs. Then, he would be incarcerated into one of the most dangerous and feared facilities in the entire United States. Wilms swallowed thickly. Rikers was a ferocious jail packed with murderers and drug addicts, hardened killers bought up on the mean streets of New York City. As a supposedly convicted pedophile, he knew what would happen to him.

'This will never work,' Wilms spat at Aaron. 'I'll never talk.'

'I don't give a damn,' Aaron replied. 'We don't need you either, Victor. All we needed was the faces of MJ-12, and the chance to lock you up for good while we start in on them. Your time is done. You're not getting out of this, either your jail time or your prison sentence, and I look forward to you screaming out loud to a judge that you're actually a member of a secret organisation called Majestic Twelve and that you'll be sprung anytime soon. They'll add an insanity plea, probably, which we'll make sure doesn't get through.' Aaron smiled at Wilms. 'You're not the one with powerful friends any more, Victor. Tell me where LeMay is.'

Wilms' face twisted in frustration and he cursed.

'Larchmont.'

Mitchell nodded once, and then looked at the driver. 'Continue to Rikers.'

'I just gave you LeMay!' Wilms screamed.

'You just saved your own life,' Mitchell said, 'nothing more. Life's going to get tough for you from now on, get over it.'

Wilms heard a scream erupt from his own throat as he lunged at Aaron, his fury and frustration unleashed in one terrible burst. The big man was too quick, however, and both Wilms' arms were batted aside as one thick fist ploughed into his skull and Victor's world dimmed to blackness and silence.

***

XXXIX

Antarctica

'I think you might want to take a look at this,' he said softly.

'Already looking at it,' Amy replied in a whisper.

The frigid blackness was now alive with billions of tiny flickering lights, as though he were witnessing the glittering majesty of a galaxy drifting past amid the blackness of space. The light flickered through the *Seehund's* cockpit in a dazzling, silent array.

'What are they?'

'Antarctic krill,' she replied. 'They're crustaceans that lives in large groups called swarms, sometimes reaching densities of thirty thousand individuals per cubic metre. In terms of biomass, it's probably the most abundant animal species on the planet with an estimated five hundred million tons of them around the Southern Ocean.'

Ethan watched as the densely packed krill swarmed past, flickering lights rippling across each of the creatures' backs, which were no longer than his little finger. Their light reflected off the submarine's hull as if it were just below the waves, and above he could see the underside of the glacier glowing blue far above them, its surface rolling and smooth, sculptured by the unseen currents of warmer water.

'The thing is,' Amy said, 'they shouldn't be here.'

'What do you mean?' Ethan asked.

'The Southern Ocean has plenty of nutrients, but krill often struggle to survive because phytoplankton doesn't seem to grow much despite the resources. These high nutrient, low chlorophyll regions were known as Antarctic Paradoxes until it was realized that there were low concentrations of iron in the same regions. Small injections of iron into the oceans there triggered large blooms of krill and other similar species.'

'So there must be a source of iron supporting these krill,' Ethan understood as he watched the swarm fly by them, so dense now that the *Seehund's* lamps penetrated only a few feet ahead, forcing Ethan to slow down further.

'Thirty eight pounds per square inch,' he said as he glanced again at the pressure gauges. 'We won't be able to go much deeper than this.'

'We're within a hundred yards,' Amy replied. 'Keep going.'

The *Seehund* crept forward through the glacial darkness, the shimmering swarm of krill drifting away behind the submarine as Ethan guided it toward the mysterious signal lingering somewhere just beyond their sight beneath the glacier.

'I've got a change in temperature readings,' Amy reported excitedly as they journeyed through the immense blackness. 'Ambient sea temperature is now eight degrees Celsius.'

'It's getting warmer?' Ethan asked in amazement.

'There must be some kind of hydrothermal vents ahead,' she replied, scanning her laptop's screen for any sign of the vents. 'They're volcanic, usually very hot, and usually found near deep-sea ridges and along the edges of tectonic plates, not here in Antarctica.'

Ethan thought back to what Doctor Chandler had said just hours previously.

'There are active volcanoes beneath Antarctica, right? Couldn't their vents have been forced sideways instead of upward by the force of the ice pressing down on the continent?'

Amy nodded, still gazing at her screen.

'It's possible that magma chambers and gas vents could have been diverted by the ice pressure and made it this far out,' she acknowledged. 'If so, that means that we'll find life out here. Most of the hydrothermal vents have been found near the coasts around the edge of the continent, not here in the interior and not ones that might be attached to Lake Vostok. There could be a whole new food chain down here, new species just waiting to be discovered.'

'We're here for Black Knight,' Ethan reminded her, 'and we're running out of time.'

'Sixty yards,' Amy reported. 'Steady as she goes.'

Ethan experienced a transient humor at Amy's sudden adoption of a nautical theme as he guided the *Seehund* along.

'I've got a seafloor,' she said suddenly, 'maybe twenty feet below us.'

Ethan prepared for any sign of the seafloor ahead of them, peering out into the gloomy darkness where the single headlight penetrated less than ten yards ahead of the submarine into waters now filled with tiny organisms that reflected the submarine's lights. To Ethan it looked almost like the classic image of a starship rocketing through space, stars drifting past amid the blackness.

'Forty one pounds per square inch,' he said as he looked at the gauges again. 'This is about our limit.'

Amy did not respond, staring instead at her monitor in silence.

'Amy?'

Amy remained silent for a moment longer, and then her voice reached him as though from afar.

'I can see it.'

For some reason Ethan felt a pulse of anxiety in his stomach as he heard her words, and perhaps for the first time he realized the enormity of what they were approaching. An object from another world, something far beyond any human experience, something that could literally change the face of humanity forever.

'What do you see?' he asked.

Amy waited for what felt like an agonizingly long time before she replied.

'It's...,' she hesitated. 'It's a sort of, glow. I can't quite make it out on the screen. Can you see anything up there?'

Ethan peered out of the dome into the blackness ahead and suddenly he could see the submarine's beams of light drifting across the surface of the sea floor. But he could see nothing beyond the barren, rocky terrain long buried beneath the ice sheets. The *Seehund* crept closer, Ethan slowing the submarine to just two knots as they closed in on the signal.

'Almost there,' Amy whispered.

Ethan peered through the dome of the submarine, seeking any possible sign of the object, and then suddenly he heard the reassuring hum of the batteries die down and the submarine's lights shut off and plunged them into darkness.

'What happened?!'

Amy's voice was twisted with panic as Ethan realized that her laptop had also switched off. He gripped the safety rails of the dome as he felt the submarine come to a halt in the black silence, completely devoid of power and in total and utter darkness.

'We've lost power,' he replied. 'Everything's dead.'

With sudden dread realization Ethan knew that coming down here had been a mistake. They should have fortified their position and awaited support and the remotely piloted vehicles that could have been sent down here into the frozen depths to retrieve Black Knight without risking the lives of the team.

'I can't see anything.'

Amy's voice was suddenly bereft of the excitement and fearless enthusiasm of just a half hour before. Now, it sounded small and afraid in the darkness.

'We could die down here.'

Amy's voice was hollow in the blackness inside the submarine's pressure hull. Ethan felt around for the pressure gauges, wondering how much air they had left without the pumps working.

'Stand by,' Ethan said as he fumbled for a flashlight.

He pulled his flashlight out of his jacket and flipped the switch. Nothing happened. He tried it again and then looked at where he figured Amy's laptop would be. Suddenly he realized that there was no good reason for both the submarine *and* the laptop to lose power simultaneously unless...

'Electromagnetic interference,' he said to himself.

'What?'

Ethan thought back to some of the briefings they had received from Chandler on *Die Glocke* and the UFO encounters reported at Kecksburg and other incidents across the United States.

'People often report that electrical systems are interfered with during UFO encounters,' he said. 'Radios don't work, compasses go awry and engines cut out. What if our proximity to the Black Knight is what knocked out the batteries? It explains why your computer isn't working either.'

He heard the rustle of Amy's hood as she looked down at the laptop and realized what Ethan was saying.

'We just need to get further away from it,' she said. 'Everything should work again.'

'But that means we can't pick it up either,' he pointed out.

'The hell with that,' Amy almost shouted at him. 'I don't want to die in this tin can down here! How can we get away?'

Ethan reached down to the ballast levers, fumbling among them in the dark and double checking that he was holding the correct ones before he released them. Immediately, compressed air from the submarine's internal tanks was released into the hull's buoyancy tanks and he felt the *Seehund* rise up in the water.

A moment of silence passed by, punctuated by loud clicks and bangs as the pressure changed slightly and the hull expanded a little as it rose up from the seabed.

Suddenly, the electric motor hummed and the lights flickered back on as Ethan heard the oxygen pumps rattle back into life. The internal lights flickered on again and he let out a loud sigh of relief as the dials and gauges appeared as a soft green glow around him.

'Jesus,' Amy uttered as her laptop began to reboot in front of her. 'I could've done without that.'

Ethan checked the gauges and then looked at the communications screen on Amy's laptop as it started up again.

'Doctor Chandler, can you hear me?'

A fuzz of static was all that was returned as they waited for a response. Ethan looked up uselessly out of the dome and figured that they had been cut off for good, for now, by the thermal channel they had passed through during their descent.

'That warm water flowing through here will rise up continuously and disrupt our line of communication,' he said. 'We might not be able to get it back until we get closer to the base again.'

'It doesn't matter,' Amy said. 'The sub's working and we're alive. Good work, captain.'

Amy whipped him a brisk salute over her shoulder, her smile bright in the gloomy hull, and Ethan saw her laptop screen and the signal upon it.

'We need to figure out a way of getting that thing up to the dock without finishing off our batteries,' he said.

Amy thought for a moment. 'Riggs said that this submarine was originally designed to be rigged with a detachable explosive charge in the bow, right?'

'Yeah,' Ethan confirmed. 'But that charge isn't in place, only the shell and...' He smiled as he realized what she was getting at. 'If the charge shell was magnetic, we could tether it and lower it down.'

'If the Black Knight is magnetic too, then the nose shell might be strong enough to pull it up to the surface on a tether. That's why we saw all those krill blooms – there might be iron in Black Knight, and iron is magnetic.'

Ethan shrugged. 'It's our only chance now, so let's give it a try. If it doesn't work we'll mark the location and hope that the support teams arrive before Veer storms the base.'

Amy wasted no time as she clambered out of her seat and made her way forward to the nose of the submarine. Although designed to be fitted with torpedoes, the *Seehund's* original plans had mimicked a similar and successful British design which carried an explosive charge in its bow.

Amy could make out the charge casing before her, sitting beyond an open pressure door the size of a dinner plate. She peered inside and saw the casing, which was attached to the submarine via a series of mechanical pins, themselves connected to a lever inside the hull.

'Seal the hull, pull the lever and she's away,' Amy said. 'I can tether it to the pin mechanism in the front here.'

'You'll need cable,' Ethan said as he reached down to his waist beneath his jacket and began pulling off a length of rappel line. 'How far are we from the signal?'

'Maybe twenty yards,' Amy replied.

The confines of the submarine made it tough to move, but he reeled off what he hoped was something more than twenty yards and handed the coil down to Amy. She shuffled her way back to the bow and looped the rappel line twice through a hoop in the *Seehund's* hull. She then coiled the line through the charge shell and back through the locking mechanism and finally clipped it in place.

Ethan peered down into the submarine and watched as she backed out of the nose and then heaved the pressure door shut.

'Make damned sure that's tight,' Ethan said.

Amy did not dignify his concern with a reply as she sealed the door shut and began heaving the pressure wheel over and over until it would go no further.

'Sealed,' she said. 'Now, get us overhead the signal.'

Ethan complied as he advanced the power lever and the submarine inched forward. He adjusted the hydroplanes and the submarine began to ascend gently through the darkness as a fresh bloom of bioluminescent creatures shimmered past the *Seehund* in the darkness, and Ethan finally caught a glimpse of something ahead on the seafloor before it was obscured by the bow of the submarine.

At first, in the brief moment that he could see it, Ethan's brain could not quite understand what he was looking at. A trembling haze of heat seemed to surround it, the heat causing the water around it to billow and shiver in much the same way that heat bent the passage of light through the air and distorted it.

A black shape, angular, unnatural, resting on the ocean floor and surrounded by a vibrant cloud of pulsing bioluminescence. Dense clouds of krill and other marine creatures swirled around the object, which was half as large as the *Seehund* itself and enshrouded in a casing as black as oil and completely unreflective, as though the submarine's lights did not exist despite their illumination of the object's surroundings.

Ethan lost sight of the object as he climbed the submarine upward and over it, going by gut instinct as he tried to maintain a reasonable distance from the device and prevent the submarine from losing power again. He knew that he had very little compressed air remaining and with Black Knight shackled beneath them he'd need every last bit of buoyancy he could get.

'Almost there,' Amy whispered.

Ethan gradually levelled the *Seehund* out as he quickly peered down into the hull and saw Amy's screen denoting the signal's origin, almost right below them.

'A little further,' she gasped.

Ethan eased the controls forward, one hand hovering over the power lever to bring the submarine to a dead stop as soon as Amy gave the word.

'Now!'

Ethan pulled back on the lever and the *Seehund* came to a stop before drifting away again from the signal.

'It's the current,' Ethan said as Amy cursed. 'We're going to have to use power to stay in position.'

'Hurry it up then,' Amy shot back. 'We need to grab this thing and get the hell out of here.'

Ethan turned the *Seehund* to the left, angling her into the current to minimize the drift as he advanced the power once more and crept overhead the signal.

'There!'

Ethan pulled off a small amount of power to hold their position as he looked down into the hull.

'Now, cut it loose!'

Amy hurried to the bow and hauled on the lever to detach the bow charge casing. A dull clunk shuddered through the hull as the locking mechanism thumped through a quarter-turn and the nose section was released.

The *Seehund* tilted slightly bow-down and Ethan eased the hydroplanes back to keep them on station as he waited. There was a long silence and then a distant clanging sound, that of metal striking metal.

'You think that's it?' Amy asked.

'I damned well hope so,' Ethan replied.

He checked his compass and then began turning the *Seehund* gently through a hundred or so degrees until he was pointing her back the way they had come. Silently, he prayed that the submarine's motor could produce enough power to draw the Black Knight away from the seabed and up toward the docks a few hundred yards behind them.

'Here goes nothing.'

Ethan pushed the power lever fully forward as he pulled back on the hydroplanes to prevent the bow from being pulled down toward the tethered weight now attached to them. The *Seehund's* electric motor hummed loudly and then she began to move slowly forward.

'It's working!' Amy clapped in delight.

Ethan reached down and twisted the oxygen valve open, bleeding more compressed air into the saddle tanks. The *Seehund* rose up gradually, and then the speed began to increase as Black Knight broke free from the seabed. The submarine's bow dipped precipitously and Ethan pulled fully back on the hydroplanes as he fought to keep the *Seehund* level.

'It's holding,' he said, 'that thing must be a lot lighter than it looks but this isn't going to be easy. All the weight's under the bow.'

Amy understood immediately and she abandoned her seat and moved past below and beside him toward the amid ship position. Ethan felt some of the stress on the controls ease as Amy's weight shifted aft, and he realized that he could have done with the moveable ballast weights originally fitted to these kinds of submarines.

He peered up out of the dome and saw the underside of the glacier above him dimly reflecting the submarine's lights as it ascended toward the base.

'Full steam ahead, cap'ain,' Amy chortled from somewhere below.

'Will you cut it out?' he said as he tried to control the submarine and account for the drift pulling him toward the south. 'We're moving with the stream, going faster, but if I don't time this just right we'll miss the dock entrance and continue on because we don't have enough power to fight the current with Black Knight attached to us. Get your hands on the ballast lever and be ready to pull on my mark.'

Amy's gloved hands appeared on the lever near Ethan's knee and she peered up at him from the hull.

'Ready when you are, skipper.'

Ethan ignored her frivolity and kept his eyes peeled ahead, and within a couple of minutes he saw the shadowy form of the vertical shaft that led up into the Nazi base concealed within the glacial ice.

'Stand by,' he warned.

Amy's grip on the lever tightened as Ethan pitched the submarine as bow high as he could and prepared to pull off the power.

'Nearly there,' he said.

Amy's scream shattered the silence as something loomed outside the viewing dome, and Ethan flinched as a huge white and bulbous form slammed into the submarine and rocked it from side to side as an alarm claxon rang out inside the hull and huge white fangs slammed against the dome.

***

XL

'What the hell was *that*?!'

Amy's terrified scream rang in Ethan's ears as he saw the huge creature lunge directly at the dome and a set of massive fangs slam into the acrylic inches from his face, a deep, red mouth lined with razor sharp teeth that scraped down the acrylic and left deep gashes in the surface.

The *Seehund* rocked to one side and threw Amy from her seat, her body slamming against the pressure hull as Ethan struggled to maintain control.

The fearsome teeth and massive body vanished instantly into the blackness, the submarine's lights illuminating a vortex of disturbed sediment and phytoplankton that swirled in eddies through the freezing black water.

Ethan's heart hammered in his chest and his breath came in short, sharp gasps as he struggled to recover from the attack. He peered out into the gloom, suddenly fearful of what might be out there in the darkness.

'I think Chandler was right,' he said finally. 'We're not alone down here.'

Amy climbed back into her seat but kept one hand pressed against the hull for balance as she sat in silence and stared into the blackness, listening for any sign of the creature that had attacked them so viciously.

The silence deepened, as did it seemed the darkness as they waited. Ethan flinched as he realized that they were still drifting with the current, the underside of the glacier moving past above them. He cursed as he realized that he had lost track of their position.

'Can you reach Chandler?'

Amy did not respond, sitting frozen in silence inside the submarine.

'Amy?'

She shook herself awake and turned to the laptop as she keyed the microphone.

'Doctor Chandler, can you hear us?'

A soft static replied to her with its empty hiss. Ethan bit his lip and cursed again as he peered up at the glacier's underbelly and sought any sign of the shaft that would bring them up into the docks.

'Damn it,' he snapped finally. 'I think we've missed it.'

Amy began to panic, her voice trembling as she replied.

'But what are we going to do? We can't stay down here Ethan, our air won't last long enough and…'

A deep boom reverberated through the *Seehund's* hull as something massive slammed into them once again. Ethan's forehead smacked into the acrylic dome as he saw something move below them in the glow of the lights. His guts convulsed as he saw the immense body of the creature move swiftly through the lights, its back a dark and mottled gray and a stream of bubbles left in its wake. Deep lesions in its surface betrayed the scars battles with other creatures both dangerous and perhaps unknown.

'Can you see it?' Amy asked fearfully.

Ethan nodded, his hands gripping the controls tightly. 'It's big,' he replied, 'maybe eighteen feet or more.'

Amy turned to her laptop and re-wound the footage. A silence consumed the submarine once more as she surveyed what her camera had detected, and to Ethan's amazement she breathed a sigh of relief.

'Thank God,' she uttered.

'Are you kidding?'

'It's a sea leopard,' she replied.

'A what?'

'A sea leopard,' Amy repeated. 'They're common predators in the Antarctic.'

Ethan peered out into the gloom. 'There's nothing good or common about that thing out there, it's huge!'

'It may have grown large due to the unusual amount of nutrients and food down here.'

'We lost our chance to surface in the dock shaft,' Ethan said, 'and I have no damned idea where we are now.'

'Did you see where it went?' Amy asked.

'The leopard seal? Yeah, south,' Ethan replied, quickly able to orientate their position and the direction in which the animal had departed.

'Good,' Amy said, 'follow it.'

'You want me to do what?'

'Follow it,' Amy insisted. 'Seals are mammals, they have lungs.'

Ethan stared down at her for a moment and then he got it. 'They breathe air.'

He turned the submarine around to point in the same direction as the current and immediately they began to accelerate as they joined the natural flow of the water.

'How are they getting their air?' Ethan asked. 'We didn't see any of them in the submarine pens.'

'No, but we did see one of Veer's men dragged into the water by something,' Amy said, 'and leopard seals are known to be large enough to kill humans. The ice in this channel beneath the glacier is highly oxygenated, and any cavities that exist will likely have breathable air in them. All we have to do is follow that seal and hope that the cavities are large enough to accommodate the submarine.'

'Big hope,' Ethan pointed out, and then something caught his eye.

Through the gloom he saw a large, streamlined shape moving through the water. From the blackness emerged an enormous seal, three times as long as a man. Ethan had seen such animals on the television but he was stunned by their incredible size and he realized that they would easily be capable of taking down a full grown man.

'That's got to weigh at least fifteen hundred pounds,' he said as he looked at it.

'The leopard seal is second only to the killer whale on the Antarctic food chain,' Amy said as she watched the animal on the screen. 'They've been known to kill humans too, dragging them off the ice sheets or attacking them in the water and pulling them down to their deaths.'

'The docks,' Ethan realized. 'It's their calls we've been hearing, right?'

'That and the turbines under pressure,' Amy confirmed. 'Leopard seals growl quite loudly both above and below the surface. Any sign of a breathing chamber yet?'

Ethan could see bubbles periodically streaming from the seal's mouth as it swam, and then it began to ascend. Ethan eased back on the power and pulled the hydroplanes back, causing the *Seehund* to follow the seal up.

Almost immediately he saw a shadowy fissure above them, perhaps twenty feet wide and of unknown depth.

'I can see surface water,' he said.

The water rippled and glittered as the *Seehund's* lights caught it, and then suddenly he saw the seal burst through the surface before diving back down into the depths again, bubbles streaming from its nostrils like shimmering chrome spheres. Ethan guided the submarine upward into the cavity and suddenly the dome broke through the surface water as the lights illuminated a concave chasm in the ice.

Ethan could tell at a glance that the formation was natural, perhaps created as the glacier had moved slowly over rocky formations on the seabed somewhere to the north and thousands of years before. Ragged, linear scars in the roof of the cave marked the glacier's progress, dark lines scoring the ice where debris and sediments had been dragged along with the ice and frozen in time.

Ethan reached out and pulled a lever, extending the submarine's breathing tube as he then reached out and opened a valve. He heard a hissing sound as the air outside, under high pressure from the water pinning it in place against the ice, bled immediately into the low pressure atmosphere inside the submarine.

A cold blast of pristine air rushed through the *Seehund* to hit Ethan's face and he breathed it in deeply.

'Damn, that's so good it hurts,' Amy gasped.

Ethan looked up at the interior of the cavity and recognized the same natural lines that adorned the ceiling of the submarine pens.

Amy joined him and managed to peer up past his shoulder to get a glimpse of their surroundings.

'This air must be millions of years old,' she confirmed. 'For all we know we could have breathed in ancient pathogens.'

'You go girl, and keep our spirits up.'

Amy did not reply for a moment, her brow furrowed in deep thought.

'This glacier is also millions of years old,' she said finally, 'and glaciers move.'

'Yeah,' Ethan agreed, 'so what?'

Amy dropped back into her seat as she stared at her laptop screen.

'The Nazi base must also move with the glacier.'

'We know that,' Ethan said, 'and that movement is slowly tearing up the turbines they built in the water channels.'

Amy shook her head.

'That's not what I mean,' she added. 'The Totten Glacier is the primary outlet of the Aurora Subglacial Basin and has the fastest rate of thinning in East Antarctica. Circumpolar deep water has been linked to glacial retreat in West Antarctica, so why not here? It's been observed here all year-round on the continental shelf a few hundred meters beneath the Antarctic surface water.'

'You're losing me,' Ethan admitted.

'The warm water currents both outside the continent and coming from within it are what created these sub-glacial chambers,' Amy went on. 'We just saw a large leopard seal, a mammal that requires large volumes of food and a reliable air supply to survive, and yet here we are some seventy miles in from the Antarctic coast.'

Ethan realized what Amy was getting at.

'There must be an existing channel still available to the open ocean that passes directly through the submarine pens, and it must be large enough and with consistent enough air pockets to allow large predators to reach this far beneath the glacier, perhaps even live here permanently. That leopard seal might be one of countless species here beneath the glacier, and we might be able to follow that channel out of here to the coast.'

Ethan glanced at the oxygen indicators and saw that the submarine's tanks were full. He closed the vents and retracted the air pipe.

'I don't want to meet any more speciess, thanks all the same. We missed the entrance to the north dock,' he said as he looked up at the lines running through the ceiling of the air pocket, 'but if we orientate with those lines we might be able to pick up the main pens and surface there.'

Amy shot him a sharp look.

'The main pens are where Veer and his men are,' she warned. 'We show up there, it will be like handing Black Knight over to them.'

Ethan knew that she was right, but he also knew that nobody knew anything about whether they had actually recovered Black Knight or not yet. With the device tethered below the submarine and submerged beneath the water even when the *Seehund* breached the surface, nobody would be able to tell what had happened to it.

'We can't stay down here forever, and we can't make a run for the coast and leave the rest of the team behind in there.'

'Riggs and his men would not hesitate to leave *us* behind,' Amy pointed out. 'That's probably why he was so keen to lead this expedition. He could have simply sailed out of here and left us behind.'

'I think Riggs has more humanity than you give him credit for,' Ethan said as he prepared to dive the submarine.

'We can escape, right now,' Amy insisted. 'We could reach the coast in a few hours, deny Veer and his men their prize and complete our mission!'

'And Hannah, Doctor Chandler and the others?' Ethan demanded. 'Either way, we can't necessarily sail out of here. Just because a leopard seal or two can make it through seventy miles of sub-glacial ice doesn't mean this submarine will, and we don't have weapons to blast our way through. Either we make it back to the base and take our chances, or we're stuck down here forever. Which would you prefer?'

Amy scowled, but she had no alternative for Ethan as he turned the *Seehund* in the water and then eased the throttle forward as he aimed the hydroplanes down.

Slowly, the submarine slid back into the icy blackness below and the cave was plunged once more into absolute blackness.

***

235

XLI

Eric M. Taylor Center, Riker's Island,

New York City

'It's this way, and pardon the convicts, ma'am.'

Lopez grinned as she followed the duty sergeant into the centre. 'I've visited before.'

Lopez walked down a service corridor as the duty sergeant signed them in and signalled a colleague nearby in a small booth surrounded by bullet-proof glass. A motor whined as unseen locks disengaged and a large steel-barred door rolled open.

Lopez walked through with the sergeant onto D-Block, a high security wing of the centre dedicated to holding high-profile inmates. The block was deserted, steel tables and benches bolted to the floor.

'Has he said anything?' Lopez asked.

'No,' the sergeant replied. 'But then, like you asked, we didn't check in on him much.'

A gruesome symphony of whoops rang out from the tiers nearby as the population caught sight of Lopez striding through the block below. She glanced up and saw dark faces appear at barred cell doors, stark against the orange correctional jump suits as they shouted and bellowed profanities at her. She ignored them as she followed the sergeant through a door at the end of the block that led to a small corridor with three heavy security doors along one wall.

'Has he been held alone?' Lopez asked the sergeant.

'No,' he replied. 'Newcomers are held in four man cells, but your guy's tests aren't due back until tomorrow. He'll go on the block overnight, then he'll be on Twelve Main after that.'

Twelve Main was the high security wing where cells were walled with stainless steel to prevent the prisoners from ripping the latrines and sinks out to use as weapons. The sergeant walked to the farthest door and unlocked it, pushing it open as he led her inside.

Cuffed to a table inside was Victor Wilms. Lopez was prepared for the fact that Wilms would have been traumatized, but she was not ready for the sight that greeted her. Wilms' face was shaded with deep, angry welts of black and blue, one eye swollen entirely shut and an unhealthy shade of purple and yellow. His hair was in disarray, dried blood caking the corner of his swollen lips where he had been savagely beaten. His head hung low on a weary neck, one eye loosely focused on Lopez as she moved to sit opposite him.

'He's up for more tests in the morning,' the sergeant revealed as he moved to close the door. 'HIV is rife in the system and let's just say your boy had a rough old night with his cellies.'

The sergeant closed the door and Lopez looked again at Wilms. His skin was pale and haggard, his gaze hidden behind bruised sclera as though he were gazing at her from the far side of the tunnel to Hell.

'Sleep well?' Lopez asked brightly.

Wilms looked at her for a moment and then a weak laugh trickled from his lips, gaps visible where several of his teeth had been knocked out. The movement provoked more bleeding and Wilms winced at the pain. His features pinched tightly as his one good eye closed and his shoulders trembled as his bitter laugh dissolved into a pitiful sob.

Lopez watched as Wilms huddled over himself, his shoulders hunched and his head almost touching the table between them. Lopez, despite her hatred, could not help but feel some sort of pity for what he must have endured in the last few hours. That he had probably been gang raped was not lost on Lopez, and the beating may have occurred before, during or after his ordeal. Pedophiles were among the most reviled of convicts, and although Wilms was innocent of that particularly heinous crime he had caused more than enough suffering in other ways during his life to be deserving of such punishment. While other prisoners would have had forged into their psyche the knowledge that to show weakness, especially in front of other men, was to condemn themselves to a life of misery at the hands of others, Wilms had spent his life hiding behind money and power. He had no defense against the rough and tumble physicality of the real world, and such people were referred to inside Riker's Island as *"food"*, for the bigger fish.

'It's going to get worse,' Lopez said, keeping her tone stern. 'We won't let you die in here, Victor. We'll make damned sure you survive the rapes, beatings and stabbings. You've got years of this to look forward to. Either tell me everything that I need to know or this visit will be the last you'll ever see of the outside world.'

Wilms continued to sob quietly as Lopez leaned forward further.

'What is KIL?' she demanded.

Wilms' sobbing died away as he sucked in a ragged breath of air and finally managed to lift his head to look at her.

'I want immunity,' he said, 'before I say anything.'

Lopez shook her head. 'You're down for life, Victor, that's not going to change.'

'House arrest,' Wilms uttered, his voice distorted by his swollen lips. 'I want out of here.'

Lopez raised an eyebrow and shrugged. 'That might happen, but I'll need something solid before I walk out of here or you're going straight back to your buddies in that cell, so start talking fast.'

Wilms sighed, and Lopez realized that every last ounce of this man's resistance truly had been destroyed by a single night in a real jail. She wondered briefly whether she could pull this stunt off with the other members of Majestic Twelve.

'What do you want from me?' he asked in a ghostly, ragged whisper.

Lopez felt a tingle of excitement that she suppressed rapidly, unwilling to reveal to Wilms her anticipation of finally learning what everything they had been fighting for was about.

'Majestic Twelve,' she said, 'who are they? What do they want? Why do they know about this base in Antarctica?'

Wilms did not look at her as he replied, his battered face staring down at the grubby Formica between them.

'The Silver Legion,' he said.

'The what?'

'The Silver Legion of America, also known as the Silver Shirts, was an underground American fascist organization founded in 1933 by William Dudley Pelley that was headquartered in North Carolina,' Wilms said. 'It was a white supremacist group, based partly on Hitler's Brownshirts. Two years after their founding, and with Nazi funding, the Silver Shirts had built a fortified headquarters in the Los Angeles hills and had some fifteen thousand members. The Japanese attack on Pearl Harbor in 1941 killed off most support for the legion, but a few die-hards remained. They were ready four years later when the Nazis were defeated to bring into America survivors of the *Third Reich* along with all of the wealth that was pilfered from Germany in the last days of the war.'

Lopez sat stunned in her chair as she digested what Wilms had told her.

'We've been fighting the Nazis all this time?'

Wilms continued to speak, his voice monotone, his eyes cast down as though he were spilling a lifetime of regret across the table between them.

'After the war, twelve former members of the Silver Legion used their new found wealth to invest heavily into the industrial-military complex, just as their Nazi comrades had done. They prospered, became powerful, and when in 1947 the first hints of extra-terrestrial technology coming into the hands of the United States government began to circulate, they were there to pick up the threads of what had begun in Germany many years before with *Die Glocke*. Majestic Twelve was formed and the rest is history, although you won't find that in any of the official records.'

Lopez sat in silence for a moment, reflecting on just how closely MJ-12's actions and power were based on the Third Reich's regime of oppression, fascism, deception and financial power. Hadn't Hitler burned down the *Reichstag* in order to declare a false-flag war against Communism and waged genocide against the Jews despite being of Jewish descent himself? Lopez was no student of history, but she knew enough to figure that MJ-12 could indeed be descended from Nazi survivors of the Second World War, which also suggested that Wilms was telling the truth. Lopez decided to go for broke.

'What does KIL stand for?' Lopez demanded again.

This time, there was no resistance.

'Kinetic Incendiary Launch,' Wilms uttered.

'What?'

'KIL,' Wilms whispered. 'That's what it stands for.'

'Explain.'

Wilms sucked in another painful breath.

'It's a satellite that my company began putting into orbit in 1974,' he mumbled, his voice altered by his swollen lips and missing teeth. 'The purpose of the satellite is to give Majestic Twelve the ability to launch a nuclear grade assault on a target of their choosing anywhere on Earth.'

Lopez stared at Wilms in horror for a long moment. 'They have a *nuclear* capability?'

'No,' Wilms replied, his voice a hoarse whisper. 'The Kinetic Launch system relies upon gravitational energy. The impact of any such weapon would equal or exceed a nuclear detonation without the complications of radioactive fallout.'

Lopez's mind reeled.

'Where is this satellite of yours?' she asked.

Wilms looked up slowly at her and despite his suffering she thought she saw a gleam of vengeance twinkling in his one open eye.

'By now, it should be almost over Antarctica.'

Lopez was out of her chair and running within an instant.

*

Defense Intelligence Agency Watch Station,

Manhattan

Lopez dashed into the watch station even as Hellerman and Jarvis were coming the other way, having driven at a breakneck pace across the city. She had called in what she had learned from Wilms straight away, but it had taken time to get back to Manhattan.

'Did you find anything?' she asked desperately. 'Was Wilms telling the truth?'

'Oh yeah,' Hellerman replied, 'he was telling the truth all right. You're not going to believe what this guy's been up to.'

Lopez had been secretly hoping that Wilms' story had been a bluff to get him out of Rikers, but now she saw Jarvis's gloomy expression as he spoke.

'Wilms' telecommunications company launched twelve satellites in the 1970s,' he said. 'Trouble is, his network only has four in orbit.'

'Wilms used NASA launches and also purchased other launch vehicles in Russia to enable him to launch more objects into orbit, all of them part of his KIL system,' Hellerman explained.

'How the hell do they work?' Lopez asked.

Hellerman showed Lopez to a computer monitor, where an image of a satellite in low Earth orbit awaited.

'A kinetic orbital strike is the act of attacking a planetary surface with an inert projectile, where the destructive force comes from the kinetic energy of the projectile impacting at very high velocities,' Hellerman explained. 'The satellite contains a magazine of tungsten rods, each some twenty feet long, and a directional thrust system. When a strike is ordered, the satellite releases one of the rods out of its orbit and into a suborbital trajectory that intersects the target. The rod accelerates as it approaches periapsis and the target due to gravity, reaching tremendous velocities shortly before impact. The rods are shaped to maximize terminal velocity.'

Lopez's mind reeled. 'How fast would they be moving when they hit the planet?'

'Roughly five miles per second,' Hellerman replied.

'That's fast,' Lopez said. 'How much damage could they cause?'

'Hard to predict because there are so many variables and as far as we know, they've never been built or tested before,' Hellerman explained. 'The Outer Space Treaty prohibits weapons of mass destruction in orbit or outer space. However, it only prohibits nuclear, biological and chemical weapons as part of its statement. Since the most likely form of kinetic ammunition is inert tungsten rods, in most cases kinetic bombardment remains legal.'

'If you can afford to build them and put them in orbit,' Jarvis replied.

'How come everybody's not doing this?' Lopez asked.

'They have done in the past,' Hellerman pointed out. 'During the Vietnam War there was limited use of the Lazy Dog bomb, a steel projectile shaped like a conventional bomb but only about one inch long and a half inch in diameter. A piece of sheet metal was folded to make the fins and welded to the rear of the projectile. These were dumped from aircraft onto enemy troops and had a similar effect as a machine gun fired vertically. Observers visiting a battlefield after an attack said it looked like the ground had been 'tenderized' using a gigantic fork. Bodies had been penetrated longitudinally from shoulder to lower abdomen.'

'Project Thor was a research program at Boeing in the 1950s,' Jarvis added, 'which is pretty much what Wilms must have based his own design on. The system most often described is an orbiting tungsten telephone pole with small fins and a computer in the back for guidance. The system described in a 2003 United States Air Force report was that of a twenty foot long, one foot diameter tungsten pole controlled with a satellite and capable of hitting any spot on the globe with a velocity of around Mach ten.'

Lopez looked at the map of Antarctica displayed on a screen nearby.

'Can we track this thing?' she asked.

'Cheyenne Mountain is already providing us with a tracking solution,' Jarvis explained. 'The team at Cheyenne are calculating orbital trajectories and such like as we speak.'

Lopez turned to Hellerman.

'How long would it take between launch and impact of one of these tungsten weapons?'

'The time between deorbit and impact would only be a few minutes, and depending on the orbits the system would have a world-wide range.'

'Damage radius?' she pressed him.

Hellerman sighed.

'In the case of the system mentioned in the 2003 Air Force report above, a six meter long tungsten cylinder impacting at Mach ten has a kinetic energy equivalent to nearly twelve tons of TNT. Some sources suggest a speed of nearly forty thousand feet per second, which for the aforementioned rod would amount to a kinetic energy equivalent to one hundred twenty tons of TNT.'

Lopez looked again at the map and she knew that they were running out of time.

'Wilms must already have tasked his satellite with the hit,' she said. 'Is there any way we can knock it out of orbit or intercept it in some way?'

Jarvis shook his head.

'There are no other options,' he replied, 'and with Wilms out of the picture Majestic Twelve would likely have taken control of the KIL Satellite.'

'And it's the perfect kill,' Hellerman said. 'The ice will refreeze the impact zone within days. Nobody will ever know what happened down there.'

'The satellite must have codes,' Lopez said, 'a way for us to hack it.'

'Get back to Wilms and get them from him,' Jarvis ordered. 'Any way you like, just get them or this will all be over long before we can get Ethan and Hannah out of there!'

***

XLII

Antarctica

'We're almost there.'

The interior of the *Seehund* was bitterly cold as Ethan guided the submarine using the electric motors toward a shimmering veil of water above them. From below he had almost missed the submarine pens in the gloom, only the faint halo of illumination coming from glow sticks tossed across the docks revealing its location at the last moment.

Ethan gently angled the hydroplanes upward and prepared to surface as he looked down at Amy.

'We don't know what's happened here since we left, so be ready for anything.'

Amy nodded, her features pinched with concern as the *Seehund* rose up and Ethan peered up out of the dome as the submarine finally broke the surface of the pens. To his relief he saw Riggs and Del Toro rush to the side of the dock with mooring lines as Ethan held the submarine in position alongside the dock and they tied the vessel down. Ethan shut down the engine and immediately reached out for the dome latches, unlocking the seals and pushing the dome up and open.

A waft of clean, cold air breezed in to the submarine and Ethan breathed it in deeply as he levered himself out of the cockpit.

'Did you get it?' Riggs asked.

Ethan nodded as he jumped down onto the dock and stretched his legs, Amy jumping down after him. 'We got it. It's attached to the cable on the bow.'

Riggs looked at the cable.

'Good,' he replied. 'Let's get it out of the water and into the base. The sooner we get this sorted, the sooner we can get the hell out of here.'

Ethan saw Hannah hurry across to him. 'We lost contact and thought that you'd both gone under.'

'We almost did,' Ethan admitted as he watched the SEALs hurriedly attach the cable to a winch on the edge of the dock. 'I don't know what that thing is but it's lighter than we expected. It came up without any trouble but it shuts off any electrical devices within a few yards of it.'

Doctor Chandler's voice reached him from behind.

'Electromagnetic interference,' he called out as he descended the steps onto the dock. 'A common event during UFO encounters.'

'And lighting storms,' Amy countered as she turned to watch the SEALs begin to winch the object up out of the water. 'Just because it's charged doesn't mean it's from another planet.'

'Doesn't mean it's not, either.'

'That's not a logical argument,' Amy protested. 'You can't prove a negative. Extraordinary claims require extraordinary evidence, and you don't have…'

'Will you two cut it out?' Hannah snapped. 'Look, you can test the damned thing to your heart's content now.'

Ethan watched as the SEALs heaved on the winch and something below them in the water loomed out of the darkness. As he watched, the water in the pen began to glow a luminescent blue as fresh bacteria plumes began appearing on the water.

The winch heaved again and the tip of the object broke the surface. Ethan could see that it was as black as night, a sort of metal that seemed entirely smooth and yet matt in appearance, reflecting none of the lights illuminating the pen. As the SEALs hauled on the winch, more of the object was lifted clear of the water and he heard Amy gasp in surprise.

The object was indeed bell-shaped, roughly twelve feet high and perhaps ten feet in circumference at its base. Ethan could already see that there were odd markings around the rim of the base as the water streamed off the object, like angular hieroglyphics that were etched into the solid metal itself. The object was lifted clear of the water, and Ethan stepped back as the SEALs swung it around on the crane and gently lowered it onto the dock.

The metal base landed with a hefty thump on the dock as Riggs stepped back from the winch, his face sheened with sweat.

'Heavy,' he said, 'but not nearly as heavy as it should be. It must be hollow or something and made of aluminum.'

'That's not aluminum,' Chandler said as he cautiously approached the object and rested his hand against it. 'The electromagnetic charge proves that.'

He pushed against the object, but he could not move it as Amy crouched down alongside the base and began making careful copies of the inscriptions in her notebook.

'Looks like ancient Egyptian, or perhaps even the Sumerian script,' she said as she worked.

Doctor Chandler nodded, a bright smile spreading on his features.

'That, my dear, would not surprise me in the slightest. The Sumerians recorded in their history the stories of gods from the skies who came down with great knowledge and shared it with the people. They repeatedly stated that these beings resided in the oceans, and that they would come from the water from time to time to help humanity.'

'And no doubt Santa Claus was there to record the events,' Amy chortled as she worked.

'Mock me all you like,' Chandler muttered in reply. 'Our ancestor's tales of ancient intervention by gods from the sky form the basis of all today's religions, regardless of what today's believers may assume to be true. This, *Die Glocke*, is the first tangible evidence of that.'

Amy shook her head in silence as she continued to work.

'I don't give a damn where it came from,' Riggs said as he stared at the object. 'It's too big to fit through the front door, so one way or the other we're going to have to get it out in pieces.'

Chandler stared at the SEAL aghast.

'Destroy it? The most precious discovery of modern times? An object that will change human history and you want to smash it to pieces?!'

'It's not going to change anybody's history if it ends up buried beneath a couple hundred thousand tons of ice,' Riggs pointed out.

'We don't know what it contains,' Amy shot back, for once on Chandler's side. 'What happens if we break it open and what's inside is lethal to us, an infection of some kind? We'll all be dead then, too, regardless of what happens to this cavern.'

Ethan stepped in. 'Look, there may be another way.'

'Tell me,' Riggs said.

'The device is light enough that it could plausibly be floated out of here using the *Seehund*, right? We could use the same sub-glacial tunnels that the Nazis used to get into the glacier and build this base. Amy and I saw those channels and there's life down there, so there must be a way out.'

Riggs frowned. 'Our support will be coming in using that same path. We can't risk the chance of a collision beneath the ice.'

'There's no guarantee that the channels are still fully open,' Chandler reminded them. 'We were briefed that our reinforcements might not be able to make it all the way here, which would mean a longer wait at the base.'

Riggs dragged a hand down the stubble foresting his chin as he looked at Saunders.

'We heard anything yet?'

'Nothing on the secure channels,' Saunders replied. 'If they're on their way, they're staying real quiet about it.'

Riggs nodded and looked at Amy. 'And you say that this object could contain things that might be dangerous to humans?'

'It's from another world,' Amy pointed out. 'Another civilization built this. We have no idea what they might have placed inside it.'

Riggs nodded as he made up his mind.

'If that's so, then we can't risk letting it out of this base and perhaps infecting the rest of the planet with some Godawful disease or virus. The only option we have is to open it here.'

'Say what now?' Hannah uttered.

'It's the only logical course of action,' Amy agreed enthusiastically, eager to be the one to open the first genuine alien artifact in human history. 'If this base is about to be destroyed by natural forces, then we know that any virus will be contained by the collapse. All we have to do is ensure that whatever's inside this bell does not make it into the water flow and out into the wider world.'

'And how would you do that?' Hannah asked. 'This whole cavern is carved from ice that flows out of the glacier, right? One drop of water infected here will be carried directly to the southern oceans.'

'The blast doors,' Ethan guessed. 'We seal them up and open the bell while we're inside. That way, it can't get out.'

'Nothing can be sealed so perfectly,' Chandler insisted. 'We cannot reliably examine this artifact outside of a proper laboratory.'

'Bit short on the laboratory side of things, Doctor,' Riggs said as he strode by and headed for the interior of the base. One way or the other, we've got to open it here and find out what's inside or this whole mission will have been for nothing, so we'll have to use the field tents instead. Get on it Amy, figure out how to open this damned thing and fast.'

*

Amy sat on the dock, huddled in her Artic coat as she stared at the bell's implacably solid side and let her mind wander free. Ethan could see her from where he leaned against the railings at the base entrance, Hannah alongside him as they waited.

'She's not going to figure this out in time,' Hannah whispered. 'Veer's men could come through the front door at any moment and we won't be able to hold them off for long.'

'Give her time,' Ethan said. 'She's desperate to see what's inside the damned thing and that's a powerful motivator.'

'You never heard of what happens to curious cats?'

Ethan smiled as he pushed off the railings and walked down onto the dock. He approached Amy from one side, saw her looking straight into Die Glocke's featureless surface as though seeking a reflection that wasn't there.

'How can it be so smooth and yet not reflect anything?' she asked him, rhetorically he guessed because he felt like the last person on Earth to have a decent answer.

'They ran out of polish?'

Amy chuckled despite her deep thinking and shook her head, then sighed and bowed it. 'I can't figure these icons out.'

Ethan looked at the shapes and symbols adorning the circumference of the artifact and shrugged.

'It's hardly surprising. It took centuries for archaeologists to figure out Egyptian hieroglyphs, and you've only got an hour at best.'

'The archaeologists had the *Rosetta Stone* to help them,' she replied. 'I don't have a damned thing, and I doubt very much that Chandler's idea of comparing these to Sumerian script is going to work.'

'I wouldn't rule it out,' Ethan replied.

Amy looked up at him in surprise. 'You don't buy into all that ancient alien crap, surely?'

Ethan felt mildly embarrassed for some reason, but he held his ground.

'I've seen quite a bit of evidence to support it, Amy, believe me. We wouldn't be sitting here looking at this thing if alien civilizations hadn't launched it here or left it behind. Kind of suggests that people like Chandler might be onto something.'

Amy scowled and looked again at the device.

'We were always going to find alien life eventually,' she muttered. 'Just because we have doesn't automatically mean that every crackpot theory about ancient aliens is suddenly true.'

Ethan looked again at the icons and frowned.

'What makes you think that they're letters or numbers anyway?'

Amy shrugged. 'I guess it's because there's no other thing that they could be. Why inscribe an artifact like this at all if not to pass on a message.'

'Yeah, but it could just as easily be a registration plate or something, right?

'Are you always this comical?' Amy asked him with a wry smile.

'Just sayin',' Ethan shrugged again. 'We're assuming this thing is of huge importance because it was left here. What's to say it wasn't just a simple vehicle left behind by a group of camping interstellar travellers who were just passing through and…'

Ethan was cut off as a deep moan reverberated through the cavern, thundering with enough force to vibrate the air in Ethan's lungs as he staggered sideways and sought a handhold. He leaned against the side of *Die Glocke* as the chamber shuddered around them and the icy black water cavitated once more, symmetrical loops shimmering in the dim light from the glow sticks marking the dock's edge.

'They're getting worse,' Hannah called as she clung to the railings nearby. 'This cavern could go any moment.'

Ethan kept his hand on the bell, and to his shock he felt it vibrating with such force that his arm went numb and he was forced to place his right boot firmly on the deck and push off from *Die Glocke* while his arm was still able to react to his commands.

The tremendous noise and shaking faded away once more and Ethan shook his hand and frowned at it.

'What?' Amy asked.

'Die Glocke,' Ethan said as he shook his arm back and forth to bring it back to life again. 'It was vibrating, made my hand go numb.'

Amy stared at his hand for a moment, then at the artifact, and then she leaped to her feet and threw her arms about Ethan's neck as she kissed him firmly on the lips. Ethan stared at her in shock as she released him.

'Warner, you're a genius.'

'I keep saying it,' he replied. 'Why?'

Amy was already running for the base. 'I know how to open Die Glocke!'

***

XLIII

'Are you sure this is going to work?'

Lieutenant Riggs seemed unsure of himself for the first time since Ethan had joined the team as he looked on nervously at Amy.

'It'll work,' Amy replied. 'You've just got to seal this side of the base off. We can't risk letting anything inside the device reach the other side, okay? It stays in here.'

'Couldn't it get through the water channels beneath the base?' Hannah asked, clearly remembering Amy's own prior concerns about quarantine.

'We'll keep it away from the dock edge,' Amy promised. 'And the tent will seal it in.'

Ethan watched as Doctor Chandler sealed the last few edges of the transparent plastic tent that they had erected around *Die Glocke*, sealing it off from the atmosphere. Nearby, a small generator was being prepared by Del Toro, ready to draw out some of the air pressure inside the tent so that nothing could escape in the event of a breach: instead, air would flow in and not out.

'And what if there's something, y'know, *alive* in there?' Hannah pressed.

Amy smiled as she pulled herself into a biohazard suit, a helmet in her hand as she sealed the last of her suit up.

'Nothing substantial can live for thirteen thousand years, Hannah,' she assured her, 'but bacteria and other forms of life have been known to last for literally hundreds of millions of years before being spontaneously brought back to life in the presence of liquid water or vapor. We're not taking any chances.'

Amy pulled the hood over her suit and sealed it shut as Doctor Chandler moved across to her, and together they helped ensure that both sides of their suits were properly sealed before Amy looked at Riggs.

'We're ready,' she said. 'Seal the tent from outside, then activate the generator. Once we're done, get inside the base and seal the door from the inside. That's about all we can do for now.'

Riggs seemed genuinely uncertain.

'I don't like this one little bit,' he replied as he led his soldiers back toward the sally port. 'Whatever you've got to do in there, make it fast, okay?'

Ethan watched as the SEALs waited as Amy and Chandler walked into the tent, and then they sealed if from the outside before switching on the generator. The air pressure inside the tent rapidly reduced, and Ethan could see the vents drawing air in instead of out, those vents lined with grills designed to stop any foreign objects or bacteria from entering the tent. Simple scrubbers cleaned the carbon dioxide out of the tent, while both Amy and Chandler had oxygen supplied via small tanks on their backs.

'They've got an hour,' Riggs said as he walked by Ethan. 'All we have to do is keep Veer off their backs and ours.'

Ethan and Hannah hurried in pursuit of Riggs as he led the team back inside the base and the SEALs worked to seal the door behind them. As soon as it was secure, Ethan hurried up to the command center where a laptop computer was now open on an abandoned workspace, the light from the screen glowing blue through the room.

'Amy, can you hear us?' he asked.

'Loud and clear!'

Amy's reply came from within the tent, where they could see her and Chandler preparing to open *Die Glocke*. Amy's voice was slightly distorted but the images were perfectly clear as she spoke to them.

'It never crossed my mind until that last quake inside the cavern, but these symbols around the circumference of the artifact are likely not alien numbers or letters but sounds, like musical notes. We have no idea how alien forms of life might communicate but as this device seems to have sought out an aquatic environment, it seems plausible that the species that created it might have communicated by some form of ultra-sound.'

Doctor Chandler cut in as he worked.

'Most marine species on earth use ultra-sound as a means of communication,' he said. *'This device cavitated at the same time as the cavern during the last quake, and likely conducts sound just like an ordinary bell. If Amy is right, then applying the correct frequencies to the artifact should open it or perhaps even activate it.'*

Hannah glanced at Ethan. 'Am I the only one thinking this is probably a bad idea? Didn't Chandler say that the Germans activated their *Die Glocke* during the war and that it melted people or something? I'd rather wait until some secret government organization can open this thing somewhere really remote.'

'We are remote, and working for a secret government organization,' Ethan pointed out.

'I mean remote from *me*.'

'It's more than likely the stuff of myth and legend,' Amy said in reply as she worked, *'but it is at the very least plausible that if this device has a defensive mechanism then sound may form a component of that. Everybody's heard an opera singer hit a note*

and shatter a wine glass: it's all to do with resonance. Match the resonance of an object with soundwaves, and you'll shake it apart.'

'The Tacoma Narrows Bridge was destroyed in 1940 by the same phenomenon,' Chandler added. *'The bridge was already known as "Galloping Gertie" because of its undulating behavior. The bridge was peculiarly sensitive to high winds. Rather than resist them the Tacoma Narrows tended to sway and vibrate, a tendency which progressively worsened due to harmonic phenomena. A forty mile per hour wind storm ripped the entire massive bridge apart.'*

Ethan looked at Riggs.

'Would the construction of this base provide any protection from something like that, a sound weapon?'

'Maybe. Extremely high-power sound waves can disrupt or destroy the eardrums of a target and cause severe pain or disorientation,' Riggs acknowledged. 'The NYPD uses the LRAD-500X sonic weapon to disperse crowds but a base this size would prevent soundwaves from such weapons from reaching us if we were on the submarine pens on the other side.'

'I heard that the crew of the cruise ship *Seabourn Spirit* used a long-range acoustic device to deter pirates who attacked the ship,' Sully said, 'so it's possible this thing could use sound as a defense. The fact that it's shaped like a bell suggests it would be effective at dispersing sound over long ranges, and if it's really powerful even the water wouldn't protect us – sound passes easily from water into the body.'

Ethan watched as Amy prepared an amplifier that they had bludgeoned together from the base's old tannoy system. Attached now to a laptop using a complex series of cables and transistors that allowed the amplifier's 1940s technology work with a modern computer, Amy had scanned in images of the icons on the artifact's exterior and then applied a computer program to detect likely audio patterns matching the symbols.

'Okay, we're ready,' she said finally. *'Here goes.'*

As Ethan watched, across the data link he heard a strange series of whoops and growls emitted by the amplifier. It sounded rather like a herd of cattle moving by, grunts and snorts that sounded similar but had no particular rhythm or pattern to them.

'That's not it,' Amy said as he looked at the artifact and saw nothing. *'Next pattern and frequency.'*

Another blast of noise hit the rear dock, this time sounding reminiscent of a boulder rolling and bouncing down a rocky hillside.

'This is going to take hours,' Riggs uttered from nearby as he listened to the stream of noises coming from the laptop. 'There must be billions of noises that program could rustle up, and none of them matching the frequency that Amy thinks will open the artifact.'

Despite the noise, Amy could apparently hear the soldier as she worked.

'Not so,' she replied. *'This is a learning program. Every time a sound doesn't work, it removes both it and its data stream from the list of possible choices, along with all variables in the same tone. Every test we run removes millions of sequences and narrows down the actual frequency and tone that matches the symbols.'*

'You ever done this before?' Riggs challenged.

'No,' Amy replied. *'But then it's not every day we find an alien device in the middle of Antarctica with the hieroglyphic version of a doorbell on it, right?'*

Riggs scowled and moved away but he said nothing as Amy continued to work.

Ethan perched on the edge of the table nearby and watched as Amy's amplifier rig emitted sound after sound, each one being systematically rejected by the computer program. Hannah joined Ethan as they listened to the noises.

'They're starting to develop a pattern,' Hannah said as she listened.

Ethan frowned, unable to hear anything that he would have called a melody or tune. 'I don't hear anything.'

'It's in the background,' Hannah insisted. 'Listen.'

Ethan closed his eyes as he heard what sounded like bubbles billowing beneath water, and suddenly he detected the same rhythm that Hannah's more sensitive ear had picked up on moments before. The random noises were gradually being replaced by a subtle, repeating signal.

'It's sounding more like ultra-sound too,' he whispered as he listened.

'We're getting something,' Amy called.

The SEALs gathered and listened too as the computer's repeated attempts to match the symbols to sounds began narrowing down the frequencies. Ethan heard a long, low whistle that sounded something like a train approaching down a tunnel, and he realized that he had heard something similar himself.

'Whale song,' Lieutenant Riggs recognized the same sound. 'Damn me, maybe she was right after all.'

As Ethan listened, so he heard something behind the gradually refining whistle, a series of whoops and low, gently rippling howls that began to sound like something approaching...

'Dialect!' Amy shouted in delight.

Ethan felt a strange sense of fear as he listened to the noises now emanating from the amplifiers in the rear dock. A harmony of warbles and indistinct noises that somehow still sounded like the conversation of intelligent beings, a rippling back and forth of sounds that he realized must literally be the words of some other species from who-knew-where across the galaxy.

'My God,' Chandler exclaimed as he worked alongside Amy, 'this is a dialect, a discernable language of some kind!'

Ethan was about to ask what Chandler thought the language, odd as it sounded, might mean when suddenly the computer beeped and Amy let out a squeal of delight. Ethan looked at the monitor and saw the computer in Amy's tent stop producing sounds and instead present her with a file that was blinking on her screen.

'This is it!' she chirped. 'It's ready.'

Lieutenant Riggs shoved his way to the monitor. 'Play it, now.'

'Hang on,' Hannah said. 'Why not let them get out of the tent first and then play the sound remotely. We don't know what's gonna come out of there.'

'Like Amy said, there's nothing alive in there,' Riggs shot back without looking at Hannah. 'Open the artifact.'

Amy did not hesitate to proceed, either not hearing or more likely choosing not to hear Hannah's suggestion as she hit a key on her keyboard. Ethan stood up as he stared at the screen and the amplifier emitted a final sound.

Even from his position looking at a small monitor Ethan could see the laptop inside the tent, the individual icons and symbols on *Die Glocke* appearing with each new note of the melody now playing throughout the base. Ethan could already tell that it was the sound of some kind of other-worldly species, a resonating series of low hums, howls, hoots and even clicks that corresponded with the symbols on *Die Glocke*.

The sequence played out and then the base returned to silence. Ethan looked at the artifact but it remained silent and still. Amy frowned at it and then stared up at the camera.

'I don't get it.'

Ethan shrugged, 'So, maybe it is just a registration plate after all?'

Saunders' voice attracted their attention away from the screen. 'We've got company.'

Lieutenant Riggs cursed under his breath as he grabbed his rifle. 'Damn it, this was a waste of time.'

Ethan accompanied him over to the shattered windows and looked down to see Veer's men fanning out toward the base.

'They're going for it,' Saunders said. 'They're attempting a full-frontal assault.'

'Their funeral,' Riggs growled. 'Let 'em in close and then we'll take them to pieces.'

'Roger that.'

Riggs looked across at Ethan. 'Time to end the games out back. If we can't open that thing up, then neither will they. Be ready to dump it back into the ocean if the base is breached.'

Ethan nodded as he drew his pistol and checked the mechanism. He hurried across to the monitor and spoke quickly.

'Amy, we're under attack. Get out of there, right now.'

They were out of time.

*

'It's over,' Chandler said. 'We just don't have the time to finish this.'

Amy held her hands to her head as she stared at the artifact.

'It *should* open!' she insisted. 'We deciphered the signal!'

'We deciphered *something*,' Chandler corrected her. 'We need to get out of here before Veer's men kill us all!'

Amy struggled to think clearly as Chandler made for the tent exit. She saw him move out of the main tent, seal it behind him, and move into the entry corridor where he could then exit the entire tent out onto the dock. Amy was about to follow him, hoping that she could return to the work before Riggs and his team sent *Die Glocke* to the bottom of the ocean, when she saw the writing on the transparent plastic before her.

DO NOT ENTER WITHOUT FIRST SEALING MAIN ENTRANCE

The words were written in reverse on the plastic in bright red letters and suddenly she realized her error.

'Left to right,' she gasped.

'What?' Chandler asked her from outside.

'We assumed that they read from left to right,' she said again, 'but even here on Earth both Islamic and Japanese script run in the opposite direction. What if we played the sequence back to front?'

'There isn't time, Amy! We have to go!'

Amy ignored him as she whirled to her computer and tapped a few keys. The program flipped the sequence and she hit the play key without hesitation.

The melody played once more, the somber whoops and calls echoing around the chamber with eerily intelligent rhythm that seemed to resonate with some deeply buried, primal memory in her mind as she stood rooted to the spot as the sequence played out.

The sounds faded away and for a long moment Amy stood in silence and stared at *Die Glocke*, but again nothing happened.

'It didn't work, Amy,' Chandler cried. 'Get out of there!'

Amy turned to leave, but then she heard it. A hiss of escaping vapor filled the tent as she turned back and saw a thin gap appear as if by magic around the tip of *Die Glocke*, as slowly the top of the device opened.

'It's working!' she yelped in delight and edged her way closer to the device.

'Stay back,' Chandler urged her. 'We don't know what's in there!'

Amy did not hear him as she moved alongside Die Glocke and stepped up onto a tool box in order to peer inside the device. She reached out for a flashlight and switched it on, then aimed the beam down into the interior.

Her heart sank as she sighed.

'It's empty,' she said.

Chandler peered in through the plastic wall of the tent. 'It's what?'

'It's empty,' she said. 'I can't see anything inside it except two cylinders, and they're hollow. How can this thing be *empty*?!'

The scientist stared at the device for a long moment and then his face fell in horror and he cried out a warning.

'Amy, get away from it!'

Amy tried to step back, and then everything fell silent and black.

***

XLIV

Antarctica

'What the hell happened?'

Ethan stood with Hannah beside the dock and stared at Amy as she lay unconscious inside the tent, Chandler scrambling into his bio-hazard suit and hurrying inside as he spoke.

'She managed to open Black Knight, and that thing shot out of it and hit her in the face.'

Ethan looked down at Amy and saw what looked like a gold disc of some kind on the dock alongside her. Chandler approached it cautiously and knelt down alongside it.

'What is it?' Hannah asked.

Chandler whistled softly as he examined the disc.

'It's gold,' he said, 'and it's inscribed with schematics of some kind.'

'A gift?' Ethan asked furtively.

'No,' Chandler replied, 'gold is valuable on Earth because it is a rare metal, but that may not be the case on other planets. It's been used because gold is extremely resistant to decay, so anything transcribed upon it and suitably protected will last for millennia. NASA did something similar with an engraved gold disc attached to the side of *Voyager 1*, the most distant man-made satellite in history – it's already left our Solar System. This disc likely explains what Black Knight is for or who made it. It's a communication, literally, from another species.'

Ethan clenched his fists. 'Good, then we got what we were looking for. Now all we have to do is get it out of here.'

Chandler did not share Ethan's enthusiasm, however, and looked up at Black Knight. 'What bothers me is why this contraption should be used to contain such a small message,' he said finally.

'Let's not worry about that,' Hannah urged. 'At least not right now. We need to leave.'

At that moment, Sully appeared at the dock.

'They're here!' he called. 'We've got contact with the submarine!'

Ethan whirled and with Hannah followed Sully at a run back up to the command center, where Riggs was manipulating the team's radio. Ethan saw Lieutenant Riggs' signals beacon flicker briefly.

'Tell me you're not mistaken,' he gasped in relief.

Riggs checked the frequencies. The radio beeped again as it connected with the US Navy submarine lurking somewhere below them in the deep.

'I'll be damned,' Saunders uttered from his position, 'better late than never.'

'The channel must be open right to the coast,' Hannah said as she looked at Ethan. 'They made it through.'

Ethan checked the magazine of his pistol as he replied above the sound of sporadic gunfire and the rumbling of the cavern around them.

'It's not going to be open for long if this cavern collapses and we don't have any way of getting past Veer's men and out to the pens.'

Riggs nodded.

'They're not going to surface while they're under fire and risk damaging the submarine.'

Ethan peered around the edge of the corridor and then looked at Riggs.

'I can hold them off here while the rest of you get aboard,' he suggested. 'Amy's the priority now along with that disc, we need her out of here and contained.'

'She's not safe,' Riggs insisted. 'She's been exposed to whatever's inside that thing. I'd rather see her buried here than take her with us, so the disc is the only thing that's coming along.'

'She's a human being,' Hannah snapped at Riggs. 'She could be cured. She's the only way we can *learn* a cure!'

'And the DIA aren't going to be happy if you and your team falter at the last hurdle and leave behind the very thing that they've been hoping for,' Ethan pointed out. 'Burying Amy under the ice and I'll bet the DIA or the Navy will bury every one of your careers the moment you get out of here.'

'This wasn't part of the mission,' Riggs snapped.

'Amy *is* the mission now,' Ethan shot back. 'She's Black Knight as much as that disc, which has also been exposed to anything that might lurk inside Black Knight!'

Riggs scowled and glanced at Del Toro, who shrugged.

'I don't like it but he's right: we take the disc, we gotta take her too 'cause if we don't the mission's a bust.'

Ethan was about to argue the point when one of the SEALs dashed in.

'They're preparing to attack,' he said breathlessly. 'Two minutes and we're done!'

Ethan looked at Riggs, and realized that he was right. He holstered his pistol and rushed toward the rear dock entrance.

'I've got an idea,' he said quickly. 'If the submarine can get in here, then the *Seehund* can still get out!'

Riggs stared at Ethan in amazement. 'Sure it can, but it only takes two people!'

Ethan stopped at the door and looked back at him.

'The *Seehund* is sealed, fully contained. If we send it east through the tunnels with Amy and the disc inside, she can be picked up off the coast by the *Polar Star* under controlled conditions and from there travel back to America.'

Riggs looked like he'd been slapped. 'And Veer's men out there?'

'Don't know about the *Seehund*,' Ethan replied. 'They're going to be looking for a large submarine trying to get into the pens, not a *small* one trying to get *out*.'

'And the minor issue of how the hell anybody can go in there with her right now, if she's contaminated in any way?'

'The biohazard suits,' Ethan said quickly. 'The pilot can handle the submarine if Amy is tied down well enough. With the current beneath this glacier they'll be out of here within an hour or two, and the *Seehund* can remain safely submerged for that long. If we put Amy inside a suit too, then they can be removed from the sub at *Polar Star* without fear of contamination.'

Del Toro shook his head. 'That's a huge risk for whoever does the driving, Warner.'

'But no risk for the rest of the planet,' Ethan said. 'I'll do it.'

'No,' Riggs snapped as he pointed at Hannah. 'You're too good a shot to be expendable. Ford, you're up. Get a suit on and fast!'

Hannah's legs almost collapsed beneath her. 'Me?'

'You know enough of the controls from your briefing and you can get her out of here,' Riggs insisted. 'It's the smartest option, ladies first and all that.'

Ethan gripped Hannah's arm. 'It's the right thing and Amy trusts you.'

Hannah baulked, but then a rattle of gunfire smacked along the wall behind them as a deafening rumble shook the base and churned the water in the pens.

'Running out of time folks!' Saunders chortled. 'Time to leave!'

Hannah grit her teeth as she glared at Ethan. 'If I get out of this alive, I'll sue you!'

Ethan grinned and tugged her toward the rear dock. 'Come on!'

They ran together to the dock, where the *Seehund* was moored alongside the oxygen tent containing *Die Glocke*. Ethan ran down the steps and across to where two of the SEALs were hurriedly preparing to push the device back into the water.

'Leave it there,' Ethan insisted.

'We can't,' one of the soldiers insisted. 'It's a part of the mission.'

'The only useful thing inside that artifact was that disc,' Ethan snapped back. 'I want Veer to think he's won while Amy and that disc get away untouched.'

Doctor Chandler had watched the exchange in silence, but now he stepped forward.

'I will go with Amy,' he said.

'You can't control the *Seehund*,' Ethan dismissed his offer.

'I may be considered a conspiracy theorist and crank but I'm not an imbecile,' Chandler replied quietly. 'Amy took an enormous risk to retrieve Black Knight and now she's in need of our help. So far I've been a passenger on this mission, but now I can see that if I go with her, it will leave you two to support the SEAL team and perhaps succeed in holding Veer's men at bay for long enough to save yourselves.'

Ethan looked at the old man for a long moment, and then at the SEALs.

'It's not rocket science to pilot this thing,' Sully replied, 'if he can hold a straight course then he should be able to make it out.'

Ethan turned to Chandler and sighed. 'There are leopard seals down there that might investigate the sub, just try to follow them to air pockets that must exist along the entire route if they can make it this far beneath the glacier. It'll keep your oxygen reserves topped up. Once we're out of here, we'll catch you up in the other submarine and help you track out of here.'

Chandler dragged on his biohazard suit as Ethan briefed him. The two SEALs looked at each other and then at Amy inside the tent.

'We'd do better to just drop the device and the tent into the water and send the *Seehund* back to the coast,' Sully said in a whisper.

'She needs to live, just like the rest of us. Do either of you want the job of piloting the sub' out of here?' Hannah demanded.

Both of the SEAL's stood up straight, refusing to be cowed.

'I'd do whatever it takes to complete the mission!' Sully snapped back.

'Then help get Amy into that suit,' Ethan snapped. 'We don't have much time.'

As if in response the chamber shuddered again and chunks of ice plummeted from the ceiling of the chamber and crashed into the frigid black water around them. The SEALs jumped into action as they opened the *Seehund's* viewing dome. Chandler zipped up his suit and turned to the tent entrance.

'Amy, can you hear me?'

Ethan looked at the young scientist, who was standing perfectly erect despite the trembling cavern and dock around them, her eyes filled with fear.

'I can hear you,' she mumbled, almost tearfully.

'We're leaving,' Chandler said, 'and we'll get you back to Polar Star and out of here, okay?'

Amy nodded. 'And the disc?'

'It's coming with us,' Chandler assured her.

'Hurry,' Ethan urged.

Chandler unsealed the tent entrance and stepped inside, carefully sealing it behind him before he moved through into the tent proper. Amy remained silent and still as Chandler gently reached for the helmet of her suit.

'Easy now,' Ethan said. 'Double check that it's secure.'

Chandler lifted the helmet and held it over Amy's head, the scientist several inches shorter than Chandler. Then, slowly, he lowered it into place and then sealed it.

'Good,' Ethan said as he glanced at the SEALs. 'Okay, here goes nothing.'

Chandler took hold of Amy's gloved hand and led her out of the tent, careful to seal the Black Knight in behind him.

'Okay, let's move,' Ethan said as he guided them both to the *Seehund*.

Ethan turned to Chandler, who was standing behind him and looking furtively at the submarine.

'It handles just fine,' he promised the doctor. 'Just let the current carry you along and reserve as much of the fuel as possible for electrical power. It's three knots at least down there, enough to pull you through the tunnels and make it out at about eight to ten knots. Two hours, tops.'

Chandler smiled unconvincingly. 'And if the chamber comes down on me?'

'It won't because you'll already be gone. The quicker you leave, the safer you'll be, now go!'

Chandler sighed again as he clambered up the side of the *Seehund* and then levered himself into the cockpit. The SEALs handed him a GPS locator beacon, already activated and transmitting on a frequency that the *Polar Star* would be able to detect, then helped him close the dome and check that it was air tight before they leaped off the hull and stood alongside Ethan on the dock.

Moments later, he heard the rumble of the submarine's engine and slowly it sank beneath the waves, Chandler's nervous expression the last thing he saw before the *Seehund* vanished from sight.

'Balls of steel, man,' one of the SEALs said.

'Let's go,' Ethan replied as he turned for the base entrance, Hannah with him. 'Veer's men will break through any moment.'

He had barely got the words out when the dock beneath him shook and the sound of violent explosions shuddered through the base.

***

XLV

Hannah ran behind Riggs and Ethan as they hurried up to the command center. Hannah staggered to one side in the control center as she felt the entire base shudder beneath her feet. A cloud of smoke drifted up past the shattered windows as a hail of gunfire swept the interior of the center and smashed out the remaining glass as she dragged herself to the entrance and looked down the corridor outside.

'Return fire!' Riggs yelled. 'Ford, downstairs, support Sully and Del Toro at the blast hatch!'

Hannah pulled her pistol and dashed for the stairwell.

A roiling haze of smoke filled the corridor, the handful of glow sticks still working casting orbs of light into the tendrils as she got to her feet and started running. She reached the stairwell and heard a clatter of gunfire as she dashed down them two at a time, trying not to slip on the patchy ice as she hit the corridor at the bottom and immediately threw herself behind a bulkhead as she saw Del Toro and Sully heavily engaged as bullets whipped past her and clanged off the walls in showers of sparks.

The SEALs were holding the corridor, directing an almost continuous stream of withering fire out to where Hannah could see that the pressure door had been forced open by the blast of Veer's explosives. She could not see if the latch was in place or whether it had been snapped off by the force of the explosion, but beyond the swirling acrid smoke she could see further down the docks to where bright muzzle flashes flickered dangerously close.

'Grenade!'

Riggs bellowed the warning as he leaped down the stairwell as Del Toro hurled himself at a small black object that bounced in from the open doorway and skittered along the ground. He caught it in his hand in an act of supreme courage and tossed it out again. Hannah winced and covered her ears as a sharp explosion rocked the base once more, Del Toro and Riggs hugging the walls to avoid the cloud of shrapnel from the blast that peppered the walls.

Hannah edged forward, ten yards behind where the two SEALs were holding firm and directing their supremely accurate fire at every figure that loomed near the doorway.

'Seventeen!' Del Toro snapped.

'Fifteen!' Riggs replied.

'Twelve!' Sully yelled.

Hannah realized that they were counting down their rounds despite the chaos and noise around them. A gunman jumped through the doorway and fired from the hip as he moved, Hannah slamming her back to the wall as he hopped through the bulkhead and tried to dodge left.

Riggs hit him first, Del Toro a moment later, both men firing a double-tap that put two rounds in the gunman's belly and then snapped his head left and right as the second rounds shattered his skull and he slumped back into the wall.

A second gunman loomed and Hannah fired without conscious thought, two shots echoing out above the roar of gunfire as the first bullet clipped the gunman's shoulder and the second whipped his head aside as it smashed through his jaw and he screamed, a cloud of blood splattering onto the ice and his boots as he reeled away with his hands covering his face.

Del Toro hit him twice again and he collapsed onto the dock, partially blocking the doorway as his screams were silenced.

Riggs and Del Toro began advancing toward the open doorway under cover from Sully, gunfire from further down the docks whipping through the corridor but coming from too far away to pick them out as they moved, the smoke covering their advance now as they pushed forward. Hannah slipped past one bulkhead and moved to occupy their former position, aiming carefully at the open hatch but cautious of stepping out into the corridor.

'Hannah, covering fire on my mark!'

Riggs's voice carried clearly enough that she knew instinctively what to do. Del Toro switched to his 203 grenade launcher and fired two rounds out onto the docks. The grenades arced through the air, landing far enough away to be out of the reach of their immediate assailants either side of the door, close enough that the blasts would injure more men.

Caught in a perfect trap, the attacking soldiers had no choice but to break for cover.

'Now!' Riggs shouted.

Del Toro launched himself forward as Hannah opened fire through the hatch, aiming down toward the tunnel mouth. At this range she knew that she could not hope to hit anyone by design but with luck a bullet or two might pass close enough to Veer's gunmen to force their heads down for a moment, enough time for Del Toro and Riggs to get the door shut.

Del Toro slid in behind the heavy hatch as bullets continued to fly through the opening, and with a wince of effort he heaved the door closed again and the heavy metal of the hatch slammed against the jam with a deep clang that echoed down the corridor.

Riggs leaped to his feet and slammed his weight behind the door as Hannah dashed forward and helped him, bullets clanging against the far side of the door as Del Toro grabbed the metal rails that had been used to keep the door closed. Both had been bent and snapped by the force of the blast, but he rammed what was left of them through the latches. The roar of gunfire was muted instantly as Del Toro turned to Riggs.

'It's only a matter of time,' he said breathlessly. 'They're gonna get through here.'

Riggs nodded and looked at Hannah. 'Good work. Let's see how many of them we managed to pick off.'

Hannah led the way back into the control center, where Saunders was still manning his post and watching the docks below with his sniper rifle. Hannah could tell that the gunfire had ceased but the windows were now completely blown out, a gaping hole in their defense against even a single rocket propelled grenade.

'Five,' Saunders said without looking at them as they walked in.

'Two,' Del Toro added.

'Two,' Sully said.

'Two,' Riggs finished off the tally, 'and Hannah here picked another one off.'

'Twelve dead for no losses,' Saunders grinned. 'I'm liking that. Can we have another go?'

Ethan leaned against the wall and peered down toward the tunnel entrance. 'I saw Veer and his team land and they had maybe a hundred men. They're down to eighty now, still heavy odds, and I'm willing to bet they'll use RPGs if they really feel that they can't get in here.'

Hannah frowned. 'That's what doesn't make any sense. They could have fire balled us by now, so why are they making all these risky moves instead?'

Riggs looked about the control center. 'There must be something up here that they want or need, something that they can't afford to destroy or endanger.'

'But the base is empty, abandoned,' Hannah replied. 'There's nothing here except what the Nazis left behind before the end of the war.'

Ethan frowned as he walked around the control center and looked at the maps protected behind acrylic cases.

'The Nazis went to a lot of trouble to build this place and to maintain its secrecy even after the war had ended,' he said. 'It's not like they suddenly revealed to our government what had been done down here or we'd have found this base long ago.'

Hannah looked about her and began to wonder along with Riggs whether something else might be concealed right under their noses.

'Maybe they used this base as a location to store secret papers, or money, or even their technology after the German surrender,' she suggested. 'The hardcore Nazis like the SS would have done anything to preserve something of the Third Reich in the hopes that one day they could resurrect their dream of an Aryan master race.'

'How would Veer's men know anything about any of this?' Del Toro asked, gesturing around him at the base. 'If our own government didn't suspect the existence of this base how could they have figured out it was here at all, let alone contains something of importance? I thought Black Knight was what got us all out here?'

'It was,' Hannah agreed, 'but Majestic Twelve goes back a long way. The DIA believe it was formed within a couple of years after World War Two ended, which would mean they would have had access to a great deal of what the Germans were doing in the late stages of the war. Maybe one or two of them did know about this base, or at least what might be inside it.'

Riggs turned to Del Toro.

'Maintain the watch, but I want two men to scout through the facility again. Leave no stone unturned. Whatever might be hidden here will likely be well concealed if the Nazis were forced to leave in a hurry.'

Del Toro moved off immediately as Riggs looked at his watch.

'We don't have much ammunition left and there's still no communication from our support team. We can't hold this position forever.'

Right on cue, they heard a voice boom across the docks from outside.

'It's only a matter of time!'

Hannah listened to the voice echo through the darkness. Riggs shook his head to forbid anybody from replying.

'The more silence he hears, the more angry he'll get,' Ethan whispered to her. 'It might force his hand and cause him to make a mistake.'

A long silence enveloped the chamber as they waited for the big man outside to shout again. His voice, when it came, was laced with rage.

'One way or the other, we're comin' through that door and there's nothing you can do to stop us! We've got ammunition, food, water, supplies and reinforcements. You've got nothing!'

Veer's voice echoed around the chamber, chasing around as though searching for them before trailing off into the distance.

'We're comin' for you! We'll get in there eventually!' Veer bellowed from somewhere beyond the thick clouds of smoke billowing across the docks.

Riggs, bored already, grabbed his rifle and was about to head back to the rear dock when he looked at the smoke clouds filling the cavern outside. He turned to Saunders, who was still manning his position, the sniper's rifle aimed down at the tunnel entrance where bursts of machine gun fire sporadically raked the walls of the base.

'Anything?' Riggs asked above the rattle of gunfire.

'They're up to something,' Saunders replied, 'but I ain't sure what. If I were them I'd create a smoke screen and get under the walls then blow the doors, but maybe they ain't as bright as us.'

Riggs didn't buy that either as he peered out across the docks. He was surprised by the fact that Veer had not yet attempted to assault the base. The only explanation for their reluctance was that they had a better plan, and that made Riggs nervous. Veer had more men, more equipment, more weapons and an active although tenuous line of supply back to the surface, whereas his team had been specifically designed to infiltrate the base without support and hold their position until reinforcements arrived.

'Anything on night vision?'

Saunders shook his head slowly, his gaze directed permanently down the barrel of his rifle.

'The ice is too thick to get a good look at what they're doing in there,' he said. 'Best guess?'

'Go for it.'

'They're setting up a mortar to fire into this command center, forcing us out and letting them cross the dock. Once that happens, it's only a matter of time.'

Riggs nodded. Veer's team must possess heavier weapons than just small arms and rifles, and it suddenly struck him that they could have used rocket propelled grenades to attack the command center from afar rather than mortar units. Easily portable and quite accurate, they would be sufficient to cover a fire team's ingress to the blast door. Sure, Veer might be concerned about explosions bringing down the cavern around them, but the blasts would be contained by the base itself if their aim was good. There seemed no good reason not to attempt it, unless they had a better route in figured out and…

Rigg's eyes drifted down to the dock itself and the black water shimmering there. The gradual flow of water through the docks was joined by the flow from the fissure in the cavern wall to his left, and it flowed away both under the glacial ice and into the tunnel where Veer and his men were hiding.

'You said that the channel runs right underneath the base?' he asked Ethan.

'Yeah, both ways.'

Hannah saw a sudden realization hit Riggs hard.

'They'll come in underwater!' he snapped.

**

XLVI

Andrei Veer slid into the black water of the submarine pen as his men maintained a steady barrage of fire and a smoke screen against the upper levels of the base overlooking the dock. The water slid over him and the sound of gunfire became muted, distant flashes of light like distant lightning in heavy clouds shimmering overhead.

The bitter cold of the water bit through even the thick thermal lining of his suit as he descended into the deep, his men visible ahead as they swam. All of them had descended at least twenty feet beneath the waves: contrary to popular myth, bullets were rapidly slowed by water, especially cold water, and were useless for hitting targets below that depth. That, and the absolute blackness, was enough to conceal Veer and his men as they moved silently through the darkness toward the rear of the Nazi base.

Veer was not much one for interest in history, but he was none the less amazed at how the Nazis had been able to create such an extraordinary base in the vast natural cavern beneath the glacier. He could just make out the huge stanchions that were buried deep into the ice either side of the cavern, suspending the base above the murky, chill depths beneath it. Veer kept a close eye open for any sign of the leopard seals that patrolled the waters, his rifle held in his gloved hands. Again, contrary to movie myth, getting water into a rifle was pretty much enough to render it useless: most soldiers pulled balloons or condoms over the barrels of their rifles when entering the water to seal the interior.

Veer swam in pursuit of his men, passing through a deep channel beneath the base where vertical stanchions reached down into the water, enormous buoyancy aids welded to their legs helping the base remain in position. Veer knew that such stanchions could not have been attached to the surface of Antarctica far below, as the glacier's constant movement would have torn them free within even a year of being built.

Something moved to his right, and through the gloom he saw a large, long black object drifting through the darkness. Veer felt a twist of anxiety wrench his innards as he thought about the scientist he had tossed into the docks that had been chewed up by something living in the water. He saw his own men giving the massive form a wide berth and watched it as it passed by on the very edge of his visibility, cruising south and away from the pens. Veer kicked off again as soon as he lost sight of the black creature, keen to get as far away from it as possible.

Above him in the gloom he saw a faint rectangle of light appear as they passed beneath the base and then he saw his men ascending up toward the rear dock. Veer adjusted his ballast and began to rise as he kicked his fins and accelerated toward the surface.

*

'Get that rig set up, now!'

Riggs yelled his warning as he jumped down onto the rear dock and hurried across to the tent. Inside, Sully was attaching a C4 charge to the side of the Black Knight, his face hidden inside a biohazard suit as he backed out and re-sealed the tent behind him. Hannah stepped down onto the dock and watched as they prepared the base to defend against Veer's men.

'Enemy!'

Sully pointed at the water, which until moments ago had been as smooth as silk. Now, ripples of motion could be seen expanding outward in concentric circles, disturbances from below the surface rippling the water.

'I don't see any bubbles,' Hannah said.

'Closed breathing apparatus, Special Forces kit,' Sully explained, and then called a warning in a harsh whisper to Riggs. 'They're coming up!'

The SEALs filtered back off the dock toward the hatch. Even as they did so, Hannah saw

that Sully had attached the C4 charges to the surface of Black Knight itself and she cried out a warning to Riggs.

'Amy said that the device might react to high-intensity sound! You blow that charge, you might set the thing off!'

'Priorities,' Riggs replied with a tight grin. 'If Veer's men come up through here they'll overrun us and any worries we might have about Black Knight will be history.'

'Chandler said that this thing melted the flesh off people,' Hannah insisted as she grabbed his arm. 'I call that a damned priority!'

Riggs looked at her, his gaze buried deep into her eyes.

'Not your call to make,' he growled back. 'You don't like it, then get the hell off the dock and away somewhere safe. Our people will be here in minutes and I don't intend to miss the ride!'

'There won't be a ride if that thing activates!'

'Good, because if this thing is so lethal it'll take out all of Veer's men!'

Riggs pushed her aside and Hannah backed off as she watched the SEALs set up their firing positions inside the main hatch. Ethan had remained in the command center, helping Saunders maintain a steady rate of fire on Veer's main force, and she wished desperately that he were here now to help convince Riggs to shut off the charge.

'Are you getting inside or what?!' Riggs demanded of her.

Hannah looked at the charge on Black Knight and she knew that she couldn't risk it blowing them all to hell. She launched herself off the stairwell and down onto the dock.

'Ford, get away from there!'

Hannah ran for the Black Knight, and then all at once she realized that she was too late as four figures broke the surface of the water, ugly black assault rifles pointing at her as the entire cavern erupted to the sound of deafening gunfire.

*

Veer's men broke free of the water just above him, and almost immediately he saw bullets zipping trails of bubbles through the water as they came under attack, heard the muted rattle of machine gun fire as they fired back. Veer pulled his rifle carefully off his back and hesitated beneath the surface, watching as his soldiers fired at their assailants up on the docks.

One of them twisted violently in the water as his head snapped back, a cloud of scarlet blood billowing in the water as he was hit in the face and killed instantly. His body rotated in the water to lay flat on its back with limbs extended, and Veer kicked for it as he reached the surface, using the dead body as a shield.

Veer broke the surface and opened fire on two Navy SEAL gunmen huddled in a narrow hatchway above the dock. Even as he fired he saw four of his men clamber up onto the dock and hurl grenades at the hatch.

'Grenade!'

The scream went up from one of the SEALs and they vanished into the corridor and slammed the hatch shut. The two grenades bounced off the closed blast door and detonated, blowing it open again. The blasts were deafeningly loud as Veer's men ducked to avoid the shrapnel burst from the weapons, chunks of metal zipping through the chamber in all directions. Veer ducked behind the corpse of his soldier before he kicked for the dock and hauled himself out of the water.

Veer turned to look at the biohazard tent and the strange object contained within, a dull black bell-shaped structure. 'Secure it!' he bellowed.

The troops swarmed over the object, two of them bursting in through the tent entrance. Veer saw them creep up to the object, their weapons held before them as they reached out to open the interior flap of the tent, and then he saw Hannah Ford hiding beneath the stairwell, crouched with her hands over her ears as she squinted and turned away from Black Knight.

'No!' Veer yelled at his men.

A sudden, deafening blast erupted from within the object and Veer ducked and turned aside as from the corner of his eye he saw their heads torn from their necks in a cloud of flame and smoke that ripped through the tent's transparent plastic.

The tent collapsed around the object, the two bodies of the dead soldiers slumping against it as blood pulsed from the ragged remains of their necks. Two thumps from inside the tent echoed through the dock as their heads bounced on the unforgiving dock beside them.

Veer, his hands clamped over his ears to prevent the blast from bursting his eardrums, saw Hannah Ford break from cover and dash to the hatch.

'They booby trapped it!' somebody shouted.

'Congratulations, genius!' Veer roared as he pointed to the base door. 'Get that open! Whatever was inside this thing has likely gone with them!'

The soldiers rushed up to the door of the base, even as Veer's radio crackled. *'General, we've got company!'*

Veer heard a blast of gunfire distort the line as he bellowed his response. 'What's going on out there?!'

'The Navy's here sir! They've got a submarine!'

Veer glared at the door of the rear of the base and realized that he'd been duped. If the submarine surfaced then reinforcements would flood the base and this would all be over – he'd be kissing goodbye to his fortune. He yelled his reply.

'Drop charges into the water and scare them into staying deep! We're on our way!'

He was about to make for the door to the main base when a strange vibration caught his attention. Suddenly, he realized that the chamber was shaking softly, and slowly his men fell silent as they all turned to look at the Black Knight.

The strange hieroglyphic text around the base of the object was glowing a bright electric blue, like a halo that was growing in intensity with every passing second. Veer squinted as a piercing pain struck his eardrums and he whirled away. Nausea wrenched his stomach and he staggered sideways and vomited onto the dock, his vision blurring and the entire dock trembling as though struck by an earthquake.

Through blurred eyes he saw and heard his men staggering about and crying out in agony as the emanations from the Black Knight grew in intensity. The water of the dock rippled and swirled in angular peaks, like a model of an impossibly uniform mountain range, and Veer grabbed at his facemask as he hurled himself toward the water.

To his left, alongside Black Knight, one of his men's agonized cries was twisted to a new and unbearable crescendo as his flesh seemed to melt off his bones, his wetsuit bubbling as though made from boiling oil. Veer saw the man's face collapse in upon itself as the chamber's walls shivered and chunks of ice began spilling from the walls and crashing into the dock.

Veer threw himself into the water and plunged deep beneath the waves.

*

Hannah felt the incredible noise coming from the rear dock sear through her eardrums as she stumbled down the corridor, and she knew that she would not be able to make it out of the building and onto the dock in time to escape the horrendous agony consuming Veer's men on the docks outside.

She hurried along the darkened corridor in pursuit of Riggs' men, and then she came up against a steel door that had been firmly closed. Hannah reached out and pulled the handles of the door, but the SEALs had fled and secured it closed behind them, preventing Veer's men from following them easily into the main base.

Hannah cursed as the noise intensified, an ear-splitting screech that seemed so powerful that it was a physical thing, as though invisible men were assaulting her all around her body, battering her with endless blows. In her pain and confusion, she turned away from the source of the sound and in doing so found herself looking at the entrance to the anechoic chamber.

And suddenly she understood.

She staggered alongside a pressure hatch and turned right, stumbling into the anechoic chamber as she turned and tried to force the door shut. Her limbs were numb, the noise reverberating through her chest like war drums and shaking her eyeballs in their sockets as she heaved the door closed, squeezing her eyes shut as she felt what seemed like razor blades piercing them and her eardrums.

The hatch sealed and some of the intolerable pain eased. Hannah sighed in incredible relief as she leaned against the hatch and twisted the valve closed. The terrible pain and the horrific noise vanished and she slumped to her knees, her vision starring and her ears ringing as though they were about to burst.

*

Veer floated thirty feet beneath the waves and watched as his men hurled themselves into the water. He could still hear the infernal noise screeching across the dock above, but down here it was sufficiently muted that he could bear it.

The bodies landed in the water, some of them missing limbs, some of them thrashing in agony and gradually falling apart, the water stained red with blood that diffused the already meagre light from the glow sticks on the docks.

Veer remained silent and still, even when the enormous form of a sea leopard loomed past him, homing in on the gruesome feast appearing on the surface of the water. The enormous creature was three times Veer's size, but it remained beneath the surface of the water until the terrible cacophony had faded away before it climbed and began tearing at the mass of flesh now clogging the surface.

Veer allowed himself to ascend slowly, saw one or two of his men appear from the darkness around him and clamber out of the water again, careful to avoid the gigantic predator feasting on the grisly remains all around them.

Veer swam to the dock and pulled himself out of the water, then yanked his mask from his face.

'What the hell happened?' one of his men asked in horror.

The dock was littered with corpses, most of them no longer recognizably human, the flesh having split from the bones and been reduced to a bloodied jelly inside the wetsuits his men had worn.

'Acoustic weapon of some sort,' Veer uttered, his voice sounding strange in his own ears as he looked at the blast door and then at his companions. Three men, of an original hundred, remained with him.

'With me, let's finish this!'

'Get that door open, and let's finish this right now!'

Veer led his men inside the corridor at a run, weapons held before them and their barrel-mounted flashlights illuminating the interior in stark beams of white light. They only covered fifty paces before they came upon the sealed blast door.

'Blow it, now!'

Veer watched impatiently as his men attached charges to the sealed door and then backed away down the steps. Veer huddled in below the door and covered his ears as the troops activated their detonator and flipped the switch.

An ear shattering blast thundered through the chamber and Veer heard the heavy door crash down as his men burst from their hiding places and rushed the door with weapons drawn.

Veer prepared to open fire even as Hannah Ford stumbled out of an adjoining door, a pistol in her hand. She saw him coming and immediately tried to aim the weapon at his face. Veer smashed the pistol from her grasp, the weapon spinning away across the dock and into the water with a splash as he jammed the barrel of his rifle up under her ribs.

'Hello again,' he sneered, water streaming down his face and across his thick beard.

'It's here!' one of his men shouted.

'Looks like your boyfriends have stood you up at the last,' he smiled without warmth. 'Don't worry though, we'll make good use of you just as soon as we get out of here.'

'Got to hell,' Hannah snapped back at him.

'You first!' Veer snapped and shoved her along in front of him.

***

Dean Crawford

XLVII

'You did what?!' Ethan yelled above the clatter of gunfire.

'Hannah's still back there!' Sully replied. 'She made a dash for Black Knight but Veer's men showed up and cut her off!'

Ethan's voice echoed down the corridor as he ran after Sully, rage seething through his veins.

'There was no time!' Sully shouted back as he raced up the stairwell to the command center. 'If I hadn't shut the door that damned thing would have killed us too!'

Ethan cursed as Riggs and his team hurried across the center to rappel lines Ethan and Saunders had thrown out of the shattered windows, secured against the thick steel legs of the planning table.

'Tell me the sub's coming up!' Ethan asked.

'They're almost here and aware of the enemy!' Riggs replied as he checked the radio set. 'Time to leave!'

'Hannah's still back there!' Ethan snapped. 'We can't leave her!'

He saw the conflict on Riggs' face, swiftly overwhelmed by mission protocol.

'We can't save everybody and she made her choice, Warner! We go now, or we stay buried here forever! You gonna cry into your cups or cover us?!'

Ethan felt like screaming as he hurried to the windows and grabbed an M-16 rifle. Riggs took one last look at the dock, the water below them churning now as something began rising up from the black depths.

'Now!'

Ethan aimed out of the command center windows as Del Toro and Saunders opened fire on the darkened maw of the tunnel opposite. Gunfire raked the icy walls of the tunnel and drove Veer's men back out of sight as Ethan lifted the M-16 rifle and aimed carefully at the tunnel entrance through the smoke drifting through the cavern.

He selected the 203 grenade launcher and fired twice. Two grenades arced from the weapon across the pens and bounced onto the icy dock as they rattled into the mouth of the tunnel. Above the rattle of gunfire from the SEALs Ethan heard the cries of panic from within the tunnel and then two blasts thundered out as bright flares of light illuminated the ragged tunnel mouth.

The grenades showered Veer's men with supersonic shrapnel and Ethan saw chunks of ice plunge from the ceiling of the tunnel to clutter the entrance as the armed men fled the assault. Ethan turned to his left and yelled across the control center.

'Go, now!'

Riggs and his men burst from the control center windows and plunged down the rappel lines as Ethan and Saunders opened fire once more, covering their descent.

Alongside the pens Ethan saw the surface of the water rise up as though some gigantic black whale was ascending from the icy depths. The water flooded over the dock as from the deep rose an enormous submarine, a glossy black leviathan that almost filled the entire pen from front to back. Even as the submarine was ascending, from its bridge leaped armed men clothed entirely in black, more Navy SEALs who rushed out of the interior and clambered down onto the hull, weapons firing at the mouth of the tunnel.

Veer's men were firing back but already in heavy retreat as they fell back into the tunnel, and through the smoke he could see them turning and fleeing.

'They're in retreat!'

Riggs and his team landed on the docks and dashed toward the submarine as Ethan turned and looked behind them down the corridor that led to the stairwell and the rear dock. He could see Veer's men running toward them and firing as they went. Del Toro hopped through the open hatch and then slammed the door behind him as Saunders pushed a heavy container in front of the door.

'Let's go, now!' Saunders snapped.

They dashed together across the command center and leaped onto the lines, descending toward the docks as Ethan covered their escape, the soldiers amassing at the mouth of the tunnel and opening fire. Ethan saw Veer's men fleeing en masse down the tunnel, firing as they went but desperately trying to escape the hail of fire being directed at them.

Riggs and his team scrambled up the ratlines thrown to them by the submarine's crew as Ethan hesitated.

'What the hell are you doing?!' Riggs yelled up to him as the chamber began to shake all around them.

'I'm not leaving Hannah with these assholes!' Ethan shouted back down.

He turned and checked the magazine of his rifle and then that of his pistol. Fifteen rounds in the rifle, ten in the pistol. Veer's men had been pushed back by the SEALs into the tunnel and would most likely flee. That left Veer's personal escort, which had looked to be about six men who had assaulted the rear dock. At least one had been shot in the water and two had died in the blast inside the tent, which left Veer plus three.

Ethan edged his way toward the entrance to the command center as he saw the flickering glow of flashlights approaching through gaps in the door. Veer's assault was over before it had even really begun but Ethan knew that the submarine would not wait for Hannah or him and would make good its escape within moments.

Ethan had only an instant to think before Veer's men would burst into the command center. He heard their boots rushing upon his position and he knew that there could be no escape.

***

XLVIII

General Veer hurried along behind his three remaining men, shoving Hannah in front of him with the barrel of his rifle as they ascended the steps to the command center entrance and came up against the blast door, sealed shut from the other side.

'You want us to blow it?' one of his men asked.

Veer shoved him aside and bellowed into the command centre.

'We've got Ford! Open up, or I'll execute her right here and now!'

They could hear the rattle of occasional gunfire from outside but nothing more.

'Looks like your men have abandoned you too, Veer,' Hannah spat, unable to prevent the cold grin that spread on her face. 'So much for your leadership skills.'

Veer did not look over his shoulder as he drove his elbow into Hannah Ford's ribs. The agent folded over the blow, her long hair hanging over her face as she slumped against the wall.

'Open it!' Veer bellowed at his men.

The soldiers rammed the door and it cracked open, the weight of a barrel on the far side pinning it shut. Two more attempts, and then as one they burst into the command center and swept it with their weapons. Veer spotted the dead bodies of two of the SEALs laying sprawled on their faces nearby, saw the shattered windows of the command center and the rappel lines now fastened around the legs of a large table.

Veer dashed to the windows with his men and saw the massive submarine sinking below the waves that trembled as the entire chamber around them rumbled with the threat of collapse.

'No!'

Veer's roar of rage was almost drowned out by the rumbling, shaking roar of the gradually collapsing chamber around them. He turned to Hannah, his grip on her arm painfully tight as he glared at her.

'This is what they do!' he bellowed. 'They've abandoned you, left you here to die! Even Warner's gone!'

Hannah's heart plunged in her chest and her shoulders sank as she saw the submarine sink into the abyss, the waves around the massive hull churning and tossing the dead bodies of Veer's men around amid chunks of ice as it vanished. She couldn't blame Ethan for taking his chance at escape, but it felt a crushing blow all the same and now she knew that there was no reason for Veer to keep her alive.

The General released her from his grip and stood back, rage and malice fighting for space upon his great bearded face as he raised a pistol to point at her head.

'The hell with you,' he growled.

Hannah managed to dredge up one last spurt of defiance. 'Good to know that you'll die down here with me.'

Veer emitted a grim chuckle as he squeezed the trigger.

The gunshot was immensely loud in the confines of the command center and Hannah cried out in fear as she felt the impact of the bullet. And yet she did not fall. She felt the blast, felt the thud, and saw Veer topple sideways as a bullet smashed into his great barrel chest and he stumbled backwards out of the command center as the pistol fell from his grasp.

Hannah whirled as she saw a SEAL laying on the floor of the center, a rifle aimed now at Veer's men as he fired three more shots in rapid succession, each seeming to blur into the next. The bullets slammed into the soldiers one after the other before they had even had a chance to realize quite where the shots were coming from. To her horror she saw Warner's face, his hair matted with blood as though he had been shot in the head, his features grim as he fired at their assailants and they fell almost as one.

Hannah cried out again as she lunged forward and yanked a pistol from the holster of one of the fallen soldiers, then whirled and fired at their bodies, putting more bullets into them and ensuring that they would not be getting up again.

She turned as Ethan scrambled to his feet.

'You didn't leave?' she gasped in amazement.

'I know,' he replied. 'I'm an idiot.'

'Veer got away!'

'Forget about him, let's get out of here!'

Ethan grabbed her hand and together they dashed from the command center. The ground trembled beneath Hannah's feet, chunks of ice tumbling from the ceilings and smashing onto the icy decks as they scrambled for purchase.

She followed Ethan down the stairwell and they rushed through the exit together and onto the dock, the water to her left turbulent as thick slabs of ice plunged into the black water and churned it violently.

She barely saw the figure loom from their right and plunge into her, massive hands wrenching the pistol from her grip and hurling her past.

Hannah rolled over in mid-air and slammed onto her back on the icy dock as Veer's voice boomed out above the din of the collapsing cavern.

'Warner!'

*

Ethan whirled and saw Hannah lying on the dock on her back, Veer looming over her with a pistol in his hand that was aimed down at her head. The big, bearded soldier glared at Ethan.

'Toss your weapons!'

Ethan glanced at Hannah and then reluctantly tossed his rifle and pistol to one side, the metal weapons skittering across the icy dock.

'Now, hand whatever you got out of Black Knight to me,' Veer growled.

Ethan winced at him. 'It's already long gone, Veer, and this cavern is about to collapse. If we don't get out now, we'll all be dead!'

'You're not going anywhere until you give me whatever you found in that device!'

'Believe me, you don't want any part of it,' Hannah snapped up at Veer. 'Right now it's floating out of here alongside the US Navy's finest submarine. You'll never catch up with them, and even if you could you'd never be able to get it back. It's over, Andrei!'

Veer sneered down at her as he took more careful aim. 'It is for you.'

'Veer!' Ethan shouted desperately. 'Right now, you can get the hell out of here and disappear and nobody will ever be any the wiser. You can still get away, but I swear if you shoot her I'll hunt you down for the rest of my days!'

Veer smiled cruelly. 'And what makes you think that you'll be leaving here alive, Warner?'

Ethan had no suitable response to the big man, and then he heard the rumble inside the huge cavern reach a new crescendo. He looked up at the walls near the rear of the base and saw gigantic stress fissures split the ice with cracks like thunder that echoed through the chamber.

'The whole place is coming down, Veer!' Hannah yelled.

Ethan glanced to one side and saw the bodies of several of Veer's men lying on the dock, their heads a mess of bloodied tissue where Saunders' unwavering aim had cut them down. Several of them were wearing diving suits, oxygen cylinders still on their backs.

'Then it's coming down on you,' Veer roared as he looked at Ethan. 'Where is the submarine going?!'

'What the hell difference does it make?!' Ethan yelled. 'You can't get it back now, it's too late. You've lost, Veer, it's over!'

Veer grinned at Ethan. 'It's not over until it's over, and I have one play left that will send that sub' to the bottom of the ocean!'

Ethan frowned in disbelief as Veer produced a small GPS device and activated it.

'What's that?' Hannah asked.

Veer did not reply as he tossed the GPS device into the water, the glowing screen a brilliant light that began moving swiftly with the flow.

'Radar guidance for the weapon that will destroy you, the submarines and everything here,' Veer roared back as he shot Ethan a malevolent glare of victory. 'If I can't have it, then nobody can!'

Through Ethan's mind ran images of the submarine's crew, Riggs' SEAL team and of poor Amy trapped aboard the tiny *Seehund* as the Antarctic base was annihilated by some unspeakable weapon deployed by Majestic Twelve.

Ethan turned and threw himself across the dock, his body sliding across the ice as he reached out. His hand plunged into the freezing water and grabbed for the GPS device as it slid past. The frigid cold bit deep into his skin, ached in the bones of his hand as he closed his grip around it and threw it clear of the water.

Veer roared and turned to aim at Ethan, and in an instant Hannah drew a knife from a sheath inside her boot and slammed it down into the bridge of Veer's boot. The wickedly sharp blade tore into Veer and he screamed in shock and pain as he tried to swing the pistol back around to aim down at her. Hannah lifted one knee, brought it right back almost to her chin as she then flicked her boot out and it slammed into Veer's groin with an audible thud.

The huge man's cry of pain was wrenched off as he doubled over. Ethan scrambled to his feet and hurled himself at Veer as Hannah rolled clear. Ethan slammed into Veer and both of them crashed down onto the ice, Ethan grappling for Veer's pistol and instead getting a hold of his forearm.

The huge soldier was far too strong for Ethan to batter the pistol from his grasp, but he wasted no time in scrambling to his feet and stomping down on Veer's wrist. He heard the crackle of bones breaking beneath the blow, Veer screeching in agony as he reached out for Ethan's jacket.

Ethan jerked away as the soldier attempted to wrench the knife from his boot, but the serrated blade caught in the thick leather and the torn flesh beneath.

'Run!' Hannah yelled. 'Now!'

Ethan turned to flee in pursuit of Hannah, but then the walls of the cavern let out a deafening roar and Ethan saw the surface of the water churn as a fresh flow burst through into the cavern from below and the surface of the dock began to surge upward.

'It's too late!' he yelled to Hannah. 'We'll never outrun it!'

Hannah stopped and stared at Ethan, who turned back to look at Veer. The big soldier was trying to stand up, but the blade in his foot was too painful and he could not hope to walk out of the chamber.

Ethan dashed to the bodies of Veer's fallen men and began unzipping the wetsuits they wore. Hannah realized instantly what he had in mind and began tearing the wetsuit off another of the dead soldiers.

Ethan hurled off his thick Arctic jacket and managed to drive his legs down into one of the suits, hauling it over his shoulders as he looked at the black water surging closer and heard the sound of the walls of the cavern crashing inward under the unbearable pressure of millions of tons of water swelling in the tunnels.

'You'll never make it!' Veer yelled as he tried to yank the blade from his boot, his features twisted with pain. 'We're all going to die down here!'

Ethan ignored the mercenary as he zipped up his suit and hefted the oxygen tank onto his back, clipping it in place as he looked across at Hannah and saw her pulling the tank of the dead soldier into place on her own shoulders. She pulled the rubber hood into place and attempted to wipe thick blood off the faceplate with numb hands. She yanked the faceplate into place and Ethan quickly sealed it for her.

He stepped out from behind her and saw Veer move.

'Down!'

Something flickered in the light as it flew across the dock, and all at once Ethan saw that the blade was out of Veer's boot. He heard a thump and felt Hannah stiffen, her eyes wide with shock as she looked around and down. Hannah slump onto her knees as the thick blade of the knife quivered in her side.

'No!'

Ethan dropped alongside her, the serrated blade buried in her flesh somewhere just below her ribs, Hannah's eyes wide and her breathing coming fast as her hands clenched around the handle of the blade.

'No, don't move it!' Ethan yelled. 'You'll break the seal of the suit!'

Ethan turned as a tremendous roar burst across the cavern and the fissures in the far wall suddenly burst open. Fierce columns of icy glacial water exploded into the docks and burst past the command center, pouring down onto the docks as frigid water flooded over the dock walls.

Ethan saw the water flood across the dock around them, and then he saw a huge, muscular and torpedo-shaped form surge from the waves and slide onto the dock.

'We're going, now!' Ethan urged as he held Hannah and let the freezing water rush across them.

He kicked off, the flow of water rushing toward the tunnel as he let the fearsome flow carry them along and looked back to see Veer's body immobile on the dock as the water burst around it. Then he saw the leopard seal, its huge form dwarfing Veer's as it lunged for his body and sank its razor sharp teeth into his leg and wrenched him toward the water.

Veer screamed as the seal hauled him off the dock but the sound of his torment was lost as the water thundered by them and carried their bodies downstream, Ethan glimpsing Veer vanish into the waves. Ethan held Hannah close alongside him as they were swept along and the current washed them off the dock and sent them careering down the tunnel and out of the chamber.

The walls of the tunnel thundered by, the roar of the rushing water amplified by the enclosed space and the sharp ice walls illuminated only by the glow from the flashlights attached to their wetsuits as they were sent tumbling through the depths of the narrow chasm.

Hannah's legs were kicking alongside his, and the knowledge that she was still conscious was hope enough for Ethan to keep fighting as the current swept them along through the gloomy confines of the tunnel. He saw the shadowy form of the Nazi soldier buried deep in the ice flicker past like a ghoul in the subglacial darkness, began to see faint bioluminescence in the water as they were rushed along by the current. The water levels began rising faster than the current could carry them, and all at once he saw the glow from their flashlights flickering across the ceiling of the tunnel, the ragged surface dangerously close to their skulls as they tore along.

'We're going to have to dive!' Ethan said as he grappled for his mouthpiece. 'Can you make it?!'

Ethan felt Hannah squeeze his hand tightly as she shoved her own mouthpiece into place as the water threatened to dash them against the ice. Ethan pushed his mouthpiece into place and then kicked away from the surface of the water, one hand around Hannah's chest as they plunged beneath the surface.

The roar of the rushing water became a dull but equally threatening rumble as they plunged through the darkness. Ethan could just make out the walls of the tunnel rushing by in a cloud of bubbles, the bioluminescent algae and bacteria in the water providing a soft blue glow. The current was immensely strong, twisting with the path of the tunnel and keeping their bodies a respectable distance from the sharp, ragged walls as they tumbled over while passing alongside powerful vortexes. He knew that if they became caught into those vortexes it would all be over, their fate the same as the Nazi guard buried for eternity in a tight corner of the tunnel.

Ethan held onto Hannah as tightly as he could and tried to look in the direction of their travel, and almost at once he flinched as he saw a dead body pinned against the surface of the tunnel, then another, then more still. He realized that Veer's team had been caught by the freezing deluge as they fled for the rappel lines that would have carried them out of the fissure. He saw dozens of bodies pinned against the tunnel walls or turning over and over in vortexes, their faces white and their mouths agape, eyes wide with the final terrible agony of drowning.

The tunnel took a swift turn to the left and Ethan reached out to his right, trying to keep both himself and Hannah on their backs in the hope of his hand catching one of the many rappel lines left by Riggs' SEAL team when they had entered the fissure.

He saw in the gloom the faint halo of the four glow sticks they had wedged into the ice appear in front of him, the soaring walls of the cliff above glowing like a sword of light distorted by the churning waves of the surface as they rushed past beneath, and to his elation he saw Hannah reach out too and search for the lines.

Something brushed across Ethan's arm and slid along it toward his wrist, and he felt Hannah suddenly jerk in his grip as she got a hold of one of the lines and hung on to it for grim death. Ethan caught the same line, slid down beneath her in the strong current, and then they both slammed against the fissure wall.

Ethan managed to hang on, felt Hannah thump into his side alongside him and he pushed her upward, knowing the pain she must be in. Hannah pulled herself slowly up and out of the flow, inch by agonizing inch. Ethan hauled himself up after her and they broke through the surface and clambered up and out of the water, hanging on to the lines as Ethan wrenched off his mask.

'Can you make it up?' he yelled above the roar of the rushing water, his face numb with the cold and his hands aching.

Hannah nodded as she tore off her mask and mouthpiece, but he could see that her face was as pale as the ice surrounding them from more than just the cold.

'I can,' she gasped wearily, her voice inaudible above the roar of the water but Ethan able to guess her words from her lips. 'Let's go.'

Ethan scrambled up the line beneath Hannah, hoping to help her if she faltered. They climbed one icy ledge at a time, the faint glow of sky far above them drawing them upward. Ethan looked up at Hannah as she climbed, the rushing water below fading away from them, and as he did so something warm dropped onto his cheek. He reached up and touched it and saw blood smeared on his finger, and he knew that Hannah could not continue on much longer.

'Keep going!' he encouraged, trying to sound upbeat, 'we're almost there!'

Hannah, one agonizing step after another, climbed the last few yards out of the fissure and Ethan reached up to help push her upward and over the edge of the trench, the thick blade still protruding from her side and drenched with blood. Hannah managed to lever herself over the edge without wrenching the blade and then she slumped onto the ice.

Ethan scrambled up the line and over the ledge, saw the same spectacular sky they had left behind many hours before, the sun was low on the horizon amid a halo of torn ribbons of cloud, black against the brilliant sunset that would not end for months.

Ethan dropped down alongside Hannah, who was lying now on her back and staring up at the heavens.

'Hang in there,' Ethan said, 'we're getting out of here now.'

Hannah managed a vacant smile as Ethan turned to the ski-gliders, and then his heart sank. Every one of them had been sabotaged, the engines reduced to smoldering wreckage by Veer's men and the parasols likewise burned.

Ethan slumped onto his haunches as he surveyed the vast wilderness around them, hundreds of miles of barren ice glowing in the light of the low sun. The silence was almost deafening.

'We're not leaving,' Hannah croaked alongside him as she turned her head and saw the damaged ski-gliders nearby. 'Looks like you're stuck with me until the bitter end.'

'I'll think of something,' Ethan promised.

Hannah smiled and rested one hand on top of his. 'We're about to be bombed, Ethan, in case you'd forgotten.'

Ethan looked down at her and then he heard a noise coming toward them, as though the sky above them were being torn apart, and he knew that it was over, that there could be no escape.

'You owe me ten bucks, asshole,' Hannah smiled.

Ethan heard the noise reach a deafening crescendo, and he squeezed her hand in return as the sky was torn apart by noise above them.

***

XLIX

DIA Watch Center,

Manhattan

Nicola Lopez sprinted down a corridor that led to the DIA's Watch Center and burst in to see Jarvis and Vaughn concentrating on the main screen with Hellerman.

'I've got it!' Lopez yelled as she hurried across to them and thrust the codes into Hellerman's hand. 'Put them in!'

Hellerman grabbed the codes and pinned them to his monitor as he began typing furiously.

'What did you offer Wilms to get them?' Jarvis asked her.

Lopez watched as letters, numbers and symbols flew across the screen and Hellerman hit *"Enter"* on his keyboard. 'I promised him solitary confinement,' she replied. 'After a night with his cellmates, he doesn't want to encounter another human being again in his entire life.'

A flurry of digital code swept across the screen as the computers accessed the KIL Satellite's controls, and then Hellerman gave a whoop of victory.

'We're in!' he yelped as he scanned the data now streaming down his monitor.

'Cancel the launch!' Jarvis ordered. 'Shut the damned thing down!'

Hellerman obeyed without hesitation and the satellite's systems began shutting down one after another as Hellerman accessed them and terminated the code managing the various systems and programs.

'As soon as I'm done,' he said, 'I'll order the satellite into a terminal descent and send it into the Pacific Ocean somewhere far from…'

'Belay that,' Jarvis snapped.

Lopez shot the old man a sharp glance. 'That wasn't part of the agreement.'

'The agreement's changed,' Jarvis replied without looking at her. 'The president himself wants the satellite placed in a new orbit, parallel to one of our new Keyhole satellites.'

'So you can monitor targets and be ready to hit them at a moment's notice,' Lopez guessed easily. 'Damn it Doug, I should've known better. This satellite is dangerous and there could be more of them.'

'We have the control codes now,' Jarvis replied. 'Majestic Twelve won't be able to use this system as leverage against other countries, nor our own for that matter.'

Vaughn was frowning at the screen. 'Oh, no.'

'What?' Lopez asked.

'We're too late,' Vaughn replied. 'Look, the data for the satellite says that it holds four weapons, those tungsten projectiles. There are only two on board now.'

Hellerman rattled off a line of code and then examined the results. 'Damn, he's right.'

Jarvis leaned closer.

'One would account for the Vela Incident,' he said, 'but the other?'

Hellerman accessed more code, his hands flying over the keys, and Lopez heard his sigh of regret as he looked up at her.

'We missed it,' he said. 'The satellite launched a second projectile three minutes ago.'

Lopez felt her stomach flip inside her. She already knew the answer to her next question, but she felt compelled to ask anyway: 'What was the target?'

Hellerman rattled off another code command and looked up to the main screen. Lopez looked up and saw an image of the Southern oceans, and there upon it an arc with a red icon upon it that was following a line of descent toward a spot in the Eastern Antarctic.

'It's already on its way down,' Hellerman said in a quiet voice, the rest of the Watch Center silent now as they observed the tiny icon. 'Velocity is approximately one mile per second and increasing.'

Lopez walked away from the desk, as though having a clearer view of the screen would somehow allow her to influence the outcome of the strike.

'Can we intercept it?' Jarvis asked hopefully.

'No allied aircraft in the vicinity,' Hellerman replied, 'and no way that our ballistic defenses could be launched in time to intercept that missile now. Two minutes to impact, it's already entering the atmosphere.'

Lopez looked across at Vaughn. 'No word from Ethan?'

'Nothing.'

Lopez looked at the screen and saw the missile accelerating rapidly, a small digital read-out reaching three miles per second already.

'Oh my God, that's going to create one hell of a bang when it hits,' Hellerman said unhelpfully as he gazed at the icon.

Lopez looked at the phone on Jarvis's desk, hoped against hope that it would ring. To her amazement, it suddenly buzzed urgently and Jarvis hit the speaker button.

'Jarvis, tell me something good!'

The line crackled with distortion as a voice reported in.

The SEAL team made it out and the artifact has been secured,' the voice replied. *'The team is clear but not everybody made it back.'*

'Where's Ethan Warner?' Lopez demanded.

'And Hannah Ford?' Vaughn added.

'Stand by.'

There was a painfully long wait on the line as the caller checked with the crew of the submarine and the SEAL team.

'I'm sorry, but Agents Warner and Ford are both unaccounted for and were last seen inside the base below the glacier, which has since collapsed.'

Lopez stared up at the main screen just as the digital read-out alongside the missile icon reached five miles per second and the weapon arced down onto Antarctica in its hypersonic terminal descent.

'It's over,' Jarvis said softly.

*

Ethan gripped Hannah's hand tightly in his own as he heard the roar of the missile plunging down toward them from the heavens and he flinched, ducked down and closed his eyes as the roar became deafeningly loud and thundered directly overhead.

The snow on the ridge was blasted aside and Ethan thought that his eardrums were going to burst as something rocketed directly overhead their position and barely above the ridge line. Ethan waited for the intense heat of the impact, the unimaginable moment when their bodies would be assaulted by the million-degree heat of a nuclear blast.

Suddenly, the great roar of noise rushed by and faded to the south, and Ethan peered from the corner of his eye in time to see a great wake of wind-blown snow left behind by the wings of a twin-engine aircraft that thumped down on the ice alongside the ridgeline.

Ethan was not an expert on aircraft but he could recognize some of the more classically shaped airframes and the one before him now was a fugitive from the golden age of aviation. The Consolidated PBY Catalina was painted white and looked like a giant dove as it turned on the ice. A veteran of World War II, the amphibious Catalina had a long hull with an equally wide wingspan atop it, two large piston engines set into the high wing either side of an angular glass cockpit with multiple windows. On her rear fuselage, two bulbous Perspex viewing bubbles that had once held cannons glinted in the sunlight. Capable of landing both on the water and on land, the Catalina had been renowned during the war for its reliability, durability and extremely long range.

All at once, Ethan smiled and said a single name.

'Lopez.'

Ethan could barely speak as he jumped up and saw the Catalina seaplane braking on the snow as it began to turn back toward the ridge line, its pilot swinging the big aircraft around like a pivot on one main wheel as he powered up the starboard engine to help turn the aircraft about.

'Come on!' Ethan yelled at Hannah. 'Our ride's here!'

Hannah's weary expression livened as she saw the airplane travelling back toward them and Ethan helped her to her feet, the former FBI agent holding the handle of the blade in her side as together they staggered out onto the ice.

The PBY Catalina taxied across to them and the side door opened up to reveal the rugged features of Arnie Hackett shouting at them above the engine noise as his wife, Yin-Lee, guided the aircraft.

'You wanna hurry the hell up?!'

Ethan almost carried Hannah the last few steps and Arnie hauled her on board the aircraft as Ethan jumped up into the fuselage and hauled the door shut.

'What the hell are you doing out here? How did you find us?!' Ethan asked in amazement.

'Got a text from a friend!' Arnie shouted. 'The smoke from those wrecked skidoos guided us in! Now strap in and shut up!'

Arnie dashed for the cockpit, shouting as he went. 'Yin, get us the hell out of here!'

The Catalina's engines roared as the aircraft thundered along the ice, her huge flaps, powerful engines and broad wings providing enormous lift as she rushed along the Antarctic ice and rotated, her nose pointing for the sky. The fuselage shuddered and vibrated as the aircraft thundered along the ice and then suddenly the shaking vanished as the aircraft lifted off and Ethan heard the undercarriage retracting as the aircraft climbed away into the frigid sky.

'Did we make it?'

Hannah's voice was weak, and Ethan crouched down alongside her as he squeezed her hand and applied pressure once more to her wound.

'Yeah,' he replied, 'you're gonna be fine now. We made it.'

Ethan heard Arnie's voice from up in the cockpit bellow back down at him. 'We're not done yet, asshole. Brace for impact!'

Ethan looked down at Hannah and managed a smile. 'Just a formality.'

Hannah almost laughed, but her mirth was choked off with pain and she winced as Ethan held on to her.

Through the windows he saw something, and for a moment he thought that a second sun had appeared high in the western sky. A bright flare of light burst against the evening sky far behind them, and then he detected for the briefest of moments a flash of something rocketing down through the sky.

The sunset behind the Catalina suddenly brightened ten-fold and Ethan squinted away as the missile hit the Nazi base with enough force to bury itself half a mile down into the glacier. He waited for a moment and then opened his eyes in time to see an immense fireball expanding out behind the Catalina, a tremendous mushroom cloud billowing out from the impact site and towering up into the Antarctic sky.

Moments later, the Catalina was hurled forwards through the sky as the shockwave from the ferocious blast slammed into the aircraft.

*

Lopez saw the missile icon strike the Antarctic and vanish without any graphic to determine what had happened, but on another screen a satellite's visual image of the Antarctic flared with light as data began spilling down screens nearby.

'Nuclear grade detonation strike!' Hellerman called as he read the data pouring down the screens. 'Yield equivalent to five megatons, impact point matches the location of Black Knight's descent into the ice fields. We're looking at a major destabilization of the glacier's northern fields and...'

Vaughn's hand on Hellerman's shoulder silenced him. 'Let's maybe leave that debrief for a bit, okay?'

Hellerman nodded as he glanced at Lopez and saw her head hanging, hidden behind her long black hair. 'Sure.'

Lopez could hear them both clearly however, and her voice rang clear in the otherwise silent room.

'What's the blast radius?' she asked.

Hellerman looked at the main screen, where the spy satellite's sensitive cameras were recording data from the impact site.

'At least one mile,' he replied, 'expanding as we speak but losing power and velocity now.'

Lopez looked up at the screen for a moment as Hellerman, working swiftly, overlaid fresh graphics on the blast zone where Lopez could already see a large cloud of flame and smoke billowing up from the surface and casting a long, dark shadow away from the impact sight across the Antarctic.

'The blast radius would be non-fatal at anything beyond two miles,' Hellerman added as he surveyed the data. 'If they got to the surface and were able to travel away from the site far enough, they could have made it.'

Jarvis shook his head.

'Ethan would have made contact by now,' he said. 'He'd know we were monitoring the situation down there.'

Lopez reached into her pocket and retrieved her cell phone. There were no messages, nothing to suggest that Ethan had tried to contact her, but then of course being so far south it was unlikely he would have any means of reaching her.

She turned to Hellerman.

'That satellite detects movement, right?' she asked.

'Sure,' Hellerman said, 'but it's not sensitive enough to detect people. They'd be too small and move too slowly. Even the ski-gliders would be too tiny to…'

'Look for something larger, doing about a hundred fifty knots.'

Hellerman stared at her. 'Say what now?'

'Just do it,' Lopez insisted.

Hellerman tapped in a series of commands, re-tasking the satellite's sensors to pick up any object of a defined size travelling at the speed Lopez had suggested in the vicinity of the blast zone.

The computer whirred for a few moments as the satellite's on board computer reset the optics for the new resolution and tracking request, and moments later a small icon appeared on the screen, travelling south away from the blast zone.

Jarvis walked closer to the screen as the satellite zoomed in under Hellerman's control, and he shook his head slowly as he recognized the pixellated form of an old World War Two aircraft, an unmistakable shape.

'That's a Catalina,' he said.

'I'll be damned,' Hellerman gasped in delight as he looked at Lopez. 'How the hell did you get him there in time?'

'The text message,' Vaughn said, glancing admiringly at Lopez, 'when we were sent after LeMay. I can see why Warner relies on you so much.'

Lopez looked at the tiny icon on the screen and then her cell phone rang and she picked it up.

*

The Catalina's fuselage was humming with the growl of the two piston engines as they labored to lift the aircraft higher into the evening sky. Ethan could see the billowing clouds of their exhaust trailing behind them, just as similar clouds had done from the C-130 Hercules when they had arrived in the Antarctic what seemed like an age before.

The Catalina had climbed high enough that it was able to achieve a data link with *Polar Star*, and from there to satellites. The links were strong enough that Ethan's cell phone had picked up a signal, and he had seen a dozen or so missed calls from Nicola Lopez.

'Ethan?'

The sound of her voice in his ear, one that he had not heard for so long, was one of the best things he could ever recall hearing. He sat with his legs out in front of him on the deck of the aircraft, slumped against the seats as he replied.

'Nicola.'

'Christ you're okay! That's another one you owe me, wise guy!'

Ethan smiled, dragged one hand down his face and realized that it came away wet.

'Yeah.'

The tone of Lopez's voice changed. *'You sure you're okay? I mean, I just called you after waking up from a coma of six months and all. Don't get yourself too excited or anything.'*

Ethan's hand still rested on Hannah's wound, and her hand was still upon his, but there was no longer any strength in her grip. Arnie squatted beside him, the medical pack and dressings he had rushed to Hannah's side with soaked in blood as he shook his head slowly.

Ethan let Hannah's hand remain where it was, not wanting to remove it, and looked into her clear green eyes. They stared in silence at the ceiling of the Catalina's fuselage, empty now of the vibrant spirit that seemed to have soared the very moment the bomb had detonated behind them.

'We're coming home,' Ethan replied, his throat tight, 'but only one of us is coming back.'

After a long pause Lopez's reply came back gently across the line.

'I'm sorry, Ethan. I'll speak to you when you get here.'

Ethan nodded, rubbed his eyes angrily. 'I'll look forward to it.'

Ethan cut the line off, and then reluctantly he lifted his hand free of Hannah's and gently closed her eyes for the last time.

***

L

Defense Intelligence Agency Headquarters,

Washington DC

Ethan Warner sat quietly on a seat opposite the DIA's Patriot's Wall, a series of hexagonal gold plaques set alongside each other in a shape reminiscent of the continental United States and flanked by the flags of both the agency and the United States of America. The wall honored DIA personnel who had lost their lives while working for the agency around the globe. Ethan knew that the wall was not exhaustive due to exclusion of agents with links to classified missions – nobody knew how many personnel the agency had lost in classified circumstances over the decades.

A new plaque now shone on the wall, emblazoned with Hannah Ford's name. Ethan stared at it in silence for a long time, and knew that if either he or Lopez had lost their lives in the battle against the enemies of their country their names would not be honored upon the wall. Unlike the CIA, contractors were not included on the DIA's wall due to the often highly sensitive nature of their work.

He was still sitting there when Doug Jarvis strolled in and took a seat alongside Ethan, the pair of them staring at the same wall.

'What intel did we get on Majestic Twelve?' he asked.

Jarvis looked at him for a moment. 'Let's forget about them for a moment. How are you doing?'

Ethan sighed and looked into his lap for a moment before he replied.

'It doesn't really matter how I'm doing, does it,' he said matter-of-factly. 'We have a job to do and it costs lives every day. All that matters right now is finishing the job.'

'You need to take some time,' Jarvis began, 'or this whole thing will…'

'It won't be for nothing,' Ethen growled back. 'Hannah gave her life for this, for what we do, for this cause that we've been recruited for. You and I both know that the only reason her name is up on that wall is because she worked for the FBI and had enough history there to warrant it. As it is, the cause of her death has been put down to terrorism.'

'It was the only way to get her on the wall,' Jarvis replied. 'Had we not opted for that, her sacrifice would have gone entirely unnoticed.'

'Which brings me back to my original question.'

'Nicola and Michael succeeded in identifying the members of Majestic Twelve in New York City,' Jarvis informed him. 'While you were returning from Antarctica our team was able to put names to those faces. We know who Majestic Twelve are, Ethan, every last one of them and we already have one of them in custody, a man named Victor Wilms.'

'The man behind the missile attack,' Ethan said. 'What about Mitchell?'

'He gave us Wilms, but is now in the wind. I can only assume that he intends to flee and live out his days on some obscure beach far from civilization, or that he intends to continue exacting his revenge on Majestic Twelve.'

Ethan shook his head. 'He won't last long on his own. A man like Mitchell always has a game plan of some kind, an escape option.'

'Perhaps,' Jarvis conceded, 'but he's getting too old for field work. If he's planning something it'll be big, something sufficient to allow him to live his life in peace.'

'The eradication of his enemies,' Ethan agreed, 'which now represent Majestic Twelve. He'll hunt them down as we do, but he won't stop at arresting them.'

'No, he'll kill them one by one,' Jarvis replied.

'I'm not going to let Hannah have died just so Mitchell can go on his revenge spree,' Ethan said, his voice hard and cold. 'That asshole spent enough time working for the bad guys and knowing it to have expended any sympathy I might have had for him. You should never have worked with him, Doug.'

'I had no choice, and the intel' he gave us resulted in us apprehending one of MJ-12's most senior members and identifying the rest. Not only that, the images we obtained show them in the company of Gordon LeMay, who is now dead. They were the last people to see him alive and we have evidence of their complicity in his death: his autopsy revealed the use of a drug called *pancuronium bromide*, slipped into champagne which the members of MJ-12 handed to him. We even have LeMay's collapse on record and MJ-12 standing around laughing at him on the floor.'

'Nothing less than he deserved,' Ethan observed.

'I'm not going to disagree with you on that score, but we have them on the run. Hannah and Mitchell's work gave us a major breakthrough Ethan, the first step on the road to crushing MJ-12.'

'What about the blast at the glacier, and the remains of the base?'

'The impact event has been put down to a meteorite strike, with NASA providing data and material borrowed from other genuine Antarctic impacts to support the assertion,' Jarvis explained. 'With the glacier weakened it will be many months before scientists can again visit the area. We have teams already monitoring the site, which is filling up once again with ice and snow as it refreezes. Our best estimates suggest that within three months there will be no remaining evidence of the impact.'

'And global nuclear detection satellites?'

'All detected the impact, as did seismic survey instruments around the globe, but all nations with sufficient resources to observe the event have taken NASA's story as gospel and there appears to have been no international enquiries about what happened. On the same vein, we have enough evidence to charge Victor Wilms with the attempted murder of United States service personnel at the site, along with the illegal missile test event known as the Vela Incident. He'll be tried behind closed doors and likely incarcerated in a maximum security facility – I felt that the one in Florence would be a nice touch to finish his story.'

'He'll get out,' Ethan said. 'These people have too much power, too much money.'

'Not this time,' Jarvis countered. 'Wilms' targets were military, which makes him an enemy combatant and effectively a terrorist. His lackeys in MJ-12 won't be able to help or reach him, and we'll be using Wilms as an example and a message to others among the cabal: we're coming for them and there'll be no escaping true justice this time.'

Ethan sighed again as he stared at the plaque on the wall.

'What about Amy?'

Jarvis shifted in his seat.

'She is in confinement in a laboratory at Edwards Air Force Base and under the strictest security, but she's doing fine and Doctor Chandler is with her. The *Seehund* submarine you used maintained a perfect seal and Chandler got her out, with *Polar Star* picking them up off shore. The DIA has the disc in its possession and we're working on deciphering it now.'

'How long will that take?' Ethan asked.

'I have absolutely no idea,' Jarvis replied, and then stood up. 'You did good work down there, Ethan. There's a light at the end of this tunnel now and it's all down to Hannah.'

Ethan nodded, and Jarvis walked away. He had barely gone when from the other side of the room somebody else approached, and Ethan looked across to see Nicola Lopez striding toward him.

Ethan stood up and practically fell into her arms, the two of them leaning into each other and saying nothing for a long time. Eventually, Lopez looked up at him and one hand touched his cheek.

'You okay, hero?'

Ethan could not prevent the awkward smile that slapped itself across his face as he tried to keep his grief inside. His jaw ached and he nodded.

'Just another day, right?'

Lopez nodded as she released Ethan and looked at the plaque on the wall. 'Would've been me if I hadn't been in a coma.'

'Napping on the job again,' Ethan replied.

'You wanna be the next plaque on that wall, asshole?'

Lopez's eyes were hot with contempt but he could see the twinkle in them. Her skin was filled once again with color and though he could see that she had lost weight, she was rapidly making her comeback.

'Does this mean we're partnered up again?' he asked wearily.

'You work for me, remember?'

'That was before we threw our lot in with the DIA again,' Ethan pointed out. 'We're on an equal playing field now.'

'You mean level playing field.'

'You know what I mean.'

'That's what I just said.'

'Jeez, I need another break from you already.'

Lopez smiled brightly, grabbed his hand and gently led him away from the memorial wall.

'We've got work to do,' she said. 'We've got MJ-12 on the run, and now's the time to strike. They know we've identified them, so they're going to do everything they can to erase their histories before we can charge them with anything.'

'And how do you propose we stop them?' Ethan asked.

'They're Nazis, right? We'll hit them where it hurts them the most,' Lopez replied with a cruel smile, 'their history and their pockets.'

*

The deepest, most secretive subterranean section of the Defense Intelligence Agency was its Research and Test facility, concealed not just from the public but from most of the agency's many thousands of employees. Most were informed that it contained the agency's archives, the record of countless covert missions, which was true enough in and of itself.

But Jarvis knew that it did not reveal the whole story.

In a far flung corner of the archives, in an area purposefully allowed to gather dust, was a door emblazoned with an aged warning sign of high voltages within. The door had a single visible lock, to which only a handful of the agency's personnel held a key. The key would not work on its own, however, for most of the locks inside the door were on the far side and controlled from a secure location in the Director's office. One could only access the door with their key if the other locks had been accessed by the director himself.

Jarvis slid his key into the lock, turned it, and waited.

Moments later he heard mechanical and electrical locks open and the door hissed open before him. He walked into a narrow tunnel filled with old fuse boxes, cables and pipes, and strode down it until he reached another door. Above this one, a dusty looking camera flashed a red light, and as the door behind Jarvis closed again so the one in front of him opened.

The laboratory within was large, manned by a dozen or so people hand picked from the agency's thousands of staff. One of them was Hellerman, who hurried up to Jarvis's side and started speaking as though he had never done so before.

'Oh my God, sir, thank you so much for letting me know about this place. I can't believe all of the incredibly cool things you've got hidden away down here and I really wanted to say that I...'

'Where is it, Hellerman?'

Hellerman controlled himself and pointed down the laboratory. 'It's just over here.'

Jarvis followed him to a workstation where a Perspex box contained a perfect chrome sphere of material that looked to him like a ball of mercury, the liquid flowing around itself as though it represented the weather patterns on a tiny planet. Beneath it was the gold disc, broken now into two pieces.

'What is it?' he asked.

'The disc was merely the container,' Hellerman enthused, 'and the Black Knight a drone of sorts, perhaps one of thousands distributed across the galaxy by an advanced species. We deciphered the symbols upon it using Amy's work from Antarctica and it opened to reveal this.'

Hellerman pointed excitedly at the sphere.

'And *this* is what, exactly?' Jarvis asked.

'Hell, I don't know!' Hellerman almost shouted, his face beaming with delight, 'that's the exciting thing!'

'An educated guess?' Jarvis pushed.

Hellerman glanced at the sphere. 'It's a computer drive,' he replied. 'It's a liquid metal, variable state memory system so advanced that I nearly pee my pants even thinking about it. It's using the quantum state of the metal in order to maintain immense volumes of information, comparable to the entire memory capacity of every single computer on Earth ten-fold.'

Jarvis peered at the sphere and saw his own distorted reflection in it.

'Can you access it?'

Hellerman's delighted expression faltered slightly as he too looked at the sphere. 'No. In fact we don't even know where to start, except to be certain that we can't take a keyboard and a USB and just plug it in.' Jarvis peered at Hellerman, who shrugged. 'Sorry, I just get real excited by things like this. Whatever it's for, Majestic Twelve knew about it and wanted it real bad.'

Jarvis nodded and stood up from it.

'Keep this to yourselves,' he ordered. 'Do everything that you can to understand what it is and how it works. If we can access it, our country will have a sufficient technological advantage over the rest of the world that will never be surpassed.'

'You got it,' Hellerman said as his head bobbed up and down like a deranged parrot.

Jarvis walked away from the laboratory and out of the subterranean section of the building. He used the elevator to return to the ground level of the agency, and then left work for the day. He did not use his cell phone until he had driven ten miles away from the agency, and then it was a burner cell that would not be traced. He dialed a number from memory and waited, the line picking up on the second ring.

'*Yes?*'

'We've got it and we'll figure out how to use it sooner or later.'

A long silence on the line before the reply.

'*We're taking an awfully big risk here, Jarvis. Keeping me out of ADX Florence and off the law enforcement radar will only last so long.*'

'It only has to last so long,' Jarvis replied. 'I want this all to come to an end, but I sure as hell don't want to spend the rest of my life looking over my shoulder. We're each other's insurance policy, Aaron: let's make sure all our cover is perfect before we both disappear.'

Jarvis shut off the line as he drove, opened his side window and tossed the phone over the side of the bridge and down into the Potomac. As he closed the window he reflected on how little time he had left to complete his mission, just like Mitchell.

***

Also by Dean Crawford:

The Warner & Lopez Series
The Nemesis Origin
The Fusion Cage
The Idenitty Mine

The Ethan Warner Series
Covenant
Immortal
Apocalypse
The Chimera Secret
The Eternity Project

Atlantia Series
Survivor
Retaliator
Aggressor
Endeavour
Defiance

Independent novels
Eden
Holo Sapiens
Soul Seekers
Stone Cold

Want to receive notification of new releases? Just sign up to Dean Crawford's newsletter via: www.deancrawfordbooks.com

ABOUT THE AUTHOR

Dean Crawford is the author of the internationally published series of thrillers featuring *Ethan Warner*, a former United States Marine now employed by a government agency tasked with investigating unusual scientific phenomena. The novels have been *Sunday Times* paperback best-sellers and have gained the interest of major Hollywood production studios. He is also the enthusiastic author of many independently published Science Fiction novels.

www.deancrawfordbooks.com